LOVE LESSONS

"Do you wish to lie with me now, Tiger?" Candel asked as she reached down to unbutton her shirt.

Nicolas's male pride was offended by her forthright approach. "How long have you been stranded on this island, anyway?" he asked. "These natives have very peculiar customs."

"What year is this?" Candel inquired.

"1814."

"Eleven years," she said. "Women dominate this island. A man's position in our society demands little of him except amusing himself and pleasuring a woman when she requests it."

"When *she* requests it?" Nicolas gasped in amazement. "Where *I* come from, men reign supreme, and you'd better not forget it."

"You didn't answer my question," Candel said softly. "Do you desire me? Now?"

The initial touch of Tiger's hands and lips stole her breath away. When he kissed her, it was as if he had kindled a magical flame deep inside her. Wild tingles flew down her spine as his lips moved languidly and his muscular body pressed against hers.

When the kiss ended, she looked up at him, smiling.

"Now," he said sternly. "Lesson number one . . ."

PINNACLE'S PASSIONATE AUTHOR—

PATRICIA MATTHEWS

EXPERIENCE *LOVE'S* PROMISE

LOVE'S AVENGING HEART   (302-1, $3.95/$4.95)
Red-haired Hannah, sold into servitude as an innkeeper's barmaiden, must survive the illicit passions of many men, until love comes to free her questing heart.

LOVE'S BOLD JOURNEY   (421-4, $4.50/$5.50)
Innocent Rachel, orphaned after the Civil War, travels out West to start a new life, only to meet three bold men—two she couldn't love and one she couldn't trust.

LOVE'S DARING DREAM   (372-2, $4.50/$5.50)
Proud Maggie must overcome the poverty and shame of her family's bleak existence, encountering men of wealth, power, and greed until her impassioned dreams of love are answered.

LOVE'S GOLDEN DESTINY   (393-5, $4.50/$5.50)
Lovely Belinda Lee follows her gold-seeking father to the Alaskan Yukon where danger and love are waiting in the wilderness.

LOVE'S MAGIC MOMENT   (409-5, $4.50/$5.50)
Sensuous Meredith boldly undertakes her father's lifework to search for a fabled treasure in Mexico, where she must learn to distinguish between the sweet truth of love and the seduction of greed and lust.

Available wherever paperbacks are sold, or order direct from the Publisher. Send cover price plus 50¢ per copy for mailing and handling to Pinnacle Books, Dept. 647, 475 Park Avenue South, New York, N.Y. 10016. Residents of New York and Tennessee must include sales tax. DO NOT SEND CASH. For a free Zebra/ Pinnacle catalog please write to the above address.

GINA ROBINS

ALWAYS AND FOREVER

PINNACLE BOOKS
WINDSOR PUBLISHING CORP.

PINNACLE BOOKS

are published by

Windsor Publishing Corp.
475 Park Avenue South
New York, NY 10016

Copyright © 1992 by Connie Feddersen

All rights reserved. No part of this book may be reproduced in any form or by any means without the prior written consent of the Publisher, excepting brief quotes used in reviews.

If you purchased this book without a cover you should be aware that this book is stolen property. It was reported as 'unsold and destroyed' to the Publisher and neither the Author nor the Publisher has received any payment for this 'stripped book'.

First printing: October, 1992

Printed in the United States of America

This book is dedicated to my husband, Ed, and our children, Christie, Jill, and Kurt, with much love.

Chapter 1

Nicolas Tiger stood at the helm of the *Sea Devil*. His piercing blue eyes were fixed on the waves that gently rocked his schooner, luring the vessel and its crew into a false sense of security. In the distance he could see the ominous mass of floating seaweed that marked the boundaries of this legendary sea within the Atlantic Ocean.

The setting sun, a ball of red-gold fire on the burnished horizon, cast an incandescent glow across the towering sails of the schooner. A faint breeze whispered through the sails, making them rustle and snap before they sagged in the calm sea air. The cables, usually as taut as harp strings, became so slack that they hung in loops, giving the masts very little support.

Although Nicolas had steered his schooner through the Devil's Triangle a score of times the past few years, there always seemed to be a mysterious presence lurking about . . .

Foolish hogwash! Nicolas scoffed at the wanderings of his mind. And yet . . .

"I don't like the looks of this sky, Tiger," Bufford

Parks grumbled as he braced his forearms on the rail. "Aye, that red glow spells trouble. I've seen it before."

Nicolas glanced down at the stout, red-haired first mate who had joined him on the quarterdeck.

"I'd rather dodge those British frigates in the blockade or even engage them in battle than sail through this Sea of Lost Ships any ole day!" Buff declared.

"Aye, my sentiments exactly," Otis Scroggs piped up. The helmsman propped himself against the wheel and followed Nicolas and Bufford's gaze across the island of waving seaweed that could hold back a ship like a vine-choked swamp. "I've heard too damned many tales of lost ships and ghost crews in these waters not to get the willies when we navigate through the Devil's Sea."

"You and Buff have spent too much of your time filling sailors' heads with wild tales," Nicolas said sarcastically. "You're beginning to believe all that nonsense . . ."

His voice trailed off when another breath of wind whispered across the planked deck, causing the sails to pop and the timbers to groan, as if phantoms were rising from their watery graves.

Then the wind died as quickly as it had come, leaving the *Sea Devil* stalled in a deadly calm. "Don't tell us you don't feel it too, Tiger," Buff said. "You've been sailing these seas for twenty years yourself. You've heard the stories and you even dared to set foot on board that ghost ship we found floating three years ago with a valuable cargo in its hold, and not one mariner on deck. Those stories you scoff at are true and you damned well know it. Jolly Roger himself is proof that strange things happen in the Sea of Fear. Why, if that parrot could talk he could tell us what happened to the crew of the *Marina*. Jolly Roger was the only living creature on that derelict ship!"

Nicolas shifted uneasily from one foot to the other, his eyes magnetically drawn to the bank of clouds in the east. He couldn't scientifically explain the abandoned ship on which he'd found Jolly Roger. But Buff and Otis had certainly contributed to the mystery by embellishing the tale and wagging their tongues all over Barataria— the headquarters of Jean and Pierre Lafitte and the other privateers. Buff and Otis had mesmerized many a sailor with their eerie speculations and wild conjectures.

"Aye, I feel it," Nicolas reluctantly admitted to the first mate and helmsman. "Intuition warns of the approaching storm. But we aren't going to panic and succumb to the outrageous myths and legends of this sea."

All three men concentrated on the ever-growing mountain of sun-dappled clouds that gathered on the eastern horizon like angry doubled fists.

"I think we ought to turn back to Bermuda 'fore that storm swallows us alive," Otis advised. "I don't want to be sittin' atop this Graveyard of Lost Ships when this hurricane unleashes its fury."

"And if there really are crew-gobbling sea monsters down below from Lost Atlantis, I'd rather not be around to become an appetizer," Buff grumbled. "Being on this quiet sea when a storm's brewing doesn't bode well. We've already got one strike against us for launching on a Friday. I don't consider myself superstitious, but I'm beginning to think I should be!"

Nicolas chuckled at his long-time friends. "The two of you have been knitting your wild yarns for so long you'll start seeing all the ghosts and sea dragons you're always jabbering about. But don't fret," he said, with encouraging confidence. "We'll weather this storm just as we've weathered all the others. And we'll live to play cat-and-mouse with another British frigate . . ."

"Good Lord!" Otis crowed when he turned back to the wheel to gaze off the starboard bow.

Even Nicolas gasped in shock when he pivoted around to see what had provoked Otis's hoot of disbelief. The sun had dipped into the ocean and luminous white streaks glowed on the darkening sea. The incandescent flumes stretched toward the *Sea Devil* like bony fingers.

"I don't like what I'm feeling *or* what I'm seeing, Tiger," Buff remarked after he recovered his speech. "I heard tell that Columbus even reported seeing this same strange glow when he first sailed to America on the *Santa Maria*. And I also heard one of the other privateers from Barataria mention a similar phenomenon while he was up on the riggings, repairing frayed sails. It's a forewarning of doom, sure as hell!"

"Buff!" Nicolas's booming voice bounced off the planked deck and reverberated around the canvas sails.

Since Nicolas rarely raised his voice, except when he had reached the very limits of his patience or when danger was at hand, Buff knew the captain was on the verge of an outburst. Buff willed the hair on the back of his neck to settle back into place and his stampeding heart to return to its normal rate. But he still couldn't overcome the feeling of cold dread that formed icicles on his spine. Disaster lay ahead—he could feel it all the way to the bone.

"I think we should call the crew from below deck to trim the sails," Buff advised grimly. "That's no slow moving storm. It could be upon us in an hour, and what with us in the middle of the Devil's Sea . . ."

"I agree, Cap'n," Otis chimed in. His gaze darted to the fingers of light that crawled toward them on the darkening sea. "We ain't makin' headway in the doldrums anyhow. Better to be prepared for the worst, I always say.''

Nicolas fought the uneasy sensations that assailed him. He had damned well better keep his wits about him because everyone else seemed to be edging toward panic. He felt those unnerving premonitions, too, but he valiantly fought them back.

"I think it ill-advised to signal the crew until that—" Nicolas peered at the silver flumes of light that streaked the sea, unsure of what to call the unexplainable glow. "—Until the sea looks normal again."

"This sea never looks normal," Buff said, scowling.

"Buff, do you recall the story about that wealthy family from New Orleans that disappeared in this part of the ocean over a decade ago?" Otis murmured as he stared at the silver streaks. "They vanished right off their schooner during a storm, as if some demon of the deep had uncurled its tentacles and plucked them from the deck."

Buff nodded bleakly. "Aye, I remember all too well, Otis. Some say it was the devil come to collect his due. Others say it was because of a curse brought on by the leaders of the French Revolution who tried to execute every nobleman who had fled from the guillotine at the beginning of the Reign of Terror. I've even heard it rumored that French spies were responsible for disposing of the family to prevent them from uniting with the other escaped nobles and lords to retake France from the peasants' hands. Other folks speculate that it was the monsters who live in the Devil's Sea that gobbled them up to satisfy their appetite for human flesh."

Nicolas sighed. "Now's not the time for your wild stories." His legendary nerves of steel weren't holding up as well as he'd hoped.

"Well, we've got nothin' better to do while we wait out those crawlin' silver fingers," Otis sniffed. "You can scoff if you want, Cap'n. But strange things occur in the Sargasso Sea and that is fact."

Buff braced himself against the rail and stared at the glow that slowly but surely inched toward them. "I remember the legend of the lost Caron family as if it happened yesterday," he declared with perfect assurance. "I was still the captain of the merchantman schooner that traded in the West Indies, England, France, and Spain. After the mysterious accident at sea, the Marquis de Caron offered a fabulous reward for information about his missing family. It was the talk of every port we entered."

"Aye, and I was yer first mate on the merchantman," Otis recalled. "At the time, Tiger was still learnin' the ropes and playin' *gopher* for every seaman on board. The marquis offered a ten thousand dollar reward. He came down to the New Orleans dock every day to question every captain of every ship. He did that for two years until his health began to fail and he could no longer keep his vigil."

"Caron?" Nicolas's gaze bounced from one veteran mariner to the other.

The name struck a familiar chord. Nicolas had met and dealt with a haughty aristocrat known as André Caron several times in the past few years when the privateers smuggled goods past the British blockade and sold them at The Temple—the auction house that Jean and Pierre Lafitte had constructed in Barataria. The Temple was a hubbub of activity where men from all walks of life came to buy and sell supplies that were hard to acquire because of America's war with Britain.

Nicolas considered André Caron to be a shrewd, conniving rascal who had tried to weasel out of paying the full price for the goods he had ordered. Teeming with self-importance, he flaunted his wealth with jeweled rings and the most elegant clothes money could buy. Obviously André preferred to squander most of his cash on his wardrobe rather than on supplies. He and Nicolas had argued over the price and had come to blows during their last encounter. Nicolas had taken the remainder of payment from André's hide and had loosened several of his teeth.

"Is André Caron related to the marquis?" Nicolas questioned curiously.

"Aye," Buff confirmed. "André and his wife were only poor relations—distant cousins to be specific—before Gustave Caron lost his immediate family in the mysterious accident at sea. Gustave had been labeled as one of the charmed French noblemen who had the foresight to pull up stakes from their native land and sail to Louisiana before the Reign of Terror took the lives of the King and his ministers." He glanced grimly at the tall, raven-haired captain. "There were all too many noblemen who couldn't escape with their lives during those cruel times. Heads and titles were lost during the vicious uprising that changed France forever."

Otis took up where Buff had left off. "Gustave Caron had but one son, a daughter-in-law, and a gifted grandchild. They were the marquis' pride and joy, 'specially the young granddaughter who was the first of their family to be born in New France. The whole lot of them were renowned scholars. The little golden-haired girl was said to be a prodigy with an incredibly keen mind and a hunger for knowledge. At the age of nine she could speak and read three languages. The family had begun to travel extensively in Europe, which may have been one reason

13

that some folks thought the Carons were trying to join forces with other French noblemen to retake the throne. The speculation of spies disposin' of the Carons could well be fact.''

''The marquis had planned to accompany his family to Spain on that particular voyage,'' Buff added when Otis paused for breath. ''But he was taken ill and remained in New Orleans. That was the last time he saw his beloved family alive.''

''The captain of the returning schooner presented his sketchy but gloomy report to Gustave Caron. The marquis very nearly went mad with grief and frustration. Accordin' to the story, a storm seized the vessel somewhere in these very waters. None of the other passengers or crewmen were lost at sea, only the three titled Carons,'' Otis went on to say. ''It was a mystery to all. The marquis sent out dozens of search parties, some of which perished at sea themselves. But the Carons were never found nor was the incident explained to Gustave's satisfaction. It was as if the threesome had disappeared into thin air. The captain found some of the floating debris from cargo that he'd tossed overboard so the ship wouldn't be settin' so low in the water when the devastatin' storm struck. But no trace of the Carons.''

''I've even heard the conjecture that a water spout passed over the deck of the ship and sucked the family up, though why they would be on deck during a storm is beyond me,'' Buff said with a shake of his wiry red head. ''It's almost as eerie as finding Jolly Roger on that ghost ship all by himself with a booty of valuable cargo for us to . . .''

A shocked gasp broke from Buff's throat when he spied the huge ball of fire shooting across the heavens to plunge into the sea near the location where the glowing fingers of silver had appeared a quarter of an hour earlier. The mass of seaweed swallowed up the fireball, as well as the luminous white light that had sprawled across the ocean. To make matters worse, distant lightning danced across the waves. A rumble of thunder mingled with the sound of water lapping against the hull of the schooner.

Nicolas gulped. If he remained on the quarterdeck much longer, listening to these two overly imaginative sailors spin their sticky theories and weave their eerie yarns, he'd be a bag of brittle nerves!

"I'll summon the crew to trim the sails," he mumbled before he lurched around and propelled himself toward the steps.

"Holy hell!" Buff cried. His wide hazel eyes popped as he leaned over the rail to note the pack of sharks and eels that encircled the becalmed schooner.

Nicolas grimaced and then gave himself a mental slap. Curse it, a few more minutes of this and he'd be as loony as his junior officers. "For God's sake, Buff, you're perfectly aware that eels and sharks migrate here in great shoals to spawn in the seaweed before their newborns follow the Gulf Stream back to Europe."

"Aye, I know all that," Buff agreed. "But why are they circling around *us* on *this* particular night? Do you suppose they were drawn by the glowing light in the sea?"

"To be sure," Nicolas replied sarcastically. "Just as the *Sea Devil* was magnetically drawn into the Sargasso Sea by the unexplainable light." He glanced sternly at Buff and Otis. "Give your wild imaginations the rest they so richly deserve. If we must ride out a storm, I prefer that my officers possess sound minds and steady hands. If the two of you don't get hold of yourselves, you'll have the entire crew in a state of panic!"

15

When Nicolas disappeared into the companionway to summon the crew, Buff glanced apprehensively at Otis. "What do you think, mate?"

Otis clamped his fingers around the wheel until his knuckles turned white. "I think it's gonna be one helluva long night. Cap'n Tiger never has been one to give in to sentiment. But I'd wager he'll be as scared as the rest of us 'fore this night is out."

Buff's gaze was instinctively drawn back to the erect fins of the sharks and the mass of wriggling eels that circled like an Indian war party. "I figured that one day I'd go to my reward in Fiddler's Green, but I hadn't reckoned on having a shark take me there." He shivered at the thought. "Hell, we could even wind up like the Carons—sucked off this ship and hurtled into the jaws of demons from the deep."

"Aye, mate." Otis nodded gloomily as he stared across the darkened sea that reflected the distant lightning. "The cap'n always seems to enjoy defyin' death and playin' with fire to sharpen his skills. This time he might get more than he bargained for. The Devil's Sea is givin' us plenty of forewarnin' of doomsday. Cap'n Tiger had better heed the signs, lest he finds hisself stuck in Davy Jones's locker for all eternity!"

While the crew of privateers gathered lanterns and made their way to the deck to check the riggings and haul in the sails on the three towering masts, Nicolas sprawled in his chair sipping brandy. During the past few months he and his men had battled two British brigantines and captured a London-bound schooner off the coast of Bermuda. It had been a lengthy but profitable voyage. They had confiscated a cargo of salt, sugar, rum, and wine.

They had even managed to haul crates of shiny new blunderbusses and ten cannons from one of the British warships before the vessel sank and its crew swam to shore at Bermuda. The fine *eau-de-vie* brandy Nicolas sipped was one of the many spoils of war he'd taken from the British . . . and he would live to do battle again, even if Buff and Otis had come to the bleak conclusion that they had been doomed in the Devil's Sea.

Nicolas nursed his *eau-de-vie* and eased back in his chair to stare at the colorful parrot that was climbing all over his wooden cage. Although Nicolas was a mite apprehensive himself about the telltale signs of danger on the sea, he had learned at the age of ten to hide his emotion and fear from those around him. He had set out to prove his strength and ability in this cruel world. Over the years he had earned a distinguished position among the Lafittes and the other privateers. His reckless daring and unfailing courage had become legendary at Barataria and throughout the swamps and bayous of southernmost Louisiana.

Yet, the unexplainable glow and the approaching storm did give Nicolas just cause for alarm, even if he refused to show it. Having spent so many years at sea, he had developed a sixth sense every bit as strong as Otis and Buff's. The only difference was that Nicolas's mulish stubbornness refused to allow him to take emotion and eerieness seriously. He remained behind a wall of self-imposed reserve, projecting that much-needed air of authority and iron-willed control that stabilized a leery crew in crucial moments. But Nicolas was no man's fool; he knew he was sitting on the brink of disaster. The goods and supplies he had confiscated near Bermuda filled his schooner's hull to capacity. The ship was already setting heavy in the water, overloaded and vulnerable to looming

17

waves that could capsize and destroy. If the storm intensified, part of the cargo would have to be sacrificed to keep the *Sea Devil* afloat in the angry seas . . .

"Hello, Tiger."

The high-pitched voice of Jolly Roger pierced Nicolas's troubled thoughts. He glanced at the colorful green Amazon parrot dancing around on his perch, chattering nervously. A wary frown knitted Nicolas's dark brows while he watched the parrot flutter restlessly from one side of his cage to the other. It was as if the bird were trying to alert his master to something that Nicolas had already sensed himself—imminent danger.

"Hello, Tiger," Roger repeated before he danced around in a circle, teetering precariously on his perch. His famous wolf whistle reverberated around the captain's spacious cabin. "Need a cracker."

The faintest hint of a smile pursed Nicolas's lips as he reached over to fetch Roger a treat of nuts and dried fruits. "I don't know about you, Roger, but I prefer a stiff drink."

Roger's neck twisted until his beak had turned one-hundred-and-eighty degrees. He babbled and chirped but refused the treat Nicolas offered. "Where's the rotgut?"

Sure enough, Roger also preferred a drink. The parrot was a lush and he had been since Nicolas had found him three years earlier on the abandoned ship. Roger's previous owner had obviously been partial to whiskey and had allowed the bird to acquire a taste for it. Nicolas poured a speck of brandy into a cup and set it at the bottom of the cage. Roger hopped down to sip and then climbed out of his cage by his beak and claws, coming to roost topside like reigning royalty surveying his sprawling kingdom.

"Need a drink."

18

"You've had plenty," Nicolas insisted. "I, on the other hand, haven't had nearly enough." As he brought the jigger of *eau-de-vie* to his lips, a monstrous wave slammed against the ship, slopping the drink down the front of his shirt and causing everything in the cabin that wasn't nailed down to slide sideways.

When the cage wobbled, Roger went berserk. He spread his wings and sailed across the dimly lit room to crash into the wall and drop to the bed. While Nicolas brushed the liquor from his chin, he watched Roger perform a strange ritual of ducking his flexible neck like a snake and then arching backward while he jabbered in a musical monologue of chirps and high-pitched squawks, giving a running commentary of every phrase he'd ever learned.

"Curse it, not you, too!" Nicolas muttered as he set the glass aside and headed toward the door.

"Where's the rotgot? Need a cracker. Hello, Tiger. Need a drink," Roger crowed as he danced around on Nicolas's bed and then scrambled inside the pillowcase.

In his haste to reach the quarterdeck, Nicholas ignored the panicky parrot. He had the inescapable feeling that Roger's odd behavior was another forewarning of catastrophe. And considering the way the wind was howling when he zoomed out of the companionway, Nicolas knew he was going to remember this night for a long time to come . . . or at least as long as he had left to live . . . From all indications, that might not be as long as he'd hoped!

Chapter 2

Panic was the byword on the main deck of the *Sea Devil*. Even Nicolas couldn't overcome the feeling of dread that swamped him when he stared off the port bow to see the huge wall of water swelling on the choppy sea. The stays that had hung in slack an hour earlier tightened with such a violent jerk that he half-expected the masts to snap like dry twigs. The ship had emerged from the deadly calm to confront fierce blasts of wind that put frothy silver caps on the boiling surf.

The crew had managed to trim the sails on the mainmast and had begun work on the riggings on the foremast before another gust of wind buffeted the vessel, sending it lurching into the trough. Lanterns swung crazily in the breeze. Canvas sails billowed and snapped. Timbers creaked and whined under the excessive pressure of the sucking wind that seemed to attack, retreat, and then surge like hell's fury unleashed.

It was as if the blustery gale were pulling at the *Sea Devil* from opposite directions at once, testing its strength and endurance. A black cloud settled over the churning waves, just behind the gigantic wall of water that resembled a prehistoric monster rearing its ugly head from the depths of the sea. The air was so highly charged with electricity that it could make a man's scalp prickle.

The looming fog bank that hovered off the starboard bow seemed unmoved by the howling wind. The milky-white haze contrasted sharply with the black clouds to the east. It was as if the defenseless schooner were adrift directly on the boundary line between calm and storm. The fog, which was composed of tiny pinpoints of translucent light, crept toward the rocking ship as it was being shoved off the beaten path of the shipping lanes. Even the canvas took on a luminous glow.

In the span of time it had taken Nicolas to summon the crew and down a few drinks, the ocean had become a churning inferno where dark met light. It was as if an undersea volcano or earthquake had erupted, shaking the very foundations of the ocean floor, while a raging storm descended from above. Tons of water pounded against the port side, sucking and gurgling around the wind-tossed ship. The sharks and eels that had circled like waiting vultures had disappeared into the choppy depths to escape impending doom.

Before another heavy squall crested over the shuddering schooner, the crew scrambled from the masts to wrap ropes around themselves. They were taking no chances of being catapulted into the boiling sea by the tremendous force of wind and water.

The stark fear that seized Nicolas when he stepped onto the deck dissolved in one second flat. His men depended on him to make crucial decisions, to inspire them. Like a speeding bullet, Nicolas shot across the deck toward the young cabin boy who was frantically trying to coil the spare ropes. Nicolas plowed into the lad when another fierce wave slammed into the ship.

A river of water flooded over the deck, changing course as the schooner was lifted on the soaring crest and then dropped into the surf. Water dribbled between the cracks of the planks and slithered down the steps to the companionway. The foaming water never had time to pour off the slanted deck before another angry wave bit at the lurching ship. Barrels of fresh water were upended to roll across the planks like bowling balls on their way to strike the group of men who hung onto the rail for dear life.

Nicolas's voice roared above the screaming wind in warning to his crew. The sailors flung themselves away from the rolling kegs which thudded against the gunwales.

"Secure the loose cargo and barrels with that coil of rope," Nicolas bellowed at his shaken men. "And you—" He whirled on the terrified cabin boy who huddled beside the mainmast, clinging to the timber like a drowning cat to driftwood. "You get down to my cabin and make sure Jolly Roger isn't having heart seizure!"

With a dazed nod, Wyatt Townsend gathered his noodly legs beneath him and staggered across the slick deck.

Why Nicolas had decided to take that young ragamuffin on his privateer ship in the first place, he wasn't quite sure. Perhaps it was because Wyatt reminded him of another young lad of twenty years past who had been left alone with no one in the world to care what happened to him. As it turned out, Wyatt's chances of seeing his thirteenth birthday were growing slimmer by the second. It could very well be that Nicolas had done the timid orphan no great favor. The lad's hours could be numbered . . .

Casting his depressing thoughts aside, Nicolas darted

toward the steps to the quarterdeck before the next wave struck with disastrous force. He clamped onto the railing like a limpet, his feet apart to maintain balance, his fists lashed to the wet wood in preparation for the dangerous pitch and roll.

"Otis! Curse it, point us into the wave!" Nicolas blared over the whining timber and sucking sails. "If we hit that wall of water broadside this battle will be won by the sea and we'll all be floundering in it!"

Otis frantically spun the wheel as the ship plunged into the trough of the wave. The sea was rising twenty-five feet high with another thirty-five-foot giant lurking in the distance, waiting its turn to swallow the *Sea Devil* in one gulp.

The crew had managed to build a barricade of kegs and strips of canvas to divert each flood as it rushed over the bow, allowing the preceding wave to drain off before the schooner was besieged by another barrage of frothy water. But the flimsy barrier proved no match for the monstrous squall that pummelled the ship. The canvas barrier bulged and water poured everywhere as the wave took the schooner high in the air. When the crest broke, the ship shot forward with the onrush of wind and sped along at terrifying speed—tail up and nose down into the churning seaweed of Devil's Triangle.

"Fetch me some rope!" Nicolas frantically ordered Otis who had been thrown aside by the wildly spinning wheel.

Otis knew what his captain planned to do. Nicolas had just volunteered to man the wheel come hell or high water, both of which had already arrived upon the scene! Hurriedly, Otis clutched at the water-soaked rope and struggled to tie Nicolas in place. It would take a strong, unerring hand on the wheel to battle the deadly waves that loomed like rows of infantrymen waiting to blast the lumbering schooner to smithereens. Otis gladly relinquished his position at the helm. He knew he was no match for Nicolas Tiger's physical strength and steel will.

Few men were, Otis thought to himself. Nicolas had come up through the ranks of privateers the hard way. He had proven his ability to lead in times of crisis. Because of his remarkable courage and valor, Jean Lafitte had honored Nicolas by presenting him with his own ship five years earlier. To this day, even the unruliest men in the crew were hesitant to challenge Tiger's authority. And no one wanted to exchange places with Tiger now, either! They had put themselves in the captain's skilled hands and their lives depended on his ability to negotiate the gigantic waves.

The sound of the mainsail twisting and slamming against the mast reminded Otis of a death knell. He prayed for all he was worth as he tied the knot to secure the rope around Nicolas's chest and hips.

"Roll out the anchor," Buff shouted to the crew on the main deck. "Everybody who isn't tied down better get that way in a hurry!" His arm shot toward the monstrous squall. "This next wave looks to be brutal, mates!"

"Boatswains! Lower the mainsail or this whole damned ship will be torn to shreds," Nicolas screamed as he clamped a stranglehold on the wheel that tugged against him as if it had a fierce will of its own.

Sea and gale crashed and howled as the crew scrambled to haul in the remaining sail. The submerged anchor had no effect on the drifting ship. The vessel was spun about by the undercurrents that tugged at the dangling anchor from beneath the choppy surface.

Nicolas had found himself in tight scrapes before—in

storm and in battle—but this was positively the worst! No matter how he strained to keep the ship facing the oncoming mountain of water, the hull seemed to skid across the canyons of the sea like a skier racing down a vertical slope. Each time the schooner nose-dived into the trough, water plunged over the deck like a waterfall, battering him and his men, sapping their strength and stealing their breath.

"Bring the cargo from the hull," Nicolas bellowed to his crew. "We're setting too damned heavy to stay afloat."

Some of the more courageous mariners volunteered to untie their protective ropes as the careening ship rose with the next looming swell. Before the vessel swooped down at a dangerous angle, the men scrambled toward the companionway.

It was impossible for Nicolas to measure the time it took for the string of sailors to haul up the crates and hurl them into the sea. He had his hands full trying to control the swerving schooner and prevent capsizing with the heavy load.

Lightning streaked overhead with crab-like fingers clutching at the black cloud. Flashes illuminated the waterlogged deck and its panic-stricken crew. Cables and pulleys, still aglow with the strange incandescent light, swung with the force of the gale. The foot ropes trailed out at ninety degree angles, poised like snapping whips ready to lash out at anyone who dared to dash beneath them. The storm was like a nightmare from which the crew of the *Sea Devil* feared they would never wake. Minutes seemed to turn into hours as the crew tossed their prize cargo overboard and then re-lashed themselves to the railings and masts to await their destiny.

Thunder crashed above the moonraker beam and stout

canvas whirled away in shredded fragments. Nicolas tried to steer the wind-battered ship but the sea was without mercy. The schooner tipped at a dangerous angle, sending men sprawling as water rushed across the deck for the umpteenth time. By sheer luck Nicolas spun the ship the instant before it was thrown on its beam-ends. He didn't even have time to catch his breath before another crack of thunder boomed and yet another monstrous wave attacked.

"Holy Mother of God!" Buff howled when he glanced skyward.

Saint Elmo's fire—the luminous flame that often settled on the mast of a ship during a disastrous storm—sparkled against the riggings of the foremast. The crew stared goggle-eyed at the gleaming light that seemed to foretell of disaster.

"We're doomed to slip our cables and depart for Fiddler's Green," someone wailed from the main deck.

"For all of us who craved the sea, this trip will wash that taste out of our mouths forever," Buff muttered dispiritedly.

"Lord have mercy on us all!" Otis howled as he extended the compass he clutched.

Nicolas used the flash of lightning to determine what had upset the helmsman to such a wild degree. His own composure cracked when he saw the nautical instrument spinning from left to right, as if it, too, had been seized by some diabolical spirit. Nicolas had heard tales of haunted waters during his childhood days on board ship. He had also heard the eerie stories that made mention of all the phenomenal occurrences that were reported by mariners in the Devil's Sea. But never in his worst nightmare had he expected to be bombarded by so many strange, unexplainable incidents at once! If his crew managed to make it back to the privateer's cove in Barataria alive, they would be spinning a tapestry of incredible tales!

Despite the overwhelming odds, Nicolas's fists knotted around the wheel when the vessel lurched and shuddered, as if assaulted by the rippling shocks of another undersea earthquake. The compass was still spinning crazily and the violent force of the wind and water shoved the battle-weary schooner sideways. The atmospheric pressure sucked at Nicolas. His ears popped and salt water stung his eyes as the incandescent fog swallowed the ship.

Fleetingly, Nicolas thought of the legend of the missing Caron family that was reported to have been plucked off the deck during a storm. Surely he was about to experience the same dismal fate, he moaned to himself. He glanced down at the point of the compass which swung back and forth, unable to determine direction. It was as if a titanic undersea magnet had befuddled the nautical instrument, making it as useless as the frightened crew. The mariners were trapped in a deadly whirlpool of wind and water that spun and sucked and opened like a black abyss to swallow them alive.

"What the hell's happening?" Buff croaked. Horrified, he clung to the mast, as if the world was about to come to an end. And damned if he didn't believe it!

Nicolas didn't answer. His eyes were transfixed on the lightning ball that sparked against the mainsail like silver fire. He sent up a hasty prayer when the surging wave lifted the waterlogged ship as if it were as light as a feather, sending it spiralling downward into the deep trough between the towering walls of water. He swore he felt the cold, suffocating rush of the surf seconds before it actually collapsed on the ship. He held his breath, wondering if it would be his last. His body was drenched with water and seaweed clung to him like the icy fingers of death.

Just when Nicolas was certain his air-starved lungs would burst, the water receded. Raindrops hammered from the overhanging clouds and lightning bolts stabbed at the ship. Nicolas flinched when a strange, death-like calm claimed the schooner and the frayed ropes sagged against the masts. In those unnerving seconds of deafening silence, Nicolas considered his life's worth and his unfulfilled dreams. He reflected on all the things he'd done and all the things he had hoped to do before he ran aground on the other side of eternity . . .

The thought had no time to take root as the howling wind returned like a choir of banshees in the night. Sheets of driving rain soaked the *Sea Devil* as she strained against the wind, fighting for the freedom to follow the wild demands of the deep.

Time crept by while thunder crashed like gigantic cymbals and lightning cut jagged slashes through the clouds. The wind wailed and sailors offered their last prayers to heaven. Nicolas, however, gritted his teeth and negotiated the treacherous waves that left the ship teetering at dangerous angles. He cursed the errant schooner as it bowed to the tremendous forces of the sea.

The crew had given up hope of surviving the violent tropical storm in this mythical sea that was often referred to as the Devil's Playground, and for good reason! But Nicolas Tiger refused to give up. He knew he could very likely go down with his ship, strapped to the helm. But by damned, he wasn't going down without a full-fledged fight and a defiant curse on his lips. He was one bastard son who was meant to make his mark on this world! He hadn't gotten as far as he wanted to in life and this cussed storm wasn't depriving him of a single moment. He was *not* going down into this churning sea! By God, he refused!

The mighty Tiger's roar drowned out the crashing of waves against the battered hull. Otis, Buff, and the crestfallen members of the crew peered at the helm where Nicolas was lashed to the wheel. Lightning reflected the flash of fire in Nicolas's silver-blue eyes as he spun the *Sea Devil* about to take the brunt of the cresting wave.

Bufford Parks had long been aware of Tiger's iron will, his brute strength, and his fierce determination. The man was the stuff that legends were made of. But until this harrowing moment on the borderline between life and death, Buff hadn't given Nicolas Tiger full credit. The man was challenging the demons of the deep, attempting daring nautical maneuvers that would have terrified a lesser man.

The ship cut through the swell like a finned shark and slid sideways on the rising breaker. Buff closed his eyes as the onrush of water hit him full force. It was unnerving to find himself engulfed in what felt like the entire ocean. But as the wave crashed across the deck, he heard another curse explode from Nicolas's curled lips. Buff didn't know another man he'd prefer to have at the helm,— with the exception of the good Lord Himself. In fact, he couldn't help but wonder if Nicolas Tiger wasn't navigating with the Master Pilot at his side.

It seemed a miracle that they had survived as long as they had. If anyone could endure this destructive storm in such dangerous waters it was Tiger, who had already survived more than his fair share of disaster. Nicolas was determined to endure, just as he had endured all of life's vicissitudes. A dynamic inner force drove this muscular giant. He refused to accept defeat at the hands of man or nature. Nicolas always challenged impossible odds with every intention of winning—as he was now, as he would until the day he died . . .

Buff hoped and prayed that day wouldn't come anytime soon . . .

Chapter 3

After what seemed a century-long battle of man against nature, the force of the storm swept eastward. Exhausted, Nicolas slumped against the wheel and breathed a sigh of relief. Rain still pounded on the decks of the battered schooner. Black clouds swallowed the stars and the compass was spinning crazily, making it impossible to determine direction without the heavenly constellations to guide them.

"Tiger, that was the finest nautical maneuvering I've seen in a long while," Buff complimented as he wormed loose from his ropes. "You deserve a rest. Otis and I will tend the helm."

Prying his paralyzed fingers loose, Nicolas freed himself from the ropes and surveyed the schooner. He may have saved himself and his crew from a watery grave, but at tremendous cost to the *Sea Devil*! Bringing a square-rigged ship about through the eye of the wind was a complicated maneuver, even when the vessel wasn't battling a heavy squall. In an angry sea and howling gales the maneuver was not only intricately complicated but dangerous. The slightest miscalculation could have led to catastrophe. Nicolas had been exceptionally fortunate, but the *Sea Devil* had not.

The cyclonic winds had taken their toll. Nicolas had been forced to race through the trough a score of times while coming about from starboard to port tack, making the critical pass through the eye of the winds. The treacherous maneuver saved lives but damaged sea vessels. The main boom and mainsail had been smashed to bits. Now the only way for the schooner to make progress—after extensive repairs to the canvas and beams—was to sail backwards. Damage to the schooner would force Nicolas to make an unscheduled stop in the Caribbean for repairs, delaying their return to Barataria.

A scant smile hovered around Nicolas's lips as he remembered the shapely beauty whose family owned a plantation in Martinique. After the death-defying ordeal he'd just survived, a little female companionship would be a welcome change. No doubt his bedraggled crew would also enjoy celebrating their escape from what had come dangerously close to a fatal disaster at sea.

"Cap'n? Shall we weigh anchor?" Otis questioned as Nicolas started down the steps. He glanced down at his malfunctioning compass. "I don't s'pose it would do much good, though, come to think of it. I haven't the slightest idea where we are or which direction we'd be headin' in we was to make progress with these tattered sails."

"We'll hold position until the weather clears," Nicolas instructed. "We might wander onto an island reef and rip the hull to shreds."

"In other words, you don't have the faintest idea where we are either," Buff snickered.

"Aye, I do," Nicolas retorted. "We're alive. For now I'll be content with that."

"Well, as for me, I hope we were blown off course far enough to escape the clutches of the Devil's Sea," Buff declared. "That wild ride is sure to turn my hair gray, but I reckon gray hair is better than being dead and gone."

Nicolas received glowing accolades from the crewmen who followed him down the companionway. They all had a long day ahead of them—mending sails, untangling cables, and bracing broken beams. Nicolas couldn't wait to remove his soggy clothes and crawl onto his cot for a catnap. Battling the storm had completely sapped his strength.

A disapproving frown gathered on Nicolas's dark brows when he ambled into his cabin to find Wyatt Townsend draped in a chair amid the strewn volumes of books that had slid off the shelves during the violent storm. The young lad had helped himself to his captain's private stock of brandy and there were only a few drops left in the bottle. Wyatt was snoring up a storm and Jolly Roger lay on his back with his claws in the air, dead to the world. Carefully, Nicolas scooped the parrot into his hand. A faint smile pursed his lips when Roger's flexible neck dropped over his thumb. The pint-sized lush of a bird had drunk himself into a coma, as had Wyatt. They were a disgraceful pair.

After placing Roger in the bottom of his cage to sleep it off, Nicolas removed his wet clothes and slid beneath the quilts. His arms and legs felt like rubber and his muscles screamed in protest as he rolled to his side to douse the oil lamp above his bed. Nicolas cocked his head when an odd sound mingled with Wyatt's snoring. He could have sworn Roger was accompanying Wyatt harmoniously. Considering the size of Roger's beak, the parrot could snore with the best of them.

"Damned drunken bird," Nicolas grumbled at the darkness. "Probably drank himself blind."

On that thought, Nicolas closed his eyes and lapsed into slumber. Even the chorus of snorers didn't faze him.

The quiet rap at the cabin door brought Nicolas gradually awake, though it had no effect whatsoever on Wyatt and Roger. Neither had moved a muscle during the night.

Grabbing a fresh pair of breeches from his sea chest, Nicolas dressed on his way to the door. He was greeted by the bleary-eyed helmsman who was obsessed with the malfunctioning compass he clasped in his hand.

"It still won't work," Otis declared without bothering with a morning greeting. "There's somethin' you need to see from the quarterdeck," he added, jumping from one topic to another like a grasshopper.

"More damage to the ship?" Nicolas questioned as he retraced his steps to gather his boots and shirt.

"Nay, somethin' even more peculiar than this spinnin' compass, if you ask me," Otis replied. "Lordy, I'd give half my prize money to know where in hell we are!"

Befuddled by the helmsman's remark, Nicolas followed him up the steps to the deck. The ship was still engulfed in heavy gray clouds that covered the sea like a blanket. Only a breath of wind stirred through the shredded sails as the *Sea Devil* rocked on the waves. When Nicolas climbed onto the quarterdeck where Buff manned the wheel, Otis thrust the spyglasses at him.

"I don't have the foggiest notion what direction that is, but don't that look like an island beyond the seaweed?"

Nicolas peered through the spyglass at what appeared to be a tiny isle like a miniature green mountain on the far side of the seaweed. Gray clouds swallowed the specter before he could focus on it. While he was trying to read-just the lenses, the island reappeared in a blur of clouds and seaweed.

"I suppose you think we should row out to determine where we are," Nicolas commented as he studied what could very well have been a mirage.

"I was about to suggest that," Otis answered. "And if ya happen onto some islanders who have a spare compass, buy it. This one's useless. It's goin' 'round in circles, just like we are."

"I'll go along with you," Buff volunteered as he stepped back to let Otis take his shift at the helm. "It's giving me the jitters, not having a clue where the hell I am."

After Nicolas wolfed down his breakfast and set the crew to work on repairs, he lowered the dinghy into the sea. Minutes later, Otis piled in beside him with his first aid kit slung over one bulky shoulder and a knapsack strapped around the other.

Nicolas arched a mocking brow and grinned at the first mate who appeared to be practicing the policy of being prepared for anything.

"Well, it's always better to expect the unexpected," Buff defended huffily. "I brought a wee bit of every-thing—just in case we meet with trouble. After what we've been through, there's no telling what we'll find out there."

Taking the oars in hand, Nicolas steered the small vessel through the water, watching the island alternately appear and vanish in the fog—as if it were a mystical castle in this mysterious sea. Nicolas rowed past several wooden barrels and crates that his men had tossed over-board during the night to save the *Sea Devil*. It seemed odd that their cargo had remained so close to the ship, considering the gigantic waves that had swamped and buffeted them. But a strange underwater current seemed to carry the cargo along in single file and pull the skiff toward the semicircular reef that guarded the mysterious island—an island which, oddly enough, was shaped like a question mark.

"Damned lucky, we were," Buff murmured as he stared at the jutting coral and jagged rocks that were visible after they'd cleared the mass of floating seaweed. "If the *Sea Devil* had scraped against this reef during the storm we wouldn't be here now, I can tell you that for sure!"

"Do you think we're charmed, Buff?" Nicolas teased as he rowed toward the hovering fog.

"*You* are," Buff specified with a cryptic smile that seemed to hint at more. His full meaning was lost on Nicolas and Buff intended to keep it that way as long as he could. "Jean Lafitte has said so plenty of times. Every time I give him a detailed account of running an English blockade or encountering a man-of-war, he shakes his head in wonder. You're as slippery as an eel, says he. And I agree."

Nicolas shrugged off the praise and concentrated on the fog that had the same incandescent appearance as the one that had drifted toward the schooner before the storm unleashed its fury. There was definitely something eerie about this island in the middle of nowhere. Even the *Sea Devil* seemed to absorb the mystical glow, making it impossible to judge distance. It was as if they were being carried along on a current that defied the oars, leaving them drifting away from what had been reality only minutes before. The heavy air absorbed sound, and the racket of hammers pounding spikes on board the schooner was enclosed in a vacuum surrounded by silence.

"Something just isn't right," Buff said uneasily.

"That's what you said yesterday."

"Well, it still isn't right today either," Buff grumped. "Did you ever feel as if you were having a bad dream and you couldn't shake yourself awake? That's exactly how I feel—like I'm suspended in infinity. Hell, I'm even afraid to trust my own eyes and instincts."

Nicolas felt the same peculiar sensations himself when the skiff became engulfed in an unexpected whirlpool of tidewaters that swirled around the island. He had to paddle like crazy to keep from being swept toward the submerged boulders that looked as if they had once been part of the island rather than the sea floor. Unless he missed his guess, an earthquake had once crumbled part of this island into the ocean, creating a surrounding death trap that could rip an unsuspecting schooner to pieces.

The closer Nicolas rowed to the island the more fascinated he became. The lapping waves were sending up a mist when they crashed against the iceberg-like boulders. The spray cast the illusion of a fog that wasn't really there. It was as if the ocean itself was protecting this island paradise by enveloping it in a mist that hovered around it like a thick curtain. Although Nicolas was a man who dealt in cold reality, he had to admit this expedition into the outward bound had piqued his curiosity and stood his nerves on end.

"Well, I'll be damned," Buff chirped when they surged through the mist to see a pearly-white beach nestled between the outstretched arms of rock. The sandy beach fronted a dense jungle of tropical palms and ferns. But what had held Buff's fascinated attention was the cluster of naked native women who swam in the surf.

Nicolas couldn't have been more stunned if an unseen fist had connected with his sagging jaw. The bare-breasted natives were tugging his floating cargo from sea to sand to inspect the treasure. But what really captured his disbelieving gaze was the golden-haired mermaid who glided in with the surf to amble along the pearlescent shore. A mass of sunlit hair cascaded over her naked body and tumbled all the way to her thighs. Just staring at her through the spyglass was enough to send a warm throb of desire pulsating through his loins.

The women had yet to notice the approaching dinghy—they were too intent on their treasures from the sea. Minutes later, a shout of alarm erupted from the congregation of dark-skinned females. Like devoted servants protecting their queen, the natives swarmed around the blond-haired nymph until she was no longer visible, even through the spyglass. In a frantic flurry, they propelled the blonde through the foliage that surrounded the lagoon.

"Tell me I didn't see what I thought I saw," Buff chirped, goggle-eyed.

"If you didn't, I didn't see it either," Nicolas croaked, his voice not nearly as steady as he'd expected.

"Where'd they go?"

"Even more puzzling, how'd they get here in the first place?" Nicolas mused aloud.

Before Nicolas could ponder those baffling questions, a cluster of scantily-dressed natives—male *and* female—forged through the underbrush, armed with primitive spears and bows. Warily, Nicolas glanced at what appeared to be an unreceptive greeting party that was complete with, of all things, women warriors!

Hurriedly, Buff stripped off his white shirt and waved it over his head like a flag of truce. Although the dark-skinned warriors kept their lances and bows poised and ready, they made no attempt to attack.

"You'd better drag out your most charming smile,

Tiger," Buff advised. "I've heard tell that Carib Indians are cannibals. These natives could be their descendants. I don't relish being anybody's midday meal so don't you dare look the least bit threatening."

With wary trepidation, Nicolas eased from the skiff when it ran aground, pulled ashore by the odd current that surrounded this mystical island. The natives' expressions were neither hostile nor friendly, only cautiously curious. Attempting to break the ice, Nicolas held up his hand in a gesture of peace and good will before moseying toward one of the crates that had washed ashore. Using his dagger as a crowbar, he opened the crate and reached inside to fetch an apple—compliments of the British Navy's food supply. Wearing his most charismatic grin, Nicolas took a bite and then offered apples to the warriors who stood like statues in the pearly-white sand.

A stout, pot-bellied native in a skimpy loincloth, whom Nicolas assumed to be the chief, waddled forward to accept the fruit. After studying it curiously, he took a bite, chewed thoughtfully, and then nodded his head. The chief spoke to his companions in their own tongue. When the entire group surged toward him, Nicolas braced himself for the worst. But the natives only swerved around him to fish the apples from the crate.

While Nicolas was trying to decide how to communicate with the natives who appeared to be a throwback from another time, four dark-skinned females carrying spears latched onto his arms and propelled him toward the underbrush. Buff emitted a loud squawk when he was accosted in like manner by four men.

Nicolas dodged the fern leaves that slapped at his face while he was pushed along the narrow trail that led into the interior of the tiny island. They wove around a tumble of gigantic rocks which looked as if they had been shaken loose from their original positions by an earthquake. He couldn't help but wonder how long this mystical island would remain in existence. Another quake could send it crashing into the sea, as if it had never been here at all. The backward civilization which lay on the borderline of the Devil's Triangle might well become another lost Atlantis.

After several minutes, the tribe and their captives arrived at a huddle of squatty huts. The thatched roofs and bamboo walls were so similar in color to the surrounding foliage that they blended into the thickets.

Glancing around the village, Nicolas swore that he and Buff were somehow involved in time travel. The islanders looked and lived just as they had been described by Columbus centuries earlier. Nicolas had thought he had brought his schooner through the eye of the wind during the storm, but it sure as hell looked as though he had sailed through a hole in the universe, defying time and space.

Buff resisted being hustled into the village, certain he was about to be roasted over an open fire and served with an apple in his mouth. But to his relief, he was shoved to the ground and handed a sea shell brimming with amber liquid. Cautiously, he took a sip, expecting poison. To his further surprise the brew tasted exactly like rum!

Nicolas sipped his drink and enjoyed watching the dark-skinned, bare-breasted females who wandered in and out of their huts with swarms of children milling around them. Having survived weeks without the pleasures a woman could provide, Nicolas let his eyes glide over their shapely bodies. Since the women dressed as scantily as the men, very little was left to the imagination. All the natives wore loincloths of silk and satin . . .

Silk and satin? Nicolas did a double take. The island

was obviously far away from the commonly traveled shipping lanes and the natives appeared to have little or no contact with the outside world. They were as curious about the unexpected visitors as Buff and Nicolas were about finding a civilization that had presumably disappeared when the Spaniards brutally overran the Caribbean Islands. Somehow, this small tribe had managed to escape the butchery that had driven most other natives to extinction. Evidently the tribe had fled to this fog-encased isle in the middle of nowhere.

Nicolas smiled pleasantly when the chief jabbered at him in his native tongue. Although Nicolas had learned French, Spanish, English, and a few of the dialects used in the Indies, he didn't have the faintest idea what the chief was saying. But that seemed of little concern to the chief, who kept right on talking and sipping his rum.

Curiously, Buff watched the bare-breasted women wander around the perimeters of the village, eyeing the newcomers with blatant interest. There was something naturally seductive about the sway of their hips and their speculative glances. Buff's chest swelled out of proportion, flattered by the attention he was receiving, even if Nicolas commanded most of the feminine stares.

Although Nicolas was hardly oblivious to the sensual gazes coming his way, he was far more curious about the position of women in this primitive society. They seemed equal . . . Good God, dare he say *extremely influential* in this civilization? And these women also knew nothing about the coquettish games practiced by civilized females. The natives' looks said it all, and quite explicitly!

"Where do you suppose they stashed the white woman?" Buff questioned quietly.

Nicolas's broad shoulder rose in a shrug. "More importantly, how did *she* get here?"

"The same way our cargo did, I suspect," Buff replied, sipping rum from his sea shell.

An hour elapsed but still the white woman hadn't graced them with her presence. Nicolas and Buff had been treated to a variety of tropical fruit and a half-dozen conversations which they couldn't begin to understand. Finally, Nicolas's curiosity got the best of him. It was as if the natives were intent on hiding the white woman, pretending she didn't even exist. Was she being held captive? Just what position did she hold in this primitive community, if any? Was she a slave, a concubine?

"Where is the white woman?" Nicolas questioned, growing tired of this evasive game.

The chief frowned, befuddled by the question.

Nicolas gestured toward his own face and arms, comparing his skin color to the chief. "The white woman," he demanded.

The chief's pleasant expression evaporated. The entire tribe clutched their weapons and took a step closer to their guests.

"I do believe you said the wrong thing, Tiger," Buff murmured uneasily. "It doesn't appear they want us to know there's a white woman among them. Now we're duck soup for sure!"

With a flick of his wrist, the chief called his warriors to arms. Lances and bows were raised into firing position. Nicolas swallowed hard while he surveyed the area, wondering how the devil he and Buff were going to escape. Before Nicolas could devise a plan, twenty warriors—seven men and thirteen women—pounced. Nicolas and Buff were pressed to the ground and held there by the points of arrows and spears whose sharp tips gave off an offensive odor which was undoubtedly some type of poison. Nicolas sincerely hoped he wouldn't have to find out for sure.

"It was definitely the wrong question to ask," Buff grumbled, staring bleakly at the dagger-like tips that hovered a hairbreadth away from his heaving chest.

Apprehensively, Buff glanced at Nicolas whose blue eyes had turned a dangerous shade of silver. Knowing how Nicolas responded to impossible odds, Buff expected the daring captain to take on the whole tribe single-handed. It would be just like Tiger to stare certain death in the face and then defy it. But to Buff's surprise, Nicolas didn't spring into action. He simply sat there, stunned to the bone. His gaze had drifted past the cluster of threatening warriors and he was held spellbound by a vision that had appeared out of nowhere.

"My Lord . . ." Buff breathed when his wide hazel eyes followed Nicolas's mesmerized gaze.

Buff sat for the longest time, stunned by the captivating image that had caught and held Nicolas in an unblinking trance . . .

Chapter 4

Candeliera Caron emerged from the hut where she'd been watching and waiting for well over an hour. She had mixed feelings about making contact with the two men who had miraculously located the remote island on which only one live guest had arrived in more years than she could count. The sight of the white men aroused emotions Candeliera hadn't faced in an eternity—emotions she thought were dead and buried forevermore. After months of nightmares, she had finally put the past behind her to begin her new life on the island. Now the past was on a collision course with the present.

If not for the probing question posed by the tall, daring buccaneer who had been enjoying island hospitality, Candeliera would have remained where she was until the intruders departed. But the bold inquiry had put the villagers up in arms. The chief was talking extermination and she felt compelled to intervene.

Candeliera had not, however, counted on the emotional jolt she received when her gaze locked with those silver-blue eyes that drilled into her with such scrutinizing intensity. The man, who looked to be thirty or thereabout, was ruggedly handsome, undeniably appealing to the feminine eye, and exceptionally muscular. A helmet of wavy raven hair capped his bronzed face. His linen shirt strained sensuously across his broad chest, gaping at the neck to reveal the dark hair beneath it. His black breeches were molded to the columns of his muscular thighs and lean hips as if they had been painted on. They were so noticeably snug around that certain part of his male anatomy that Candeliera found herself staring in curious fascination. Black Hessian boots extended to his knees, creating the intriguing picture of incomparable athletic physique and raw masculinity in its purest form.

Having known no white men near her own age, she found herself staring at him in feminine curiosity and rapt appreciation. True, several of the native men possessed well-structured bodies, but none of them compared to this six-feet-four-inch, two-hundred-and-twenty-pound giant of a man who kept drawing Candeliera's eyes and triggering sensual speculations.

When Nicolas's penetrating gaze flooded over her like slow-flowing molasses, Candeliera flinched inwardly at the startling effect. Indeed, if he had reached out to touch her she doubted she would have been even more shocked by her own reactions. Tamping down those unfamiliar sensations, Candeliera raised her chin to stare the daring intruder straight in the eye.

She knew how to deal with the natives, having learned their customs and beliefs. But she was completely inexperienced in dealing with her own kind after this long isolation. She was taken completely aback when the swarthy rake rolled agilely to his feet, defying the lances that had been thrust at him. This powerfully-built rogue seemed to have a complete absence of fear. He would have had a spear buried in his back if she hadn't lifted her hand to forestall the actions of one particular female native whose lance was poised to strike. Ironically, the same woman had paid him plenty of attention earlier. It only served to prove how quickly the natives turned when their priestess was threatened.

Nicolas quickly recalled what Buff had said earlier about feeling as if he were drifting in a dream. For certain, this breathtakingly lovely princess belonged in a man's fantasy, satisfying all his lusty desires. Stung by impulse—something Nicolas rarely followed—he moved deliberately toward her, despite the threatening spears that could easily turn him into a human pincushion.

Although Nicolas had seen and enjoyed the intimate charms of more than his fair share of females, he couldn't call to mind even one woman who possessed this fairy princess's exotic beauty. Her thick spun-gold hair covered the bare torso of her upper body like a tantalizing cloak that concealed her sun-kissed flesh and yet exposed just enough to leave a man aching up to his eyebrows. Nicolas could vaguely see the colorful silk loincloth beneath those flowing tendrils of hair that extended to her thighs. And gorgeous thighs they were, too! he mused. Lady Godiva had nothing on this bewitching sprite. This island princess definitely deserved a legend of her own and Nicolas was making one up with each step he took toward this luscious beauty whose state of undress was burning him into a pile of smoldering coals.

Eyes like polished amethysts peered up at him, as if *she* were every bit *his* equal. She appeared totally unashamed of her lack of proper clothing in the presence of a man. Her oval face was tanned from extended hours in the sun—something civilized females abhorred. Proper ladies went to great pains to protect their alabaster skin, but this female's wholesome beauty was proof positive that a golden glow could arouse a man's interest to the extreme. And if this siren's bewitching face, heart-shaped mouth, and lustrous mane of silver-blond hair wasn't enough to turn a man's head and inspire his erotic fantasies, she possessed what appeared to be a voluptuous body that begged for intimate caresses.

At first sight, Nicolas's thoughts detoured down the most erotic avenues imaginable. Put quite simply, he was spellbound and overwhelmed by a vision of such enchanting beauty.

Exhibiting the polished manners of a gentleman—and he could play the gentleman if he were so inclined, though he was not inclined very often—Nicolas offered tribute to this exquisite female who had captivated him. Like a gallant knight paying respects to his queen, Nicolas knelt on bended knee. Surely his respectful display would get those pesky natives off his back . . . and bring him ever closer to the epitome of feminine perfection, thought he. He thought wrong. The instant he grasped Candeliera's hand, a stampede of offended natives swarmed around him.

Candeliera winced at the feel of this handsome rogue's strong, callused hand curling around her fingers to press a kiss to her wrist. It was a warm, confident hand that hinted at incredible strength, as did his sinewy physique. Another jolt of awareness sizzled through her nerve endings when Nicolas raised his raven head to disarm her with a rakish grin and a most provocative wink. Long velvet lashes that any woman would envy surrounded those glistening pools of silver-blue. Candeliera felt her knees wobble when he turned on the charm and flashed her another winsome smile. But if she hadn't raised her free hand to forestall several of the natives who were itching to run him through, that would have been the very last smile to grace his lips. The natives wanted blood!

Buff very nearly suffered heart seizure when Nicolas dared to approach the dazzling beauty so boldly. And what really rattled Buff was that Tiger was making such a spectacular display of gallantry. In the past, Tiger had only one use for females and he rarely displayed more than nonchalance in their presence. His gestures were completely out of character. For certain, Tiger had been bewitched by this white woman's unexpected appearance and astounding beauty.

"I have traveled far and wide, my lady," Nicolas murmured in a rich baritone voice that hummed with velvety seduction. "But I have never met a woman as lovely as you. You have utterly bewitched me."

Well, at least Tiger knew he'd been bewitched, thought Buff. That explained his unprecedented behavior.

It had been eons since Candeliera had heard or uttered a word of English, Spanish, or French. It took her several moments to translate and to puzzle out this bold rogue's intentions toward her. He seemed to be showing an interest in sharing her bed, but he hadn't openly admitted it. How odd to talk circles around truth, she thought. The natives made no bones about their sexual encounters. If they desired to be physically satisfied they came right out and said so.

Since her arrival on the island, the natives had looked upon her as their priestess, sent to them by their sea god. She had been set apart from the natives and refused the sexual liberties which the islanders practiced in their daily lives. This ritual of seductive courtship which this man was employing on Candeliera was a new experience, a game she had never played. She was miffed by it. Any native who dared to cast Candeliera a provocative glance or touch her could expect severe punishment. She was offered worshipful respect.

Candeliera had grown up in a civilization that was obscure and unfamiliar to men like Nicolas Tiger. This unexpected cultural collision caused Candeliera considerable confusion, not to mention the unexplainable sensations that flooded through her the instant he dared to touch her.

When the indignant chief stamped forward to hammer Nicolas over the head in hopes of teaching him some manners, Candeliera flung up her free hand in another deterring gesture.

"I do not believe the white man means to be disrespectful," she assured the affronted chief. "He simply does not understand our ways. He has only come to offer his friendship in the only manner he knows."

Although Nicolas didn't understand a word of what Candeliera had said, he listened to her soft, melodic voice as it tumbled from those kissable lips. He felt another wave of desire ripple through him, causing a knot of longing to coil in his loins. Aye, he had occasionally played coquettish games in his quest for passion. But he had to admit those pretentious rituals seemed sacrilegious when he offered them to this gorgeous sprite who held herself with such regal poise and unshatterable confidence. In fact, Nicolas almost felt the need to apologize for flinging effusive flattery at her, well-deserved though it most certainly was.

There was something oddly unique about this curvaceous female who wore nothing more than a cape of shiny gold hair and a skimpy silk loincloth. To him, she was far more appealing than a proper lady who'd spent the entire day primping before getting into her extravagantly expensive gown and putting on exaggerated airs to call attention to herself. This island nymph was one of a kind, blithely unaware of all the devious games people played in civilization.

"Forgive me, my lady," Nicolas whispered as he lithely jumped to his feet. "I had no intention of offending, only to pay tribute to such dazzling beauty."

The island princess said nothing. Her curious gaze traveled over his linen shirt and tight black breeches. Apparently she was still assessing him. And since he was overdressed, considering the local standards, Nicolas had the feeling she was doing a little speculating of her own about how *he*'d look in nothing but a loincloth. She was certainly entitled, thought Nicolas. He had made no attempt to disguise the fact that he was looking at her to see all he could!

"My lady, can you understand me?" Nicolas persisted. He felt the urgent need to communicate with her in a common language. Or better yet, to speak to her in ways that required no words. But remembering the chief's huffy protest, Nicolas imagined what he had in mind would be out of the question. *"Parlez-vous Français? Español?"*

"You must be patient, sir," Candeliera replied after a moment. "It has been a long time since I have spoken English, French, or Spanish. I have no need for it here."

While Nicolas was attempting to communicate with the island priestess, Buff sat cross-legged, staring owl-eyed at the pendant which encircled Candeliera's neck and sparkled through that glorious mass of blond hair. He recognized that distinguished crest on sight. Even though Nicolas had yet to make the connection, Buff certainly had. He couldn't logically explain what the Marchioness de Caron was doing on this obscure island in the middle of nowhere, but she was definitely here—all grown up and looking exactly like a princess from a fairy tale!

"Good Lord . . ." Buff gulped in stupefied astonishment. If the marquis was still alive—and Buff wasn't sure he still was—Gustave Caron would pay a king's ransom to have his granddaughter back. She was heiress to a staggering fortune, a living legend who had miraculously survived the disaster at sea. What an enthralling tale, and Buff couldn't wait to tell it!

"These men are a threat," the pudgy chief asserted. "I was prepared to treat them with kindness since they have survived what so many others have not. I had planned to send them on their way. But now that they have confronted you so boldly, they must be destroyed!"

Candeliera didn't agree with the chief's logic any more in this instance than she usually did. The chief was nothing more than a figurehead in this tribe which was dominated, and understandably so, by females. It was the women who were the core of society. They were the ones who prepared the food and raised the children while men enjoyed their leisure and the sexual privileges the women offered them at their convenience and pleasure. Women held all the authority and she, who had been called Priestess Pyreena—descendant of the sea god who provided the islanders with all their needs—reigned supreme.

"I am aware that we wish no contact with the outside world," Candeliera replied. "I know your ancestors escaped the other islands to avoid the butchery of white invaders. But you will be no better than the Spaniards you so despise if you practice the same cruelties. These men will leave as they came." Her tone of voice was firm and insistent, her gaze direct. "We have no riches

51

here to lure them back, only the prizes that the sea god sends to us. These men pose no dangerous threat. Take them to their skiff and let them leave in peace.''

Although Nicolas would have dearly loved to know what the conversation was about, Candeliera didn't bother to enlighten him. But it was easy to conclude that the chief had been offended by Nicolas's bold approach. For some reason, these natives were extremely protective of this lovely siren. She obviously held a lofty position in their society, even if she wasn't one of them. She spoke to the disgruntled chief in a decisive tone which indicated she thought herself to be his equal, or better. What a strange civilization, thought Nicolas. The day *he* let a woman boss *him* around was the day he laid down and died! But in this particular situation, Nicolas found himself rooting for this shapely sprite who appeared to be defending him. More power to her.

''Offer these men gifts of fruit, nuts, and trinkets,'' Candeliera instructed. ''Send them back to their world safely and they will leave us alone in ours.''

With a disgruntled snort and an inarticulate mutter, the chief conveyed the order to the warriors who had converged on Nicolas. The white men were swiftly herded back in the direction they had come. Gifts of food were dropped in the skiff before Nicolas and Buff were shoved into it. The chief's stubby arm shot out like a bullet, indicating that the white men were to go at once. His stern countenance implied that a return visit would not be well received.

''It looks as though we overstayed our welcome,'' Nicolas said with a smirk as he peered at the waving ferns and palm leaves through which the scantily-garbed natives had disappeared.

When Nicolas grabbed the oars to strain against the

incoming tide, Buff gaped at him in amazement. "That's it? You plan to leave without taking the girl with us? Are you mad?"

Nicolas frowned at his indignant first mate. "I was under the distinct impression that Princess Whoever-she-is happens to be content on the island. I've made it a practice to mind my own business and I've no intention of changing at this late date."

"I saw the way you were looking at her. Don't think I didn't," Buff snorted. "Anybody with eyes in his head could tell what you were thinking. I may be getting old, but I'm sure as hell not going blind, Tiger!"

"So I was thinking about her," Nicolas retorted with a nonchalant shrug. "So what? I've cast an interested eye at more than one lovely lady. And bewitching though this one most certainly is, she apparently holds a prestigious position in that backward society. Those natives have every intention of keeping her and she seems to have every intention of staying right where she is. If you ask me, we're damned lucky to escape with our lives. Now let's just forget it, shall we?"

Typical Tiger, Buff thought sourly. He was a natural charmer when he wanted to be, especially when it came to women. But once a particular female was out of sight, Tiger had a tendency to put her out of his mind, or at least he always gave that impression. Why was Tiger being so infuriatingly typical now, after he had been so unbelievably uncharacteristic earlier? His behavior had suddenly become impossible to predict!

"You imbecile!" Buff scowled as he clamped his fingers on Nicolas's forearm. "Don't you ever listen to a word I say? Haven't you figured out who that girl is? Or were you too damned busy ogling her? Didn't you notice the pendant around her neck?"

Nicolas grinned wryly. "Actually, there were other parts of her anatomy that demanded my attention."

"Well, you should have taken a good long look at the necklace around her throat," Buff snorted in disgust. "That was the Marchioness de Caron! The reward for her return could bring us a sizable profit, not to mention easing the mind of the marquis—if he's still alive and wondering where the deuce his family got off to."

Nicolas blinked. "Caron? As in your mysterious tales of legends of the lost?" He scoffed at Buff, whose chest swelled up like a bagpipe in offended dignity. "You, my friend, were out in the rain too long. The salt water rusted the cogs in your brain. That pendant you *thought* you saw could have come from anywhere. It certainly looks as though the natives have all sorts of supplies floating in on the tide, ours included."

"There's nothing wrong with the workings of my mind," Buff muttered. "And even if that female isn't who I think she is, we're still obliged to rescue her. What kind of life will she have here, leagues away from her own kind? As near as I can tell, she's considered a goddess of some sort. Those islanders won't allow their men to lay a hand on her and they weren't all that crazy about you touching her, either. It almost got you killed in case you didn't notice. If she remains here, she'll wind up a shriveled old spinster."

A pensive frown furrowed Buff's brow as he glanced toward shore. "These natives must be like some of the Indian tribes in America that designate a virgin as their medicine woman or guru or whatever they call them. They are supposed to be able to communicate with the gods and are to avoid intimate contact with men. Now what kind of life is that for a woman?" Buff asked somberly. "Women are meant to bear children, to be cared

54

for and protected by their men. If you ask me, this tribe has everything backwards. Why, hell, even that pudgy chief backed down to the priestess. That's not natural. They're warping her thinking with their bizarre ideas!''

"And how do you know the priestess and the chief were arguing?'' Nicolas lifted one thick brow and grinned at his ruffled companion. "I didn't know you spoke their native tongue. You should have said so.''

Buff glared daggers at the ornery rake. "I could tell by the tone of their voices that they were disagreeing,'' he replied with a scowl. "I've heard enough arguments in various languages to recognize a difference of opinion when I hear it. I'd wager the marchioness just spared our lives and we owe it to her to spare her from a long, lonely existence in a primitive culture.''

Nicolas stared at the foggy mist that concealed his distant schooner. "And just what do you propose we do, Oh Pearl of Wisdom? March back to the village—you armed with your flintlock and me with my dagger? Are we going to slay the natives to save the priestess who may or may not be the missing member of the Caron family?''

Buff was thoroughly annoyed with Nicolas's sarcasm. "Well, hell, I don't know how to go about doing it. But my conscience and my sense of what's right won't let me leave without her. And if you won't go with me then I'll just have to swim back and find a way to tote her to the schooner by myself.''

Nicolas flung Buff a withering glance. "The lady has the whole tribe eating out of the palm of her hand. She seems to like her life just the way it is,'' he countered.

"Only because she doesn't know better,'' Buff contended.

"And you could get yourself killed trying to discover

55

if she really wants to leave this island,'' Nicolas shot back.

"Maybe, but I'll have to take that risk. The marchioness deserves to be living in the lap of luxury in New Orleans. She should be enjoying all the privileges of her pedigree and wealth. If her fortune were gone it would be an entirely different story.'' His gaze was lost on Nicolas, who refused to meet his probing stare. "But it's not like that for her, and eligible men will come flocking around her like bees to nectar when she returns to civilization. She deserves to be reunited with her grandfather if he's still alive. And by damned, I aim to see that she is!''

Although Nicolas was the first to admit he found the princess wildly attractive, he wanted no complications and entanglements. He had plenty already without antagonizing a bunch of backward natives. He could very easily come away looking like a porcupine with dozens of poison-tipped arrows buried in his flesh. Nay, Nicolas had defied death the previous night to save himself and his men from the violent storm. He wasn't testing fate again so soon and certainly not for a mere woman! None of them was worth it in his estimation.

And anyway, who could say for certain if the woman was the Marchioness de Caron? The story Buff told may or may not be true. And perhaps the pendant Buff thought the girl wore had floated to the island, just like the crates of apples. Surely crates and trunks from wrecked ships had followed the current to this obscure island time and time again. That certainly explained the silks, satins, and jewels which obviously weren't mined or manufactured on the island. They were scavengers living off the disasters of lost ships and they were content with their way of doing things, and with their priestess.

When Nicolas tried to battle the current and aim toward the distant schooner, Buff grabbed his arm a second time. "You of all people know what it's like to grow up without your own flesh and blood, to be cast out alone in this world." His hazel eyes bore into Nicolas. "But you're a man and she's only a defenseless woman. She must have been even younger than you were when she was left all alone, hundreds of miles from the things that were familiar. And what about her poor grandfather? Think of the anguish and grief he's suffered all these years, not knowing if his family was dead or alive. How would you feel if you had a loving family awaiting word about you, Tiger? Or worse, how would you feel if someone you loved was stranded on a primitive island and those who could have brought that loved one back to you simply turned around and rowed off without the slightest bit of compassion or consideration?"

Buff stared at Nicolas long and hard. "I'll admit that you and I and the other privateers spend most of our time looking out for ourselves and each other. We've become selfish mercenaries. I don't know about you, Tiger, but I've still got at least one sentimental spot in my heart. And if you won't help me rescue that poor girl then I'll do it by myself. All I ask is that you await my return. If I'm not back by dark, then leave without me because I'll likely be roasting over the fire. But at least I'll die knowing I tried to do the right thing for once in my life. After last night's storm and our brush with death, I promised the Lord above that I'd be a better man if He got me through that disaster. I guess now He's giving me the chance to prove it."

Nicolas peered at the woolly-faced first mate before he glanced at the pearly-white beach. A muffled mutter tumbled from his lips. Buff's newfound sense of integrity was probably going to get them both killed. Although

Nicolas had briefly considered abducting the priestess for his own lusty pleasure while he was immersed in his titillating fantasy, he'd discarded the idea when he realized how fiercely protective the tribe was of their golden-haired treasure. And he didn't need money so badly that he'd rescue her just for the reward. Hell, he'd acquired a sizable fortune the past few years from raiding Spanish galleons and looting British frigates. The reward was hardly worth risking his life!

Yet, despite Nicolas's staunch belief that it was best not to interfere in another individual's destiny, Buff was determined to intervene because of his misdirected sense of decency. Curse it, since when had this old coot turned out to be so conscientious? Buff was letting the harrowing experience of the storm influence him. Valor in battle was one thing but *this* was something else again—the something else that could get them both stabbed, boiled, and served as a main course!

"I'm going back," Buff proclaimed as he took control of both oars.

"If you have to be so damned noble all of a sudden, at least be sensible," Nicolas grumbled as he jerked the oars from Buff's hands. "Don't you think those natives are crouched in the bushes, watching to be sure we depart? If you're determined to rescue that she-male, we had better lose ourselves in the mist first and then circle around to come ashore elsewhere. My guess is the islanders will spend the remainder of the day scanning this lagoon."

Buff had occasionally pointed out the flaws in Nicolas's character—like being insensitive toward women, unemotional, and self-oriented. But he had never once complained about Nicolas Tiger's analytical logic. The man always thought with his experienced mind, never his sentimental heart. Buff never considered Nicolas to be the careless sort. Brave? Aye. Daring? Indubitably, but never thoughtlessly careless. Or at least he hadn't been until he swaggered toward the priestess, defying danger for a closer look at feminine perfection. But when it came to doing battle, Nicolas always had a plan.

Settling himself in the dinghy, Buff waited until they had glided through the foggy mist before he took up an oar to help steer them out of the current and around the massive arms of rock that surrounded the cove.

"Trust me, Tiger. We're doing the right thing," Buff said with perfect assurance. "That girl will thank us a dozen times over for saving her from this primitive existence. Her grandfather will be indebted to us forevermore for returning his blood kin."

Nicolas didn't respond; he simply rowed. Damn that Buff and his noble ideas. True, Nicolas wouldn't mind the pleasure of the woman's company. But an innocent maid on board a privateer, surrounded by a crew of love-starved men? It seemed to Nicolas that they were inviting all sorts of trouble, even if they did manage to abduct the chit and escape with their lives.

Curse it, Nicolas was beginning to think there was something to those eerie tales about the Devil's Sea. Peculiar things seemed to happen in these waters, making people behave uncharacteristically. He wondered if he'd live to tell about the peculiar things he was being forced to do against his better judgment. He had already pressed his luck and he wasn't sure how much he had left.

Nicolas cast Buff a mutinous glance as they circled the island. The man had always been taken in by a pretty face. It was his worst fault. Nicolas, on the other hand, was usually capable of controlling his impulsiveness, relying on cold, sound logic. This wasn't logical and his instincts were rebelling against this rescue mission. It was bound to cause trouble. *More* trouble, Nicolas silently amended. There was a war going on and here he was trying to rescue a female who didn't seem all that anxious to be rescued. Surely he had more important things to do. And he'd be off doing them now if Buff hadn't hit him with those remarks about being left alone in the world.

That must have done it, Nicolas decided as he aimed the skiff toward a secluded spot surrounded with vines and dense foliage. Buff had known just which nerve to tap to get Nicolas to agree. Curse it, if they got out alive, Nicolas vowed to rake Buff over the coals for resorting to the one scrap of sentiment that touched him when nothing else could!

Chapter 5

Candeliera ambled toward her private hut on the edge of the village, just as the sun started its descent toward the sea. The appearance of the white men earlier in the day had a disturbing effect on her sense of well being. For more years than she could count she had accepted her fate and resigned herself to an uncomplicated life with the natives on Lost Island—as they called their isolated home. In past years, several bodies had washed ashore—victims of violent storms and ruthless piracy, no doubt. But no one had arrived alive except for her and that had been by a sheer miracle. Since she had been only nine at the time, she had been able to crawl onto the floating wooden keg which had held her high enough out of the water to prevent drowning in the rolling waves.

The white men's unexpected appearance had stirred uneasy feelings of another life in another civilization beyond the sea. Their arrival had triggered the haunting memory of her childhood—a nightmare that had been dead and buried until it rose again like a demon from the deep. Candeliera was reminded of her own arrival on the island and the tragic incident that had left her an orphan . . .

Her rambling thoughts screeched to a halt when she entered her thatched hut. She found herself trapped within a pair of brawny arms. Before she could shout for assistance, a cloth was stuffed in her mouth and she was hauled up against the rock-hard wall of a man's chest.

Nicolas had taken the precaution of employing a gag. He didn't believe this female was as thrilled with the prospect of being rescued as Buff seemed to think she was. Sure enough, Nicolas was right!

Candeliera's composure came unraveled when she twisted around to view the dark face that loomed above her. With mounting alarm, she gazed into those silver-blue eyes that burned into her with stern intensity. The realization of what was about to happen hit Candeliera like a doubled fist. Years earlier, another man had clamped hold of her and dragged her to the deck of the schooner upon which she'd been sailing with her parents. Candeliera found herself reliving that tormenting nightmare, fighting those deeply embedded fears which sprang back to life in less than a heartbeat.

Nicolas couldn't believe the battle he suddenly had on his hands! It was as if he had latched onto a ferocious wildcat who was spiked claws and thrashing legs. She was every bit as determined to extricate herself from his clutches as he was to hold onto her. If she escaped to alert the villagers, Nicolas and Buff could kiss the world good-bye!

Circling back to the island had been one of Buff's very bad ideas, Nicolas realized. He sorely wished he'd paid no heed to his first mate's plea. As lovely and bewitching as this woman was, she was also a five-feet-two-inch bundle of remarkable strength and fiery determination.

She had already clawed the top layer of skin off his cheek and had kicked his shins to splinters. If her brutal blows had been directed at more vulnerable parts of his anatomy he would have been doubled over, howling in pain.

Anxious to come to Nicolas's assistance, Buff fished the rope from his knapsack and grabbed Candeliera's ankles. After Nicolas had shed his shirt and forced Candeliera into it, Buff bound her wrists. With swift efficiency, Nicolas tossed her into a jackknifed position over his shoulder. When she raked her claws down his bare back, he bit back a screech of pain. Gritting his teeth, Nicolas slipped through the slit he had cut in the back of the hut and plunged into the jungle of palms and vines.

Desperate, Candeliera bucked and writhed and clawed to free herself, but to no avail. She even resorted to pounding her doubled fists against his spine, but her blows didn't seem to faze the muscular giant. If they did, he was keeping his discomfort to himself, depriving her of even the smallest satisfaction.

While Buff was leading the way through the thick underbrush to return to their skiff, a shout of alarm arose in the village.

"Damn, somebody must have gone to check on the priestess," Buff speculated, glancing apprehensively over his shoulder toward the distant glow of the campfire. His eyes widened in concern when torches blazed against the darkness of the tropical jungle. "They're following us!"

Nicolas quickened his pace, cursing this female and her devoted followers with every hurried stride. By God, he had refused to allow the previous night's storm to destroy him and his men; he wasn't about to wind up as mulligan stew, either! Blast it, this was all Buff's fault! He and his newfound ethics!

"Remind me never to honor your foolish requests again," Nicolas scowled as he ducked beneath a palm branch and thrashed through the dangling vines.

"The lady will thank us for this, just you wait and see," Buff asserted between puffs. "She's scared, that's all. And those natives are only thinking about what's best for them, not their priestess."

Candeliera was having difficulty keeping up with the hushed and hurried conversaion while she bounced along on Nicolas's shoulder. It had been too long since she'd heard English spoken and she had to force herself to concentrate on translation.

Still furious about being carted away against her will, Candeliera hammered on Nicolas's muscular back, wishing she had a spear that would inflict enough pain to force him to put her down. But the brawny brute seemed invincible. Nothing she did discouraged him.

"Holy hell!" Buff hooted when an arrow whizzed past his shoulder to snag in the dense underbrush. "If we don't reach the skiff—and quickly—we'll be human pincushions."

Those were Nicolas's thoughts exactly. Arrows—poison arrows, he suspected—were buzzing around them like a swarm of angry hornets. Frantic, he zigzagged around the clump of trees and jogged down the beach. With more haste than gentleness, Nicolas dumped his wriggling captive in the dinghy, plopped down atop her to hold her in place, and scooped up the oars. Although Candeliera desperately tried to worm loose and fling herself overboard, Nicolas held her flat and rowed for all he was worth. Arrows hissed through the air to plunk only inches away from the sides of the dinghy. Nicolas's notorious growl indicated he was nearing the end of his fuse as he battled the whirlpool current that sought to send them gliding back in the direction they'd come.

As Nicolas strained against the tide, constant shouts echoed across the sea. Voodoo curses were being hurled at them, and he assumed he and Buff were being condemned for stealing the priestess.

The islanders were very determined, Nicolas realized when he spied a fleet of fishing boats cutting through the sea like a flotilla of sharks. The rescue brigade refused to turn back, even after Nicolas had negotiated his way around the monolithic arms of rock that reached out into the ocean.

In the distance, he could see the oil lantern swinging in the twilight, guiding him toward his waiting schooner. But he couldn't reach the storm-ravaged vessel quickly enough, he thought gloomily as he flashed a piping-hot glare at Buff.

When Nicolas was within shouting distance of the ship, he barked the order to weigh anchor and unfurl every sail, tattered though most of them still were. Thankfully, the crew had been hard at work making repairs during his absence. The ship could make some headway in the breeze, even if it did have to sail backwards because of the damage to the yardarms, riggings, and canvas.

"What the hell's goin' on?" Otis called from the helm.

Nicolas wasted no time in explanation. "Toss out two grenades while you're loading the twelve pounder," he yelled. He gestured toward the fleet of natives who were in hot pursuit, spouting voodoo incantations with every angry breath.

Amid the spray of lantern light, Nicolas could see the crew scurrying to load the cannonade on the main deck.

Two of the men scooped up the grenades as the captain had ordered. The grenades—bottles filled with gun powder, small shot, and pieces of iron—were set aflame and heaved toward the natives. The unexpected blasts sent the natives into another barrage of curses.

Nicolas swiveled around on his perch to monitor the loading of the cannon which would definitely deter the irate natives paddling toward him. The loader and sponger pulled the plug out of the muzzle which had sealed the barrel during the storm. With the cannon readied, the crew awaited the next command.

"Load!" Otis shouted into the speaking trumpet.

The powder monkey, as Wyatt Townsend was referred to when he manned his battle station, slid the bulky cartridge from its case and handed it to the loader who tossed it to the head cannoneer. Hurriedly, the cartridge was rammed into the barrel and the sponger shoved the cartridge home. The other men retreated a safe distance before the loader and powder monkey pushed the cannon against the bulwark of the ship in preparation for firing.

"Prime!" Otis bellowed as he surveyed the approaching fleet of natives.

The priming wire was shoved into the cartridge and gunpowder was dumped into the pan of the lock. When fire had been set to the fuse, Nicolas dropped his arm in a signal to fire.

The cannon boomed and a cloud of smoke rose into the overcast sky. The cartridge whistled through the air above Nicolas's head and exploded in front of the lead canoe.

"Fire again when ready!" Nicolas roared as he frantically rowed toward the stern of the *Sea Devil*.

A second cartridge was rammed home and its fuse detonated. The shot sent a spray of water over the canoes, forcing the natives to abort their rescue mission or risk being blasted head-on. Still spouting furious curses, the natives reversed direction to retreat to their island beyond the mist.

Nicolas breathed a deep sigh of relief as he latched onto the rope ladder that had been tossed down to him. Safe at last!

His gaze fell back to the squirming bundle of femininity. Without bothering to question his protective instincts, he reached over to fasten the shirt he had hurriedly wrapped around her earlier. However, the garment had been doused with water during their hasty retreat and the shirt had become almost transparent, revealing what lay so temptingly beneath it.

Although most of the men in his crew obeyed orders without question, that did not necessarily apply to their dealings with women. This she-cat's presence was bound to incite a great deal of lust. This curvaceous priestess was destined to become the object of ravishing gazes and hungry speculation. The less the mariners saw of this lovely imp in her clinging garments the better, Nicolas decided. She could find herself backed into a dark corner and mauled, especially in that soggy shirt that enticed more than it concealed.

Terror had a fierce and mighty hold on Candeliera. Only one other time in her life had she been hauled away from the security she had known. That nightmarish incident had drastically changed her life, and now she was forced to endure a similar ordeal. Everything inside her rebelled when Nicolas jerked her up under one powerful arm and started up the ladder. She swung wildly with her bound hands, only to have him whip her around so that her knuckles connected with the hull of the ship, causing her to shriek in pain.

Candeliera resented everything about this man, up to and including the scent of cologne that clung to the shirt she wore. Not only that but he was whisking her away from the island to . . . to what? Her emotions were being torn out by taproots and she soundly cursed the men who had abducted her and caused this upheaval. She struck out with her long nails again, hoping her captor would drop her and leave her to drift back to the island where she belonged.

"Ouch! Damn it, woman!" Nicolas growled at her shapely derrière which was draped over his shoulder. "I'm going to cut those claws the first chance I get!"

The instant Nicolas's head appeared above the railing two of the mariners relieved him of his squirming baggage. One of the men retreated a step and stared at Candeliera in disbelief before he composed himself and dashed forward to retrieve her before she hurled herself over the gunwale. Although she bucked and screeched in indignation, they weren't about to let her go.

"Lordy! A veritable mermaid," one of the crew crowed.

"And an angry one, too," another added with a snicker.

With her long hair shimmering like gold dust in the lantern light and the lower portion of her body undulating in her attempt to burst free of restraint, Candeliera did resemble a mermaid. Her presence brought all activity on deck to a standstill.

The instant Nicolas set foot on deck, he scooped Candeliera up and headed toward his cabin. The wench hadn't been on the schooner one minute and already she'd drawn the fascinated attention of every man on board. Curse it, this feisty hellion was bound to cause trouble. He could see his men thinking the same lusty thoughts that had

68

darted through his mind earlier that day the instant she had emerged from her hut.

Definitely trouble, Nicolas concluded as he opened his cabin door.

"Hello, Tiger," Jolly Roger chirped in response to the whine of the door. After fluffing his colorful feathers, the parrot hopped onto a higher perch to have a look around.

When Nicolas roughly tossed Candeliera on his cot, he also sprang the trap on her temper. She could guess what this scoundrel wanted—to violate her, to molest her without a moment's consideration of her feelings. If this blackguard had been on the island and had handled her so disrespectfully, he would have been strung up on bamboo poles and tortured within an inch of his life!

Furious with her captor, Candeliera bounded up to latch onto the first makeshift weapon she could find. With a venomous hiss, she hurled a nearby chair at him and then scooped up the empty brandy bottle from the table.

Nicolas sidestepped the cartwheeling chair and ducked before the bottle could slam into his skull. The leg of the chair broke when it crashed into the wall. The bottle shattered in a zillion pieces. In less than a minute his immaculate cabin was in a shambles and Roger was bouncing off the sides of his cage, terrified by the wild hisses and loud crashes.

"Enough!" Nicolas roared. He flung up his hand toward the she-cat as she launched another bottle of his finest whiskey. "A truce. I won't harm you if you promise not to harm me."

It took several seconds for Candeliera to translate his words. Even when she did, she wasn't sure she should trust this formidable rapscallion who towered over her. He could be luring her into a false sense of security before he pounced. Well, he'd never get that close, she vowed furiously. She'd claw the hide off his handsome face first!

Despite the request for a truce, Candeliera grabbed another liquor bottle and cocked her arm, prepared to put her improvised weapon to flight.

"I *wouldn't* if I were you," Nicolas warned.

Candeliera decided she *would*—the consequences be damned!

When the bottle sailed across the room, Nicolas scowled at the wild woman's defiance. Agilely, he shot out a hand to catch his fine stock of brandy before it splattered against the wall. Then he stalked toward Candeliera, who didn't have the sense to realize she'd been defeated.

"Now look, lady," he growled as he slammed the bottle onto the table, his eyes glittering ominously. "We're trying to do you a favor by rescuing you . . . am I going too fast?" He studied her flushed face while she wrestled with his rapid-fire soliloquy. "Now curse it, sit down and listen!"

Candeliera had never been treated so rudely. It also disturbed her that he was such a powerful, overwhelming male. There was an intensity about him that she wasn't sure she could handle. Candeliera was appalled that she felt incapable of handling any man under any circumstances! On the island she was treated like royalty. Her wishes were obeyed without question. But on this ship, she was being ordered about by this overbearing brute who was oblivious to a man's proper role in the presence of a woman. Candeliera wasn't used to sitting down when she was *ordered* to do so. She tilted her chin to a militant angle and flashed Nicolas a scathing glare.

"When I say sit, you *sit*!" Nicolas insisted as he

clamped his hands on her rigid shoulders and shoved her down onto the cot.

Damn the woman. She didn't react in the way he had come to expect from those of the female persuasion. Thus far, this she-cat had him stymied and forced *him* to respond in a most unprecedented fashion.

Candeliera refused to be cowed by his bullying and high-handed manner. The nerve of this rascal! He was ordering *her* around and telling *her* when and where to sit? The very idea!

When Candeliera bolted back to her feet, Nicolas's temper snapped. With a roar and a thunderous scowl, he shoved her down again. The back of her knees collided with the edge of the cot and she flopped down, despite her attempt to keep her feet. Nicolas followed her to the cot to straddle her belly, shackling her bound wrists with one steely hand.

The sight of this bare-chested giant looming over her in a most compromising position brought all Candeliera's self-preservation instincts to life in one second flat. She raised her knees and rammed them into Nicolas's back. Caught off guard by the blindsided attack, he settled on top of her, forcing out her breath in a whoosh. Levering himself up again, Nicolas glared at the defiant hellion who still refused to be dominated.

It was into this scene—with Nicolas half-sprawled on his irate captive—that Buff walked. He quickly surveyed the broken bottle and chair and then glowered at Nicolas, whose intentions toward Candeliera appeared less than respectable.

"Tiger!" Buff barked as he watched Candeliera squirm frantically beneath Nicolas's bulky form. "What the devil has gotten into you?"

It definitely wasn't what Butt was thinking, Nicolas mused as he sank down beside the human tigress. True, the first time he'd laid eyes on her, she had stimulated his desire. But after this most recent fiasco, he was tempted to strangle her swanlike neck and be done with it!

"What I'm doing is trying to teach this spitfire a few manners," Nicolas muttered before calling Buff's attention to the ransacked cabin and his scratched face. "She tried to tear me *and* this place all to hell."

Buff eased the door shut and carefully veered around the broken glass. "She's frightened," he said in her defense. "Once she realizes we have her best interests at heart, she'll calm down. You might have tried to explain instead of manhandling her!"

"I did try to explain," Nicolas grumbled, refusing to release his captive for fear she would pick his bones clean with those dagger-sharp nails. "Either she can't understand or she's simply too damned stubborn to listen to reason."

Buff approached, wearing a peace-treaty smile that revealed the wide gap between his two front teeth. "Not to worry, my lady," he crooned, "No harm will come to you. We're only taking you back where you belong." He spoke slowly and distinctly, as if English were her second language.

Careful not to frighten Candeliera more than she already was, Buff reached out to offer his hand to help her up into a sitting position. That done, he removed her gag and then bowed courteously. "There. You see? We don't want to hurt you, only to help you."

"Speak for yourself," Nicolas snorted as he inspected the claw marks on his cheeks and forearms. "She took her anger out on my hide and I'd dearly like to reciprocate.

Clapping her in irons and giving her a few lashes with a cat-o'nine-tails might cure what ails her.''

Their captive understood Nicolas clearly enough—the glare she hurled at him was hot enough to burn the iron off a skillet. Thoroughly disgusted with the events that landed him in a battle royal with this fiery female, Nicolas rolled to his feet and unpopped the cork on his brandy bottle. Mockingly, he raised the flask to toast the violet-eyed horror before taking a generous swig.

Candeliera had felt an unprecedented stirring of physical attraction the first moment she had seen this swarthy, midnight-haired rake. But those feelings had gone up in a puff of smoke when he dared to whisk her away from her safe, secure world. When Nicolas raised his glass in ridiculing salute she felt the compulsive urge to claw out those taunting blue eyes of his!

Giving way to the impulse, Candeliera bounded up like a jackrabbit, knocking Buff to the floor on her way to pounce on Nicolas. In one spectacular kangaroo hop, she launched herself at him, sending his bottle slamming against the wall. A furious bellow followed when whiskey splashed on his chest and his head collided with the wall.

Nicholas deflected the oncoming blow to his cheek and snaked out his free arm to lift the feisty heathen off the floor. Damn, he thought to himself. This misfit was in for a rude awakening when she set foot on American soil. If she behaved like this in New Orleans, someone was likely to box her ears. He'd like to be the one to do it, too!

"Buff, go fetch us some supper," Nicholas ordered as he watched his stunned first mate get to his feet and dust himself off. "We'll feed this wild hellion and then

I'm going to make a lady out of her, even if it kills both of us!''

Nodding mutely, Buff massaged his bruised backside on his way to the door. He paused to glance back at the squirming bundle whom Nicolas kept clutched under one arm. Perhaps his noble deed hadn't been such a good idea after all, Buff mused pensively. He had never seen a woman behave in such an uncivilized fashion. Even his quiet, soothing voice hadn't fazed her. This blond-haired beauty was a seething mass of volatile temper!

When the door eased shut behind Buff, Nicolas carried the squirming bundle over to his cot and dropped her unceremoniously into a heap. With a menacing scowl, he sank down on top of her once again to hold her in place. Candeliera, who was not accustomed to being restrained in any manner whatsoever, squirmed vigorously and spouted insults at him in the natives' language.

Nicholas couldn't say for certain why he employed the method he chose to subdue this wriggling firebrand. But the technique did serve to shock Candeliera long enough to get her attention. His mouth descended on those luscious pouting lips, kissing the resistance clean out of her. He wondered if it was the first time a man had dared any type of amorous assault. It certainly would have seemed so, judging by her stupefied reaction. Her curvaceous body stilled beneath his as he uncoiled to lie full length upon her. And before she had time to gather her scattered wits and fight back, Nicolas found himself kissing her again. This time he utilized a far gentler technique that he rarely bothered to use on his lovers in various seaports from hither to yon.

At first, Candeliera had been too stunned to react. And seconds later she was still too bewildered to resist. Her naive body responded to this rake's pulse-jarring kiss in ways she'd never dreamed possible. Wild tingles flew down her spine as his lips moved languidly upon hers and his muscular body blended into her feminine contours.

The civilization in which she'd lived had not permitted her to experiment with her femininity, although the natives took a very liberal approach to sex and practiced passion with a variety of partners. Candeliera had always been curious about sexual encounters, but any man who dared to approach *her* with lust on his mind had become an example for others who might be tempted to forget their places. All she knew about the wanton desires of the flesh was what this darkly handsome rascal was teaching her with such tantalizing expertise. There was something wickedly pleasurable about his touch. Candeliera decided she liked this blue-eyed giant far better when he was kissing her than when he was growling and attempting to restrain her in that forceful, domineering manner.

Although this firebrand was clearly inexperienced in kissing, Nicolas was startled to realize how fiercely attracted he had become in a matter of minutes. He had never forced himself on a woman because, quite honestly, he'd never had to. Women usually came to him with little invitation. Until now, he'd never treated a female so roughly, though there were a few he'd have liked to beat the tar out of. This hellion had deserved to be manhandled after she'd come at him with claws bared. And yet, the instant his mouth slanted over those dewy soft lips and his male body came into contact with her delectable curves, Nicolas felt a fire burning inside him. The pleasure this imp had given him had almost been worth the pain and frustration she'd put him through.

The only thing Nicolas didn't know was how to retreat without leaving himself at a disadvantage. This feisty beauty had thrown him into a tailspin. He had suddenly found himself kissing her for the mere pleasure of it rather than to shock her into submission.

Levering up on an elbow, Nicolas peered down into the enchanting face surrounded by a waterfall of shimmering, silver-gold hair. Lord, what a beguiling creature she was! He could well imagine how eagerly this temptress would be pursued in New Orleans society, if she could be properly trained and tamed. Why, lines of prospective suitors would be forming behind her, especially if she was who Buff thought she was. With her vast fortune and stunning good looks, she would take the city by storm! And what a fashion statement she would make, he thought wickedly, if she sashayed into civilization dressed in her native dress—or rather the lack thereof!

"I'll untie you if you promise to behave like a lady," Nicolas offered.

Candeliera stared into his bronzed face and fascinating eyes which were now a sparkling shade of silver instead of hard glittering blue. Her body still tingled with sensations caused by his masterful kisses and the feel of his masculine flesh.

It had been impossible not to notice the change in his anatomy while he lay upon her. Being a typical man, he had been physically aroused by a woman, and without any provocation. That was to be expected, Candeliera reminded herself. Males of the species were governed by animal instinct, not by their rather limited intelligence. They were motivated by primitive desires for food, shelter, and sex, and not necessarily in that order. She decided to employ what she knew about those of the male persuasion to gain the advantage. But she would be remiss if she didn't remember that she was dealing with a creature of lesser intelligence—common man.

In the island society where women were dominant, females permitted male companionship when they desired physical pleasure. Candeliera decided to use the same tactic on this swarthy captain and treat him the same way the native women handled their various lovers.

Lifting her hands, Candeliera silently requested that Nicolas set her free. "I won't attack you," she assured him in English.

A wary frown puckered Nicolas's brow. He had seen the ponderous expression that captured this nymph's elegant features while she was silently scrutinizing him. He wondered if he dared to trust her. Considering her previous track record, she might decide to launch herself at him the instant she was free. If she did, he wouldn't have an inch of skin left on his face or chest. She was deadly with those long claws and he had the scratches to prove it! But his male pride prompted him to accept her word. The day Nicolas Tiger couldn't handle a female—even one as feisty and unconventional as this one—would be the day he gave up on this world!

Casting Candeliera his most charismatic smile, Nicolas untied her ankles and then loosed her wrists. To his amazement, the curvaceous blonde shrugged off the shirt he had lent her. With the utmost poise and grace, she rose from the cot, wearing only her silky loincloth. His gaze immediately fell to the roseate tips of her breasts that were barely concealed by the cascade of curly hair that tumbled over her shoulders. Nicolas swallowed hard as his eyes wandered over the trim indentation of her waist, the alluring flair of her hips. He was as captivated as he'd been when she emerged from her thatched hut to command his undivided attention. Curse it, no woman deserved to be this attractive, this well-structured, he mused.

"We will use each other's bodies for our pleasure, Captain," she told him with her usual air of authority. "Afterwards, you will return me to my island and leave us in peace."

Nicolas's jaw dropped open; his eyes feasted on ultimate temptation. Although this imp's English was slightly choppy from lack of use, her tone of voice indicated she was accustomed to giving commands rather than taking them. Now why didn't that surprise him? And what a command it was, too! Candel had been so disarmingly direct that Nicolas was thunderstruck. He could barely think straight while his eyes drank in the luscious sight and his mind was awhirl with erotic speculations . . .

The rattle of the door jarred Nicolas's malfunctioning brain back to proper working order. In a flash, he bounded to his feet to cover Candeliera's appetizing figure with his shirt. But in his haste, his fingertips brushed against the peak of her breast, triggering another tidal wave of reaction that left him weak-kneed.

"Come in," Nicolas answered, his voice an octave higher than usual.

Candeliera had thrown him for a loop and he wasn't sure he could handle her as well as he had thought he could. But then, Nicolas thought in his own defense, he had never met a female who didn't know her place and ordered *him* around as if women were the superior gender! What sort of weird culture existed on that island? For damned sure, it wasn't the kind with which Nicolas was familiar!

Chapter 6

Nicolas's broad shoulders sagged in something akin to relief when Buff and Otis trooped into the room carrying trays of food. With each passing moment it was becoming alarmingly difficult to be alone with Candeliera. She stirred too many emotions inside him.

While the men were surveying the damage to the cabin, Nicolas fished out a clean shirt. He kept a watchful eye on Candeliera all the while, just in case she considered going on the rampage again.

Otis extracted the compass from his pocket, thumping the case with his finger, attempting in vain to jar the instrument into functioning properly.

"Three days and still this confounded compass won't work," he grumbled. "Darned if I know what to make of this, Cap'n."

Having voiced his concern regarding the compass, Otis repocketed the instrument and tipped his hat to the scantily-dressed woman. "How do ya do, ma'am. Glad to have ya aboard," he added politely.

Candeliera nodded haughtily, annoyed at the interruption that delayed her attempt to bargain with the captain and convince him to return her to the island.

"I'm glad to see you finally realized we have no wish to harm you," Buff piped up. "What's your name, my lady?"

"Pyreena, priestess of the Sea God," she informed the men.

A wry smile pursed Nicolas's lips as he pivoted to face Her Aloof Majesty. "I think Buff wanted to know your name *before* you came to the island."

Candeliera glared at the towering giant who eclipsed the lantern light and left her in his shadow. When her chin tilted to a rebellious angle, Nicolas glanced at her with casual menace.

"Don't force me to employ strong-arm tactics again," he muttered just loud enough for her to hear.

Candeliera fumed at the remark, which reminded her of their tussle and that breath-stealing kiss which had thrown her completely off balance.

"My name was Candeliera Junfroi Caron," she said begrudgingly.

"Was I right or was I right?" Buff asked with a gloating grin. "I told you that's who she was?"

"Caron?" Otis chirped. "My Lord!"

"Candeliera . . ." Nicolas rolled the provocative sounding name off his tongue as he reached out to comb his fingers through the thick tangle of silver-blond hair that cascaded over her shoulders. "Such a sophisticated name. But it doesn't suit such a wild-hearted woman. Since you have a temper that's so easily set to flame, I shall call you Candel."

"I wish you wouldn't," Candeliera insisted as she sidestepped his caress. "I prefer to be known as Pyreena."

It had been a long time since anyone had referred to

her as Candel. The nickname was one that her family had given her a lifetime ago. Now they were gone and so was the life she only vaguely remembered. Candeliera refused to face the tormenting memories of days gone by. It had taken years to recover from her traumatic experiences and she refused to face the ghosts of her past—again.

"Don't you understand, my lady?" Buff questioned. "We plan to take you back to New Orleans where you belong. There's a fortune awaiting you. Your grandfather, the Marquis de Caron—"

"He's still alive?" Candeliera queried anxiously, staring at the bushy-haired first mate in astonishment.

Buff shifted uneasily from one foot to the other when those startling lavender eyes focused on him with such intense curiosity. "Well, I can't say for sure. It's been a long while since the marquis came down to the docks, hoping to receive word about your family. He was taken ill and I haven't seen him since. But I know some of your kinfolk are in New Orleans. Captain Tiger has dealt with the Carons on several occasions."

Unpleasant dealings they were, too, Nicolas silently added. He had no respect for André Caron. In fact, that manipulative weasel was partially to blame for Jean Lafitte's and the other privateers' problems in New Orleans. After Nicolas had refused to settle for the price André had announced he would pay—and not a penny more—for goods delivered according to their original agreement, an argument had ensued. Punches were thrown and André had caught most of them. Intent on teaching Nicolas and Jean a lesson about doing business with influential men, André had gone to Governor Claiborne, demanding that he clean out the "pirates" in Barataria. Nicolas had considered himself a privateer, never a pirate. But because of André and the governor, Baratarians were no longer able to walk the streets of New Orleans as freely as they had in previous years.

"I have no wish to be reunited with my kinfolk," Candeliera protested. "I wish to return to the island immediately."

Even as a child, she had never felt comfortable in the presence of her distant cousins. André and his prissy wife Yvonne had been cool and aloof for no reason that a child of nine had been able to comprehend. Their air of self-importance seemed unjustified. Candeliera imagined André and Yvonne would be as thrilled to see her as she would be to see them—which was not at all!

"But yer an heiress—the Marchioness de Caron!" Otis reminded her. "Why would ya want to return to a primitive island when ya could have the whole world at yer feet?"

When Candel looked as though her temper was about to erupt once again, Nicolas intervened. "Otis, I'd like you to man the wheel and set a course to Martinique to make repairs."

"And how am I to get there from here when this compass is still spinning in circles?"

Nicolas rolled his eyes, pleading for divine patience. Candel had already depleted his personal supply. "Surely you noticed sunlight glowing in the clouds sometime during the day. You're a seasoned mariner. Use your instincts to figure out which direction is west of here and open sail."

"In this befuddlin' sea, no place is west," Otis grumbled as he headed for the door. "But I'll do my best to get us out of wherever we are. Just don't blame me if we wind up in Africa."

"I *demand* that you return me to my home . . . NOW!" Candel shouted.

She was infuriated that these men had not obeyed her wishes as the natives had always done. Curse these sailors to eternal hell! They didn't seem to know their place in the presence of a woman. To defy her would have earned them a dozen lashings on the island!

"Buff, take command of the ship," Nicolas ordered as he watched the feisty blonde fume. "Candel and I need another private chat."

"Pyreena," she corrected with a scornful glare.

"Whatever you say," Nicolas said with a careless shrug and a dismissive flick of his wrist.

"Aye, Tiger." Buff followed Otis out the door.

When they were alone, Nicolas turned to his ungrateful guest. Considering her temper, he knew it would be foolhardy to turn his back on her for more than a few seconds.

"Do you wish to lie with me now, Tiger?" Candel questioned as she reached down to unfasten her shirt. "The sooner you appease your lust the sooner I will be returned home."

Nicolas's hand clamped over her tapered fingers before the shirt fell open. Damn it all! This unorthodox female kept knocking him sideways with her blunt references to sex. His male pride was offended by her forthright approach. He was accustomed to taking the initiative in romantic encounters, none of which had *ever* proceeded like this!

A muddled frown knitted Candel's brow when Nicolas refused to allow her to disrobe. "Do you not find me appealing?" she questioned point-blank. "While it is true that I have never been permitted to lie with the natives because of my position, I have no doubt that I can learn what I need to know quite quickly."

"Will you stop all this talk about sex!" Nicolas exploded in frustration. "How long have you been stranded on that island with those natives and their peculiar customs?''

''What year is this?''

''1814,'' he informed her.

''Eleven years, and there is nothing peculiar about the native society,'' she replied, highly affronted. ''Women dominate the island, as well they should. The chief has only attained that honored position because he is the son of one of the most respected and influential women in the village. The customs of sex are part of the daily routine and women have no qualms about selecting a partner to satisfy their urges. A man's position in our society demands little of him except amusing himself and pleasuring a woman when she requests it.''

''When *she* requests it?'' Nicolas gasped in astonishment.

He had heard that some Caribbean islanders had functioned in similar cultures until the influence of the Spanish, French, and English had been forced on them. But what Candel was suggesting was outrageously insulting to the intelligent males of the species. This poor woman would be in for a cultural shock—the likes of which she couldn't begin to imagine—when she returned to New Orleans. It also looked as though the task of grooming Candel to adjust to normal society after a long absence was going to fall to him. For certain, neither Otis nor Buff could handle this high-spirited firebrand who simply didn't know her place. His officers were too caught up in who she was—the Marchioness de Caron—rather than what she had become during her formative years on the backward island.

And just how long would it take this willful misfit to accept the fact that women didn't rule the outside world? Nicolas wondered. Why, she was socially retarded and completely out of touch with the rules of etiquette, protocol, and propriety. She didn't know half the things he did, even if she had been a child prodigy of nine when she tumbled from the decks of a schooner and washed ashore on that uncivilized island. Hell, America was at war with Britain and she didn't even know it. Napoleon had been exiled from France and was attempting to regain power and it was news to her.

"Sit down, Candel," he ordered in a firm voice.

Her chin tilted a notch higher. Candel only sat when it was her wont, not that of a man! How dare he think she would honor his commands, now or ever!

Nicolas sighed in exasperation. Silent obedience was obviously something this unconventional female didn't understand. Somehow he doubted she ever would. She possessed all the arrogance of an empress.

Clutching her forearm, Nicolas drew her down with him to the edge of the cot. "Since you deal in plainspokenness, I'm going to be frank with you."

Her brows knitted in bemusement. "Is that your name? Frank?"

A bubble of laughter reverberated in his chest before he could contain it. "Nay, my name is Nicolas Tiger."

"Then why do you wish to be Frank with me and no one else?"

" 'Tis only a figure of speech," he assured her, biting back another amused grin.

Candel nodded in understanding. Come to think of it, she did recall a few phrases from her childhood, though she hadn't thought of them in over eleven years. "I see. Like counting your ducks before they fly."

"Counting your *chickens* before they *hatch*," Nicolas corrected. "But that is neither here nor there—"

"What is?" she asked, totally confused by his clichés.

Nicolas flung up his palm to forestall her questions. "Just listen to me, Candel. You have been living in a backward civilization for over a decade. Considering your unfortunate circumstances, I can understand why you refused to dwell on your past, anticipating no hope of rescue from that uncharted island. Indeed, I'm not sure I know where the hell it is myself and I've traveled the shipping lanes of the Atlantic for almost twenty years. But we're at war and I can tarry no longer in these waters. My ship needs repairs and I'm carrying ammunition and weapons that I've confiscated from the enemy—weapons that can aid our cause."

"Who's at war?" she questioned curiously.

"America and England. The English were impressing American sailors and capturing ships for their battle against Napoleon. They even blockaded American seaports to prevent us from trading with our allies. Of course, Napoleon was practicing the same infuriating policy to muster men for his navy, even though he decreed he wouldn't waylay any more of our ships. I suppose the crowned heads of Europe operate under the theory that all's fair in war, especially now that Napoleon has been exiled to Elba."

When Nicolas found himself digressing, he heaved a sigh and concentrated on trying to make Candel understand his position. "The point is the Americans are girding up for more battles and our cargo of weapons is essential. After we make the necessary repairs in Martinique, we'll be sailing to New Orleans." His eyes focused somberly on Candel. "You are coming with us, like it or—"

Candel refused to admit defeat. She wasn't concerned about *who* was at war *where*! All she wanted was to go back where she belonged and she didn't belong in New

Orleans! Without warning, she bounded off the cot and shot toward the door like a speeding bullet. She would prefer to leap overboard and swim to the island rather than put herself through another emotional upheaval. Without the assurance that her grandfather was still alive, Candel had no desire to return to her previous life. She had made a place for herself on the island and there she would remain until the end of her days!

Nicolas was unprepared for Candel's abrupt flight across his cabin. She was out the door and gone before he'd completed his sentence. With a thunderous scowl and a furious curse, he bounded after her.

Although most of Nicolas's female acquaintances weren't known for their athletic ability, this nymph could run like the wind! Before Nicolas reached the main deck, Candel dashed toward the bow of the ship—which was now the stern since the *Sea Devil* had to sail backward.

Feeling as if he were moving in slow motion, Nicolas charged forward and managed to latch onto her ankle before she leaped overboard. Her momentum came to an abrupt halt when Nicolas yanked her into his arms, pinning her hands to her ribs so she couldn't claw at him.

For the life of him, Nicolas didn't know why he hadn't allowed Candel to jump ship and take her chances with the demons in the Devil's Sea. He had been perfectly content to leave her on the island in the first place—now he seemed determined to hold her captive out of pure contrariness. If ever there was a woman who needed to be tamed, it was this wild witch. She had rattled him with her propositions of sex in exchange for her precious freedom. But what really rankled was that she had planned to use him. *Him!* A confessed womanizer who had only one use for females until this point in time. It offended his pride to know his legendary charm hadn't fazed her one whit. In fact, he was sure she would toss the same outrageous proposition at any member of his crew if it got her where she wanted to go—back to her beloved island with its primitive natives and their backward civilization that was an insult to intelligent men everywhere!

"Buff!" Candel beseeched when Nicolas carted her past the bewildered first mate. "If you'll take me back to the island, I'll give you my bo—"

Nicolas clamped his hand over the lower portion of Candel's face and cursed vehemently. She had confirmed his suspicions and trounced on his pride—again. Nicolas was seriously considering putting a padlock on that runaway tongue of hers. Damn her! She didn't even have the decency to look ashamed after she'd flung that outrageous proposition at Buff. Candel had so much to learn about being a proper lady that it was downright scary. It was obvious that he would have to teach her everything she needed to know. There was no telling what would happen to this hopelessly naive creature if she hurled those outlandish requests at the rest of his crew.

What a time to be saddled with such responsibility, thought Nicolas. There was a war going on and here he was, trying to civilize this wild heathen of a female who tossed the word *sex* around as if it were a common preposition! Hell, she didn't even know what she was talking about. She'd admitted it herself. Well, maybe he should bed her, just so she'd know what she was planning to offer everything in breeches in her attempt to return to the island. Of course, as independent and domineering as she was, she'd probably insist upon initiating lovemaking and calling all the shots. After all, she was living under the ridiculous impression that women ruled the world. That would be the day!

By the time Nicolas reached his cabin, he had regained control of his emotions. He had allowed this violet-eyed harridan to get under his skin but that wasn't going to happen again. He would expect the unexpected from Candel from this moment forward. He wasn't going to let himself be surprised by anything she said or did. She was a child-woman who hadn't been old enough to understand life before the tragedy left her marooned on Lost Island. The natives had indoctrinated her into their way of thinking and put her on a pedestal. She had lived in a vacuum for a decade and now she would have to adjust to the world outside, a world that had changed considerably since she left it.

Even though it would be a spiteful trick to return Candel to her cousin André—weasel that he was—just as *she* was, Nicolas couldn't bring himself to do it. Candel would suffer the most, not her scamp of a cousin. She would have to learn to function in white society again, to adjust to the changes. And by damn, Nicolas was going to instruct her, whether she wanted to learn or not!

Determined, Nicolas slammed the door with his boot heel, carried Candel to his bed, and pinned her to it.

"Hello, Tiger," Roger chirped automatically. Nicolas ignored the parrot.

"Now, young lady, your instruction begins," he growled into her flushed face. "You are not going back to that island ever again. Do you understand me? Life as you knew it is officially over. You are going to be cooperative and you're going to learn everything I demand of you!"

"Only when the arctic freezes over!" she spewed furiously.

"When *hell* freezes over," he corrected her gruffly.

"And as far as you're concerned, it just has. You may have been the high priestess of Lost Island but I'm the captain of this ship and I'm the master of your soul now. Where *I* come from, and where *you're* going, men rule supreme and you'd better not forget it!"

"Is that so?" she sniffed sarcastically. "Then kindly explain how Elizabeth came to be Queen of England and why Cleopatra once ruled Egypt?"

Nicolas gnashed his teeth, annoyed that this chit was not only extraordinarily lovely but also sharp-witted. She was always quick to challenge him. "The queen is no more than a figurehead while Parliament's men make the laws. And Cleopatra knew she wasn't fit to rule so she killed herself."

"That's a lie," Candel scoffed. "Cleopatra just didn't want some emperor telling her what to do. I can certainly understand that!"

She lay there looking so insufferably superior that Nicolas wanted to shake her, but he resisted the urge.

"The fact remains that you're going to do as I say because I'll be one step behind you to ensure that you do," Nicolas ordered brusquely. "Women are not dominant in *this* world. If I give you a command, you will obey it. Women refrain from speaking until they're spoken to and when they are invited to speak they are not to disagree with the opinions of men. Neither do women offer intimate favors to pacify men as if they were starved dogs being tossed a bone. Women are not in a position to demand the allegiance of their menfolk as if men were the inferior gender. 'Tis the other way around in civilized society. And if *I* wish to make love to you, then *I* will say so and *I*'ll say when. 'Tis not your place to offer your body to every man who passes by unless you desire to become a prostitute who sells her flesh to make her living.

Since you have a fabulous fortune waiting you, that will hardly be necessary.''

Candel couldn't visualize the picture Nicolas was painting. She had been too young to understand society before the tragic incident at sea and had grown up in a world that contradicted everything Nicolas described. Women bowed to men like conquered slaves and offered sex at a *man*'s convenience? The very idea! Women sold their bodies for money? Ridiculous! And what was that unfamiliar phrase about *making* love? What was there to make? Either a woman loved or she didn't. And what did that have to do with sex anyway? This blue-eyed rake was talking crazy. She'd never understand his world and she had no desire to return to a civilization that functioned in reverse from the natural order of things. Men the superior gender? Impossible! Their brains were located below their navels and their lower form of basal intelligence did not easily adapt to the reasoning process. They were motivated by their sexual drive . . .

"What does this *making love* mean?" Candel suddenly wanted to know.

Nicolas stared into those thick-lashed eyes brimming with naive innocence. Perhaps she understood the mechanics of propagating the species but she obviously knew nothing of the art of loving and the simple pleasures of womanhood. The prospect of teaching her the difference between sex and lovemaking sent a throb of desire pulsating through his loins. Nicolas had encountered his share of experienced women who knew how to appease a man's needs. But he had never seduced a virgin . . .

Before his mind wandered down such dangerous avenues, Nicolas gave himself a mental reprimand and concentrated on her question. "Sex," he informed her, "populates the country or satisfies primal needs. Making

91

love entails a great deal more, my lady. It involves giving and sharing pleasure and emotion between a certain man and a special woman. 'Tis more of a spiritual than a primitive encounter.''

Candel pondered his words. She supposed that was what her parents had shared and she had been too young to understand. Their relationship had seemed different from the casual sexual practices she'd witnessed on the island.

"So you're saying that you do not want my body because you prefer making love to sex,'' she concluded. "Where is the woman you like to make love with? What makes her so special that you desire no others?''

Candel found it fascinating to watch Tiger's face turn red each time she blurted out the word *sex*. Who would have thought a simple three-letter word could rattle a man so much!

Nicolas knew right there and then that he'd waded in over his head. What Candel needed was a woman's point of view. Unfortunately, there wasn't a woman around to enlighten her and the responsibility fell to him.

Feeling uncomfortable with this subject, Nicolas chose to dodge the issue until he was better prepared to offer explanations that would clarify rather than confuse.

"Let's drop this love business for now and concentrate on the basic differences in civilization,'' he suggested as he eased down beside her. "When we reach Martinique, I'll see that you have all the fashionable paraphernalia a woman needs to be properly attired. And in the meantime, we'll discuss suitable female behavior and acceptable social amenities.''

"There is nothing wrong with the way I act,'' Candel protested, highly offended by his insinuation.

This was the first wrestling match he'd had with a woman, the first time he'd had his hide peeled off by a clawing female. There was no telling what would pop out of her mouth or how she would react to his comments. And worse, she had grown up without modesty, tramping around half-naked! She was unaware of what a tantalizing effect she had on the men of the civilized world who weren't accustomed to seeing so much bare flesh unless they had privacy. Candel was going to have to change her ways, and quickly!

"Lesson number one," Nicolas announced.

He rose to his feet and then doubled over at the waist to drop into a courteous bow. After he'd straightened himself he struck a sophisticated pose.

"We're going to take our meal together and do it in an acceptable, dignified manner," he told Candel as he offered his hand to draw her to her feet.

Nicolas flashed Candel his most charming smile and played the role of a gentleman to the hilt. "Dinner awaits, my lady. Please join me. I am looking forward to your delightful company."

"Nay, you aren't," she contradicted him. "You don't like me and I certainly don't like you."

"But that is neither here nor—" Nicolas caught himself before he tossed out the cliche that had miffed her earlier. "That doesn't matter," he insisted. "Being courteous and polite doesn't mean that you have to be painfully honest about your feelings. You must behave in a socially acceptable fashion whether you feel those particular sentiments or not. Now *pretend* you find my company pleasurable and I'll do likewise."

Hesitantly, Candel accepted his proffered hand. She wasn't at all sure that she wanted to pretend what she

93

didn't feel, but she wasn't totally ignorant of white society. Her mother had taught her proper table manners, though she had little chance to use them on the island where one's fingers were all the eating utensils one needed.

With a sensuous sway of her hips, Candel sashayed across the cabin and sank into the chair Nicolas pulled out for her.

With a disapproving frown, Nicolas noticed Candel's seductive gait. They would have to do something about that provocative walk. The hypnotic sway of her hips was far too titillating to a man who was walking behind her. She naturally inspired a man's fantasies but this was definitely not the time for Nicolas to entertain one of them. He had his work cut out for him if he wanted to correct her personality and behavior!

Although it had been quite some time—more than half her lifetime, in fact—since she had used a knife and fork, Candel had to concentrate not to be awkward and clumsy with the utensils. But when she touched the napkin to her lips, just so, Nicolas arched a thick brow and smiled approvingly. For some reason his gesture was immensely satisfying to Candel. Why she should care what this blue-eyed rake thought of her she couldn't imagine. She had never needed a man's approval before.

"If I am being forced to return to New Orleans . . . against my wishes," she added meaningfully. "I think you should tell me what has occurred in my absence."

"For one thing," Nicolas began between bites. "Napoleon gave New Orleans to Spain so England couldn't get control of it in case he was defeated in battle. Later Spain returned New France to Napoleon. While Spain was in control of the port, smuggling became a regular occurrence. People wanted the supplies they couldn't acquire under Spanish rule and the goods had to be sneaked past Spanish authorities.

"After Napoleon took New Orleans back, he found himself in need of cash to support his European wars," Nicolas continued. "He sold his holdings to America and Louisiana became a territory in 1803 before joining the Union two years ago."

"So when I return to New Orleans . . . against my wishes," she repeated in the same emphatic tone, "I will be an American citizen rather than French. So what else has changed since I left?"

"Steam-powered vessels are very popular on the Mississippi River these days," Nicolas informed her, stabbing a chunk of potato. "Steamboats transport cargo and passengers up and down the river. From the ever-expanding custom houses in New Orleans, supplies are shipped to the eastern seaboard . . . *if* the schooners can outrun the British blockade, which is hampering American economy. If not for privateers such as myself and Jean Lafitte, very little trade would be possible."

"Privateer?" Candel eyed him dubiously. "I thought that was another name for a pirate. You're a pirate?"

His dark browns narrowed over his eyes. "I am *not* a pirate. Despite what your c—" He clamped his mouth shut before he blurted out the word *cousin*. "Despite what some snobbish citizens choose to think, we carry a letter of marque with orders to battle the British and seize their merchant ships."

Candel regarded him with consternation. "You make your living stealing cargo for profit and selling it in New Orleans. That, as I recall, is considered piracy."

"Curse it, this is war!" Nicolas roared. He held back his temper when Jolly Roger squawked in response to the loud outburst.

"And you have a temper," Candel noted with wicked glee. "A tiger's temper, it seems." She nodded thoughtfully. "You were well-named, Captain."

"I do *not* have a temper!" Nicolas blurted out a little too loudly to sound convincing.

Or at least he'd *had* an even disposition until his confrontation with this saucy misfit. He had prided himself in his ability to maintain control of his emotions. But this female had an incredible knack of getting to him. She flustered him with her directness, her keen wit, and her remarkable beauty. He felt a magnetic attraction and he fought it because he wanted no emotional ties with any woman. In his estimation, women were the root of all evil. Relationships were to be kept shallow, brief, and impersonal.

Thanks to his own selfish mother he had been cast off without an anchor, set adrift in life's stormy sea at a vulnerable age. And until this moment Nicolas had so little regard for women that he used them to amuse him and satisfy his sexual desire, nothing more. This relationship with Candel contradicted his previous encounters and philosophies. And if he thought he could have trusted Otis and Buff to take her under their wings and teach her what she needed to know, he would have foisted the responsibility onto them. But the older sailors were too tender-hearted where women were concerned. In fact, Buff's protest was what had caused this amethyst-eyed sprite to be here in the first place.

Disturbed by his meandering thoughts, Nicolas rose from his chair and ambled toward the door. "I'll go see if I can find some shears to clip your hair to a more acceptable length and fetch more suitable garments for you while you're on board," he offered. "That skimpy loincloth is not proper in our society. Women don't display their charms for all the world to see."

Candel frowned, puzzled. "I thought you said women were to display their femininity since they were only the objects of sex—"

"Curse it, Candel, forget what I said," Nicolas blustered. This woman was making him crazy with her constant references to sex. "Do you wish to be a proper lady?"

Watching this muscular giant become rattled by her straightforwardness was the only amusement Candel had enjoyed. She found herself badgering him for the mere sport of it.

"I think I would like to be a prostitute. Then I'll know what these sexual encounters are all about. Why, I might even find someone to make love with me so I can know the difference," she declared, just to get another rise out of him. Sure enough, she did.

In four swift strides, Nicolas retraced his path to brace his hands on the table and glare into her twinkling eyes. "You are not going to be anybody's whore. That's what my mother was and by damn, I intend to see that you don't pursue that profession!" He yelled as if she were deaf, provoking Jolly Roger to chirp and screech. "I vowed to make a lady out of you, even if it kills us both. And if you don't cease flinging the word *sex* around so carelessly, I'll turn you over my knee and throttle you!"

"You don't like sex then?" she questioned in mock innocence.

"Of course I like it," Nicolas muttered in exasperation.

"Then why should I be deprived of it?"

"Because you're—" Nicolas broke off in inarticulate

curses as he stalked over to retrieve a book from the shelves. "I suggest you occupy yourself in my absence by reading." He thrust the book at her. "And here, use these." He tossed a pair of clippers at her.

Her gaze slid over the clippers and focused on the book. "Is it about sex?"

Nicolas threw up his hands in resignation. "Curse it, Candel!"

She was beginning to think *Curse it, Candel* had become her new nickname. All this roaring Tiger could think to say was: Curse it, Candel *this* and Curse it, Candel *that*!

"I'm not at all certain the civilized world is ready for you," Nicolas finished with a hopeless shake of his raven head.

"Nor am I ready for it," she replied as she thumbed through the classic she'd read as a child. Her version had been in French—this one was in English. "It only proves that you should return me to the island immediately. 'Tis more than obvious where I belong. I am never going to live up to the expectations of proper society."

It was only after Nicolas breezed into the companionway that he realized what that clever lady was up to. She had been harassing him unmercifully in hopes that he would change course and take her where she wanted to go. Well, it was too late for that now. And from now on, he wasn't letting that ornery sprite rattle him with her brash remarks and outrageous declarations about becoming a concubine. He would make a lady out of her, so help him! She wasn't going to turn out like his mother.

Damn it, Candel had hit an exposed nerve. She had triggered unpleasant memories about *his* past. True, he had never hesitated to turn to women of easy virtue, despite his lack of respect for them, but . . .

98

Nicolas scowled at himself. His encounter with Candel served to remind him that his basic philosophies in life were built on contradictions. He had been reasonably well-adjusted until that female hurricane blew into his life. Perhaps he *should* hand her over to Buff and Otis. Let them see how well they could keep their sanity when bombarded by her unsettling questions!

Chapter 7

"Well, Tiger, did you get the marchioness calmed down?" Buff questioned the instant Nicolas stepped onto the quarterdeck.

Calmed down? Candel? Nicolas doubted any man could accomplish that. "At present she is polishing up her English by reading a novel and filing down her spiked nails," Nicolas reported as he peered across the sea. "I borrowed a set of Wyatt Townsend's clothes to replace that skimpy loincloth she was wearing."

" 'Twas a mite too provocative to have her running around like that, I'll admit," Buff replied. "I'm not sure we could trust some of the members of this crew with her. She sure is a pretty little thing, isn't she?"

"She's also a holy terror," Nicolas muttered.

"That should be a welcome change for you," Otis inserted with a snicker. "Yer accustomed to dealin' with the kind of women who melt at yer feet instead of clawing out yer eyes."

Aye, he was. And he certainly wasn't used to fielding the kind of questions Candel asked without batting an eyelash, either!

"Well, I'll be damned," Otis declared as he stared at the nautical instrument in his hand. "Would ya look at that! The compass is finally workin' properly."

"I told you nothing functioned properly in the Sargasso Sea," Buff snorted. "Not a compass, not the prevailing winds, nothing. After what we've experienced the past few days, we're damned lucky even to be alive."

"Set the course for Martinique," Nicolas ordered as he surveyed the tattered sails and broken yardarms. "With a favorable wind, we'll be there soon."

"*If* we don't run into trouble first," Otis stipulated. "I'd hate to meet with a British frigate while we're limpin' to port. We couldn't outmaneuver 'em, even if our lives depended on it."

The prospect of exposing Candel to a sea battle and endangering her life was an unnerving thought. Nicolas was accustomed to fighting, but she certainly wasn't. She had lived a peaceful, secluded existence for over a decade. There was so much she didn't understand. And being a woman . . . Nicolas smiled slightly at the thought. Nay, he reminded himself, Candel could never be considered an ordinary woman, not by any stretch of the imagination. She had come from a society in which men were considered second-class citizens. Knowing her confident, independent nature, she would probably think it her duty and obligation to engage in battle, just as a man.

Her philosophies on life were completely backward. He sympathized with all the men who dared to court her when she returned to New Orleans. They would be in for the same shock he'd received and he didn't even consider himself a proper gentleman, not with his breeding. Those dandies would be sitting on their heels after Candel tossed out a half-dozen of her unsettling questions and treated them as if *they* were the fairer sex.

"I think I'll try my hand at repairing the topgallant sail," Nicolas murmured as he strode toward the mast. "We need the extra canvas to take advantage of the wind."

While Nicolas concentrated on making repairs, his mind kept wandering to the female in his cabin. Odd, she occupied a great many of his thoughts. No woman ever had before. She wouldn't, of course, after he'd indoctrinated her into American culture, Nicolas convinced himself. Once she behaved in an acceptable fashion he could deal with her as easily as he dealt with all the others. Aye, in two weeks Candel's alluring flame wouldn't burn so brightly. And he was *not* buckling to the impulsive urge to teach her everything she wanted to know about sex, either! Tempting though that prospect sounded, he would keep his distance—for her sake as well as his own.

There would be at least one woman on the continent who entered marriage as pure as driven snow. She would be totally unlike his mother who had never married and left him with a difficult stigma to overcome in his youth—the whore's child. Nicolas had been an unexpected problem for his mother. Cecile Tiger hadn't even bothered to keep him with her but had chosen to leave him with his grandmother, Helene. When his ailing grandmother had passed on, Cecile had taken Nicolas to the harbor and shoved him at Buff who was the captain of a merchantman. It had been Otis and Buff who'd raised him and saw to it that he was educated far better than either of them had been. Nicolas had learned his lessons well in those early years. He understood how it felt to be alone, unwanted, and unloved. The emotional scars of his youth were deeply buried and there they would remain.

Life was what a man made of it. That was what Buff had always told him. Nicolas had acquired a stockpile of wealth from privateering to compensate for those early years of poverty and torment. He'd spent most of his life at sea, trying to satisfy the restlessness within him, searching for that part of himself that seemed to be missing. On the high seas there was danger and adventure to test his skills to the very limits. This was the life he loved—bound by no restraint. He was the master of his fate, just as Candel demanded to be the mistress of hers . . .

Nicolas hoisted the topgallant into position and then glanced toward the dark companionway below him, remembering he had better check on Candel. Although he'd locked her in his cabin to prevent her escape, she was imaginative enough to find a way to swim off to her island where women were women and men weren't really men.

After shinnying down the mast, Nicolas made a beeline for the companionway. God, how he hoped that firebrand had drifted off to sleep. And if she had, he wouldn't dare wake her up. This was the most peace and quiet he'd had all day!

A faint smile pursed Nicolas's lips when he quietly eased open the door. The lantern light gleamed in the wild tangle of silver-gold hair that formed a glittering pool around Candel's bewitching face. She was curled up on the cot with the book clasped to her bosom, fast asleep. The enchanting pose was definitely appealing. She looked so tempting, so serene . . .

For a moment Nicolas stood there, contemplating where he was going to sleep. If he stretched out beside her on the cot he would be flirting with temptation. He'd been without a woman for more weeks than he cared to remember. This particular woman cast a lure like a seine flung into the open sea. But he had promised himself to curb his lust where she was concerned. She deserved to enjoy a proper courtship with a man from her station in life. Seducing her would satisfy his physical desires, to be sure. But she was a virgin, for God's sake—a naive maid who liked to speak of intimacy, if only to rattle him, which it damned sure did. However, that was one topic they would not broach, not in the physical sense. Nicolas did have a few scruples, though there were those who would adamantly deny it.

He tiptoed over to the most comfortable chair in his cabin. He would sleep sitting up. Tomorrow he would fetch a hammock to string up in his quarters. Candel would be safe with him. Hell, he could be as noble as Buff if he wanted to be. And for this little misfit he was going to try. This was his noble deed for the month . . . for the year, he amended silently before he drifted off to sleep . . .

Candel felt a firm hand around her waist, propelling her through the darkened companionway. Before she could cry out in alarm, another gloved hand covered her mouth. She was being dragged across the rain-slickened deck, struggling to maintain her balance while the ship pitched and rolled in the angry sea. Wildly, she fought for escape from the imprisoning arms of the masked man who whisked her up the steps toward the railing. Through the torrent, she could barely make out the crew members at the far end of the deck as they frantically tossed barrels and cargo overboard to save the ship from taking on too much water.

Terror filled Candel's eyes when she saw her parents being led up the steps by another masked man. Her mother was crying, whimpering her daughter's name. Wildly, Candel thrashed for freedom, desperate to reach the safety of her parents' arms. A scream of terror gurgled in her throat when she was lifted into sturdy arms and dangled over the railing. The sound of frantic footsteps mingled with the pelting rain, but there was no one there to save her from her horrifying fall. She clawed at the air, twisting to reach up in a silent plea for mercy. All she saw before she hit the water was a wooden keg being hurled beside her . . .

"Candel!" Nicolas shook her a second time, but she didn't respond. It was as if she were trapped in the arms of a hellish nightmare that refused to release its grasp. "Candel, wake up!"

Candel's flailing arms smacked against the side of Nicolas's head. Easing down beside her trembling form, he cradled her against him, soothing her with every consoling word that came to mind. But still she writhed as if she were attempting to thrash her way up the wall, battling some invisible monster that sought to swallow her alive.

"Candel!" Nicolas finally resorted to giving her a hard shake that sent her head snapping backward. "You're safe. Do you hear me? Nothing is going to harm you. I swear it."

His deep baritone finally forced its way through the terrifying specters, sending them back into their shallow graves. With a muffled sob, Candel threw her arms around Nicolas's neck and clung to him while her body quivered with the haunting memory of her nightmare. She squeezed her eyes shut against the ghastly visions and the echoing voices from her past, but the sounds and images were still there, just beyond consciousness, waiting to engulf her . . .

"It's all right," Nicolas whispered, nestling his chin against her tear-stained cheek. "It was only a dream."

"But it wasn't!" Candel sobbed hysterically. "It was real. I was . . ." Her voice trailed off as she gasped for breath and shuddered convulsively.

It had been more than ten years since the tragedy at sea—eight years since she'd begun being plagued by the recurring horrors of that fateful night. Now she had been whisked away from the secure world on the island, just as she'd been stripped from her parents' arms and left to perish . . .

Tenderly, Nicolas curled his fingers beneath her chin, raising her misty lavender eyes to his reassuring smile. "Sometimes it helps to talk about it."

"Nay, it doesn't," she insisted, her voice wobbling with emotion.

The feel of his arms surrounding her was welcome relief after the sensation of falling through infinity into the sea. When she had first been assaulted by this nightmare, there had been no one there to comfort her. The natives had set her apart from the very beginning, unaware of the traumatic experiences she'd suffered. Candel had been left to battle the haunting demons alone as a terrified child. The only possible way for her to cope was to shut out the past as if it had never existed, as if reality itself had been a bad dream. That strategy had worked reasonably well until she had been uprooted from the island and toted off into the unknown for the second time in her life.

Gently, Nicolas combed his fingers through the dishevelled tendrils that spilled over her bare shoulders. He couldn't help but wonder if the uncertainty of her new life had triggered her nightmare, unveiling those vulnerable feelings that she had buried deep inside her. On the outside, she had grown a protective shell. But on the inside were the insecurities and fears she preferred not to confront.

After hearing Buff and Otis give their account of the Caron legend, he wondered if perhaps Candel had faced unspeakable horrors that Buff and Otis hadn't even considered. As of yet, Candel had refused to mention the incident that had left her stranded.

"What happened that night, Candel?" he questioned softly.

Nicolas met her watery gaze with sincere curiosity, but Candel stubbornly shook her head as the tears boiled down her cheeks, catching the light from the porthole, glistening like a river of diamonds.

"Once you confront your fears they will no longer hold you hostage. I need to know what happened and you need to speak of it," he insisted.

"What do you care?" she burst out, hating the tears that welled up behind her eyes and flooded down her cheeks.

Nicolas eased down beside her and looped his arm over her bare hip. "When I was young, I was left to face the world alone," he confessed. "I'm not so old that I don't remember the fear, the resentment, and the loneliness. I wondered what I'd done to deserve my miserable fate. But Buff and Otis were there to help me through the bitterness and the insecurity, to care about me when no one else did." His index finger trailed over her cheek, rerouting the stream of tears. "Now I'm here for you, little one, just as they were there for me. Let me slay your dragons for you."

The sincere tone of his voice brought another round of tears to her eyes. The feel of his muscular body lying next to hers provided the kind of protection she'd never known. Finally, Candel took a shuddering breath and offered her account of that tragic night as she remembered it through the eyes of a nine-year-old child.

The story Candel related about being abducted by a mysterious stranger in a flowing black cloak and being dragged to the railing to be tossed overboard was nothing like the legend Buff and Otis had recalled. From the sound of things, Candel had become the bait to lure her parents close to the railing to be disposed of during the storm by the mysterious stranger's accomplice.

Nicolas set his ponderous musings aside when Candel drew a steadying breath and continued her bleak tale. "As I plunged into the sea and resurfaced to clutch at the wooden barrel that had been tossed down to me, I could see my parents above me. The darkly-clad man who had brought them on deck was hovering beside them. I saw a flash of silver before my parents toppled from the railing. I tried to paddle toward the spot where they had fallen overboard, but they . . ." Her voice cracked and a gush of tears flooded her eyes. "I screamed at them but they sank into the frothy waves as if they were . . ."

"Go on, Candel," Nicolas murmured as she succumbed to the terrifying images that engulfed her. "What did you do then? How did you get to the island?"

When an icy chill slithered down her spine, Candel felt the compelling urge to sidle closer to the warmth and security of Nicolas's body. "I clung to the wooden barrel that had been tossed down to me," she forced herself to choke out. "I sprawled on top of it, riding the waves wherever they took me. I don't remember much about the night because I cried myself to sleep, not caring if I ever awoke. When the barrel ran aground, along with the crates of cargo that had been tossed overboard, I found myself surrounded by natives. They seemed to think I was a gift from their sea god. They made no inquiries, even after I learned to communicate with them in their language. They believed I had been sent to them for some supernatural purpose which they were not to question, only to accept.''

Nicolas felt a strange tug at his heartstrings when Candel revealed the terrors of her past. Although he always tried to keep his emotions in cold storage, the tragic tale melted him. He felt the urge to protect and console her, to make up for the disaster that had befallen her. Ah, how well he remembered that feeling of loneliness and despair when he was pushed into unfamiliar arms and rejected by his own mother. For Candel it must have been ten times worse because she had been wanted and loved and then cast out into the unknown. At least Nicolas had been surrounded by seamen who spoke English and had given him plenty of chores on the merchantman to preoccupy him. But she had awakened into a world that was totally unfamiliar, just as she had now. To Candel, Buff's good deed was nothing remotely close to a blessing. It was another nightmare.

Nicolas almost wished he had refused Buff's demand to rescue her. Candel had coped with her previous tragedy—now she would be forced to deal with even more turmoil. He regretted making life so difficult for her, knowing how many obstacles she had yet to overcome before she adjusted to another civilization.

"Just hold me, Tiger," Candel sobbed against the lapel of his shirt. "Eleven years ago I would have given anything for a shoulder to cry on. I didn't think I would ever recover from the awful pain and aching emptiness. Did you feel that way, too? Did you want to be held and loved and reassured?"

Aye, he had longed for those same things that Candel

needed then and now. He'd wanted to know someone cared, to know he wasn't just an extra person in this cruel world . . .

When Candel inched away to peer up at him, Nicolas's heart stumbled like a faltering steed and he clutched desperately at the trailing reins of noble restraint. But those violet eyes cast a potent spell. He could see all the unfulfilled needs in her enchanting features, feel the imprint of her voluptuous body on his. She needed compassion and he felt the fierce stirring of desire. He longed to make her forget her haunting memories, to love her the way she deserved to be loved, not as some regal priestess but as a woman.

Even as his head moved deliberately toward her honeyed lips, his conscience warred with his desire. Candel was willing to satisfy her curiosity about the intimacies between a man and a woman in an effort to forget what she preferred not to remember. His eager body was a little too willing to accommodate her inquisitiveness, her need to be held and reassured. Nicolas had vowed to keep his distance, but the promise in her kiss tore all rational thought from his mind. He'd never felt so vulnerable in the presence of a woman, and never cared so little that he did.

She tasted like warm wine and he couldn't seem to get enough of her. Candel was so pure and naive and trusting, so certain there would be magic in this intimate encounter which had eluded her all the days of her life. She was accustomed to watching the natives practice their liberal views on passion and she was oblivious to civilization's taboos. He could almost feel her ripe body begging to learn what he could teach her about herself and the mysteries of desire. He could feel his traitorous hands gliding over her ribs to swirl over the gentle curve of her hips.

When she made no attempt to resist his caresses, he couldn't muster the will to stop himself from exploring every delectably-formed inch of her.

It had been too long since Nicolas had enjoyed the pleasures a woman could provide and this innocent maiden was such an incredible temptation! When he deepened the kiss, her soft moan of surrender compelled him to lead her into the mystical dimensions of passion, to ensure that she enjoyed every breathless second of their lovemaking.

Suddenly Nicolas felt no selfish intent, as he usually did when he took his pleasures with a woman. He longed to give rather than take, to share the tingling sensations that danced on his nerve endings and made his body shudder with heightened awareness.

He wouldn't rob Candel of her virginity, Nicolas told himself as his hands drifted over her satiny thigh to unfasten the skimpy garment that covered her hips. He wouldn't dare go that far. He would only introduce her to the world of passion. He would partially appease her curiosity and curb the hungers that gnawed at him. He would stop before he reached the point of no return . . .

Famous last words, came the taunting voice from deep inside him. This bewitching female had the ability to suck emotions out of him like a human hurricane. He had never been able to detach himself from his feelings since the moment he'd met her. She played havoc with his mind, as well as his body. Already the air between them was so heavily charged that it was a wonder a lightning bolt didn't spear through the decks to strike him!

When Candel's inquiring hands slid beneath his shirt to explore the breadth of his chest, Nicolas knew that he was only fooling himself if he thought he could be content with a few kisses and caresses rather than total possession. Her responsive kiss hit him with the force of a sledgehammer, scattering his noble intentions and confusing his powers of reason. He was lost—like a drowning victim going down for that third and final time. There was no help for it. He'd secretly wanted this lovely mermaid since he'd first laid eyes on her. It may have been a purely physical impulse but it was a fierce, obsessive need that overwhelmed logic and left him a prisoner of his own ravenous desire.

Candel inhaled the masculine scent that filled her senses, reveling in the unprecedented sensations that swamped her. Her pulse pattered like driving rain while he introduced her to the mysteries of intimacy. She was eager to learn.

The initial touch of Tiger's hands and lips on her body stole her breath away. Candel recalled hearing the muffled moans that wafted from the village huts and she had been curious to know what prompted those sounds. Now she was beginning to understand the heady sensations that drew gasps of indefinable pleasure. This man was a masterful lover with plenty of practice to his credit, no doubt. He knew how to make a woman ache for his touch and yearn for his kisses. It was as if he had given her life and made her breathe, as if he had . . .

When his fingertips skimmed over the taut peaks of her breasts and his sensuous lips followed to tease and excite her beyond bearing, Candel felt her body throbbing with the most remarkable sensations. It was as if he had kindled a magical flame inside her that radiated heat through every square inch of her body. When his hands coasted down her belly to trace the ultrasensitive flesh of her inner thigh, a throb of indescribable pleasure pulsated through her. But nothing he did seemed to appease the maddening craving that uncoiled inside her. The sensations multiplied, feeding upon each other, leaving her writhing in his arms, craving release.

When his knowing fingers found her womanly softness, Candel clutched at him and gasped for breath. Bullet-like sensations riveted her innocent body and she arched toward him, silently begging him to end this delicious torment.

Nicolas marveled at Candel's passionate responses. She was as wild and uninhibited in love as she was in life. Candel knew nothing of practiced seduction, only spontaneous reaction. She made no attempt to disguise what she felt or to conceal her needs from him—needs that he alone had aroused. The fact that this was her first experiment with passion had a staggering effect on him. He was watching her respond to each wondrous new experience, teaching her all he knew about the potent effects of physical desire.

For the first time in his life, he wasn't simply going through the paces of lovemaking for passion's sake. He was giving of himself for a woman's pleasure as well as his own, and yet pleasing this uninhibited siren was oddly satisfying in itself. It was as if her breathless pleasure was his own . . .

When her hand drifted over the band of his breeches to caress him as familiarly as he had caressed her, Nicolas gulped and forgot how to breathe. Her innocent explorations struck with the intensity of an erupting volcano, turning muscle, bone, and flesh to molten lava. How was it possible that such an inexperienced woman could arouse him so quickly, leaving him trembling with such feverish desperation? No female had ever caused him to lose control to the point that his willpower was on the verge of self-destructing. His emotions seemed to bounce off each other like a logjam in a river. The heated closeness of their bodies aroused him until wanting her had become a tangible thing. He was on fire and Candel was the flame that triggered every sensual impulse inside him . . .

For a man who arrogantly believed he had learned all there was to know about passion, he was certainly learning things from this innocent. Maybe she did possess supernatural powers, just as the natives believed. She definitely had Nicolas convinced that she could weave magical spells that mesmerized and entranced. What she was doing to his brain and body defied description!

A groan of unholy torment rattled in his chest when her hand enfolded him, caressed him, excited him into a frantic sense of urgency. Passion burgeoned inside him until his need for her bordered on mindless desperation. He was like a wild man, governed by such obsessive desire that nothing was as important at that moment as satisfying this burning hunger that consumed his body, mind, and spirit.

Bracing himself on one arm, Nicolas drew Candel's supple body beneath his. Holding her passion-drugged gaze, he guided her legs apart with his knees and settled intimately above her. The feel of her silky flesh melting into his body pushed him right over the edge into oblivion. With one penetrating thrust he broke the fragile barrier between them and then instantly regretted his lack of sensitivity and tenderness.

Candel could feel the muscular length of him contracting against her—invading, dominating, overpowering. She gasped in pain and pushed against his bulging forearms, attempting to shove him away. Her frightened gaze focused on the dark face that hovered a few inches above hers. What had seemed so glorious and pleasurable had suddenly become a mixture of searing pain and panicky uncertainty.

When Nicolas glanced down into those animated violet eyes surrounded with thick curly lashes, he cursed himself a dozen times over. Candel had been so trusting and he had failed to prepare her for the inevitable discomfort he'd known she would experience. Carefully, he withdrew and then bent to brush his lips over her kiss-swollen mouth before imitating the wildly intimate gesture of lovemaking with the thrust of his tongue.

"Forgive me for hurting you, little one," he whispered before he took her parted lips under his once again. "As in life and in passion, sometimes there must be pain before we can fully appreciate and understand the meaning of pleasure. Surrender your body to me, Candel. I long to become the flame inside you. And I promise I'll never hurt you again . . ."

Gently, he reentered her, moving slowly at first until she relaxed beneath him. He saw her pain dissolve while he watched her become a woman in the most intimate sense of the word. Ever so gradually he drew her with him into the hypnotic cadence of passion. He longed to heighten and intensify her pleasure until she came willingly with him into that hazy dimension of sublime ecstasy. When he felt her moving in perfect rhythm, caught up in the same wondrous sensations that seized him, his body drove into hers, seeking ultimate depths of intimacy.

Burgeoning passion commanded Candel to answer each deep thrust as they skyrocketed through space like a shooting star. She desperately clutched at Nicolas as the wild, sweet cadence of rapture engulfed her. Her senses reeled as she clung to him, feeling his steel-hard muscles flex and contract as he communicated with her in a language that needed no words.

The searing pain had ebbed long ago, her body becoming no more than a shell that housed a hot, numbing ache that intensified until she wondered if she could survive it. Such immeasurable pleasure seemed to demand the supreme sacrifice of life itself. She was going to die, of course. She couldn't even breathe and she couldn't even remember why she should have to . . .

And die she was sure she had, when the tidal wave of indescribable ecstasy buffeted her. Uncontrollable tremors seized her body as Nicolas shuddered above her, clinging to her as if he were falling through infinity. It was as if the erratic pulsations that consumed him were echoing from his body to hers, as if they were one vital essence living through each other, for each other. Phenomenal, she thought dazedly . . .

Much later, when the dense cloud of passion evaporated, Candel's lashes fluttered up to see Nicolas propped on his forearms, staring at her in pensive deliberation. Impulsively, she reached up to limn his sensuous mouth, remembering the wild splendor they had shared. She had come to realize that Nicolas Tiger was more man, inch for square inch, than any man alive. He made her want him with every fiber of her being before he fulfilled her in ways words couldn't begin to express.

"So that's what sex is all about," she pondered aloud.

"Lovemaking," he amended with a soft chortle. He should have known the topic he'd artfully dodged earlier in the evening would crop up again. After all, Candel possessed insatiable curiosity.

"If this is what harlots do for a living, I cannot imagine that one would need to be paid for it," she said with her customary candor.

116

"They have sex, Candel. I told you there's a differ-ence. They have no emotional attachment for the men who share their beds," he explained. "What we shared was personal and private."

A pensive frown knitted her delicate brows as she traced the smile lines that bracketed his mouth. "Does that mean we are bound together by emotion? Does that mean you love me, Tiger?"

See there, Tiger? See what happens when you shoot off your mouth without first engaging your brain? he scolded himself. Now what was he supposed to say with-out confusing her? Nicolas had only intended to involve his body in this encounter, not his heart and emotions. He had never permitted a woman free license to his body before. What they'd shared had been a little *too* personal. In fact, the moment had been a little *too* much like love and that unnerved him. Nicolas had never professed to love anyone—ever. He couldn't possibly love this gor-geous, wildly exciting woman. He'd only just met her and he was a means to satisfy her curiosity.

Now how in the hell was he going to explain the difference between sex and lovemaking when he had just admitted they had experienced more than mutual lust? Damn, he should have simply rolled away and returned to his chair where it would have been wiser to have stayed in the first place!

Nicolas quickly thought it over and decided to take the coward's way out—much to his disgust. He had never considered himself fainthearted but he chose to avoid the question by posing one of his own.

"Do you love me, Candel?"

"Why, of course not," she replied. What a ridiculous assumption, she thought. She didn't even know what love was!

Well, she didn't have to be so damned straightforward about it, he thought irritably. The comment cut to the quick, though he couldn't imagine why it should. It should have come as a relief to him. He hadn't wanted her to read more into their amorous *tête-a-tête* than he had intended, had he? So why was his pride smarting?

"But maybe I will come to love you after I share the same experience with the other crew members," she said candidly, knocking Nicolas's knees clean out from under him. "If I don't find as much pleasure with the other men, then perhaps that means I—"

"Curse it, Candel. You aren't going to experiment with every hot-blooded sailor on this ship!" Nicolas exploded. "If you want more practice then you can practice with me."

No man wanted to discuss the other lovers who might eventually take his place while he was still abed with a woman, he raged to himself. Scowling at the odd feeling of possessiveness, Nicolas rolled away and grabbed his breeches. Candel's brash remark really irritated him, even when he knew damned well that it shouldn't have. He had whetted her appetite for passion, and like a child introduced to the taste of candy, she craved more! He'd created a monster!

A mischievous smile pursed Candel's lips as she watched Nicolas thrust his legs into his breeches—backwards. Scowling, he yanked them off and started all over again while she muffled a giggle. She had quickly learned that Nicolas Tiger prided himself in being in control. And, being a bit ornery by nature, she enjoyed shocking him out of his dignity. She had learned in her dealings with the male natives that it was best never to give them any advantage. Men had a tendency to let power go to

118

their heads. They functioned better if their roles in life centered around making a woman happy rather than the other way around. Candel wasn't giving Tiger any advantages in their relationship, even if she did find him incredibly handsome and sexually appealing. She hadn't a clue what he expected from the women he took to his bed, but she certainly wasn't about to become subservient just because she liked him a great deal more than she had anticipated she would.

"I'm going up on deck for some fresh air," Nicolas announced on his way to the door.

"I'm coming, too," she replied, inviting herself.

"Nay." Nicolas lurched around to glare at her as if she'd committed some breech of etiquete. "I . . ."

His voice trailed off when Candel gasped at the telltale stains on the sheet. Her alarmed gaze flew to Nicolas and he couldn't help but grin at her incredible naivete. " 'Tis only the sign of your lost virginity. There's no cause for alarm . . . It was a first for me, too."

Having confessed that truth—and why the hell he had, Nicolas didn't have a clue—he spun around and walked out.

For a moment Candel stared at the door and the lingering image that formed in front of it. Remembering the intimacies they'd shared sent a warm tingle flooding through her. Despite what she had heard about pirates as a child, this raven-haired giant didn't seem so wicked and cruel. In fact, he had been remarkably gentle and sensitive. Candel imagined that all his women found him fascinating and amazingly skillful . . .

The thought provoked an odd feeling inside her. Jealousy perhaps? Surely not. She had no right to be possessive, no right at all. Like the native women, she would

119

accept their intimate encounter for exactly what it was—a physical release. But she did admit the thought of practicing what Nicolas had taught her did sound very appealing. He was very good at sex. But quite honestly, she couldn't imagine that an encounter with another man could be better. What he hadn't taught her about the magic of passion she didn't think she cared to know. Indeed, how could sex be better than this? Why, Tiger even had the power to dissolve pain into indescribable pleasure and make her forget there was another world outside his arms.

A drowsy smile on her lips, she snuggled beneath the quilt to let her dreams take up where reality had left off. Ah, reliving the wondrous sensations Nicolas had evoked from her was far better than enduring that unnerving nightmare. When those disturbing thoughts assaulted her in the future, she would remember the way it had been with that blue-eyed rake. His memory was sure to chase those tormenting fears away . . .

"Something bothering you, Tiger?" Buff inquired as he watched Nicolas circumnavigate the quarterdeck for the third time in less than two minutes.

"Aye," Nicolas murmured, pausing to lean his forearm on the railing and stare at the sea.

"Candeliera Caron, I expect," Buff predicted. "A very unusual woman, that one, eh, Tiger?"

"Extremely," he admitted.

"I reckon it's difficult to keep your distance, knowing she's a lady of quality and all."

Buff didn't know the half of it!

"Mighty tempting though it must be to have her bedded down on your cot, she's different from the rest of your

120

conquests." He studied Nicolas, whose well-disciplined expression gave none of his thoughts away.

Nicolas winced inwardly as if he'd been stabbed in the back. Things had progressed far past temptation, but Nicolas wasn't about to divulge that information to Buff. For some reason Buff felt responsible for that unconventional hellion who said the damnedest things and responded to passion in ways that made a man's self-control shatter like eggshells.

Although he had noticed the probing glances Buff kept tossing in his direction, Nicolas wasn't a man to kiss and tell. His dalliances had been private and discreet, even if Buff did have an annoying habit of trying to make Tiger's love life his business. And before Buff gathered the nerve to pose questions that Nicolas didn't want to answer, he diverted his first mate's attention.

"Candel told me about the incident that took her parents' lives," he said. "She was having nightmares about it."

"I wondered if she would discuss it. It must have been difficult for her. Those things usually are," Buff commented as he propped himself against the wheel.

"The tale she told me sounded suspiciously like attempted murder, not an accident."

"Murder!" Buff crowed in disbelief. "You mean to say she thinks somebody meant to kill her and her family?"

"Tried to and did succeed in disposing of her parents," Nicolas clarified. "She was shoved overboard by an unidentified stranger while his accomplice stabbed her parents."

"God a-mercy. Who would want to kill the family? Do you suppose it was the work of spies who disposed of the Carons for fear of a conspiracy against the new regime in France? Or maybe the Carons were just carrying a great deal of cash and jewels that were too tempting to ignore.''

"We may never know what prompted the murders,'' Nicolas said pensively. ''But it does leave me to wonder if the men responsible will see a threat in her return from the dead. We could very well be putting her life in jeopardy by taking her back to New Orleans. Candel may know more about the mysterious men than she realizes. She has tried to block out the torment for eleven years. In time, she may remember more about that night. She strikes me as the type who would take matters into her own hands and try to solve the mystery herself.''

Leaving Buff with that disturbing thought, Nicolas returned to his cabin to sleep in his chair—the one he shouldn't have vacated in the first place. He wasn't accustomed to making vows he couldn't keep. He'd broken his promise to give Candel a wide berth almost as quickly as he'd made it; now his conscience was beating him black and blue. Candel had turned his mood green with her remarks about dallying with his crew. Curse it, he never felt in control where Candel was concerned. It was like riding the rolling waves in a storm, being tossed wherever the wind took him. Somehow or other he had to teach that female whirlwind her place before he forgot *his*—again!

Chapter 8

With a quiet groan, Nicolas rose from his chair and began to work the kinks from his back. When he glanced toward his cot, he was jolted fully awake by Candel's absence. He would have thought that the high priestess of an island would be accustomed to lounging in bed until mid-morning. He should have known better, considering her abundance of energy. Where the hell had she gone?

Scowling at the amount of time he was spending fretting over her, Nicolas stalked out the door. His frantic search through the hold of the ship turned up nothing. When he finally stepped onto the main deck, there she was, in the clothes he'd brought for her, chatting with Otis who was taking his shift at the helm. Watching Otis grin from ear to ear at whatever witty remark had tumbled from Candel's luscious pink lips did nothing to sweeten Nicolas's sour disposition.

Until this saucy imp came along, Nicolas had been reasonably good-natured and difficult to rouse. And what really got him hot under the collar was the cluster of crewmen who seemed to have found chores to attend to in Candel's proximity. They were *all* admiring the tantalizing scenery.

Nicolas had thought the clothes he'd borrowed from young Wyatt Townsend would have been large for Candel. He was wrong. She filled out the thin white shirt and black breeches alarmingly. Since she owned no undergarments, the shirt emphasized the fullness of her breasts and her curvaceous hips. And when she sauntered around the quarterdeck with that hypnotic walk of hers . . .

Nicolas swore under his breath when every pair of masculine eyes focused on her shapely derrière. Candel was all sunny smiles, delighted with the attention. Nicolas well remembered the remark she had made the previous night about experimenting with the crew. He knew she would get herself into serious trouble if she didn't watch her step. On this ship she was an available woman, not a priestess. She seemed to be enjoying her sexuality to the hilt, curse her gorgeous hide!

One of the sailors who had helped Candel on board the previous day slid a tattooed arm around her and pulled her close to whisper something in her ear. Evan Rollings had seemed stunned by the sight of her the previous night. Nicolas had presumed that the mariner was simply surprised to find a woman on board. What other explanation could there have been for the startled expression on Evan's weather-beaten features? However, along with the others Evan had certainly adjusted quickly to the idea of having Candel on board. Now he was all eyes, roguish smiles, and lusty speculation.

Watching Evan flirt so outrageously with Candel caused Nicolas's temper to boil. Rollings was the least trustworthy member of the crew. He strutted about, boasting of his prowess with women. He also had an annoying habit of bragging about his past. True or not, Nicolas didn't know, but for damned sure Evan Rollings was not the kind of man whom Candel should allow in her company under any circumstances.

"Rollings! Take your hands off the lady!" Nicolas roared as he stormed toward them, his silver-blue eyes glittering at Evan with deadly menace.

Evan Rollings had always been a troublesome man who resented authority and envied Nicolas's position as captain. His dark eyes swung to Tiger as he approached.

"It don't seem the lady minds me touchin' her all that much," Evan smirked disrespectfully. "I don't know why the hell you should."

The remark and the lusty leer Evan turned on Candel didn't set well with Nicolas. He didn't know why he felt so possessive and overprotective, but he did. Candel's experience in making the right choices when it came to men was limited. She didn't know a thing about choosing respectable male companions or dealing with the cunning techniques men employed to get women in their beds.

"I said . . . take your hands off her." Nicolas's rumbling voice was reminiscent of a tiger's growl.

Evan defied the command and returned the glare—dagger for dagger.

While the crew waited with bated breath, wondering how Tiger would handle one of his many conflicts with Evan, the *Sea Devil* unexpectedly swirled sideways, throwing everyone off balance. The vessel dipped into the trough and whirled like a runaway carousel. It was as if the flow of the Gulf Stream and the southern currents had crossed in the Sargasso Sea, forming a gigantic eddy that spun like a whirlpool, catching unsuspecting ships in its deadly trap.

Evan, who had been leaning against the taffrail, clinging possessively to Candel, was flung sideways by the lurching ship. The swift momentum of the schooner caused Candel's and Evan's heads to whiplash as the deck dropped out from under them. When the hapless ship plunged beneath the circling swell of waves, they were tossed back against the rail. Like acrobats performing back somersaults, Evan and Candel tumbled overboard. Two other sailors who had been standing near the rail fell headlong into the sea as well.

Candel's terrified shriek cut through Nicolas like a knife. He was torn between his frantic urge to rush to the railing over which she had disappeared and his desperate need to dive for the wheel which was spinning out of control. The unexpected whirlpool had seized the wheel, tossing Otis aside and leaving him sprawled on the deck. Hurriedly, Nicolas made the decision to take control of the ship, hoping to guide it from the eddy. It would do no good whatsoever to rescue Candel if the entire ship went down like a toy boat being sucked down a drain.

Nicolas lunged at the spinning wheel that threatened to fling him aside as easily as it had Otis. He braced his feet on the slanted deck and gritted his teeth as the wheel, as if it had a mind of its own, challenged his control.

"Otis! Toss out the lifelines while I free the ship from the eddy," Nicolas shouted.

Three crewmen responded to the command before Otis could get his sea legs. In a matter of seconds, every man on deck was scrambling to unfurl the sails, tattered or not. Taking advantage of every gust of wind to power the ship away from the dangerous whirlpool, Nicolas aimed the vessel into the circling wave that marked the boundary of the eddy. Holding the rudder straight, he sliced through the crest. The vessel threatened to pitch as the fierce current tugged at it, but with a hard right turn of the wheel, Nicolas steered away from danger. Only then did he glance back to monitor the rescue mission.

"Man the wheel," Nicolas hurriedly demanded of Otis.

The instant Otis scurried over to replace him, Nicolas dashed toward the rail to see a mane of blond hair floating near the vortex of the whirlpool. Although the three men who'd toppled overboard possessed the physical strength and knowledge of the sea to swim away at an angle, Candel was struggling to catch her breath as she was being pulled down by the current.

Nicolas's heart stalled in his chest when he saw a curling wave crest on Candel, just as she burst to the surface to gasp for air. She hadn't spied the lifeline that had been flung out to her. Nicolas felt the icy fingers of panic closing around his throat when Candel was swamped by the wave. Forcing his paralyzed body into action, he yanked off his boots and shirt and bounded off the rail. He plunged feet first into the sea and stretched out to latch onto the trailing rope before he hit the water. Wasting not a moment, he dragged the floating line with him, frantically searching for that glowing mass of blond hair amid the seaweed.

Candel was sure her lungs were about to burst wide open! The forceful pull of the eddy made it impossible to maintain any sense of direction. She reasoned that if the magnetic draw of the whirlpool was down that she should be surging in the opposite direction, but she couldn't seem to find her bearings. Terrified by an experience so like the tragedy that had left her a castaway on Lost Island, she thrashed her feet and stretched out her arms, hoping to find air somewhere. For several horrifying seconds she was sure she was being sucked into eternity. The sea was closing in on her and all she could hear was the rapid pulsations of her heart and feel the burning pain in her chest . . .

An unseen hand clamped onto her outstretched arm, jerking her upward like a cork popping from a bottle. Candel sputtered and choked and gasped for air. Her body slammed into hard masculine flesh and she dug her claws into her rescuer like a drowning cat anchoring itself to driftwood.

"Curse it, Candel, I thought I told you to file down those spikes," Nicolas growled.

Candel released one arm to rake the mass of hair out of her eyes and arched backward to stare into the bronzed face above hers. Never had she been so relieved to see anyone in all her twenty years! She displayed her gratitude by flinging both arms around Nicolas's shoulders. After hugging him, she graced him with a thankful kiss.

Why Nicolas was stung with such a jolting sense of pleasure and relief, he wasn't certain. He'd rescued victims who'd fallen overboard before, but saving Candel from catastrophe was far more satisfying. Seeing her topple into the sea had really scared him. The fact that Evan Rollings had abandoned her to save his own worthless hide infuriated Nicolas.

Watching Candel come within a hairbreadth of being sucked into the powerful current had him suffering all the torments of the damned. It was as if he were the one who'd almost drowned.

"Thank you, Tiger," Candel murmured as she cuddled up against him while the sailors hauled in the lifeline.

"You little fool," Nicolas muttered. "If you hadn't let that varmint put his hands on you this wouldn't have happened."

Candel blinked at his harsh tone. Was he blaming her

for the whirlpool? How utterly ridiculous! And Evan's friendly gesture certainly hadn't caused the ship to pitch and roll. How could this incident possibly have been her fault?

Before she could correct Nicolas's faulty reasoning, one of the crew hoisted her onto the deck. Without another word, Nicolas stalked off before Candel could point out the error in his thinking.

"Oh, damn!" Otis croaked when he wheeled back around to stare in the direction the ship was heading. He had been too preoccupied with the goings-on at the rail to notice the ship that was sailing directly toward them. Hurriedly, he clutched the spyglass to determine the type and nationality of the approaching vessel.

"It's the *H.M.S. Gallant*," he grumbled in disgust. "And here we are with our American flag floppin' in the breeze. Ten to one the commander intends to engage us. Hell, we couldn't outmaneuver nobody in this broken down tub!"

Nicolas snatched up the spyglass to study the British man-of-war and saw that it was armed to the teeth.

"Now what, Cap'n?" Otis questioned apprehensively. "We can't outrun 'em and we can't outmaneuver 'em. We can barely sail backwards now that we're in irons. What are we gonna do? We'll wind up prisoners of war, sure as the devil. I for one don't wanna be rottin' in Mill Prison. I hear it's a rat hole."

Nicolas carefully contemplated his options while he studied the ship that cut through the water like a barracuda.

"Roll out the twelve pounders," he ordered.

Otis and the entire crew stared at him as if he were insane.

"Cap'n, we can't fight 'em. They'll blow us to kingdom come when we try to turn the helm a-weather to answer fire. Look at the size of that brigantine! Why, she's a monster compared to us and we can barely cruise along at a limp, much less negotiate complicated nautical maneuvers," Otis complained.

"I said load the cannons," Nicolas demanded in a voice that invited no argument. "Fire two simultaneous shots at the *Gallant*."

The crew reluctantly manned their battle stations. The loader and powder monkey tended their tasks in grim resignation. While the mariners prepared to fire, Candel peered up at Nicolas, who stood on the quarterdeck with feet askance, glancing this way and that. Her curious gaze followed his from the sea to the approaching frigate.

A wry smile pursed Candel's lips when she realized Nicolas's intentions. She knew what he was thinking. She could almost see him thinking it. For a man, he was shrewd and calculating, she had to admit. While his crew was doubting the sanity of his tactics, Nicolas proceeded to deceive his own men, as well as the pursuing brigantine. But what he was doing was presenting a cunning illusion to lure the British to him. He knew the *Sea Devil* was too severely damaged to engage the gigantic man-of war. He was also perfectly aware that his schooner couldn't outrun disaster with its battered sails and frayed riggings.

When Nicolas glanced down to the main deck, he spied Candel in her wet, clinging clothes. His dark brows arched when his gaze locked with hers. He watched those lively amethyst eyes twinkle knowingly up at him while her heart-shaped mouth curved in that impish smile she wore so well. Her gaze darted in the direction they had come and the slight nod of her head indicated silent approval.

Nicolas couldn't help but grin. It was as if their minds were running on the same course. She knew what he intended to do, even though no one else had figured it out. His smile evaporated when he gestured for her to take cover in the cabin and she tilted her chin obstinately.

This she-male was definitely a participant of life, not a bystander, Nicolas decided. She insisted on being where the action was, no matter how dangerous it turned out to be. Nicolas could certainly understand that. Candel resented being restrained or deprived of freedom of choice. In fact, if she had remained within the protective confines of her hut on the island, Buff would never have puzzled out who she was. But even after Candel had been uprooted and carted off, she refused to cower in a corner. She embraced life, adventure, and challenge with open arms. She was a free spirit who believed in living life to its fullest.

Nicolas could have kicked himself for not insisting that Candel seek shelter in case his scheme went awry. But curse it, what man could deny her? She had been isolated far too long and her irrepressible spirit and curiosity demanded satisfaction. Nicolas, as callous as he could be when necessary, didn't have the heart to drag her below and lock her in his quarters before their confrontation with the British.

When Candel bounded up the steps two at a time to join him at the helm, Nicolas stared her squarely in the eye. "Your thirst for adventure carries risks," he warned before glancing over at the crewmen loading the cannon. "I hope you realize that, minx."

"You know perfectly well I couldn't hide in the cabin when I'm so eager to see how well your scheme works," she replied. "I believe in grabbing the moose by the antlers, too, you know."

"*Bull* by the *horns*," Nicolas corrected.

"Same thing," she countered with a reckless shrug.

"Fire!" Nicolas ordered when the cannons were primed and ready.

The schooner shivered and lurched backward when the cannons discharged, sending clouds of smoke drifting across the deck.

"Fire again when ready," Nicolas commanded.

Candel anchored herself to Nicolas's arm when the ship reverberated with the second set of explosions. Her gaze followed Nicolas's to see the cartridges send up a spray against the bow of the *Gallant*. The frigate spun about to answer with a resounding explosion of missiles that missed the crippled *Sea Devil* by a mile.

"Port tack," Nicolas called through the speaking trumpet.

The crew glanced up toward the quarterdeck, baffled by the unexpected order. Otis opened his mouth to object, thought better of it, and then latched onto the riggings to adjust the sails for the maneuver. When the vessel came through the eye of the wind, its sails and timbers groaning, Otis could no longer suppress his feelings.

"For God's sake, Tiger, yer takin' us right back to that whirlpool!"

A scampish grin hovered around Nicolas's lips when every man on board turned curious eyes to him. "Aye, Otis. But we know exactly where the eddy is. Our British cousins don't. I'd say that would put them at a distinct disadvantage, wouldn't you? It might be a bit difficult for them to wage battle against us while they're fighting that fierce current."

Understanding dawned on every face on the main deck. A raft of snickers wafted in the breeze as the crew scurried to reload the cannons and set the sails for another sharp turn.

"Yer a clever one, Cap'n," Otis called up to him.

"Sly as a tiger," Candel added.

"Sly as a *fox*," Nicolas automatically amended. "We are going to have to give you lessons in figures of speech. You butcher more clichés than any woman alive."

"Will it be as much fun as lessons in sex?" Candel teased him outrageously.

Nicolas flung her a condescending frown. "Be still, woman. That word is not to be bandied about except in privacy. This isn't the time or the place."

"You certainly have strange taboos," Candel replied, undaunted.

"Nay, your uncivilized natives are the ones with the bizarre taboos," he grunted in contradiction. "Now clamp down on that runaway tongue of yours. I need to concentrate if I'm going to lure in the British."

Just as Nicolas predicted, the *H.M.S. Gallant* unfurled its moonraker and sped toward the sluggish schooner. Another cannon blast sent a wave of water splashing over the privateers. Nicolas held his course until he spotted the rise of surf that indicated the perimeters of the gigantic whirlpool. Veering starboard, he ran the trough while the unsuspecting frigate chartered a straight course to apprehend their foe and attempt to fire at the privateers' broadside. Like a mouse swallowing the bait and instantly caught in a trap, the brigantine spun about, taking the commander and his crew by complete surprise.

The privateers watched with wicked glee as their enemies battled the fierce crosscurrents that left their vessels tilting at a dangerous pitch. The British were obviously packing a cargo of ammunition and artillery, judging by how low they set in the water. Nicolas had initially planned to leave the British commander to test his nautical skills while the *Sea Devil* sailed merrily on its way to Martinique. But the prospect of seizing more British weapons to use against them was too great a temptation. His mind whirled with alternatives, trying to determine the best way to take the man-of-war as his prize.

"Are you planning to seize their cannons and supplies as your booty, Tiger?" Candel questioned as she watched the British frigate spin like a top.

"Aye, I'd like to," he admitted. "I just haven't figured out how to make the most of their disadvantage." He peered at her mischievous grin. "I suppose you have a suggestion."

"I do," Candel replied. "Your ship can be a decoy. If you give the order to abandon the vessel before it goes down, your crew can pretend to scramble overboard by dangling from the ropes on the port side. The British can barely see us over the swell of water. They'll think we are caught in the same predicament. And when they abandon their frigate—"

"We'll secure our grappling irons and tow the ship free," Nicolas finished with a devilish snicker. "I couldn't have devised a better plan myself."

"I know." Her lavender eyes twinkled up at him. "Only the female mind is capable of such shrewd calculation."

Nicolas gnashed his teeth until he very nearly ground off the enamel. This sassy chit had just stated her philosophy in a nutshell. Too bad she had it exactly backwards.

"Go tell the crew what we're about," Nicolas muttered.

She scampered down the steps to pass the word. Ropes were hauled to port, secured, and tossed overboard. Even the lifeboats were lowered to give the illusion Nicolas wanted to create.

"Abandon ship before she goes down in the eddy!" Nicolas bellowed into the speaking tube.

His bugle-like voice carried to the British frigate that swirled past the starboard bow, tilting out of control. Thinking both ships were doomed, the British commander sent the same distress signal to his sailors, who tossed their blunderbusses aside and scampered over the railing. Nicolas waited until the abandoned frigate came around again like a horse on a circling carousel before he shouted the order to hurl out the grappling irons to snare the vessel. Suddenly his crew appeared to man their stations.

Nicolas maneuvered the *Sea Devil* into prime position so that the frigate passed closely beside them. Although the force of the spinning current sent the privateers skidding dangerously close to the boundaries of the eddy, they remained on the safe side of the trough. Sails popped and timbers creaked with the extra weight the *Sea Devil* was forced to pull. But within ten minutes, the brigantine rose upon the crest of the wave and glided free of the entrapping whirlpool.

A shout of victory resounded among the privateers, praising their ingenious captain. After coming alarmingly close to succumbing to the forceful currents themselves, the privateers took great satisfaction in bamboozling the haughty British, who considered themselves the masters of the seas.

When Nicolas steered away from the eddy, Candel was shocked to see the Goliath of a man who stood at the helm, receiving glowing accolades for the scheme which had been *her* idea. But what really infuriated her was that Nicolas was leaving the British sailors stranded!

"You aren't going to leave them to die!" she railed.

Nicolas glanced discreetly around him to gauge his crew's reaction to Candel's outburst before he gave her a dark look. "I gave the British a choice," Nicolas countered icily. "They can sink or swim. That's more choice than they would have given us if we had done battle against them. Besides, their presence on board could cause complications."

"Every incident in life has complications," Candel contended. " 'Tis no excuse for you to turn your back on your fellow man." She looked down her nose at him from the lofty heights of common decency. "I *demand* that you take prisoners instead of leaving them helpless in the sea!"

This pint-sized snip was giving *him* orders? And right in front of his crew, too! Nicolas swore he'd skin her alive the first chance he got.

Before Nicolas could take her to task, Candel darted toward the coil of ropes that lay on the deck. She knew too well the terrifying feeling of being adrift in that turbulent current. She never should have divulged her idea to such a heartless barbarian. If she'd known he'd intended to take no prisoners she definitely would have kept her mouth shut.

"Oh, very well," Nicolas grumbled as he spun the wheel to ride the wake on the perimeters of the eddy. "We'll gather our prisoners and ransom them to the British. They may have valuable information that can aid the American cause."

The mariners scurried over to assist Candel, who was determined to rescue the victims, enemies or no. Like drowned rats, the British clutched at the lifelines that were hurled out to them. Once the waterlogged prisoners had latched onto the ropes, Nicolas brought the ship about, dragging the British sailors behind him like laundry on a clothesline.

"Never *ever* defy me in front of my men again," Nicolas hissed when Candel rejoined him on the helm.

"Never *ever* make a foolish decision that forces me to cross you, Tiger," she flung back. "Perhaps you are a man without a conscience but I'm not."

"You aren't a man—period!" Nicolas spewed in annoyance. "And I do wish you would try to remember that. You resigned your position as the all-powerful priestess when you left Lost Island. You are now in *my* domain and under *my* command."

Candel's volatile temper snapped like a brittle twig. "I will never be under your command, Nicolas Tiger," she fumed, violet eyes flashing. "I am and shall always be my own person, no matter how hard you try to make me conform to your ridiculous standards."

Candel turned on her heels and stamped down the steps into the companionway. Nicolas drew an exasperated breath. Damn it to hell, he was letting that brazen she-male get away with murder. He should have chewed her up one side and down the other in front of his men after she'd challenged his decision. How could he maintain discipline on the *Sea Devil* when he set such a disgraceful example of control? Just wait until he got her to himself! He was going to lay down the law and she would follow it to the very letter. Curse her! She'd make him the laughingstock of this ship if he let her.

"What's going on?" Buff questioned groggily when he met Candel, who was stalking angrily toward the captain's cabin.

"Nothing much," she mumbled. "We nearly sank in

a whirlpool and then we were pursued by a British frigate. That's what the exploding cannons were all about," she added flippantly. "You must be a sound sleeper."

Candel latched onto the knob and half-turned to face Buff's shocked expression. "We captured the British man-of-war, too. It's being towed along behind us, if you care to have a look, now that you're awake."

With that, Candel slammed the door behind her, leaving Buff standing in the companionway with his jaw sagging and his eyes popping. Damn, this ship was jumping alive with activity. A man couldn't even catch a much-needed nap after standing watch at the helm all night without missing something. Obviously, he had helped himself to a tad too much rum before he dozed off. The pounding headache he thought he remembered having was no headache at all, but rather the rumble of cannons. He could have just as easily slept through an earthquake!

Scurrying up the steps, Buff discovered that Candel's brief account of the past few hours was right on the mark. But what he couldn't understand was Nicolas Tiger's black mood. The man should have been strutting about like a conquering warrior while he marched his prisoners across the deck. His impressive accomplishments didn't seem to faze him. Nicolas stalked around, firing orders like bullets, snapping at anyone and everyone who came within snarling distance—Buff included. And all Buff had done was sleep through the morning adventure like Rip Van Winkle!

Chapter 9

When Nicolas breezed through the door of his cabin, he was met with a glare, which he returned with equal intensity. "Let's get one thing straight here and now, Your Royal Majesty," he growled as he stalked over to Candel, who was propped on his cot with a book in hand. "I am, and will always be, in command of this ship. You aren't giving the orders around here and I will not tolerate your disrespect in front of my men!"

Candel slammed down her book. Not to be outdone, she glowered right back at the swarthy giant who loomed over her. "And you had better get one thing straight, *Your* Royal Highness," she sneered in the same ridiculing tone. "I am not, nor will I ever be, one of your dutiful sailors. I am here against my wishes, in case you have forgotten. And if I see injustice, then I will defend against it to the best of my ability! No matter who is at war, 'tis inhumane to leave fifty men adrift in shark-infested waters. I expected you to rescue them just as you saved me!" She drew an angry breath and raged on before Nicolas could wedge in a word. "You are nothing but a vicious mercenary and a black-hearted pirate!"

"I am *not* a pirate," Nicolas retorted, blue eyes blazing.

Candel didn't call him a liar but her glare clearly implied that she thought he was.

"Get up," Nicolas demanded gruffly. "My men and I are taking control of the *H.M.S. Gallant* so we can tow the *Sea Devil* to Martinique for repairs. This vessel will become our prison ship for the time being."

"Since I am a prisoner here myself, I will remain where I am."

Nicolas snorted. "I intend to put you in a place where I can keep an eye on you. Knowing your temperament, I expect you'll try to rally the British prisoners into attacking. And to discourage you from resorting to mutiny, and to punish you for defying me in front of my men, you'll be confined to quarters for two days."

She had to admit the thought of mutiny had crossed her mind after the fiasco on deck two hours earlier.

When Candel didn't deny the accusation, Nicolas smiled sardonically. "So you have already toyed with the idea," he muttered. "Your very expression gave you away. You're too plainspoken and honest, Candel. If you're going to adapt female ways in society, you'll have to learn to be more deceptive and conniving."

Since their first confrontation Candel wasn't certain if Tiger despised all women in general or simply her in particular. But judging from his last remark, he obviously had no respect for women. Well, that made them even, she reckoned. She didn't have all that much regard for men, either. The male natives were weak creatures who were ruled by their primal needs. They felt little responsibility to anyone but themselves. They were pleasure seekers, nothing more. And as far as Candel could tell, society of any kind ran smoother when females were in charge.

It was obvious she would never adapt to the civilization she had left behind a decade earlier. She had become a misfit, an outcast of the world into which she'd been born.

Nicolas stamped over to retrieve Jolly Roger's cage and then clutched Candel's hand, uprooting her from the cot. "We're taking up residence in the commander's great cabin on the *Gallant*," he declared. "We'll have more room there."

"If you're going to be there, too, it cannot possibly be big enough," Candel sniped, thoroughly put off by Tiger's high-handed manner, his unreasonable decree of punishment, and his merciless plan to leave the British sailors to face certain death.

True, she had found him physically attractive, but the better she got to know him the more she disliked him. It was just as well, she decided while she was forcefully propelled up the steps and across the deck. Nicolas Tiger didn't seem to like her all that much. They had contrasting views on so many issues. Her sense of decency did not coincide with his and she simply could not understand how his mind functioned. What seemed logical to her appeared ridiculous to him and vice versa. They had absolutely nothing in common except sexual magnetism. Although Candel had enjoyed their first passionate encounter, Nicolas seemed reluctant to come near her again. He appeared unable to separate sex from the rest of their relationship and Candel could not fathom what one thing had to do with the other. In her opinion sex was a separate entity which should have no bearing on the rest of one's daily life, just as it had no earth-shaking influence on Lost Island.

And what was even more exasperating to Candel was that she couldn't seem to function with any consistency in Nicolas Tiger's world. He had tried to force his beliefs about society on her, but as objective as she tried to be she couldn't see the reason for many of his actions or his behavior. It was all so confusing and overwhelming that she had difficulty adjusting to this cultural shock. Indeed, her whole world had become topsy-turvy . . .

Her thoughts trailed off when she spied the British prisoners who had been bound together like a string of horses. The sails of the *Sea Devil* had been trimmed so that it could be towed behind the man-of war. Only a skeleton crew of Nicolas's men had remained on the damaged schooner to guard the prisoners. Candel had been all set to sympathize with the British until their eyes feasted on her like hungry sharks ready to devour their next meal.

Men were all alike, no matter what their creed or color she thought with disgust. They all harbored a primitive mentality, even though they considered themselves the dominant sex. Candel knew, there and then, that she was destined to live a miserable existence in America. She couldn't change all men everywhere. After her experience on the island, she was too set in her ways to adapt to a world where men dominated women. Ah, how she longed to return. But she could never go back again—that bleak thought left her frustrated and depressed.

When Nicolas ushered her across the gangplank between the two ships, Candel cast a preoccupied glance at the crew. Evan Rolling's intense gaze caught her attention as she was hustled to the man-of-war. Now there was a man who also had a natural tendency to defy Nicolas Tiger. Candel had the spiteful urge to enlist Evan's assistance to break free of her captivity. Problem was, there was something about Evan that disturbed Candel. Unfortunately, her most recent conflict with Nicolas didn't allow her the time to figure out what it was. Perhaps when they reached Martinique she would enlist Evan's aid, despite her unexplainable dislike of the man who had draped his arm around her as if she were his . . .

"Stay away from him," Nicolas growled in Candel's ear when he noticed where her eyes had strayed. "He's trouble—more trouble than even you can handle."

Candel jerked up her head to fling him a venomous glare as he shuffled her toward the great cabin. "You will not dictate to me, Tiger," she spumed. "Nor will you restrain me. You are *not* God Almighty!"

"Nay, and you're not His sister, either," Nicolas retaliated in a caustic tone.

"Hello, Tiger," Jolly Roger squawked when Nicolas accidentally banged his cage against the doorjamb on his way into the new room.

Nicolas absentmindedly apologized to the parrot for slamming his cage into the wall and then found himself wishing he had a cage to stuff this blond-haired hellion into for safekeeping.

Candel was surprised to see such an elaborate cabin on board the brigantine. It made Nicolas's quarters on the *Sea Devil* seem cramped in comparison. Four spacious windows lined the bow and were covered with expensive red velvet draperies. Tuft chairs encircled the hand-carved table. A spacious bed replaced the narrow cot on which she'd slept. It was apparent that the commander of the *Gallant* preferred to sail in style. Now if only Candel could find some way to rout this brutish giant from the cabin, she might be able to tolerate her voyage to Martinique and devise an escape from the Tiger. Nothing would make her happier!

For the moment, Candel decided to set aside her irritation with Nicolas. Her astounded gaze fastened on the stacks of British newspapers and the collection of books above the commander's liquor cabinet. If she was to be confined for the next few days, at least she would have a distraction. She could catch up on all the activities and events that had occurred since she had been isolated on the island.

A reluctant smile pursed Nicolas's lips while he watched Candel brush her fingertips over the volumes. He remembered what Otis and Buff had said about Candeliera de Caron being a child prodigy who had been blessed with a bright, inquiring mind. She had displayed her love of books while on the *Sea Devil*, despite his meager collection. If he was lucky, this lavender-eyed terror would occupy herself with reading and quit giving him so much trouble.

Curse it, Candel had already put his emotions through a meat grinder. Nicolas needed to regroup and analyze this maelstrom of feelings that hounded him. Candel was trouble from head to toe. She had scared the pants off him when she cartwheeled overboard. She had burned the fuse clean off his temper when she defied him in front of his men. But he had been unduly impressed by her quick mind and her clever idea of taking the frigate as a prize. And, of course, there was this gnawing craving that she had instigated the previous night . . .

Nicolas cursed himself when his betraying eyes wandered over her shapely derriere and he visualized Candel as she had been while she was warm and willing in his arms. To become so intrigued and emotionally involved with this misfit of a female was suicide, he warned himself. Candel wasn't the usual, predictable woman he'd dealt with in the past. She thought too much like a man and yet she was all woman—a most desirable one who could crack a man's iron-clad control like a hammer shattering a mirror. God, he hated that about her!

When Candel pivoted with book in hand, she became instantly aware of Nicolas's all-consuming gaze. One delicate brow arched curiously when he finally got around to staring her squarely in the eyes.

"Did you wish to practice sex again, Tiger?" she asked with her customary candor.

Damn it, he'd never adjust to her straightforward manner! She minced no words and had the unnerving knack of reading his mind. She had done it with amazing ease when he'd planned to lure in the British. Now she could decipher his most erotic thoughts as if they were stamped on his face in bold letters.

Half-turning to avoid her probing stare, Nicolas set Jolly Roger's cage in the corner. "I doubt you would be as eager and receptive to me now as you were the first time," he remarked as blandly as possible. "Most women use their feminine wiles to gain limited or temporary power over men. When they are angry or annoyed they reject amorous advances for pure spite. After a man tires of the childish game he presents her with a costly trinket and she offers her body to him."

"That's bribery!" Candel gasped.

"Aye, and that's women for you," Nicolas assured her cynically. "Females in the civilized world have no position of authority so they manipulate and maneuver to get what they want from men. They don't openly confront or defy men the way you have a tendency to do."

Candel mulled over what he'd said, aware of the bitterness in his voice. It was obvious that Nicolas Tiger had only one use for women. But in all fairness, she had never believed there were all that many practical uses for men either. The spontaneous passion she and Tiger had shared seemed a place out of time, a fantasy beyond reality . . .

Heaving a sigh, Candel massaged her aching temples. All this introspection was giving her a headache. She found that her previous theories on life were meeting with contradictions that forced her to reevaluate herself and the men of the world. It was maddening to attempt to comprehend anything at all when she was still trying to judge everyone by the standards she had developed on the island.

"Confused, Candel?" Nicolas chuckled softly when he noticed the perplexed frown that knitted her brow. "No need to fret. The great thinkers and philosophers of the world have been wrestling with the dilemmas of life for centuries. Yours isn't to reason why, only to adjust the best way you can. When you reach New Orleans and settle into the routine you were born to, perhaps you can make sense of it."

Nicolas ambled toward Candel and gestured for her to sit down so he could clip her long hair off to a more manageable length as he had intended to do the previous day. A wry smile curled his lips as he wondered if clipping her thigh-length hair would destroy her strength of will, as it had when Delilah had sheared off Samson's. It was worth a try, Nicolas decided.

Cautiously, Candel parked herself in the chair, miffed by the ornery grin on Nicolas's lips. She couldn't help but wonder if he was thinking of shearing off her head rather than her hair.

"Don't try to make sense of life as it is on the open seas in times of war," Nicolas advised between snips of the shears. "Aye, at times we seem an undisciplined lot of heathens. I suppose my men and I are just like you—

misfits of sorts, searching for our own niche. But who knows? With your family's fortune and backing, perhaps you can change the civilized world to suit the life you knew on the island. And with your impressive pedigree, you will probably be able to make up your own rules as you go along. Your neighbors will call you eccentric, but I doubt you care much what anyone else thinks. And with your keen mind and fiery independence, you might very well change your corner of the world and the people in it."

"But *you* have no wish to try," she said thoughtfully. "That's why you chose the sea as your home." Candel nodded her head and then sat as still as a statue when Nicolas grumbled about her moving while he was trying out his barbering skills. "Perhaps if I return to New Orleans to find a fortune at my fingertips, I will buy a ship and become the captain."

Nicolas threw back his head and laughed at the vision that popped to mind. "You and your crew of females, no doubt," he speculated.

The sound of his bright ringing laughter was oddly pleasurable and contagious. Candel grinned impishly. "Aye, but we would have one man to satisfy our sexual appetite," she teased good-naturedly.

"Better make that two men," Nicolas suggested with another grin that seemed to come too easily when he was alone with her. "You and your female crew would probably wear one man out."

A reverse harem, Nicolas mused as he handed Candel a mirror so she could see his handiwork. Candel Caron would certainly set the civilized world back on its heels with her outrageous philosophies.

Impulsively, he pivoted in front of her to drop a kiss to her lips. "Amuse yourself with your stack of books, my lady. I need to acquaint myself with the workings of our new ship. I'll have Wyatt Townsend bring your supper tray down after the cooks have prepared our evening meal.''

"Do not think for one minute that you have been forgiven for locking me in this cabin," Candel remarked as he swaggered toward the door. "You are punishing me for doing what I believed to be fair and noble just so you can save face in front of your crew and give the illusion that you hold the same power of position over me that you hold over them." Her aloof gaze locked with his narrowed blue eyes. "Perhaps other women can be easily pacified and distracted by idle conversation, but I cannot. I knew exactly what you were doing. I only *allowed* you to do it."

Nicolas peered at the rebellious tilt of Candel's chin and the defiant sparkle in her eyes. She was still annoyed about the incident with the British, just as he was aggravated with her for challenging him in front of his crew. This seemingly friendly episode in the cabin had changed nothing whatsoever. They still held contrasting points of view. Nicolas hadn't really thought he'd outsmarted her. He'd only hoped to share a few moments that weren't filled with conflict, even if he did intend to follow through with the punishment to teach this firebrand a lesson in male superiority.

When the door eased shut behind Nicolas, Candel brushed her fingers over her tingling lips, marveling at the pleasant sensations that streamed through her body when she came into close physical contact with Nicolas. The scent, feel, and taste of him triggered arousing memories of their night together. Despite the fact that she'd been furious with him, his sudden, brief kiss had dissolved her irritation and she'd had to muster her defenses to maintain her combative attitude.

What a puzzling phenomenon Tiger was! One moment she liked him and the next she despised everything he represented. True, she had never been one to hold a grudge but she had almost felt she neeeded to in this instance because Nicolas's kisses could make her forget everything that happened before his sensuous lips touched hers.

What strange hold did this pirate have on her? Why did she feel that wild stirring inside her, just remembering his intimate caresses and kisses. Sex was sex, wasn't it? There were no emotional bonds that governed simple passion, were there? Why, half the time she almost hated Tiger for being so callous and domineering. He was such a complicated man and she couldn't understand what made him tick. Why was he the one her confused heart desired?

Determined not to dwell on such thoughts, Candel circumnavigated the cabin. Perhaps it was improper to rummage through the belongings of the previous occupant, but Candel wondered what the British commander had stashed in his sea chests, wardrobe closet, and cabinet drawers.

"Hello, Tiger," Roger chattered as he sidestepped along his perch to pick at the dried fruit Nicolas had left for him.

"Hello, *Candel*," she prompted the colorful parrot. "*Candel, Candel, Candel!!!*"

Roger jabbered and pecked while Candel sorted through the commander's wardrobe to find another set of clothes. Her garments were stained with seaweed after her unexpected dunking in the ocean and they smelled like stale fish. Although the clothes she confiscated were several sizes too large, Candel rolled up the sleeves and breeches to fit, then cinched up her waist with a colorful cord from the drapes. Employing a bright red sash from a uniform, she tied her recently trimmed hair out of her face and silently complimented Tiger's abilities as a barber. Was there anything the man couldn't do?

When Roger let loose a wolfish whistle, Candel flinched and wheeled, expecting to see a man standing in the doorway. She relaxed when she realized it was only the parrot mimicking a sound he'd heard hundreds of times.

"Where's the rotgut?" Roger chirped, pecking at his fruit.

Candel fished through the cabinet to give Roger a nip of his favorite liquor. All the while, she repeated her name to the parrot. If she was going to have to learn to adjust to an unfamiliar society, Roger could darn well learn to utter her name. It had to be better than hearing this blathering parrot call to Tiger every other minute. Candel didn't need to hear his name echo around the room. Nicolas Tiger disturbed her in ways too numerous to mention as it was. She needed no reminder of their befuddling relationship . . .

A curious frown creased Candel's brow while she sorted through the stack of papers in the British commander's desk. The official-looking documents drew her interest. Her eyes widened when she read the document that gave orders for the *H.M.S. Gallant* to sail to the Gulf in preparation for the attack on New Orleans.

Candel sank cross-legged onto the floor. How could she hope to settle into her old life and adjust if war was being waged on her birthplace?

The rap at the door jolted her from her thoughts. Be-

150

fore she could accept or decline her guest, a young lad of twelve stepped into the room, balancing a tray in one hand. His dark, soulful eyes focused on Candel and he offered her a timid smile.

"Cap'n said to bring ya some food, ma'am," Wyatt mumbled self-consciously.

"Hello, Tiger," Roger crowed.

"*Candel, Candel, Candel!!!*" she insisted to the babbling parrot.

Meekly, Wyatt advanced to set the tray on the table. "Sure hope yer all right after takin' that awful spill this mornin'," Wyatt murmured, failing to meet Candel's direct stare. "I was sure worried 'bout ya. I fell overboard once while I was repairin' sails. Cap'n saved me, just like he did you. If not for him, I wouldn't be here."

If not for Tiger's meddling, Candel wouldn't have been here, either! She'd have been frolicking in the lagoon on Lost Island, perfectly content with her way of life.

"I know you and Cap'n have had words a time or two, ma'am, but he's really not a bad sort, once you get to know him as good as I do."

Candel rose from the floor and sat down at the table to take her meal. When Wyatt stood there with his hands clasped behind him, Candel motioned for him to pull out a chair and then offered him a portion of the food.

"Hello, Tiger," Roger chattered as Wyatt's chair screeched across the planked floor.

"*Candel*, you stupid bird," she grumbled at the noisy parrot. "Hello, *Candel*."

Wyatt relaxed slightly as he munched on his meal, but it was difficult to completely relax when he was so bewitched by Candel's radiant beauty. Since she'd come aboard, he'd found himself staring in her direction on dozens of occasions. Watching her was like studying a priceless masterpiece, finding some unique detail that he'd overlooked the time before.

"Why did you sign on with these pirates?" Candel questioned with her usual bluntness. "Aren't you a mite young for this way of life, Wyatt?"

"I'd have no life at all if not for Cap'n," he assured her between bites. "Bein' an orphan and all, I was livin' in the streets of New Orleans when I met Cap'n. I stole some food from a shop on the wharf and the proprietor was whippin' the life outta me. The man was all set to drag me to jail, but Cap'n paid for the food and took me to Barataria before we sailed off for Bermuda. I was starvin' to death. I never knew where my next meal would come from or where I'd sleep 'til Cap'n took me under his wing to teach me 'bout the sea."

Candel regarded the freckle-faced cabin boy, puzzled by Tiger's generosity. Who would have thought the mighty Tiger had a soft spot in his rock-hard heart for street urchins?

"Cap'n has been teachin' me to read," Wyatt informed her before sipping his drink. "And he always insists that I use all the proper table manners, too. He says when I'm given my share of the booty I can set myself up as a gentleman and I'll be every bit as good as them stuffy dandies who prance about town in their fancy clothes."

"You're very fond of Tiger, aren't you?" Candel queried. *Idolized* Tiger was nearer the mark, she silently realized.

"Aye, ma'am," Wyatt confirmed. "He's the bravest, smartest, kindest man I ever met. I thought we was gonna die for sure when we was besieged by that ferocious hurricane in the Devil's Triangle. But Cap'n tied hisself to the wheel and defied the gigantic waves. And when we're doin' hand-to-hand combat with the British, he's downright amazin'. Nobody can wield a sword, saber, or pistol as good as Cap'n, 'cept maybe for Jean Lafitte.''

Candel digested the information along with her meal. She wondered if perhaps Nicolas had purposely sent Wyatt to sing his praises, hoping to soften her up a bit after their last argument. Is that what Nicolas had meant about learning to be more cunning and deceptive when coping with the world and the people in it? Had he used that tactic on her through Wyatt?

"Thank you kindly, ma'am, for lettin' me take my meal with ya," Wyatt said politely before touching his napkin to his lips. He leaned over to offer Roger the bread crust he'd saved for the chattering parrot. "If ya need anythin' just let me know. Cap'n said to make sure ya lacked for nothin'. He's very thoughtful.''

Wasn't he, thought Candel. Unfortunately, she wasn't blind to Nicolas Tiger's many foibles. Wyatt might have thought Tiger was God's brother but she certainly didn't think him perfect, not by any means. He and Candel would never see eye to eye because they saw the world through two contrasting perspectives. They were bound to clash often and she wasn't going to be sweet-talked into submitting to any man's orders, not even the great and wonderful Nicolas Tiger!

"Hello, Tiger," Roger babbled when the door whined shut behind Wyatt.

"Shut up, Roger," Candel growled before launching a leftover pea at the parrot. Between Wyatt's glowing accolades and Roger's constant chirping, she wasn't likely to forget the man who put her emotions in turmoil and kept them there. Nicolas Tiger made his presence felt—in spirit and thought, if not in body.

Candel made a firm vow not to be influenced by Wyatt's praise. She was going to form her own opinion of Tiger as it pertained directly to her. And she would never become passive or subservient to any man—ever! If Tiger wanted her cooperation and respect he was going to have to earn it the hard way. And until he treated her as his equal they were destined to clash.

"How did you find Candel this evening?" Nicolas questioned when Wyatt appeared on deck.

"Well, she didn't seem to be angry," Wyatt reported. "I did what ya told me. I said lots of nice things 'bout ya."

Nicolas grinned wryly. "You're a good man, Wyatt. I knew I could count on you to soften her up."

"I don't know if I softened her or not," Wyatt replied thoughtfully. "She just sat there studying me while I rambled on."

A worried frown creased Nicolas's dark brows. "You don't think she figured out what you were trying to do, do you?"

Wyatt shrugged his thin-bladed shoulders. "I can't say for sure, Cap'n. But she didn't argue. She just stared at me."

When Wyatt ambled off, Nicolas leaned leisurely against the railing to peer at the ship bobbing behind them. Maybe he'd committed an error in judgment by sending Wyatt to soothe Candel's ruffled feathers. Nicolas didn't know why he had resorted to such a devious trick. It must have been that parting kiss that he and Candel had shared that had clouded his thinking and made him anxious to return to her good graces if possible. He kept remembering how loving she had been in his arms, before another of their half-dozen power struggles. Per-

154

haps he had been trying to maneuver, much like a woman usually—

Nicolas winced uncomfortably. Wasn't he being manipulative by resorting to such tactics to win Candel's favor? Damn, he felt like kicking himself for sending Wyatt to Candel. She probably hadn't been fooled for a minute, considering how perceptive she was. And why did he even care what she thought of him? He was only toting her back to New Orleans for the reward, wasn't he? He hadn't really wanted to become physically or emotionally involved in the first place. It had just happened. He was determined to do what he'd vowed to do and nothing more. He would transform her into a proper lady, deposit her at the Caron estate, and be on his merry way. There was a war going on, after all. He would probably never see Candel again after they reached New Orleans. Their paths would never cross because he would make sure they didn't.

Aye, theirs would be a brief acquaintance and he would strive for a friendship. He would have to be content with that, even if he did fall victim to that gnawing hunger that occasionally sneaked up on him. The instant he set foot on Martinique, he would find a female to accommodate him and he would keep his distance from Candel. He should never have touched her in the first place and he was never going to make that mistake again. It would be best for both of them if they didn't become involved. This was no time for a man to be playing with fire. And Candel Caron was one flame that could easily become too hot to handle if he didn't watch out!

Chapter 10

After being confined to quarters for two days, Candel was allowed to come topside. Thoroughly annoyed with her undeserved punishment, she stared across the sea from the helm of the *Gallant*. Beside her, Buff manned the wheel, sailing under a favorable breeze toward the French colony of Martinique in the West Indies. In the distance, Candel could see the volcanic mountains that jutted up from the tropical green foliage.

"There's Mont Pelée," Buff pointed out. "Martinique is a beautiful island. You'll like it."

"I would have liked my own island better," Candel muttered resentfully.

"Now, Candel, you'll adjust to the outside world," Buff said with perfect assurance. "It'll just take a little time. We'll find you some suitable clothes in Fort-de-France and you won't have to wear those garments anymore."

"I hardly think a new set of clothes will right all the wrongs," Candel grumbled, perplexed by her sour mood.

It wasn't like her to be so negative. She had always maintained a positive outlook on life—until Nicolas Tiger turned her world upside down and left her floundering in uncharted emotional territory. The past two days had been stressful in the most peculiar way. It wasn't that she'd had any more unpleasant encounters with Tiger. Indeed, he had avoided her completely. Nicolas had taken the night watch at the helm, leaving Candel to lounge in the soft feather bed alone. He took his meals with his crew, allowing her to dine only in the company of Wyatt Townsend and that infuriating parrot that squawked Nicolas's name at regular intervals. Candel constantly repeated her name to Roger, but the stupid bird hadn't caught on.

What disturbed Candel was the *lack* of conflict between her and Nicolas. There was no challenge, no matching of wits or fencing of words, only dull monotony. She hadn't thought she would grow tired of reading all those volumes in the British commander's library, but she had. Being isolated on a remote island was one thing but being isolated in a cabin on a ship was quite another.

How it could possibly be that she missed Tiger she wasn't certain, but she did. He had become polite but very distant when they did cross paths and Candel found herself resenting his indifference. She had concluded that once Nicolas had taken her to his bed, he had no more use for her. He had temporarily satisfied his male needs. She couldn't think of one sensible reason for her to feel insulted or bitter. After all, she didn't attach emotional ties to sex after living with the liberal attitudes on Lost Island. The islanders didn't associate emotional bonds with sexual encounters so why should she . . . ?

"You're awfully quiet," Buff observed, drawing Candel from her reverie. "Do you want to talk about what's troubling you?"

"Nay," she insisted without glancing at the red-haired first mate.

"Neither did Tiger." Buff chuckled and tossed Candel a discreet glance. "It leaves me to wonder if what's bothering him is the same thing that's bothering you."

"I doubt it," Candel sniffed. "Nicolas Tiger has no heart, soul, or conscience as far as I can tell. 'Tis impossible to squeeze juice out of a rock."

"You mean squeeze *blood* from *stone*," Buff corrected and then snickered. "Tiger was right. You do have an amusing way of slaughtering common figures of speech."

"Forgive me, Buff," she muttered in a tone that was nowhere near apologetic. " 'Tis been over ten years since I've lived in Louisiana. I've forgotten what you consider standard cliches so I'm forced to make up my own as I go along."

"I'm not complaining, mind you," Buff hurriedly assured her.

"But I'm sure the mighty Tiger is," she scoffed sarcastically. "He complains about everything I do and the way I choose to do it."

"I don't know how you and Tiger got crosswise of each other, but he's not a bad sort. Your family will be most grateful to him for returning you. Indeed, they will probably even increase the reward they offered as a way of expressing their gratitude. And despite what you might think, he's one of the most respected and revered captains in these parts."

So she kept hearing. Perhaps the men of the world considered Tiger some sort of idol or legend, but her relationship with that silver-blue-eyed rapscallion left a great deal to be desired. And it cut to the quick to know she had been ultimately abducted for profit!

"I prefer to know about Martinique," Candel requested. "I know all I want to know about Tiger."

Buff heaved a sigh and shook his tousled red head. Most women found Tiger intriguing, but for some reason Candel seemed to have her heart set on hating him. Ah well, Buff had heard it said there was always a horse that couldn't be broken, a storm-tossed sea that couldn't be sailed, and one woman who couldn't be wooed—even by the best of men. This was obviously the woman.

"Most of the people in Martinique are of black African descent and Latin ancestry," Buff informed her. "The chief crops on the island are sugar cane, cotton, pineapple, and bananas. We'll be docking at one of the largest plantations on the island. Tiger has known the St. Croix family for several years. They are relatives of Josephine de Beauharnais, Napoleon's wife. Josephine was born at Trois-Ilets in Martinique."

Buff threw Candel a meaningful glance. "You can see how far Josephine went from her island home to the royal courts of France. Lucky for her that she didn't drag her feet about adjusting to the world outside. She's made quite a name for herself in history."

Candel imagined she'd make her mark, too. Very likely, she would be the first woman hanged for attempting to free her oppressed sisters from bondage and elevate them to their rightful positions of respect and authority. The type of men in civilization wouldn't take to the natives' customs any better than Tiger had. Candel wanted to fight the system and change the world while Nicolas expected her to adapt to fit the "civilized" world as he chose to refer to it . . .

Her thoughts trailed off when Nicolas appeared at the helm, looking fresh and clean-shaven and irritatingly handsome. Curse the man for having the ability to send

159

her pulse leapfrogging at the mere sight of him. This fierce physical attraction she felt for him was bound to cause her more trouble than it already had.

Nicolas nodded a silent greeting to Candel before taking Buff's place so the first mate could enjoy his noon meal. For several minutes Nicolas stood beside Candel, watching the breeze riffle the spun-gold tendrils of her hair and the sunlight caress her face. Lord, she was lovely. He wished he wasn't so aware of that enchanting face, those animated violet eyes, and that dynamic personality that radiated with irrepressible spirit. After taking a wide berth around her for two days and lecturing himself about being too preoccupied with her, it only took one look in her direction to put his hormones in a tailspin. Curse it, he was going to have to try harder to keep himself under control.

But no matter what, he would remain polite but distant. He would be sure that Candel was well dressed and well taught in the proper social graces of aristocrats. When he and Candel parted company that would be the end of their relationship. He would have done his good deed, even if she didn't think it was necessary to return her to civilized society. He had made a careless mistake by letting desire get the better of him once, but never again. From now on their relationship would be strictly platonic.

"You have been avoiding me," Candel said in her customary forthright manner.

That was Candel through and through, thought Nicolas. She didn't bother with tact and diplomacy. She said exactly what she meant and she meant exactly what she said. 'Twas a shame he had such difficulty responding to her challenging directness.

"Avoiding you?" Nicolas echoed with an ever-so-slight lift of his brows.

He was not going to lose his temper or become rattled by anything she said because that would signify emotional involvement. If he felt nothing particular, he could remain nonchalant and remote.

"Very well then, you have been *ignoring* me as if I don't exist," she clarified.

"On the contrary, I have only been giving you time to yourself, just as you demanded," he replied as blandly as possible.

Aye, she had said she wanted to be alone in a burst of temper, but she hadn't expected Tiger to take her seriously.

"My mistake," she replied, lifting a proud chin. "Thank you for your consideration, Captain Tiger."

"Nicolas," he replied.

"As you wish," she said with a shrug. "Will I also be allowed plenty of time alone at your friends' plantation?"

"Aye," he affirmed. "You will also have the opportunity to observe the gentry firsthand. The St. Croix family is proper and dignified to a fault."

"And you must be that one fault," Candel sniped. "Why would such distinguished aristocrats associate with a pirate like you?"

Nicolas put a stranglehold on the wheel, wishing it was her swanlike neck. "Not all my acquaintances consider me vermin, a scoundrel, and a pirate," he managed to say without showing his anger.

He had promised himself not to get angry. He was in perfect control of his emotions. Nothing this sassy firebrand could say would upset him—much.

"Then there must be a strain of idiocy in the St.

161

Croix family," Candel replied with a devilish grin as she watched Nicolas's knuckles turn white while he held a death grip on the wheel. Even the muscles of his jaw clenched. She had irritated him, even if he didn't want her to know it. "Anyone with intelligence could tell at a glance that you are a rascal through and through—a coyote in a rabbit's coat."

"Nay, damn it, a *wolf* in *sheep*'s clothing!" Nicolas burst out. "Can't you even get one cliche right?"

"So you admit it," Candel shot back, grinning from ear to ear while Nicolas fumed and cursed himself for losing his composure. "I wonder if the St. Croix family will welcome you with open arms—I got that cliche right, didn't I?" she added, just to agitate him further. "If they knew what a rapscallion you really are they would kick you off the premises."

"When are you going to stop giving me hell?" Nicolas muttered, flinging her a disdainful glare.

"When you no longer deserve it, that's when," she flung back. "Buff made mention of the fact that you plan to collect a reward for my return. That's why you dragged me off Lost Island in the first place, wasn't it? It had nothing to do with whether I *wanted* to go. You saw me as a means for monetary gain, didn't you?"

"Nay." Nicolas was so irritated that he let go of the wheel and thrust his face into hers. The ship swerved and he hurriedly shot out a hand to keep it on an even keel—unlike his temper. "The fact is, I would be willing to pay your relatives a generous sum to get you off my hands. I only hope to God they want you. For certain, I will have had more than my fill of you by the time I dump you on their doorstep!"

It hadn't bothered Candel to fling insults at Nicolas.

162

But when he hurled them back, it cut her to the quick. Why should she care what he thought of her? She didn't, she tried to reassure herself.

"Have Wyatt notify me when we dock," she insisted with her customary air of authority that could make Nicolas grind his teeth in annoyance. "I will be in my cabin."

"*Your* cabin?" Nicolas hooted. "You're—" He slammed his mouth shut when he saw Buff climbing the steps to the quarterdeck.

When Candel scurried on her way, Nicolas held back his temper and focused his boiling glare on the white caps on the sea.

"What's the trouble between you and Candel?" Buff inquired as he strode up beside the stiff-necked captain.

"Nothing," Nicolas snapped.

"I see." Buff stifled an amused grin. "I suppose that's why I could hear the two of you growling at each other from the main deck."

"Mind your own damned business, Buff," Nicolas retorted with a scowl.

"Whatever you say, Tiger," he obliged. "I don't have any trouble getting along with Candel. Funny that you should."

"And what the hell is that supposed to mean?"

"Why, nothing, Tiger," Buff replied, biting back a chuckle.

It had been a long time since Nicolas had been mad as a wet hen. He was usually the epitome of self-control and unerring logic. But on the topic of Candeliera de Caron, he was like a grenade waiting to go off. Tiger and Candel set off sparks in each other and Tiger just couldn't seem to decide what to do about it.

"Well, just don't get any foolish notions," Nicolas

huffed. "That human firecracker means nothing to me, nor I to her. What we have is a personality conflict. That's all it is."

"Aye, whatever you say."

"And stop patronizing me!" Nicolas roared as he turned around and stalked off.

When Nicolas was out of earshot, Buff released the laughter he'd kept bottled up. Come to think of it, Buff couldn't recall one instance when Nicolas Tiger got so steamed up over a female. It was probably blowing holes in his male pride that Candel wasn't swooning over him the way most women did. She stood up to him and gave him a piece of her mind whenever she felt like it. Candel was definitely a handful with her straightforward manner and her feisty temperament. Nicolas wasn't accustomed to being crossed by men *or* women—especially women! The fact that Nicolas couldn't dominate Candel was irritating the hell out of him.

What a lively pair they'd make, thought Buff. Of course, Nicolas's first love was the sea and always would be. He would never settle down. But Buff guessed that Candel could come closer to satisfying a man with Nicolas's thirst for adventure better than any woman alive. Just imagine a man like Nicolas married to a marchioness. They would be perfect for each other . . .

It would never happen, Buff told himself realistically. Too bad. It would be a fascinating marriage between two strong-willed individuals. But whatever Nicolas was feeling for Candel, it was nothing like the luke warm feelings he'd had for the females who had come and gone from his life. Women had never been his antagonists until Candel came along. They were only his temporary lovers . . .

That was the problem, Buff realized. Nicolas was

afraid to touch Candel because she was as pure as driven snow and he wasn't accustomed to dealing with such women. That was what was frustrating Tiger. He knew he couldn't tamper with an innocent marchioness without being hounded by his conscience. Nicolas wanted Candel the same way he wanted all other women but he couldn't have her. Oh, the attraction was definitely there, to be sure! Buff had seen the way Nicolas watched Candel when he thought no one was around. Nicolas had even been seen hovering around the great cabin when she was struggling with her recurring nightmares. He had wanted to go to her, to comfort her, but he hadn't allowed himself to get that close.

Buff shook off his wandering thoughts and steered the vessel toward Martinique. As Nicolas had pointed out, this affair was none of Buff's concern. It was best to let fate take its course. Whatever would be, would be . . .

"Nikki!" Camille St. Croix fairly bounced toward Nicolas as he swaggered off the ship. Giggling delightedly, she drank in the sight of the swarthy captain who moved toward her with tiger-like grace. When he was within arm's length, Camille greeted him with a zealous kiss—right on the lips.

Candel felt a disconcerting pang of jealousy while she watched the attractive brunette drool all over Nicolas. Never had she witnessed such a disgraceful display of affection in public. It had been taboo on the island to make such overt gestures. The native women often flung their men come-hither glances but that was the extent of it.

"It seems you have had a productive cruise," Julian St. Croix remarked while his sister hugged Nicolas vigorously. "There will be one less British man-of-war for President Madison and Napoleon to fret over when the Royal Navy comes calling." As Camille inched away, Julian extended his hand in greeting. " 'Tis good to see you again, Nikki . . ."

His voice trailed off when he spied the enchanting face that had been partially blocked by Nicolas's broad shoulders. Julian's sea green eyes slowly took in the unconventional but alluring attire that fit Candel's voluptuous physique like a glove.

"And who is this breathtaking beauty, Nikki? A goddess you fished from the sea?"

Without awaiting proper introduction, Julian sauntered forward to clasp Candel's hand in his own. With a flair for the flamboyant, he doubled over at the waist, tossed her a rakish smile, and pressed a kiss to her wrist. "*Bon jour*, mademoiselle."

"*Merci*, monsieur," Candel replied. "*Je suis* Candeliera Caron."

"Julian St. Croix at your service, *ma cherie*." He made another sweeping bow.

Keep that up, Julian, thought Nicolas, *and this particular female will be leading you around on a leash.*

"I'm bewitched at first sight," Julian murmured, all eyes and roguish grins.

And you're a fool on all counts, Nicolas added under his breath. If Julian kept fawning and crooning, Nicolas would never be able to get Candel under control. She would think Nicolas had fed her a bunch of lies about men being the authoritative figures and women their dutiful, devoted companions. Damnation, just what he needed— a gushing, oversexed French Casanova to hover around Candel, plying her with flattery and treating her like royalty!

"Come, *ma cherie*," Julian requested. "I will show you to your room. Camille will gladly offer you some suitable clothes, though I assure you that you look stunning just as you are."

Without offending Camille, who was still draped over him like ivy, Nicolas untangled himself and blessed her with his most charming smile. "I'll see you later, *ami*," he assured her. "Buff, Otis and I need to venture to Fort-de-France to gather supplies and begin repairs on the *Sea Devil*."

"Take as many wagons as you need, Nikki," Julian generously offered before he led Candel away. "We'll see that Candeliera is settled comfortably into a room."

Nicolas frowned at the familiar way Julian wrapped his arm around Candel. Up until now, Nicolas had found Julian a likable sort with only a few flaws. Now the man seemed rife with them—his fanatical obsession with Candel being the worst.

In amusement, Buff studied Nicolas, whose attention was focused on Julian and Candel to such an extent that he was aware of no one else. Nicolas had certainly become protective all of a sudden. It was as if he couldn't decide whether to allow Candel out of his sight, even when she was in good hands—a little too good, it appeared.

"Come on, Tiger. She'll be fine," Buff insisted, leading Nicolas toward the stable. "The worst tragedy she could suffer would be suffocation from all Julian's attention."

"I'm not the least bit concerned," Nicolas declared.

"Did I say you were?" Buff smirked. "I merely said she would be well-tended."

"*Mauled* is nearer the mark," Nicolas grumped as he headed toward the barn.

What did he care? He was thankful to foist off his

responsibilities for an hour or two. Aye, a couple of hours without that spitfire underfoot would do wonders for his disposition. He'd almost forgotten what life was like without that tigress giving him hell. No doubt, every second of peace and quiet would be most welcome.

Nicolas found himself whizzing down the road to Fort-de-France at breakneck speed. He even paid several vagrants loitering in the street to help him load supplies. Nicolas left Buff in command of the field while he dashed off to tend another errand. In record time, he zoomed down the street to purchase proper clothes for Candel and then bounded into the wagon to thunder toward the St. Croix plantation.

"Hell's bells, Cap'n, slow down!" Otis croaked when Nicolas negotiated a bend in the road on two wheels. "You've nearly thrown me off the seat twice!"

Buff merely grinned and clamped hold of the seat to keep from being flung off his perch. Unless he missed his guess, Nicolas couldn't wait to return to the plantation to check on Candel. He had arrived at that conclusion when he was left to pay for the supplies while Nicolas scurried to the boutique and returned with enough new clothes to keep her well dressed for a week. For a man who feigned no particular interest in Candel, Nicolas was certainly behaving strangely. *Mighty* strangely, Buff amended. Why, if one didn't know better, one would think Tiger had more interest in Candel than he allowed himself or anyone else to believe . . .

Chapter 11

Candel wandered around the elegantly furnished boudoir on the second story of the St. Croix mansion. A flood of long-forgotten memories seeped from the corner of her mind as she brushed her fingers over the intricately carved dresser and washstand. The plantation home and this room reminded her of the house where she'd lived near New Orleans as a child. For so long she had tucked the childhood memories away. But lately, remembered images kept cropping up—the worst of them taking the form of terrifying dreams.

Although Candel still had mixed emotions about returning to her birthplace when so much had changed, most of her troubled thoughts centered around the dashing pirate captain. She found him so physically attractive and yet so maddening at the same time. How was it possible to desire someone she wasn't sure she should even like? Their philosophies of life were in direct contrast. Candel had discovered sexual awareness and her own femininity for the first time and Tiger demanded that she stifle it. She was accustomed to having her requests obeyed and Tiger resented her authoritative attitude. She openly displayed her independence and he demanded *her* obedience by trying to repress her independent nature. They were in constant conflict.

Candel heaved an exasperated sigh. Nicolas Tiger was too complicated to figure out. Sometimes he seemed to be a walking contradiction. Now she was even beginning to doubt what he'd told her about the role of women in the civilized world and the attitudes of men toward the opposite sex. Julian St. Croix hadn't tried to dominate her the way Tiger had. In fact, Julian treated her like the natives on the island had—rushing forward to see to her every whim, showering her with effusive flattery and glowing compliments. He was simple to understand, eager to please, and difficult not to like. Julian didn't take life as seriously as Tiger did. And yet, Candel didn't feel that same spark of magnetic attraction for Julian. It was that midnight-haired swashbuckler who triggered a dozen different emotions, but . . .

Her pensive musings trailed off when her gaze fell on the delicate gown Camille had brought for her to wear. It had been years since Candel had fastened herself into such frilly garments, and never without her mother's or her maid's assistance. Candel couldn't imagine how she could manage all those tiny buttons on the back of the garment without contorting her body into a dozen different positions!

With her jaw set, Candel peeled off her shirt and drew the lacy gown over her head. To her dismay, the garment was unusually tight across the bodice, allowing her no room to breathe without splitting a seam. Reaching around behind herself to wrestle with the buttons was every bit as tedious as she had imagined. The task required two sets of hands.

While Candel was in the process of tugging the plunging neckline upward to cover the peaks of her breasts the door creaked open without warning. She blinked bewilderedly at the walking stack of packages that tramped into her room. She could barely make out Nicolas's face among the pyramid of boxes that plowed toward her like a moving mountain.

"Damnation!" Nicolas crowed when he caught a glimpse of her.

Shocked beyond belief, Nicolas dropped the carefully arranged stack of packages which tumbled to the floor like a rock slide.

"Julian has been drooling all over you already. If he sees you in that gown . . . you aren't wearing it and that's that!" Nicolas declared as he kicked the door shut with his boot heel.

The garment displayed so much bare flesh it was difficult to determine where the neckline ended and the waistline began! The sight of her creamy, sun-kissed skin hit Nicolas like a doubled fist in the groin. The form-fitting men's garb which Candel had been wearing on board ship was bad enough. But this lacy creation was even worse! It was torture to any man!

"Take that thing off this instant," Nicolas demanded.

When Candel tugged on the sleeves, exposing her full breasts to his all-consuming gaze, Nicolas flung up his hand to halt her. "Curse it, Candel, put that back on!"

She stood there, her breasts bare, staring bemusedly at Nicolas, who couldn't seem to make up his mind whether she should dress or undress. "Well, which is it?" she questioned irritably. "Am I to put it back on or take it off?"

"I didn't mean for you to disrobe right now," he grumbled, even though he couldn't take his eyes off of her for a second.

Nicolas Tiger was flustered, and Candel delighted in it. "On the island women never wear garments to cover the upper portion of their anatomy; that was true for me, too, on most occasions," she informed him while she watched his Adam's apple bob when he swallowed with a gulp.

"Does this look like your island?" Nicolas inquired sarcastically as his arms swept the perimeters of the room. He hurriedly tossed her the discarded shirt. "Here, cover yourself up."

When she had wriggled into the garment, Nicolas took a steadying breath and cursed himself for being so rattled by Candel's lack of modesty. He'd seen naked women in daylight before, dozens of times. But this was different. Seeing her indecently dressed made him go hot all over. She had the most incredible knack of turning him wrong side out and he didn't like the feeling!

"I purchased all the paraphernalia a proper lady requires," Nicolas chirped, his voice nowhere near as steady as he would have preferred. He scooped up a package and quickly unwrapped it. "These garments go under your gown."

Candel peered at the sheer chemise, petticoats, and pantaloons. One contraption was reinforced with whale bone and looked more like an instrument of torture than an undergarment. The bulky, awkward petticoats with their yards and yards of fabric were bound to trip her up!

"I'll smother in all those layers," Candel protested. "This gown would have been bad enough."

"Nevertheless, this is what a lady wears," Nicolas assured her. "And you are going to be a lady, right down to your ruffled pantaloons."

"Well, if you're so fond of these pantaloons, then you wear them. I won't!"

In three long strides Nicolas was looming over her with a determined glitter in his silver-blue eyes—eyes that reminded Candel of chips of ice.

"We're going to do this right," he said through clenched teeth. "We're starting from the bottom up—with the pantaloons—and you're going to dress exactly as I tell you!"

Mischievous by nature, Candel decided to make this rascal as uncomfortable as possible if he was going to force her to conform to his standards. With a defiant tilt to her chin, she stripped off the dress and stood before him bone naked. Sure enough, Nicolas began to growl like a tiger, frustrated by his own impulsive desire to abandon his noble vows and take her in his arms. He ached to lose himself in the magic he'd discovered and had refused to allow himself to enjoy again. He was extremely vulnerable with this gorgeous woman who saw nothing wrong with prancing around in the altogether as if it were the most natural thing in the world. Hell and damnation! How could he concentrate on dressing her properly and teaching her sophisticated manners when his body and his mind were in total disagreement?

With his jaw clenched, and battling the hunger that gnawed at him like a ravenous beast, Nicolas plucked up the ruffled pantaloons and thrust them at her.

Ever so slowly and provocatively, Candel wiggled into the garment.

"Now the chemise," Nicolas insisted, pitting his noble intentions against his lusty desires.

Candel bit back an impish grin when she noticed the bulge in his breeches which he'd tried to conceal by holding another package in front of him. He was definitely aroused. Good. She hoped he was also in considerable pain as well. It served him right for making such a big to-do about something that was as natural as breathing. And sex—that offensive word which caused Nicolas to cringe each time it popped from her mouth—seemed to be something he was quite uncomfortable discussing.

When Candel left the front of the lacy chemise gaping, Nicolas muttered under his breath and reached out to fasten the silk ribbons. His fingertips brushed against her creamy flesh and he became all thumbs in a matter of seconds. His accidental touch sent warm tingles ricocheting down Candel's spine and a hot throb pulsating in her loins. She wanted Nicolas's touch, craved the pleasures he had once taught her—the pleasures of which he'd deprived her every day hence.

Why was he so determined to deny the physical attraction between them? It had been the only time they were compatible. They had shared wondrous moments and Candel had no qualms about repeating the experience. Obviously Nicolas did. But he seemed to find her desirable, so why was he fighting it? Another of his baffling quirks that she couldn't comprehend.

"There," Nicolas announced, pleased that he'd completed the task—without pouncing on her as he ached to do. It was sheer heroism that he had managed to control himself as well as he had. "And now for the gown."

He opened the box and removed a lavender dress, knowing it would accentuate the startling color of her eyes. After the two of them wrestled with the full skirt and tugged the garment into place, Nicolas stepped behind her to fasten the stays. From his vantage point, he had an unobstructed view of cleavage and he cursed his choice of this gown. Since Julian was nearly as tall as Nicolas, he'd be granted the same tantalizing view.

Candel had no idea how bewitching she was. All she

knew was that she felt restricted and smothered under all the clothes. The fabric itched like wool and she had the urge to scratch, and so she did.

"Quit that," Nicolas ordered as he grabbed her hands and jerked them back down to her sides. "Now stroll around the room."

Candel stood in profound concentration, wondering how she was going to walk without entangling herself in the yards of fabric that surrounded her. She had only taken two steps before her heel caught on the hem of the gown and she was forced to flap her arms to regain her balance. But the tight apparel made it difficult to hold her arms out at the necessary angle to counter her forward momentum. Before the floor flew up and hit her in the face, Nicolas shot forward to catch her. Candel anchored her hands on his shoulders to steady herself while she untangled her feet from the ruffles and lace. She found her gaze locked with sparkling silver-blue.

Instinctively, her index finger traced the sensuous curve of his mouth, longing to feel his lips moving expertly over hers as they had that night a week ago. This brawny pirate aroused her and she wanted him. Why was he so determined to refuse her when she had no desire to restrain the pleasurable sensations he could arouse in her?

Nicolas felt his knees buckle when he peered into those luminous violet eyes that danced with living fire and irrepressible spirit. Seeing Candel in various stages of undress had taken its toll. He could no more deny himself a taste of her honeyed lips than he could have opened sail and cruised to the moon. A week of wanting had overwhelmed him. He had been testing his willpower, determined to prove he wasn't vulnerable. But the instant her lips parted he found an invitation that he had to accept, despite all his silent pep talks and firm vows. Candel had always been too willing to test the attraction between them, too curious, too uninhibited . . .

A moan broke from Nicolas's throat when her lips melted beneath his like summer rain. Instantly his body caught fire. He clutched Candel to him, crushing her into his hard masculine body, lost to the sweet memories of a night when he'd discovered more about the potency of passion than he'd ever dreamed of knowing.

Candel didn't resist his embrace, not for a second. The feel of his sinewy arms encircling her was pleasure she had longed for. The taste of his kiss was all the nourishment she needed. Titillating sensations sizzled on each nerve ending as she arched against him to savor the feel of him molded suggestively against her. Her breath came in ragged spurts while they clung to each other, trembling with needs that Nicolas had stubbornly denied them.

When his hand began to wander at will, Candel swore she'd faint from sheer fiery desire. She wanted Nicolas to utter distraction. She yearned to recreate that erotic magic that had been forbidden to her all her life. He made her feel wild and desperate. He made her body pulsate with indescribable pleasure. He made her ache with newly discovered desire that had increased by maddening degrees, only to be stifled by a week of total abstinence.

Nicolas closed his eyes and mind and stopped fighting the tormenting whispers of his conscience. He'd tried to be a gentleman, to become this beauty's mentor. He'd tried to keep his distance for the sake of propriety, for *her* sake as well as his own. But a man could be tempted just so often before his control shattered. Candel was the kind of woman who could bewitch a man and push him past the point of no return. She was responsive, deeply passionate, and Nicolas wanted her with every part of his being!

Candel was so open and generous with her affection and he almost hated her for it, just as he had hated his mother who had offered her body to any man with coins in his pocket. And deep inside, Nicolas had always despised females who easily succumbed. He also despised himself for his own desperate needs. He was such a hypocrite, motivated by so many contradictions that there were times when he couldn't tolerate *himself*!

And then along came this pure, naive maiden whose sexuality had been restrained far too long. She was alive with curiosity, totally unconventional, and he was trying to make a proper lady out of her despite the fact that she had no inclination to be something other than the desirable woman she was. His own mother had never been a proper lady and Candel probably never would be either since she still didn't have the foggiest notion what a lady was. And yet Nicolas still wanted Candel to obsession, despite the riptide of emotions that warred in his mind. This mental wrestling with deep-seated anger, base desire, and noble intent was driving him crazy . . .

"Candeliera? Are you dressed, *chérie*? I've come to escort you to dinner," Julian called from the other side of the door.

The Frenchman's cheerful voice shattered the moment like a rock crashing through a glass window.

"Give me a few more minutes," Candel called, her voice thick with desire.

When Julian's footsteps receded, Nicolas pried himself loose and struggled for hard-won composure. "Shall we try walking again, my lady?" he questioned, his voice rattling noticeably.

"I'd rather practice s—"

Nicolas spun her about before she could blurt out that offensive word again. "And that's another thing, minx, don't say S-E-X in the presence of Julian and his family. You'll shock them out of their stockings."

When Candel sashayed off in her own unique style, Nicolas began to mutter grouchily. "And don't take such long seductive strides," he commanded. "Take dainty steps and quit swinging your hips so much."

She glanced over her shoulder to see Nicolas's eyes gliding over her derrière in obvious appreciation. She liked having his eyes on her almost as much as she adored the feel of his lips against hers, whispering promises he had only once fulfilled.

"Extremely provocative," Nicolas reluctantly observed. "Too much for your own good . . . and mine."

Concentrating on her task, Candel attempted to glide across the room without falling flat on her face. After a few minutes she got the hang of maneuvering around the thick petticoats without losing her balance.

Nicolas leaned against the bureau and marveled at the enchanting transformation from the lovely island girl to the astoundingly classical beauty. Candel's re-entry into New Orleans society was sure to knock the highfalutin gentry dead. Of course, the upper crust would be bewildered beyond belief by her forthright questions about sex—and he hoped she never tried to saunter around half-naked the way she had on the island.

A grimace thinned Nicolas's lips as he realized what a hopeless contradiction this woman was. She possessed the odd combination of naivete and a lack of inhibition—a clash of civilization and culture all rolled up into one devastating package of stunning beauty, quick wit, and undaunted spirit.

And ah, what an enigma *he* was, even to himself! Every time he got near Candel he was forced to face the contradictions in *his* personality. In the past Nicolas had allowed himself to consort with the kind of women he detested—loose-moraled females like his mother. It was a weakness in his character. He couldn't abide the strait-laced ladies of Louisiana who were so prim and proper that they bored him to tears and suffered their own idiosyncrasies about passion. And then, of course, there were those married women who had wed for prestige and position. But he knew for a fact that there were dozens of unfaithful wives because he was the one they'd been unfaithful with! Sometimes Nicolas wondered if he accommodated those females just to reinforce his low opinion of women. And yet his own gender was no better. Many an unfaithful husband kept his mistress at his beck and call . . .

Come to think of it, he mused, world morality was in a sorry state. Civilization was built on ideal theories that crumbled when it came to practicing what was preached. What Nicolas wanted was a lady who was open and honest and passionate—like Candel. He wanted a woman who would remain devoted to him alone—*unlike* Candel, who had been taught to believe that sexual encounters weren't all that personal or binding.

In truth, both of their philosophies were so warped it was laughable! What a preposterous pair! She was a notch below royalty with a pedigree and he was the bastard son of a prostitute who probably didn't know for certain who had fathered her chld. At least, he had never been told who his father was. He would never be accepted in high society with his background but Candel was a marchioness. If anyone in New Orleans knew he and Candel had been intimate she would be ridiculed and shunned the moment she returned. And even if Nicolas considered marrying this lively lady—which he couldn't possibly—the Carons would be outraged. There were dozens of good reasons why he had to keep his distance, even if he hated every minute of it . . .

"Did I do something else wrong?" Candel questioned when she turned to see Nicolas frowning at her.

"Nay," he said with a disgruntled sigh. "Let's go practice your newly acquired manners on the St. Croix family." He offered her his arm in a courtly gesture. "Just don't start tearing the food apart with your fingers," he teased. "It will spoil the whole effect."

Julian had just started back up the steps to meet Candel when she and Nicolas appeared at the head of the steps. "*Mon Dieu!*" he breathed in awe. "*Extraordinaire!*"

Candel stared down at the blond gentleman as he scurried eagerly toward her, all eyes and gushing praise. Odd, wasn't it, she thought, that she had been more delighted by Nicolas's slow, deliberate appraisal than she was with Julian's lavish compliments. It was too easy to win Julian's attention and affection. Why was she more intrigued by a challenge? Learning to understand what made the brooding Captain Tiger tick was far more fascinating. Contradicting vibrations from him constantly piqued her curiosity. No doubt, she simply wasn't worldly enough to understand why Nicolas Tiger was the man he was. Since he kept his own counsel, she'd probably never really know him. Perhaps she should settle for a likable, amusing companion like Julian who responded to her in ways that were similar to her experience on the island.

When Julian shouldered Nicolas out of the way to escort Candel to the dining room, Nicolas had to bite his tongue to keep from protesting. He had no right to be possessive, Nicolas reminded himself as he followed a step behind. He should look upon Candel as his ward, consider her his sister. Aye, that was what he'd do. Now if he could only convince his body that this was a purely platonic relationship—except for that one splendorous night that should never have happened. If only he could forget the way she looked lying beside him, the way he felt while they made wild, sweet love . . .

"There you are, Nikki," Camille gushed as she glided through the hall to stake her claim.

Now here was a woman Nicolas could easily handle. Camille was infatuated with him and she had been since she was a starry-eyed teenager. She had grown up idolizing him from the first time he sailed to Martinique five years earlier. Nicolas could tell Camille anything and she was prone to believe him, unlike Candel, who argued with him for the mere sport of it and who had the crazed notion that she had never been wrong about anything in all her life!

Nicolas could give or take as much as he wanted from Camille without becoming tangled in a crosscurrent of emotions. Of course, he'd never compromised his friend and associate's little sister, but he and Camille could exchange a few kisses and caresses while they lingered in the shadows. And tonight, Nicolas would venture back to Fort-de-France to seek out a woman whose profession it was to satisfy a man's needs—no strings attached. That was what those women expected and deserved—the hard-hearted, callous ones like his *dear sweet* mother who had tired of dragging him around like an albatross and had foisted him off on Buff before disappearing from her son's life forever . . .

Chapter 12

After a full, rich evening of watching Julian fawn and drool over Candel, Nicolas was on the verge of shoving the amorous Frenchman into the sea to cool him off. Julian was complicating Candel's indoctrination into civilized society. She would never learn *her* place while Julian was doing all within his power to earn himself a place in her bed. The rake!

Why, Nicolas couldn't even enjoy Camille's attention since he had to keep such a watchful eye on her lecherous brother. It was as if Julian had never been in the company of a beautiful woman. That was laughable. With Julian's good breeding, wealth, and charismatic charm, women flocked to him. So why had he set his cap for Candel? Friendly rivalry perhaps? Nicolas wasn't sure, but Julian was so obvious in his intentions toward Candel that his constant smiles were making Nicolas nauseous.

Sighing in frustration, Nicolas bid Camille good night after she had covered him with kisses in the shadows of the hall. As he ambled to his room, he met Julian. The Frenchman, however, glanced the other way as they passed shoulder to shoulder. Julian spoke not one word as he strode toward his boudoir. Frowning curiously, Nicolas reversed direction to follow in his wake. He came to a startled halt when the lamplight fell across the left side of Julian's face. A pulsating red welt—looking suspiciously like a handprint—was emblazoned on Julian's cheek. A claw mark made by overly long nails marred his neck.

"What happened?" Nicolas demanded to know.

"It seems my affections weren't as well received as I had anticipated," Julian muttered as he inspected his stinging jaw with his fingertips. "Candeliera Caron packs a mighty wallop."

Nicolas felt himself growing madder by the minute. Don Juan St. Croix better not have been practicing his seductive techniques on Candel! He would skin him alive—friend or no!

"Curse it, Julian, what did you do to her?" he growled as he grabbed the Frenchman by the lapels and glared at him eye to eye.

"I tried to seduce her, of course," Julian growled right back. "Since she has been pleasuring you and every member of your crew at sea, I naturally expected—"

"What?" Nicolas had the impulsive urge to wring his so-called friend's neck. "You imbecile, she isn't the ship's whore!"

"Then who the blazes is she?" Julian snapped. "She arrived here without decent clothing and without a chaperone or a lady's maid. She may be gorgeous but from all indication she isn't from proper stock."

"She happens to be the long-lost Marchioness de Caron, heiress to a vast fortune in New Orleans," Nicolas breathed against his neck.

Julian blinked like an owl. "You should have told me who she was before. I . . . well . . . you know . . ."

183

"Nay, I don't know," Nicolas seethed. "Suppose you tell me."

Julian looked decidedly uncomfortable. "I'd rather not discuss it. I'm embarrassed enough as it is. I doubt she has cooled off enough to accept my apology just yet. I thought she was playing hard to get just to tease me and I became a mite too insistent, thinking she had offered her charms to every sailor but not to me."

Scowling, Nicolas released his stranglehold on Julian's velvet jacket and spun on his heels. Without bothering to announce himself, he burst into Candel's room, only to find it empty. With a curse and a growl, he whizzed into his own room, hoping Candel had sought refuge there. But she was nowhere to be seen.

Perhaps she had decided to return to the ship to spend the night in the cabin. Where else could she have gone without funds to take a room at an inn?

Nicolas cringed at the thought of Candel boarding the schooner. She might find herself faced with another overzealous suitor. By now, Nicolas predicted that his crew would be celebrating the capture of the man-of-war in their customary fashion. They could be a rowdy mob when they were well into their cups, especially after several months at sea.

Quickening his step, Nicolas jogged down the hill to the docks. In the distance he could hear the sailors' bawdy chants and uproarious laughter. God, he hoped Candel had gone directly to Otis or Buff to inform them of her return. Otherwise . . .

Nicolas forced himself not to dwell on the distasteful possibilities. He only wanted to track Candel down and apologize for Julian's mistaken notion that she was a concubine who had been spreading herself among his crew. Damn, this was all his fault, Nicolas thought sickly.

He should have explained Candel's presence on board ship so there would have been no misunderstandings. But he had been too jealous to notice that Julian had leapt to the wrong conclusion after he noticed the improper way Candel had been dressed when she disembarked.

Nicolas frowned as he wondered why Candel had even bothered to repel Julian's advances. For a week she had insisted that she was going to experiment with men after she'd been deprived of affection for twenty years. Had she only said those things to irritate him? Even if he lived to be one hundred and ten he would never understand the workings of that misfit's mind. And here he thought *he* was a walking contradiction!

Candel muffled a sniff as she hopped from the gang-plank to make her way to the cabin on the British brigantine. Several mariners were sitting on kegs at the port bow, playing cards, drinking straight from their bottles, and singing at the top of their lungs. They didn't notice her, which was just as well. Candel wasn't in the mood for conversation and companionship. She'd had quite enough for one evening!

Self-consciously, she tugged at the torn gown that drooped at the shoulders. Damn that Julian, she fumed as she veered around the railing to follow the steps into the companionway. He had kissed her full on the mouth without giving her the chance to accept or reject his advances. When his hand dived down the front of her dress, Candel had pushed herself away, only to hear the rending of cloth. The beautiful gown Nicolas had given her had suffered irreparable damage and that enraged her. She had slapped Julian hard when he lunged at her a second time.

And if that incident wasn't enough to infuriate her, one of the stable boys at the St. Croix plantation had grabbed hold of her as she scurried around the corner of the barn to·return to the ship. She'd been pawed twice in less than fifteen minutes. Candel had decided, there and then, that she didn't like "civilized" men nearly as well as she thought she would. They were worse than the natives. They all had cave man mentalities! These so-called civilized brutes thought they could pounce on a woman without her invitation. Candel was beginning to understand what Nicolas had meant about women being dominated and used by men. Males seemed so cocksure of their superiority. At least the natives had learned their place in society. They waited for a woman to show interest before they pursued. These aggressive men in society waited for nothing!

What really upset Candel was that the one man who interested her was not the one who pursued her or attempted to gain her favor. Her pride had been smarting all evening while she watched Camille attach herself to Nicolas like a leech. And Nicolas, curse his handsome hide, had promptly charmed the French girl out of her pantaloons. Candel decided to swear off men forevermore. She hadn't realized how fortunate she had been to remain isolated on the island, treated like a queen . . .

"Well, well, what do we have here?" Evan Rollings drawled drunkenly as he staggered around the corner with a bottle of rum in one hand, the other braced against the wall to support himself.

His hungry gaze traveled over Candel's shapely figure and focused on the creamy flesh revealed by her sagging bodice. Before Candel could twist open the latch and slam the door in his face, Evan lunged at her. The smell of whiskey and perspiration assaulted Candel's senses and she quickly shoved Evan backward.

"What's the matter, luv? Did you have a spat with the Captain?"

"Leave me alone," Candel hissed when he wedged her between his bulky body and the door.

"What you need is a man who knows how to make a lady feel like a woman before I—"

What she needed was solitude. What she got was another lusty male who didn't bother to await invitation—which he definitely wasn't getting!

An indignant shriek burst from Candel's lips when Evan snaked his arm around her and pushed her into the cabin. She didn't have a chance to slap his whiskered face before he pinned her arms at her sides and backed her toward the bed.

"Let me go, Evan," she demanded furiously.

"I've been doin' a lot of thinkin' about you lately, little mermaid," he chuckled wickedly as he tossed the empty bottle aside and shoved her onto the bed. "One never knows how things are goin' to work out, does one? Seeing you was a shock, but now that you're back . . . ooofff!"

Candel was too overcome by fear to comprehend what Evan meant. She threw up a hand when he tried to sprawl on top of her, but all she succeeded in doing was knocking the breath out of him for a half-second. In his drunken and lusty state of mind, he wasn't easily discouraged. The harder she fought the more he enjoyed exerting his will over her. Candel panicked when she heard the rending of cloth for the second time in one night. No matter which way she twisted and turned, Evan's face loomed above hers, tormenting her with crude remarks about his intentions. When his mouth came down on hers and his hands groped at her, Candel felt her skin crawl with revulsion.

Suddenly, she understood the difference between the tender lovemaking she'd experienced with Nicolas and brutal ravishment. Nicolas had been sensitive and receptive to her needs—Evan had only one purpose—to take his pleasures at her expense. He had no concern for Candel and it outraged her that she couldn't prevent him from molesting her!

Another indignant shriek interrupted his suffocating kiss when he shoved his knee between her thighs and reached down to yank up the hem of her gown. Candel dug in her nails, but nothing fazed this inebriated brute. Evan was as determined to violate her as she was to escape him . . .

A growl that sounded almost inhuman echoed through the room. To Candel's astonishment and relief, Evan sprouted wings and flew across the room to bounce off the wall. When she glanced up, her breath froze in her throat at the sight of Nicolas wheeling toward the dazed seaman he had set to flight. Never had Candel seen such cold-blooded rage in Tiger's eyes. It was frightening, even when she wasn't the recipient of his smoldering fury. If she hadn't been eager to see Evan served his just desserts, she would have pitied the drunken mariner.

Like an uncoiling spring, Nicolas pounced on Evan as he staggered to his feet. With killing force, Nicolas leveled a blow that jammed Evan's spine against the wall. When Evan instinctively doubled over to gasp for breath, Nicolas's meaty fist connected with the sailor's jaw, sending his head slamming against the wall. A bloody groan gurgled in Evan's throat when Nicolas delivered another brain-scrambling blow. Evan's knees folded beneath him but Nicolas hadn't fully satisfied his vengeance. He clamped hold of Evan's shirt to jerk him upright when he slid down the wall.

Candel grimaced when another teeth-rattling smash connected with Evan's lips, sending blood trickling down his whiskered chin. She had only thought she'd seen Tiger at the height of his fury on rare occasion, but she had never witnessed the dark side of Tiger's personality until now. It was frightening to see a man so filled with murderous wrath! She was afraid Tiger would never cease his brutal punishment, that he'd tear the drunken seaman apart with his bare hands.

"Tiger!" Candel screeched, shocked by his venomous rage.

Nicolas's hand stalled in midair while he held the noodly-legged Evan by the throat. Half-crazed though Nicolas was, Candel's pleading voice broke through the red haze that clouded his mind. Yanking Evan up by the nape of his peacoat, Nicolas stalked toward the door. His booming voice echoed down the corridor like an exploding cannon. In less than a minute, Otis and Buff arrived upon the scene.

"Get this disgusting vermin out of my sight!" Nicolas snarled. "And throw him off this ship." His glittering eyes bored into Evan like a termite into rotten wood. "If you ever come near me or Candel again, I'll kill you. That isn't a threat, Rollings. That's a promise . . ." His rumbling voice echoed through the dark companionway like a death knell.

"You haven't seen the last of me, bastard captain," Evan muttered out the side of his mouth that wasn't quite so swollen. His puffy-eyed gaze glanced off Candel. "And neither has *she* . . ."

After Buff and Otis grabbed Evan's arms to lead him

away, Nicolas slammed the door shut. Inhaling a steadying breath, he pivoted to stare down at Candel who was clutching her torn bodice. Claw marks marred her breasts and on the exposed flesh of her thighs were the beginnings of several bruises. The look in her violet eyes cut through Nicolas like a double-edged knife. It was as if she were silently asking him what she'd done to deserve such brutal attacks. Her unpleasant encounters with men the past hour had shattered her idealistic beliefs in the basic good of mankind.

When shiny tears streamed down her flushed cheeks and she burst into a sob that she could no longer contain, Nicolas honestly wished he'd beaten the life out of Evan Rollings. Candel was struggling to find her niche in a world that was unfamiliar to her and she was met with nothing but violence.

Candel was confused and disillusioned, just as Nicolas had been when his mother had given him away like a used shirt. She had no one to love her, no one to turn to. She was far too inexperienced to understand how much protection she really needed in this so-called civilized world which must seem a baffling contradiction. The harrowing incidents had destroyed her trust and deflated her spirit. She was huddling in the corner of the cot like a frightened child. No doubt, she felt just as she had after enduring the disaster at sea eleven years earlier.

Nicolas took a step forward and Candel shrank back. "Just go away, all of you," she sobbed. Her entire body quivered with the violent aftershocks of her near-brush with catastrophe. "Just go away . . ."

"Candel, I'm—"

"Leave me alone, damn you! And damn all men everywhere!" she cried, spluttering through another onslaught of tears. "Go back to your precious Camille. I'm sure she'll be waiting with—" She winced and swiped at the tears with the back of her hand when the salt seeped into the claw mark on her cheek. "What's that stupid figure of speech about waiting with fish bait?"

Nicolas frowned momentarily, trying to decipher her meaning. When the light of understanding finally dawned on him, he smiled. "You mean waiting with *bated breath*?"

"Aye, that's the one," she said with a muffled sniff.

Nicolas didn't leave when she showed him the door, as if he had not the slightest idea where to find it. He ambled toward the washstand to dip a cloth in the cool water. Gently, he sank down beside her to brush the cool compress over her cheek and breasts. When Candel tried to swat his hand away from her chest, he brought her trembling fingertips to his lips.

"I tried to warn you. You were too confident, too trusting. I'm sorry you had to find out the hard way what can happen when you find yourself in the clutches of certain men. There are too many Evan Rollings in this world, I'm sad to report."

"And what of your dear friend and resident lecher, Julian St. Croix?" Candel sniffed distastefully.

"Julian is very sorry about what happened," Nicolas assured her. "He was laboring under the misconception that you were the kind of woman who enjoyed entertaining a variety of men. He deeply regrets his mistake."

"If that's supposed to make me feel better, it doesn't," Candel muttered. "I've lost all respect for the male of the species."

"Even me, Candel?" Nicolas questioned softly.

She withdrew her hand from his grasp and stared at

the air above his shiny dark hair. "Even you," she insisted. "I don't need you either, Tiger. I don't need anyone!"

Ah, this little cast-iron butterfly was displaying her independent nature once again. She was determined not to let him know she had suffered another emotional blow, but Nicolas understood this phase she was going through. He had entered and emerged from it himself those first few years after he'd been cast out alone into the world. He had been out to show everyone that he needed no one. He'd built a wall around his wounded heart, just as Candel was trying to do now. Well, he wasn't going to let her suffer the way he had. She'd endured too much anguish already.

"Candel, listen to me," Nicolas whispered as he tilted her face to his. "I don't want to see you hurt more than you've already been."

"What do you care, Tiger?" she shot back. "You're the only man I ever offered an invitation. After you accepted it once, you've purposely avoided me. Your behavior speaks for itself. I'm sure you prefer your women with more experience, instead of a novice misfit who can't understand the world she left behind a decade ago. You're only being nice to me now because you pity me. Well, I don't want your pity or your misdirected feelings of obligation. Just leave me be!"

Candel managed to keep her voice from breaking until she had finished. But then her composure cracked. She didn't even care that Nicolas saw her reduced to blubbering tears and body-wrenching sobs. It was no longer important what he thought because she didn't care about him or anything else!

She had tried to make Tiger desire her once too often

and all for naught. This silver-blue-eyed rogue had been a foolish infatuation that would only cause her more heartache. He wanted nothing from her—not passion, not even friendship. She had tried to tease him into liking her. She had stood up to him time and time again, trying to gain his notice and his respect. But everything she did seemed to backfire. Well, she was through trying to catch his attention. He could take that gushing, eyelash-batting Camille to his bed if it pleased him. She was never going to try to make Nicolas like her ever again. She would be waspish and critical until she finally drove him so far away he would never come back!

"Candel, you're upset," Nicolas murmured.

"Of course I'm upset!" she retorted through her tears. "How would you feel if you were thrust into a world that wasn't remotely close to anything you thought it would be? I find myself scolded for speaking my mind after I was expected and encouraged to do so for a decade. Until a fortnight ago I was ruling over a society of men who obeyed my wishes and now I'm told that men are to rule over me and that I am not to disagree. I have been subjected to *your* authority as if *you* were my master and I your slave. I was forced into two days of solitary confinement for doing what I thought was right so you could reaffirm your lordly position."

Candel drew a shuddering breath and raged on in hopeless frustration. "You have whisked me away from my sensible, secure world for the reward you can get for my return. You have tried to make me into something I'm not. I don't even know who I am anymore and what I'm supposed to believe! You tell me how I'm supposed to behave, how to react, how to think, how to walk, and even how to dress! And when I garb myself in these restricting contraptions as you commanded, along comes some lusty, simple-minded man who tries to rip these garments off me!''

She peered up at him through anguished eyes and streaming tears. "How would you respond if I told you that everything you knew and understood was a terrible misconception and that you were to obey *my* wishes, no matter how illogical and ridiculous they sounded?''

Nicolas felt compelled to reach out to her, brushing his fingertips over her flushed cheeks in a consoling caress. "Candel, I—''

"Don't touch me!'' she railed, close to another hysterical outburst. "I've had enough groping and mauling to last me a lifetime!''

Nicolas stood up and stared down at the tangle of blond hair splayed around her tear-stained face. He felt terribly inadequate trying to comfort Candel when she was so close to hysterics, when she was so cynical and disillusioned. Perhaps this wasn't the time to try to force her to accept his friendship. Maybe she needed to have a good cry and wash away all the frustrated emotion that churned inside her. Tomorrow she would be her old self again and they would make a fresh start.

Reluctant though he was to leave Candel to wallow in misery, Nicolas retreated. When the door clanked shut behind him, she burst into tears and pummeled her pillow to relieve her anger and exasperation. But nothing helped. She felt so cold and alone, so utterly depressed and confused.

What she needed was to grow a shell to protect her emotions so that no one or nothing could ever hurt her again. She would become as strong and invincible as Nicolas Tiger. He would look at her and he would see his own reflection. She would allow no one to come close

194

again. And when Nicolas toted her back to her childhood home she would walk away from him without looking back. That raven-haired giant didn't matter to her, not one whit. He was nothing but a pirate, after all. She hoped his ship sank. She hoped his hair fell out. She hoped one day he would be as miserable and unhappy as she was now!

Chapter 13

Nicolas was concerned to note that Candel was *not* her old self by the dawn of a new day. She had turned her frustrations within, harboring them, letting them fester. When Julian had come to the docks with his tail tucked between his legs, humbly apologizing for the distress he'd caused her, Candel was distant and aloof, showing very little emotion. Although she declared Julian forgiven, she spoke with such controlled indifference that Nicolas felt he'd lost that one vibrant spark that had recently come into his life. Gone was the saucy, lighthearted beauty who zealously embraced life and defended against injustice. From the look of things, Candel had suffered serious emotional damage and she had decided to withdraw from the world. Nicolas knew the feeling only too well.

Although Nicolas was involved in returning his schooner to its former seaworthy condition, he kept a constant eye on Candel. She rarely mingled with the crew or smiled. Otis and Buff were permitted to share her company—but only on occasion. It was as if Nicolas and the rest of his men were no more than background scenery on the stage across which she walked to play her role.

Nicolas hated Candel's transformation. He felt the loss of communication with her in ways he'd never expected. He had allowed himself to get too close. He had become too aware of her needs, her anguish. When she was hurting, he bled. He couldn't just sit back and let something so vital and refreshing wither like a fragile blossom in a hard frost.

He decided he *was* going to do something before extreme damage was done to Candel's optimistic outlook on life! He'd make her mad enough to fight back if he must, but he would drive some sort of emotion out of that wall of self-imposed reserve which she had erected around herself. After three days of watching her mill aimlessly about, Nicolas had completed most of the repairs. Now the time had come to repair another kind of damage that one catastrophic night had caused.

With determined strides, Nicolas marched to the cabin. He was greeted by Candel's disinterested glance and Jolly Roger's customary "Hello, Tiger." Although Candel flashed the parrot a disapproving glance, she returned her attention to the book she was holding in front of her like a shield to prevent meeting Nicolas's probing stare.

"It's time we talked," he announced.

Candel's gaze rose above the book, eyeing him as if he were a misplaced stick of furniture. She said nothing.

"We'll be setting sail for New Orleans at first light. I have no intention of letting you be re-united with your family in your present state of mind."

Still nothing but silence. Candel wasn't cutting him one bit of slack.

"Curse it, Candel, I realize you've suffered a number of emotional blows the past two weeks, but you're behaving as if every tragedy in life has befallen you *alone*," Nicolas told her in a straightforward manner.

Candel coolly marked her place on the page with her forefinger and tilted the book downward, then met Nicolas's annoyed stare. "I'm sorry, Captain Tiger. Did you say something important? I wasn't paying attention."

With a muttered curse, Nicolas stalked over to yank the book from her hands and hoist her to her feet. Holding her at arm's length, he gave her the shaking he hoped would snap her out of her emotional vacuum. "Damnation, woman, I want you back the way you were!"

"And I want you out of my life as fast as possible," she flung back.

"Nay, you don't," he contradicted with an intimidating sneer. "Three days ago you wanted me in your bed, teaching you all I know about sex."

"Now look who's tossing *that word* around, would you?" The audacity of this conceited ogre, she mused. Who does he think he is?

"And furthermore, I think you're in love with me. But you're just too naive to realize it yet. That's why you resented my lack of attention." Of course, his declaration was a bold-faced lie but he figured a preposterous statement would get a rise out of her. Anything to crack the shield of indifference and start her talking again!

"Love you?" Candel parroted. "Don't make me laugh, Tiger."

"I doubt that you even remember how, cynic that you've become," he countered, relieved that he'd finally riled her. "You boasted about experimenting with other men for mere sport and curiosity. But when Julian made

198

amorous advances, you left your fingerprints on his cheek. When Evan assaulted you, you fought like a tigress. It was only *me* you wanted, wasn't it? Despite all your nettling remarks that were meant to annoy me and make me jealous.''

"You arrogant, insufferable lout!" Candel spewed, her amethyst eyes snapping. "Why would I want the affection of a mercenary pirate? I may be ignorant of the ways of civilization but even I could do better than the likes of you! You may have a magnificent body, but you're as approachable as a wounded rhinoceros!"

"Is that so?" Nicolas replied with a smirk.

He had forgotten how much he enjoyed fencing verbally with this quick minded Venus. She lashed back at him in ways no other woman had ever dared to do. And it was good to see that spark in her eyes again.

"Aye, 'tis so," Candel affirmed with great conviction. "You have the personality of an oyster without its pearl."

As usual, she was making up cliches when she couldn't remember the customary ones, thought Nicolas. He'd even missed that about her.

"Whatever physical attraction I might have had for you, now 'tis gone forever," Candel firmly assured him.

One thick brow arched to a mocking angle. "Then prove it," he challenged.

"Gladly," she replied enthusiastically.

"Kiss me and then look me squarely in the eye and tell me you feel nothing at all."

Candel glared at him. That scoundrel, she thought angrily. He was so sure of his ability to arouse all women everywhere. Well, she'd kiss him and pass his stupid test. She would be totally unaffected because she *didn't* care.

Determinedly, Candel tilted her face upward but Nicolas drew back. "I said . . . kiss *me*, not the other way around."

"Fine," she grumbled irritably. "Though I can't imagine what difference it makes who kisses whom. A kiss is just a kiss."

Her arms encircled his neck, drawing his head toward hers. Candel pressed her lips to his, determined not to respond. She was pleased that she felt nothing . . . until his arms glided around her waist, pulling her against him, reminding her of more intimate moments which she had been so determined to forget. When his sensuous lips pressed against hers and his tongue probed the hidden recesses of her mouth, she felt her defenses wobble. His teeth nipped at her lips before his head made another descent to savor her mouth in an exquisitely tender kiss.

Candel braced herself when her heart began to pound. Things weren't going as she'd anticipated. It obviously took longer than three days to forget what a fierce magnetic field of attraction surrounded them. When his adventurous hands cupped her derriere to press her familiarly to him, Candel felt tingles of betrayal vibrating through her body.

It was only because passion was still so new and fascinating that she responded so instantaneously, Candel reassured herself. It meant nothing at all. She could break this tantalizing kiss and retreat from his erotic caresses whenever she chose to.

When Nicolas's hands wandered up to trace the throbbing peaks of her breasts, Candel's brain seemed to malfunction. She suddenly couldn't remember what she was trying to prove. All she felt was that indescribable stirring of pleasure that this one man could evoke. Nicolas Tiger knew exactly where and how to touch a woman to make her yield to him, even when she'd been determined to remain unaffected.

Nicolas was having one devil of a time remembering his original purpose—drawing Candel into an argument then challenging her until she emerged from her shell. He found himself wanting what he swore he'd never permit himself to enjoy again. But touching her left him wanting her with every fiber of his being. Nicolas knew he was on the verge of losing control when Candel's hand moved inside his shirt to trace the tendons of his back and the muscles of his belly. Her touch set him ablaze. Suddenly nothing else seemed as important as feeding the fire that seared his flesh.

Nicolas likened himself to a rudderless ship, drifting wherever the current took him—and the incredibly fierce current was towing him under. A quiet groan reverberated in his chest when a tight knot of desire contracted in his belly and then in all directions at once.

Effortlessly, Nicolas lifted Candel in his arms and laid her on his bed. He was mesmerized by the glow of desire in her eyes. As he stretched out beside her, his hand slid beneath her baggy shirt. But beneath the loose-fitting garments were the luscious curves that had been indelibly etched in Nicolas's memory.

Like a man feasting on a banquet after years of starvation, his lips fluttered over the silky flesh of her belly, hungering to taste every part of her, yearning to satisfy this incredible craving. For more than two weeks he had denied himself the wondrous pleasures he'd discovered in Candel's arms and he'd hated every tormented minute! And as much as he wanted her now, for his own selfish purposes, he longed to touch her somewhere deep down in her soul, to bring her back to life after she'd withdrawn.

Although Candel tried to control the forbidden longings that bombarded her, she felt her traitorous body surrender to the potent spell this raven-haired wizard wove around her. His masterful kisses and caresses melted skin from bone. She was far too inexperienced to resist a man with Nicolas's practiced skills. There had been a time not so long ago when she had eagerly accepted his affection. But now she resented her inability to restrain the wayward yearnings of her body and her heart. His gentle caresses made her ache for his special brand of tenderness. He made her want to reach out to him, to feel and experience those emotions she had vowed to leave dead and buried. He made her forget the cruelties she had suffered, all the torment she'd endured. When she was in Tiger's protective arms, the world faded into oblivion.

A tiny moan bubbled in her throat when his hands swirled around the throbbing crests of her breasts and his lips followed. Tremors of sweet agony rippled through her, causing her to arch shamelessly toward him, begging for more. Her pulse hammered like hailstones as his fingertips caressed her quivering flesh. With tender expertise, he peeled away the layers of clothing that prevented him from touching her in the most intimate ways.

Candel gasped for breath when his kisses and caresses became even more daring and arousing. It was as if he'd sprouted a dozen hands to sensitize every inch of her quaking flesh, making her burn with a fever for which there was no cure.

While she lay there, filled with spasms of immeasurable pleasure, Nicolas drew her hand across the dark hair on his chest, inviting her caress. His lips feathered over hers in the slightest breath of a kiss that left her aching for a dozen more just like it to appease the hunger that gnawed at her.

"Now love me back, sweet nymph," he murmured. His lips parted in a faint smile as he stared down into her flickering violet eyes burning with passion. "I want you just as you were the very first time—warm, giving, uninhibited. I need what we had that night an eternity ago . . ."

His resonant voice was like an incantation that drew her into his hypnotic trance. Her hands began to weave across the broad expanse of his chest, feeling the energy and strength that lay beneath her fingertips. Although Candel was dazed by the fierce longings that engulfed her, she wanted to return the pleasure he had given her. She was intent on making him want her as much as she wanted him.

When her petal-soft lips skimmed over his nipples and her exploring hands moved over the muscles of his belly, Nicolas felt as though his lungs had filled with water, making it impossible to breathe. She used the same titillating techniques he'd used on her, adapting them to suit her purpose. He marveled at her natural feel for it, thrilled to the feel of her supple body gliding over his in the most evocative way imaginable.

The tips of her breasts teased his chest as she spread a row of butterfly kisses over his cheeks, eyelids, and forehead. Lower and lower still her lips moved, leaving him shuddering with anticipated pleasure. When her hands enfolded him, Nicolas clutched her to him, assuring her that she pleased him beyond words, that he wanted her like hell on fire.

Candel found herself glorying in this newly acquired power she held over this fascinating man. Bold and inventive by nature, she created a dozen different ways to elicit his desire, to make him crave her as if she were life itself. She cherished him with her hands and lips. She made him a willing slave to her seductive spell, just as she had become the eager captive of his.

Perhaps Nicolas didn't really want her to be a part of his life, she thought, but she would make him want the pleasure she could offer. She would carve her initials on his heart and he would remember these moments of passion they had shared. That would be her solace for caring more than she should have about a man—*this* man in particular.

Nicolas felt as if he were about to explode as Candel worked her unique magic on his body. She had led him to the edge of oblivion and he wanted her so badly that he ached all over. Gentleness escaped him when he rolled sideways to pull her beneath him. Breathlessly, he lifted her to him, yearning to feed the fire that burned him alive. Needs as ancient and as instinctive as time itself pulsated through him as he thrust deeply within her, obsessed with the need to become a living, breathing part of her body and soul.

Although Nicolas feared he would squeeze this dainty beauty in two as he urgently clutched her to ride out the cresting waves of splendor, he couldn't ease his bone-crushing grasp. If he dared to let go, he would tumble into infinity. And yet, even as tightly as he held onto her, he could feel himself slipping away, falling to the bottom of his heart—to that previously untouched place that he kept isolated from the rest of the world . . .

When the spasmodic rapture assaulted him, Nicolas knew he was lost. When he was in this lavender-eyed angel's arms he forgot the meaning of self-control. He was governed by pure emotion, never logic. And there was certainly no logic in what he felt when his body burst into flame and passion totally engulfed him. There was only sublime satisfaction . . .

It was a long moment before the blissful ecstasy dissipated. Even the emotional turmoil Candel had experienced in the past couldn't compare to the maelstrom of feeling that rushed through her like flood waters surging over a dam. Nothing in her previous experience prepared her for what she felt for this magnificent man.

Was Tiger right after all? Had a greater love evolved from this fierce physical attraction? Was that why she felt such a strong need to win Tiger's acceptance and respect and draw his attention? Was that why she had been jealous of the affection he had bestowed on Camille earlier in the week? Was that also why she had been put off by Julian's advances and repulsed by Evan's forceful attack?

"I want you back, Candel," Nicolas rasped as he treated himself to another intoxicating kiss. "You're like a breath of spring in my life. Your vibrant spirit is like sunshine on a cloudy day. Argue with me, harass me if you like. But don't withdraw so that I can't reach you. I was afraid you were gone forever."

His words touched her heart. In his own way, he was confessing that he needed her, if only temporarily. And she needed him, too. Candel had tried to become self sufficient, to put herself apart from the rest of the world. But it had been lonely and unsatisfying to bottle her emotions when she had been open and demonstrative all her life.

Her impressions, beliefs, and perspectives had undergone a transformation that Candel still wasn't sure she understood or accepted. Her life had become a kaleidoscope of ever-changing views and opinions linked with her past and influenced by the present. At times it seemed as if her very foundation was crumbling beneath her and she found herself reaching out to clutch at one stable thing, one dependable constant. As baffling as Nicolas could be at times, he was the only one who could comfort Candel's troubled soul and untangle her confusion. She had come to need him in ways she never dreamed possible for a woman to need a man, despite all the contradictions.

Candel decided not to frustrate herself by attempting to analyze this new environment. She intended to take one day at a time and cherish the enjoyment she had found with this raven-haired man, even if she couldn't quite comprehend or explain why he made her feel the way she did.

"I will become your mistress," she murmured as she toyed with the wavy hair that tumbled over his forehead. "I want no man except you to share these wondrous sensations you have taught me. I think I—"

"Tiger! Camille is here with a picnic lunch," Buff called from outside the door. "She even sent some fruit for Jolly Roger—"

Buff made the crucial mistake of barging into the cabin, as he'd had a habit of doing over the years. He had never expected to find Nicolas and Candel lying abed with only a sheet draped over them. His jaw fell open and his eyes popped in shock.

"Nicolas Stéphane Tiger! What the bloody hell do you think you're doing?" Buff exclaimed in an uncommon burst of temper. "Damn you, Tiger!"

During their long acquaintance, Nicolas could not recall a single instance when he had so thoroughly disappointed or infuriated the man who had taken him in and taught him all there was to know about the sea and about life. But the old sailor's disdainful glare branded Nicolas as a scoundrel of the worst sort. And Nicolas didn't even recall telling Buff his middle name. So how had Buff come up with that tidbit?

"I think you'd better leave, Buff," Nicolas advised as he drew the sheet protectively over Candel's bare shoulder.

Buff didn't budge. His thick chest inflated like a balloon and his ruddy complexion turned a darker shade. "Damnation, Tiger! She's a bona fide marchioness! I trained you better than that!"

"Buff . . ."

Buff was too irritated to heed the threatening growl in Nicolas's voice. He had vowed to become a better man after he survived the hurricane that had nearly claimed the crew of the *Sea Devil*. And by damned, Nicolas Tiger was going to be a better man, too, like it or not! He was going to accept full responsibility for what he'd done to Candel Caron. After all she had endured this past decade, she deserved more than to be one of the "somebody elses" who wound up in Tiger's bed.

That rapscallion! Tiger had taken advantage of a trusting maid who had been pure and innocent. Tiger was going to pay in full for his careless indiscretion. He had defied the restrictions of propriety. Damn it, a man didn't bed a lady of such high quality; he courted her good and proper!

"Now you listen to me, Nicolas Stéphane Tiger," Buff raged, waving a clump of bananas in Nicolas's face. "I took you in when you were still in knee breeches and I taught you to be a man. I never said anything when you were old enough to test your manhood with the kind of females who—"

"Buff, that's enough," Nicolas interrupted before his self-appointed conscience overspoke.

But Buff was just gathering a full head of steam and

he wasn't about to clam up until he'd said his piece. "If I would have thought you had something besides honorable intentions for Candel when you took her into your cabin, I'd have found her another place to stay. I sailed with a captain in my early years who took females on his voyages for his own fiendish pleasures. I hated him for it! And for a man who gets all het up when anybody refers to him as a pirate rather than a privateer, you're damned sure showing all the signs of a ruthless pirate!"

"Buff, get out, NOW!" Nicolas bellowed as he made a stabbing gesture toward the door.

"I'll leave when I'm finished and not a second before," Buff fumed, refusing to be intimidated by Tiger's thunderous scowl. "You are going to marry this girl and that's all there is to it. I'll be here to see that you leave no child to face the humiliation. And you'll not leave Candel—the Marchioness de Caron—to face a scandal, either. You will accept your responsibilities. Do you hear me, Nicolas Stéphane Tiger?"

Having had his say, Buff spun on his heels and stamped toward the door. He paused only long enough to peel a banana and thrust it at Jolly Roger who had been chattering nonstop while Buff read Nicolas the riot act.

When the door slammed shut, Nicolas sighed deeply in frustration. Hell and damnation, what lousy timing! No doubt he'd smolder like glowing coals in a hearth until Nicolas did as he'd been ordered. But curse it, if that outraged old goat would have stopped to think about what he was saying, he would have realized that marriage wasn't the answer either.

In the first place, Nicolas had had some unpleasant dealings with André Caron the previous year. And in the second place, he was the bastard son of a whore. He and Candel weren't in the same class. Snobbish aristocrats of New Orleans only married their offspring to other snobbish aristocrats. It simply was unheard of for a marchioness to wed a man who was nothing more than a . . . mistake.

Candel watched Nicolas mutter and scowl. His reaction assured her that he had no intentions of marrying her or anyone else. If he had been eager to enter the institution of marriage that seemed such a valued part of civilized society, he would have done so long before now. Nay, he wanted the pleasures a woman could provide without commitment. And obviously Nicolas had made his own fortune as a privateer, as he chose to call himself. He had no need of the wealth her family had amassed since her grandfather sailed from France to avoid the cruelties of the revolution. But Tiger did seem to find her an amusing pastime. For now that was enough. Candel dared not ask for more after all the turmoil she had endured the past eleven years.

Nicolas cast her a discreet glance, trying to determine how she had reacted to Buff's tirade aand his ultimatum. To his surprise, he was met with her impish smile. She glided her leg between his and curled her arms around his neck.

"Do you still wish me to be open and honest with you, Tiger?" she queried as her lips brushed invitingly over his.

"Aye, very much so, little nymph," he murmured huskily.

"It seems to me that we cannot possibly offend Buff more than we already have," she reasoned as her hands skimmed over his chest to swirl around his hips. "I prefer to enjoy this delicious sin once again before I'm to be scorned for it at Buff's convenience.''

Nicolas grabbed her straying hand before his brain broke down and his vocal cords collapsed. "Camille is on deck with her picnic basket," he reminded her.

Candel wormed her hand free to caress him boldly, making him groan in tormented pleasure. "Aye, she has the lunch basket," she affirmed in the most provocative tone imaginable. "But you have my love, Tiger. Decide which you desire most at the moment—food or sex . . .''

Ah, he did delight in her playful, plainspoken manner. It was good to have the old Candel back again. "Camille can keep her lunch basket," Nicolas decided as he bent to press his lips to her honeyed mouth. "But I do wish you would cease referring to this magic between us as sex. Let's call it making love instead . . .''

And in truth, Nicolas was beginning to wonder if that was what it was . . . or at least something damn near like it. Never in his life had he truly felt as if he needed anyone. Never had he wanted to need anyone since his mother had forsaken him at such a vulnerable age. But he did need Candel's irrepressible spirit, her youthful enthusiasm, her unrivaled passion. The past few days he felt as if he were only half a man, going through the paces of living. He had missed their verbal sparring and Candel's outgoing manner. Hell, he hadn't even had a good argument after she withdrew and shut him out.

Aye, they would enjoy each other for a time, even if Buff stamped and snorted and sneered. The secluded moments Nicolas was allowed to spend with Candel before he returned her to her family were too precious and dear. He had been noble for as long as he could. But he was long past the point of caring what propriety—or Buff—dictated.

Candel had spent her formative years in a liberal society and he had become an outcast of the one he had left behind to sail the high seas. They were making up their own rules, living each day as it came. The truth was that being with this feisty, unconventional little lady was the most fun he'd ever had. He wasn't giving her up to pacify Buff or anybody else. He was going to enjoy her. Propriety be damned!

"Mmm . . ." Candel whispered as his skillful hands coasted over her responsive flesh. "You're extremely good at this loving business, Tiger."

Nicolas grinned rakishly at the compliment. "I do aim to please, my lady."

"It must be all the previous experience that makes it possible for you to please so well," Candel said, and then wished the thought hadn't stung as much as it had.

"All the better to love you with, *chérie*," he rasped against the rapid pulsations of her throat. "Thank goodness I learned enough to please an extraordinary woman like you . . ."

Candel couldn't take offense when he put it that way. Even if she didn't mean anything special to Tiger, he could make her feel as if she did. And this certainly wasn't the time to quibble over previous affairs, not when his kisses and caresses were driving her mad with pleasure. And besides, Candel knew of no rules that decreed a man had to love the woman who loved him. She had the instinctive feeling this was definitely love—at least on her part. It involved all her emotions. Perhaps in time Nicolas would come to love her, too. And if it was meant to be . . .

211

That was the last analytical thought to enter her mind. When Nicolas came to her, Candel held nothing back. She responded in total abandon, reveling in the rapturous sensations that swamped and buffeted her. Even if this indescribable pleasure couldn't last forever, it was worth the sacrifices she had to make in the future. At least once in her life she had found her place in the sun.

Chapter 14

"Oh my goodness, I almost forgot!" Candel sat straight up in bed and blinked like an owl.

Nicolas pried one heavily-lidded eye open and stared in bemusement at the tangle-haired beauty who had been sleeping peacefully beside him. They had made wild, sweet love until slumber overtook them. But for some unknown reason Candel had bolted upright. Was it another of her traumatic nightmares? Most likely, Nicolas decided.

When she bounded out of bed like a mountain goat and sped toward the shelves to retrieve a book, Nicolas frowned in bewilderment. "What the blazes are you doing?"

"I found this document in the British commander's desk," she explained as she retrieved the paper.

Nicolas levered himself up to light the lantern and read the orders the commander of the *H.M.S. Gallant* had received. The rumors of attack by the British in the Gulf had been buzzing along the coast for almost a year. But according to the document the British were gearing up to make their strike very soon! Lost in troubled thoughts, Nicolas rolled to his feet and headed toward the door.

"Uh . . . Tiger?" Candel called after him, smiling wryly. "Have you decided to adapt to the natives' ways?"

Nicolas glanced over his shoulder and frowned in confusion.

Candel giggled lightheartedly and then gestured toward his mid-section. "If you plan to go above deck, perhaps you should don some breeches."

Nicolas stared at his naked torso and chuckled at his own preoccupation. Just how did this vivacious female manage to make him laugh at himself even when he made a mistake? Before she came along he would have been chastising himself for being so distracted. Now he merely shrugged off his blunder and grabbed his breeches.

"I like you better wearing nothing," Candel assured him with a saucy wink.

Nicolas waved the document at her. "My thanks, minx. I'll be sure to repay you later for this valuable information. You may have just saved the Americans from defeat."

After dressing on the way to the door, Nicolas charged up the steps to the deck. His mind buzzed with tasks that needed tending before they set sail at dawn. He would have to unload his British prisoners and leave them in Martinique instead of ransoming them. He was not about to give the British sailors a chance to fight against him if battle did break out on the coast.

Although Nicolas was all business when he strode across the deck, Buff greeted him with a cold shoulder and a contemptuous glare. "I expect you'll be wanting me to skedaddle into Fort-de-France to fetch the minister," Buff said meaningfully.

Nicolas ignored the stern hint and the angry glare. Hurriedly, he shoved the document under Buff's nose, which was noticeably out of joint after their previous encounter. "Take word to Fort-de-France that the British plan to attack New Orleans. They are sending part of their fleet from the east coast blockade to cut off the Gulf."

"What?" Buff crowed in shock.

"Aye, the British are girding up for battle in hopes of sealing off the trade centers on the Mississippi. They plan to march down from Canada, while simultaneously surging up from New Orleans to take control of the interior."

"But I thought our ambassadors were hard at work in Belgium trying to negotiate a peace."

"I don't see either side calling a truce while the Americans and British try to negotiate a treaty, do you, Buff?" Nicolas scoffed. "There are only a few American warships in the harbor to provide protection for New Orleans. At last count the Americans had only seven hundred army regulars to defend the city. If the Americans lose New Orleans, they'll lose the war as well and there won't be any compromising treaties signed in Belgium. According to this report, the British plan to burn New Orleans to the ground, just as they did Washington. They have already captured Detroit and they are prepared to move south."

Nicolas paced the deck in measured strides, contemplating the information in the document. "Alert every freebooter and privateer in Fort-de-France. They all have a vested interest in New Orleans. If I know Jean and Pierre Lafitte, they'll enlist all their men to come to the Americans' aid. We need all available privateers in the Gulf as fast as they can get there to heckle the British."

Casting his irritation with Nicolas aside, Buff lurched

215

around to summon Otis and Wyatt to assist him in spreading the word around the docks. When they scurried off, Nicolas started barking orders to be sure the *Sea Devil* was prepared to sail at first light. With the British man-of-war at his disposal, he could use the frigate as a free passport into the harbor. In fact, he might just sail past the blockade on board the *Gallant* and leave Otis and Buff with the *Sea Devil*. Aye, that was exactly what he'd do, Nicolas decided. Nothing would infuriate the cocky British Royal Navy more than to have one of their own brigantines blocking the channel, firing back.

Nicolas went through his checklist of supplies, intending to ensure that the schooner was battle worthy if it went up against the British. And when he had time, he was going to thank Candel properly for rummaging through the commander's belongings to uncover such an important document. Her curiosity may well have saved the day. Nicolas could have kicked himself for not thinking to search the commander's belongings.

He had been too preoccupied battling his obsession for that delectable nymph and keeping his distance from the cabin where she'd been staying. Aye, he was definitely going to thank Candel in private . . . later . . .

After several days of clear sailing into the Gulf of Mexico, Candel found herself in a turmoil of conflicting emotions. She was certain now that she was in love with Nicolas and she freely admitted and demonstrated her affection, despite Buff's condescending frowns and snide remarks. And Nicolas had stopped fighting the attraction between them. Although he never said those three words Candel longed to hear, he no longer behaved as if he resented the torrent of passion between them. They never

216

spoke of the future, but lived for each stolen moment in the present. Yet, the closer they came to New Orleans, the more uneasy Candel became. She had no idea what to expect when she arrived at her family's plantation after an eleven-year absence.

What concerned her most was the imminent battle and the fact that Tiger wouldn't be with her. More and more, Nicolas became distracted by thoughts of the British invasion. He was the kind of man who craved challenge and adventure and Candel had the unshakable feeling that he would spend all his time aiding the Americans, leaving no time for her.

All these years, Candel had had no one upon whom to bestow the love bottled up inside her. The islanders had set her apart from them, offering respect and devotion. But it had never been the same as being needed and loved for herself. Now that she had found someone she truly loved, Tiger was about to be stripped from her arms and placed in harm's way. The thought of never seeing him again reminded her of those agonizing months of her youth when she had lost her parents and found herself in a totally unfamiliar environment. She was about to suffer another emotional upheaval. Curse it, she wished Tiger had left her where he'd found her. It would have been simpler than coping with more torment!

"Does this look familiar?" Nicolas questioned as he walked over to Candel on the quarterdeck of the *H.M.S. Gallant*. He offered her the spyglass to survey the outstretched fingers of land that formed the delta below New Orleans.

Candel peered into the distance of time and space, trying to remember what life had been like before the tragedy at sea. At the time she and her parents had sailed off to Spain she had been too young to recall much about

New Orleans. And later, she had tried to put all thoughts of the past out of her mind forever. Never once had she clung to the hope of rescue.

"I regret to report that the only familiar thing around here is you, Tiger," she replied as she returned the spyglass. "And before long, I suspect you will be just a haunting memory."

Candel couldn't help herself. She was becoming more sentimental by the second. She had tried to remain lighthearted, carefree, and playful, but it was difficult when the happiness she had so recently discovered was slipping away from her.

"Don't, Candel," Nicolas murmured as he reached out to smooth away her frown. "Don't spoil what precious time we have left. We'll still see each other if that's what you want."

What *she* wanted? Nothing had ever been the way *she* wanted since she'd found herself hopelessly attracted to this rugged swashbuckler. She didn't want to be an heiress who lounged in the lap of luxury with nothing to do after she'd been active and involved on the island for eleven years. She simply wanted to be with Tiger, chasing rainbows and embracing adventure wherever they found it.

What good were titles and wealth without a loved one with whom to share it? She had learned that position and respect hadn't been enough once she'd experienced the emotions Tiger had evoked. Nothing would fill the emptiness he would leave in her heart. What was she to do with the love and emotion she felt for Tiger when he walked out of her life?

"Tiger!" Buff called through the speaking tube from the *Sea Devil* which sailed directly beside them. "We're veering west to Barataria. We'll meet you at Jean Lafitte's home on Grande Terre.''

Nicolas lifted his arm, signalling confirmation. He intended to sail the brigantine right into the British blockade before marching his crew into the life boats and setting the vessel ablaze. That should stun the British into wondering what other cunning tactics the Americans had up their sleeves!

True to his word, Nicolas cruised right between two man-of-wars and dropped anchor. Since his crew had already prepared the port and starboard cannons for firing, it was a simple matter of shoving the cartridges home to lambaste the frigates on either side of them. After Candel and the crew scurried into the skiffs, Nicolas set fire to the long fuse of gunpowder he had dribbled across the deck.

The eardrum-shattering blast sent fire and debris rocketing high into the air. The British sailors gaped at the holes blown in their ships and half collapsed in astonishment when the massive explosion destroyed the man-of war between them.

When the shock waves from the erupting vessel rippled across the water, Nicolas curled a protective arm around Candel and braced himself as the small boat surged on the wave and nose-dived into the trough to shoot toward shore.

Candel had never before ventured into the treacherous marshes and swamps that encircled the small islands of land forming Barataria—the home of criminals, smugglers, pirates, privateers, fishermen, and trappers. Nicolas had assured her there were good, kind people living in the swamp lands, as well as undesirables who were hiding from the authorities in New Orleans. He had also made it a point to tell her that there was a special code in the swamps. The Baratarians minded their own business unless the criminals caused trouble. The Baratarians had their own ways of handling troublemakers and the swamps kept their secrets from the rest of the world.

As the skiffs zigzagged past Last Island—the farthermost isle that stretched into the Gulf, Candel surveyed the forbidding shadows that engulfed the gnarled oaks, cypress, and Spanish moss-bearded trees. Occasionally she spied a deer splashing through the duckweed-smothered bayous that meandered through the wet wilderness. Patches of sunlight gleamed across the stagnant water, leaving the only bright spots in a gloomy domain that easily triggered active imaginations. Any second now, Candel expected to see a prehistoric monster surge to the surface of the swamps to gobble them alive. She couldn't imagine anyone purposely living in Barataria.

Although Nicolas had never said so, she wondered if this gator-infested marsh was the place he called home. How anyone could navigate through this labyrinth when the surroundings looked so monotonously similar was beyond her. Candel was sure she would have lost all sense of direction the instant they cruised into such unfamiliar territory!

Nicolas pointed out the chênière—an island of white shells covered with sprawling oaks. It lay amid the trembling prairie which constituted Jean Lafitte's kingdom of Barataria.

"There is another chênière to the northwest known as The Temple," he informed his goggle-eyed companion. " 'Tis there that auctions of smuggled goods are held by the privateers. Because of the British blockade, Louisiana depends on us to sneak in supplies and much-needed staples. According to legend, an Indian tribe once used the island for rituals and human sacrifices."

Candel peered at the gigantic oaks on the tiny island, trying to imagine the meeting place Nicolas had described. She had to admit the chênière was a fascinating location amid a natural fortress of swamps and marshes, but she still preferred a tropical island paradise surrounded by sea and white sand.

When they floated past Grand Isle, Candel spied the clumps of palmetto-thatched huts that housed fishermen, trappers, and, no doubt, smugglers who shipped contraband into New Orleans.

An astonished gasp broke from Nicolas's throat when they reached Grande Terre—the privateers' main headquarters. Beyond the crude fort where Jean Lafitte's elegant home once sat was a pile of charred rubble. The mansion had been filled with the finest imported furniture, silver, and china. The home, several cottages, and the warehouse—where supplies and goods had been stored—were demolished. The storehouses had also been smashed to bits and the quaint cabin Nicolas had called home was nothing but blackened timbers and ashes.

Hurriedly, Nicolas secured the skiff and led the stunned procession around the remnants of the fort. Relief washed over his features when Jean Lafitte stepped from the shadows of the towering oaks to greet them.

"I had planned a grand reception for your long-awaited return, Tiger," Jean remarked before he glanced at the remains of what had once been an elaborate home in the swamps. "But as you can see, you are met instead with my humble greeting." His gaze darted past Nicolas to focus on the petite beauty in form-fitting men's clothes.

"And who is this lovely vision, Tiger?" Jean questioned curiously.

Candel peered up into Jean's black eyes and his handsome, pale-skinned face. Jean was lean and elegantly dressed and stood only a few inches shorter than Nicolas. The privateer's face was clean shaven except for a dark beard that extended down the lower curve of his cheeks. The suave, debonair Frenchman had a certain way about him that was irresistibly attractive to women. Those big dark eyes roamed over Candel like slow-moving honey, visually assessing her and silently assuring her that he definitely approved.

"Steady, *mon ami*," Nicolas chuckled and then clucked his tongue at his friend's seductive stare. "The lady is with me."

"*Now* perhaps," Jean teased as he swaggered up to press a kiss to Candel's wrist. "But what of later?" His all-consuming gaze flooded over her a second time. "What is your name, *cherie*? I must have a name to attach to such an enchanting vision."

"Candeliera Junfroi Caron," she replied, flashing him a smile that earned her raised eyebrows and another roguish grin.

"No relation, I hope, to André Caron who considers himself the reigning king of New Orleans, as well as Tiger's predator," Jean mused aloud.

"Her cousin, I'm sorry to say," Nicolas grumbled.

"But I would not think of holding you accountable, *ma chérie*," Jean assured her, giving her the once-over a third time. "I don't know how one so lovely could have come to have such a relative. An ironic twist of fate, I suppose."

"What the hell happened here?" Nicolas demanded impatiently.

He had grown tired of Jean's flirtatious games. It reminded him of Julian's blatant overtures. He was also feeling a twinge of jealousy. And with just cause! Jean had a reputation as a ladies' man. Jean, who was five years older than Nicolas, had taught him the art of gentlemanly persuasion and sophisticated manners. Nicolas preferred not to see Jean testing his skills on Candel.

The question Nicolas posed stripped the smile from Jean's lips. His countenance sobered as he gestured for Nicolas and Candel to follow him toward the sloop that would take them to his temporary headquarters at Chênière Caminada.

"How did you know we were coming?" Candel blurted out as they threaded through the trees and underbrush.

Jean tossed her a charismatic grin. "Nothing goes on in Barataria that doesn't reach my ears, *chérie*. We are a tightly-knit network of friends who guard each other's backs. I knew the dragoons were coming to destroy our village, but I didn't raise a hand to fight them, especially not now."

"Who did this?" Nicolas demanded to know. Thus far, Jean had eluded his direct questions and he was becoming impatient to know who to blame for demolishing his home and all his worldly possessions!

Jean assisted Candel into the dinghy and took up a set of oars. "The American forces under Commodore Patterson paid us a visit. They were a very unsociable group, as you can see."

"Americans?" Nicolas croaked, staring frog-eyed at the shambles.

"They came under Governor Claiborne's orders," Jean muttered as he negotiated the winding bayou. "You have been gone a long while, Tiger. A great many things have changed these past few months."

"Obviously," Nicolas muttered as he stared pensively at what had been his cottage on Grande Terre.

"We weren't able to salvage your belongings," Jean informed his friend when he noticed where Tiger's gaze had strayed. "The Americans confiscated everything of value. What little we have left is at our new headquarters on Chênière Caminada."

While they rowed toward the island, Jean explained the complicated events that had brought disaster to Barataria. "As you well know, Governor Claiborne has long resented our power and prestige, not only here but in New Orleans. He insists on calling us *banditti* and he hasn't been the least bit grateful that our privateers have managed to elude the blockade to bring goods to the city. In fact, the wine that graces the governor's table at the Cabildo came from us. I should have let him drink swamp water," Jean snorted disgustedly.

"Aye, you should have," Nicolas muttered in annoyance. "I was ready to drag Claiborne out and let him navigate his way through these swamps after he had you and Pierre arrested last year. Now I'm twice as eager to dump him in the bayou!"

"Pierre has been apprehended again," Jean grimly reported. "Claiborne has kept my brother in chains at the Cabildo, even though his health has not been the same since his stroke four years ago. Dominique You, Beluche and seventy-eight other privateers were arrested during last week's raid. Now they're all locked up with Pierre."

"Has the governor gone mad?" Nicolas questioned. "I've confiscated a document that indicates the British are gearing up for an attack on New Orleans. The Americans need all the help they can get to defend the city and they have the best fighting men in these parts mildewing in jail! Preposterous!"

The Publishers of Zebra Books Make This Special Offer to Zebra Romance Readers...

AFTER YOU HAVE READ THIS BOOK WE'D LIKE TO SEND YOU 4 MORE FOR *FREE* AN $18.00 VALUE

No Obligation!

ONLY ZEBRA HISTORICAL ROMANCES "BURN WITH THE FIRE OF HISTORY" (SEE INSIDE FOR MONEY SAVING DETAILS.)

MORE PASSION AND ADVENTURE AWAIT... YOUR TRIP TO A BIG ADVENTUROUS WORLD BEGINS WHEN YOU ACCEPT YOUR FIRST 4 NOVELS ABSOLUTELY *FREE* (AN $18.00 VALUE)

Accept your Free gift and start to experience more of the passion and adventure you like in a historical romance novel. Each Zebra novel is filled with proud men, spirited women and temptuous love that you'll remember long after you turn the last page.

Zebra Historical Romances are the finest novels of their kind. They are written by authors who really know how to weave tales of romance and adventure in the historical settings you love. You'll feel like you've actually gone back in time with the thrilling stories that each Zebra novel offers.

GET YOUR FREE GIFT WITH THE START OF YOUR HOME SUBSCRIPTION

Our readers tell us that these books sell out very fast in book stores and often they miss the newest titles. So Zebra has made arrangements for you to receive the four newest novels published each month.

You'll be guaranteed that you'll never miss a title, and home delivery is so convenient. And to show you just how easy it is to get Zebra Historical Romances, we'll send you your first 4 books absolutely FREE! Our gift to you just for trying our home subscription service.

BIG SAVINGS AND FREE HOME DELIVERY

Each month, you'll receive the four newest titles as soon as they are published. You'll probably receive them even before the bookstores do. What's more, you may preview these exciting novels free for 10 days. If you like them as much as we think you will, just pay the low preferred subscriber's price of just $3.75 each. *You'll save $3.00 each month off the publisher's price.* AND, your savings are even greater because there are never any shipping, handling or other hidden charges—FREE Home Delivery. Of course you can return any shipment within 10 days for full credit, no questions asked. There is no minimum number of books you must buy.

4 FREE BOOKS

4 FREE BOOKS

TO GET YOUR 4 FREE BOOKS WORTH $18.00 — MAIL IN THE FREE BOOK CERTIFICATE T O D A Y

Fill in the Free Book Certificate below, and we'll send your FREE BOOKS to you as soon as we receive it.

If the certificate is missing below, write to: Zebra Home Subscription Service, Inc., P.O. Box 5214, 120 Brighton Road, Clifton, New Jersey 07015-5214.

FREE BOOK CERTIFICATE

4 FREE BOOKS

ZEBRA HOME SUBSCRIPTION SERVICE, INC.

YES! Please start my subscription to Zebra Historical Romances and send me my first 4 books absolutely FREE. I understand that each month I may preview four new Zebra Historical Romances free for 10 days. If I'm not satisfied with them, I may return the four books within 10 days and owe nothing. Otherwise, I will pay the low preferred subscriber's price of just $3.75 each; a total of $15.00, *a savings off the publisher's price of $3.00.* I may return any shipment and I may cancel this subscription at any time. There is no obligation to buy any shipment and there are no shipping, handling or other hidden charges. Regardless of what I decide, the four free books are mine to keep.

NAME _____

ADDRESS _____ APT _____

CITY _____ STATE _____ ZIP _____

TELEPHONE ( ) _____

SIGNATURE _____

(if under 18, parent or guardian must sign)

Terms, offer and prices subject to change without notice. Subscription subject to acceptance by Zebra Books. Zebra Books reserves the right to reject any order or cancel any subscription.

GET
FOUR
FREE
BOOKS
(AN $18.00 VALUE)

ZEBRA HOME SUBSCRIPTION
SERVICE, INC.
P.O. Box 5214
120 BRIGHTON ROAD
CLIFTON, NEW JERSEY 07015-5214

AFFIX
STAMP
HERE

The news caused Jean's expression to turn bleaker than it already was. "Another crisis to deal with," he said with a frustrated sigh. "But perhaps this news will change Claiborne's mind about considering Baratarians his enemy."

Jean strained against the oars and composed his thoughts to brief Nicolas on all the events that had taken place during his absence. "Since you left Barataria we had a visit from the British, who decided to clear us out. Perhaps they thought to weaken the defense of New Orleans if they do plan to attack, just as you claim. When a British sloop anchored near Grand Isle a group of marines clambered ashore to seize control. When we attacked them they retreated after suffering heavy losses. Since the British couldn't defeat us, they tried to bribe me into fighting on their side."

"And did you accept since you and Claiborne are on such unfriendly terms?" Candel interrupted in question.

Jean shook his dark head. "Nay, I asked for time to make my decision. The British sweetened the bribe by offering me the rank of captain and thirty thousand dollars in cash. And in the meantime, I wrote to Claiborne personally, offering the privateers' skills in battle to aid the American cause."

"And what did the esteemed governor say to that?" Nicolas asked with a smirk.

"He posted notices all over New Orleans, offering a five hundred dollar reward for my head," Jean grumbled.

"Why that ungrateful lout!" Nicolas exclaimed. "I'd like to have *his* head!"

"So would I," Jean agreed with a wry smile. "That's why I had my men tear down the posters and nail up notices declaring that I would pay fifteen hundred dollars for the governor's head. Most of the good citizens in New

Orleans found my counter-offer highly amusing, except for Claiborne, of course.''

"And not to be outdone, I suppose Claiborne sicked his army on you to burn all of you out,'' Candel speculated. "That certainly implies that he has no intention of accepting your offer to aid the Americans.''

"The governor might change his mind when he receives word that Tiger has a document ordering an attack on New Orleans,'' Jean mused aloud. "This sudden threat might convince Claiborne to join forces with us. General Jackson has just arrived in New Orleans to head the American defenses in case of battle. But he has only a thousand Tennessee regulars and the Mississippi dragoons under his command, plus an additional seven hundred stationed around the city.''

"And according to the document, the British are sending seven thousand soldiers to take the city,'' Nicolas added gloomily. "Claiborne and Jackson are fools if they don't accept your offer.''

"*Mon Dieu! Seven thousand soldiers*!'' Jean bleated. "Curse that idiotic Claiborne. His army destroyed seven of our privateer ships which could have served the American cause. I ought to fill his wine bottles with poison. It would serve that billy goat right!''

When Jean reached Chênière Caminada, he assisted Candel from the skiff and ushered her toward the cottage which had become his new headquarters. Otis, Buff, and the mariners who had brought the *Sea Devil* up the deep water pass near a sheltered cove on Grande Terre had already arrived upon the scene.

"*Now* shall I fetch a clergyman before all hell breaks loose in the Gulf?'' Buff muttered angrily for the umpteenth time as Nicolas strode past him. "I'd like to know what you plan to do with the marchioness.''

Nicolas flung his first mate a withering glance. One crisis was following hot on the heels of another and Buff was still stewing about propriety. Hell, there may be no need for propriety if the British burned New Orleans to the ground.

"First things first, Buff," Nicolas hissed.

"If you ask me, you should have thought of that before you dallied with the Marchioness de Caron," Buff snorted sarcastically.

"Nobody asked you," Nicolas shot back with an annoyed frown.

"Well, you should have," Buff insisted before he stormed off.

Candel was led into the quaint cottage which boasted incredible luxuries. The spacious table where Jean Lafitte and his men dined was adorned with the finest china and polished silver. Black servants scurried about to accommodate Jean and his guests. He sent one of the servants to the storehouse to retrieve a gown and all the accessories Candel required.

Candel blinked, bewildered, when the gorgeous gifts were bestowed on her. "Where did you get such expensive finery?" she questioned her benefactor.

Jean merely smiled slyly and shrugged a broad shoulder before gesturing toward the bedroom where she could change for dinner. When Candel disappeared behind the closed door, Nicolas peered somberly at Jean.

"I'm curious to know what instigated this new feud between you and Claiborne," he said point-blank—a habit he'd unconsciously picked up from Candel. "I realize Claiborne has never approved of our activities in Barataria, but amid such critical times with the British I should think he would be more tolerant and compromising."

Jean sank into his chair to pour Nicolas and himself a glass of wine. "The feud came to a head a few months ago when an American merchantman known as the *Independence* was attacked by pirates on its way back from Africa. The ship was seized off the coast of Havana," he explained. "Every member of the crew except a seaman named Williams was murdered. Williams managed to leap overboard and was rescued by a vessel bound for New Orleans."

Jean's gaze shot toward the door to the room Candel occupied. "A group of our enemies—including André Caron, who delegated himself the spokesman—went to Claiborne. They insisted that you and I were responsible for the confiscation of the cargo and the brutal murders."

"That's ridiculous," Nicolas said indignantly. "I wasn't even in the area and we've never raided American ships. Claiborne knows perfectly well that isn't our style. And if the merchantman was seen in Africa 'tis obvious that it was carrying the illegal cargo of slaves. I don't suppose this Williams character mentioned that, did he?"

"Nay, he didn't," Jean replied. "No doubt, Williams wanted to save his own hide. He could even have been bribed to point an accusing finger at us. But the incident was a good excuse for Claiborne to lay the blame on us, especially since André Caron was putting up such a fuss about having you and the rest of us cleared out of Barataria." He frowned thoughtfully at his darkly handsome friend. "Just what did happen between you and André last year? He has been egging Claiborne on every chance he gets."

Nicolas squirmed uneasily in his chair and stared at the contents of his glass. "That haughty dandy decided not to pay me the original price for the goods I delivered to him. We exchanged harsh words and then he tried to strike me." He glanced up from beneath long black lashes. "I loosened his front teeth and bloodied his upturned nose. He swore to get even."

Jean nodded thoughtfully. "André seems to be a man of his word. He's been pressing the governor to destroy our operation and the Americans definitely caused us serious setbacks."

"I'm sorry I've caused you more trouble because of my personal feud with André," Nicolas apologized.

Jean shrugged and sighed. "My regret is that I have to be so discreet in my visits to New Orleans these days. Although you and I will always be welcome in the homes and at the social gatherings hosted by our friends and associates, the streets are no longer safe with Claiborne's men on patrol. The governor's and André's opinions are still in the minority, even if Claiborne is in power. You will have to be extremely cautious in the city. If you are recognized, you can expect to rot in jail."

Jean leaned across the table to peer somberly at Nicolas. "With Pierre, Dominique, and Beluche in the Cabildo, I have only you to depend on. I need a favor, Tiger."

"All you have to do is ask," Nicolas assured him. "It was your generosity that granted me privileges here that I never would have had anywhere else."

Jean eased back in his chair and chortled at his friend's modesty. "Nay, it was your trustworthiness and your heroism in the face of adversity that won you a place in our ranks. I can hardly take credit for your cunning skills and keen wit. But I will take advantage of your loyalty in this instance. I want you to deliver your document to New Orleans and ensure Claiborne sees it with his own eyes. I have a trusted contact on Bourbon Street. Jacob Wells will see to it that you are safely accompanied to the Cabildo. Perhaps Claiborne will back down from his stubborn stand when he learns the British intend to attack with killing force.''

'' 'Tis done,'' Nicolas affirmed.

"You can see to the matter tonight. I will keep the young lady occupied in your absence,'' Jean volunteered—a mite too eagerly to suit Nicolas.

"And in return, I ask a favor of you, Jean,'' he requested with narrowed eyes. "I will gladly share all I have with you as a gesture of continued friendship. All except Candel . . .''

Jean arched a thick brow and regarded his companion for a long, thoughtful moment. "You are already playing with fire, Tiger, considering your own feud with André Caron. Are you so certain that Candel won't suffer because of this?''

Nicolas hurriedly explained the circumstances surrounding Candel's return after an eleven-year absence. "I've decided it best to let Buff accompany Candel to the Caron plantation for her reunion. André need never know about my . . . friendship with his cousin.''

"Friendship?'' Jean chuckled in amusement. "If that's all it is, why are you warning me away?''

"Because you never could resist a pretty face,'' Nicolas countered. "Aye, entertain Candel in my absence, but . . .''

His voice trailed off when Candel reappeared in a stunning gold silk gown. Seeing her in the elegant dress caused an instant and total response from Nicolas. It also drove home the point that the time he would be allowed to spend with Candel had dwindled down to a precious few hours. He'd grown so accustomed to having her around that he couldn't quite imagine life without her.

He had allowed her to matter more than she should have and now he was forced to pay the price.

"Tiger, I'm going to be sorely put upon to honor your request," Jean murmured before he rose to escort Candel to the table.

Nicolas didn't doubt Jean's words for a minute. With Candel's striking good looks and quick wit, she naturally drew men like flies to sugar. Jean Lafitte was an incorrigible flirt who could conquer even the most cautious of hearts. He had damned well better not practice all his charms on Candel or he would put a strain on their friendship!

"You're drooling," Nicolas said as Jean sank down beside him, still ogling Candel from across the table.

Jean pried his gaze away for a few seconds to grin unrepentantly at his friend. "Ah, to have Tiger's luck," he said with a woeful sigh. "She's a prize, Tiger. I cannot imagine how you're going to give her up."

Nicolas couldn't imagine how he was going to give her up, either. It sure as hell wasn't going to be easy, but it was in Candel's best interest. She deserved better than a man with his bad breeding and checkered past. They had shared a special magic for a time, but that time had come and gone. And Nicolas had damned well better start thinking of this violet-eyed nymph in terms of the past— a past that could not possibly have a future . . .

Chapter 15

"Jean told me what you're planning to do and I'm going with you," Buff declared when Nicolas ambled toward the waiting skiff.

"I suppose Jean just also happened to suggest that you accompany me," Nicolas said as he glanced back at the house.

"As a matter of fact, he did," Buff confirmed as he fell into step beside Nicolas.

"Now Jean will have Candel all to himself. That sly rake," Nicolas muttered.

He had been a mite too possessive of Candel the past few weeks, it was true. But the thought of another man enjoying her company turned him as sour as curdled milk. In the past, Nicolas had teased Jean about his flirtations. Now it wasn't quite so amusing.

"Well, if you had married Candel the way you should have, you would have a justifiable complaint," Buff countered, giving Nicolas the evil eye. "If Jean charms her while we're gone then I'd say you deserve it."

When Nicolas pulled up short, Buff plowed into his backside. "Now look, Buff, we've been through this a dozen times already. André Caron is Candel's cousin. I don't need to remind you how that uppity muckamuck feels about me and what he's done to Jean to get back at all of us. He was partly responsible for the American raid on Grande Terre. The man likes to throw his weight around and I'll not have him taking his irritation with me out on Candel. I'm a mistake of nature with a tarnished heritage and bad breeding. She's a blueblood. It would never work, especially now that Baratarians are under fire from the governor's office."

"You're every bit as good as she is," Buff insisted.

"Come now, Buff. You know better than that," Nicolas snorted.

Aye, Buff knew lots of things he'd never told Tiger and he still wasn't sure the time was right. "If your past is bothering you, you should have considered that before you decided to treat the marchioness like your mistress. I wish I'd never demanded that we bring her back to New Orleans. My good intentions and your lack of discretion have turned out to be disastrous!"

Leaving Buff to mutter and fuss, Nicolas quickened his step toward the dinghy. After Buff had plunked down like an ill-tempered bear, Nicolas took up the oars to navigate through the darkened swamps.

"You're going to let her go, just like that?" Buff grumbled a mile later. "I'm beginning to doubt your moral fiber, Tiger. I think the girl feels something special for you and you for her, though you would probably cut out your tongue before you admitted any such thing to her, me, or even to yourself."

"What does *she* know about love?" Nicolas smirked at his sulking friend. "You knew her situation on the island. I was the first man she had been with. And what do *I* know about affection, for that matter?"

"You could learn from her," Buff suggested. "Personally, I think she's got it all figured out."

"I don't wish to have this discussion," Nicolas said with mulish stubbornness.

"Good. Then you can sit there and listen while I talk. Now damn it, Tiger, I want you to marry Candel!"

While Buff was shooting his mouth off about why marriage was the only logical answer, listing all the reasons why it was important to "do the right thing," Nicolas was mentally plotting his encounter with Claiborne at the Cabildo. He had come prepared to make the most of the situation—that is, if Buff would shut his trap long enough for Nicolas to organize his scheme. Curse that old coot. He knew Nicolas understood no other way of life except the sea. Did Buff expect him to marry Candel and drag her around with him indefinitely? Or was Nicolas supposed to sacrifice all he'd known to compensate for his inability to resist temptation? Candel hadn't asked for any commitment, so why was Buff being so vocal with his objections?

"And another thing, Tiger, what's going to happen to Candel if—"

Nicolas flung up a hand. "Enough!" He tied the skiff and stepped to the dock below André Caron's plantation. "We're supposed to proceed discreetly. We don't need to call extra attention to ourselves. Your constant blathering is bound to draw attention. Use a little stealth and cunning and, for God's sake, clamp up!" Nicolas hissed.

Thoroughly disgusted that all his arguments had fallen on deaf ears, Buff tromped up the hill to the path that led to New Orleans. He didn't like the way things were shaping up in Louisiana, not one damned bit. Pandemonium was about to break loose and Nicolas intended to set Candel adrift. The young fool. He would regret his decision. Buff had a bad feeling about the whole state of affairs. But if Buff talked long and hard enough, maybe he could convince Nicolas to do what was right, even if he couldn't do a damned thing about those confounded British who were girding up for a full scale battle!

Candel burst out laughing at Jean Lafitte's outrageous flattery. For more than two hours he had escorted her around the small community, introducing her to his comrades and the other inhabitants of Barataria. Some of the men she had met earlier on the *Sea Devil*, while countless others sailed on ships in Jean's extensive fleet—minus the ships that Claiborne had ordered burned, that is.

"Really, Jean, you're wasting your time with me," Candel declared when the charismatic privateer heaped a few more compliments on her.

" 'Tis never a waste when a man finds himself in the company of such an intriguing woman," he replied with another round of provocative smiles that seemed to have no effect on this beguiling beauty who had the uncanny ability to see through him in one minute flat.

Jean sighed forlornly when Candel admonished him for flirting with her for the hundredth time. It was obvious she wasn't familiar with men's courting rituals. As Nicolas had explained, Candel was a child-woman who had been isolated from civilization, unaccustomed to the games people played.

"I cannot imagine what you see in Tiger that you cannot see in me," Jean said deflatedly.

"There is much about him to like and I have known him longer," she replied with her customary candor. "But what puzzles me is what *you* could possibly see in *me*. You have been blessed with an excessive amount of charm. I should think you could have any woman you so desire." She scrutinized Jean with appraising eyes that hinted at a flareup of mischief. "Or is it that you want *many* women for your desires?"

Jean chuckled at her keen perception and her impish smile. "Ah, Candel, I can see why you caught Tiger's eye. You have such a unique approach to life that you are positively beguiling. You don't know how to play these coquettish games yet. 'Tis your honesty that is so fascinating. You are unpretentious and direct in your dealings with men. The aristocrats won't know how to handle you. These affairs between men and women in civilization are like the fencing of swords—a parry here and there, an advance, a retreat. For certain, you're going to throw the proper dandies in New Orleans off track when you refuse to respond to their well-rehearsed lines in the customary feminine manner."

He brought her hand to his lips to brush a kiss over her fingertips. "But nonetheless, *chérie*, I am taken with you. And if ever you should require my assistance or my companionship, do not hesitate to send for me. With Tiger at sea so much of the time, you might be in need of a friend, even if that is all you will ever allow me to be."

"And with so many women enthralled by the suave and debonair Jean Lafitte, I doubt you could find the time for me," she teased.

"I'm quite serious," Jean assured her. "I consider myself fiercely loyal to my friends. I count you among them."

"Jean! *Allez-vous tout de suite!*" one of the privateers called from the darkness.

The urgent summons caused Jean to stare toward the silhouettes of the men who stood beside the swamps.

Wavering in indecision, Jean's gaze bounced back and forth between the stunning blonde and his men.

"I can find my way back to the cottage without difficulty," Candel assured him when he hesitated.

"If you're certain, *amie*," Jean murmured.

"I am quite capable of taking care of myself," Candel said with absolute certainty.

With a courtly bow, Jean excused himself before striding toward the grove of trees that appeared like gnarled hands stretching up toward the full moon. When he ducked beneath the low-hanging branches, he spied the skiff that glided through the bayou, sending silver ripples fanning out in all directions. A curious frown knitted Jean's brow as he studied the four occupants of the approaching dinghy. A shocked gasp bubbled in his throat when he recognized his brother, who had been locked in chains for the past few months. With his sword flapping beside his leg, Jean dashed toward the planked dock. And sure enough, Pierre and three black slaves who had been imprisoned in the same cell clambered from the boat.

A shout of delight wafted through the trees, sending the birds from their perches. While the privateers dashed off to spread the good news, Jean gave his brother an affectionate hug. For months Jean's lawyers had been trying to effect Pierre's release, but to no avail. Claiborne had stood firm. Yet miraculously, Pierre had escaped confinement.

"How . . . ?" Was all Jean could manage.

Pierre grinned broadly. "With the right tools, a man can wrest free of his chains and find a skiff awaiting him."

"But who . . . ?"

Another sly smile pursed Pierre's lips as he ambled through the brush toward the cabin. "An old friend arrived at the Cabildo this evening. He was allowed to pay me a call before he visited with our dear friend Claiborne.''

"Tiger?'' Jean chirped.

Pierre nodded affirmatively. ''Tiger sent a message back with me, though I don't quite understand its meaning. He said in return for the favor, he would greatly appreciate it if you would turn your legendary charm elsewhere.''

Jean burst out laughing at the subtle request to keep his distance from the ravishing blonde who had piqued his interest. Releasing Pierre was a favor Jean would not soon forget. He would see to it that Candel lacked for nothing during Tiger's absence and he would generously repay Tiger the first chance he got.

"Come along, Pierre,'' Jean insisted as he offered his ailing brother a supportive arm. "You can meet the beguiling temptation Tiger was warning me away from. I only hope you are up to it. I promise you this is one woman whose blinding beauty will knock you off your feet.''

While the servants bustled about to welcome Pierre back to Barataria in style, Jean ambled over to knock on Candel's bedroom door.

"*Chérie*, I have someone I want you to meet. Thanks to Tiger, my brother has returned.''

He waited for her response. Receiving none, he opened the door. "Candel?'' He was met with silence.

Reversing direction, Jean strode back outside to glance in every direction. Men and women were milling about while the sound of harmonicas and banjos filled the muggy night air, but the silver-blond beauty was nowhere to be seen. Concern etched Jean's brow as he shouldered his way through the crowd, posing questions as he went.

Jean had left Candel alone only for a half-hour and poof! She had disappeared into a puff of smoke. None of his men would dare to molest the marchioness, he reassured himself. Although Jean had always tried to be fair-minded in judging the disputes that arose in his domain, every inhabitant of Barataria knew he would be dealt with severely if he broke the code of the privateers. True, there were those among the privateers who preferred to think of themselves as pirates. But if any of those ruffians had dared to harm one hair on Candeliera Caron's head, the man would be signing his own death warrant. And if he didn't locate Candel before Tiger returned from his jaunt to New Orleans, *Jean* would be inviting the Tiger's wrath. Curse it all, where could that woman have wandered off to at this time of night?

Candel had been on her way to Jean's cottage when calamity struck. She had veered around the corner of one of the cottages when a grimy hand clamped over her mouth, giving her no time to react. The sharp point of a dagger had been thrust at her throat, daring her to resist. She didn't have the faintest idea who had abducted her and she wasn't sure she would live to see another sunrise.

A pained grimace claimed Candel's features as she strained against the rough-hewn rope that bound her ankles and wrists. A foul-tasting gag prevented her from screeching in protest. And what was infinitely worse was the blindfold, making it impossible for her to determine which direction she was being carried.

Panic spurted through her veins when she felt the man who carried her jackknifed over his shoulder dump her none too gently into a skiff. The sound of oars cutting through the water mingled with the croak of bullfrogs and the warble of birds in the labyrinth of swamps. Candel squirmed uneasily on the seat, only to be jabbed by a wet oar.

"Sit still, bitch. You'll be where you're goin' soon enough."

A muddled frown knitted her brow as she tried to remember where she'd heard that voice before, but she was too rattled to attach a face to it. Having met so many people during the course of the day, it was impossible to determine who had whisked her off—or why.

Candel didn't have long to wait to discover who had abducted her. When the blindfold was jerked from her eyes, she gasped in terror. There sat Evan Rollings, grinning in sinister amusement.

"I'm sure you thought you'd seen the last of me, didn't you? Just as I thought I'd seen the last of you when I—" Evan caught himself before he conveyed more information than Candel needed to hear. "I stowed away on a ship bound for New Orleans after Tiger threw me off his schooner without my pay. Now both of you are goin' to pay the price for my inconvenience."

Candel gulped apprehensively when Evan paused from his rowing to grab her bodice and jerk her upright so he could jeer into her face.

"We didn't get to finish what we started that night in Martinique. But this time Tiger won't be around to interrupt us," he said with a sneer of fiendish triumph. "And when I'm through pleasin' myself with Her Royal Highness, I'll collect the reward for your return to New Orleans and send you back where you belong."

Candel didn't have time to fully digest what Evan meant because he rushed on, cackling sardonically all the while. "You'll be sorry you rejected me, bitch. I'm goin' to enjoy seein' you beg for mercy . . . argh!"

Candel struck with the quickness of a coiled cobra. Her bound fists connected with Evan's jaw, knocking him sideways. Frantically, she clutched at the oar, hoping to hammer him over the head a couple of dozen times and put him out of her misery long enough to cut herself loose. The plan was a good one, to be sure. But Evan's skull was like a chunk of rock and it took too many blows to crack it.

With a vicious snarl Evan blocked the oncoming attack and backhanded Candel across the cheek. Stunned though she was, she fought back with every ounce of strength she could muster. Her assault had only infuriated Evan who had waited over a week to satisfy his revenge for the beating he'd taken in Martinique.

When his fingers curled and he lunged forward to clutch her throat, Candel lifted her legs. Her knees connected with painful accuracy in the most sensitive part of his anatomy. Another howl of pain wafted across the swamp, followed by an enraged growl that could have sent the alligators into hiding.

The boat tipped and rocked as Evan half-collapsed, gasping for breath. Taking advantage of his momentary retreat, Candel clutched the oar and swung wildly, catching him on the side of his head. The blow dazed him long enough for her to pounce on the dagger on his belt. Although Candel was sorely tempted to stab him, she jerked up the knife to cut herself free. She only had time to cut her ankles loose before Evan shook his head to clear his senses.

When he leaped at her again, Candel lunged with the knife, only to have it knocked away. The moonlight glistened in his eyes as he cursed her fiery resistance. Candel had the sinking feeling she had only succeeded in pushing this maniac into a murdering fury. Evan no longer cared about the reward for her return or about molesting her for his own demented pleasure. He was out for blood—hers!

A muffled shriek loosened Candel's gag as she bolted to her feet the instant before Evan grabbed her by the neck. The skiff wobbled precariously when its occupants shifted position. Candel was flung off balance and landed with a splash. Diving beneath the surface, she took off, swimming for all she was worth without daring to look back.

Twisted reeds and tree roots hampered her progress, and the heavy gown kept snagging on unidentified objects that lay in the marsh. Candel swore she felt slimy creatures slithering over her arms and legs as she struggled to put a safe distance between herself and the man who had decided he liked her much better dead than alive.

Her lungs burned as she fought her way through the tangle before daring to rise to the surface to yank off the gag and inhale much-needed air. Her eyes widened in alarm when she twisted around to seek Evan. As bad luck would have it, he had spotted her the same instant. Cursing in fluent profanity, Evan jerked up an oar and pounced with his makeshift weapon.

Inhaling deeply, Candel submerged to grope through the weeds in hopes of finding footing on solid ground. Again her lungs threatened to burst and again she waited until the last possible second to grab a breath. The instant her hands struck rock and mud, Candel burst forward and scrambled up the jutting roots of the tree that stood half-in and half-out of the swamp.

Behind her, she could hear Evan swearing foul oaths as he fought his way through the stagnant bayou. Candel clawed the moss from her face as she blindly stumbled over the crab-like roots that hampered her flight.

Her heart was pounding so frantically against her chest that she was sure her ribs would crack under the pressure, but she refused to slow her pace or look back. One careless step and she would be flat on her face, awaiting the unspeakable horrors Evan had planned for her. She could hear him thrashing through the underbrush, closing the distance between them. Candel would have given most anything if she had still been dressed in men's clothes. These full skirts were caked with mud and they weighed her down and tripped her up. Each time she stumbled she managed to right herself before she skidded in the mud, but all her floundering was granting Evan time to gobble up the space between them.

A pained yelp erupted from Candel's lips when Evan cocked the oar he carried with him and hurled it like a boomerang. The paddle slammed into her shoulder but she gritted her teeth, hiked up her soggy skirts, and ran for her life. Although she knew it would do no good whatsoever, Candel opened her mouth and screamed bloody murder. She doubted there was anyone in this section of the swamp who could answer her call. More than likely the slimy creatures of the bayou would be eager to make a meal of her, and the man behind her was furious enough to battle any beast to get his hands on her first!

Chapter 16

Nicolas tied up his skiff and stepped ashore, feeling quite pleased with the evening's activities. Buff had even ceased his preaching after the incident at the Cabildo. Nicolas expected to hear the sounds of celebration at Jean's headquarters. That, however, wasn't the case. The village was as silent as the grave.

Sensing trouble, Nicolas made a beeline toward Jean's cabin to find Pierre sprawled in bed, recuperating from his extended term in jail, and the servants anxiously wringing their hands.

"What's going on?" Nicolas demanded to know.

"It's Miz Candel," one of the servants explained. "She's missin'. Jean questioned everybody 'til he finally found a young lad who saw somebody totin' her toward the swamps. The whole village is out searchin' for her now."

Nicolas felt that all too familiar sense of panic which gripped him when Candel was in danger. He hated this feeling of helplessness and vulnerability that overwhelmed him when her life was in jeopardy. He always found himself sweating blood until he was certain she was safe and sound. God, he had really let that rambunctious female get to him!

Nicolas plowed out the door and bounded into his skiff. Gasping for breath, Buff clambered in beside him and clutched his chest.

"Lordy, I'm getting too old for this," Buff wheezed.

Nicolas took just enough time to be sure Buff wasn't about to have a stroke before he rowed into the swamp. The older man wasn't the only one on the verge of collapse—Nicolas wasn't coping all that well himself.

Curse that woman! Knowing her independent nature, she'd probably wandered off without realizing the risks involved. There was no telling what kind of scalawags were hovering around the area—what with Claiborne's promise to jail every would-be privateer, smuggler, or pirate this side of the Appalachians. The governor had practically invited every scoundrel and thief on the Mississippi to take up hiding in the swamps to elude his "Wanted" posters. There was no telling what variety of rapscallion had latched onto Candel for his own perverted purpose.

In the distance, Nicolas caught sight of a flotilla of flaming torches that reflected off the waters of the bayou. Jean's rescue brigade was out in full force. Nicolas could hear the occupants of the skiffs calling back and forth to each other as they searched the area. From the look and sound of things no one had sighted Candel . . .

A terrified shriek caught Nicolas's attention. He swiveled on his seat to stare to the east. Plunging the oars into the swamp, he veered his skiff around to paddle toward the unnerving sound that went right through him, leaving an empty ache in the pit of his belly.

"That's her," Buff insisted as he strained against his oars. "I know it's her. I've heard that eerie sound before. It gave me the willies then and it still does now—"

"Shh . . ." Nicolas flashed Buff a silencing gesture. It was difficult to determine which direction the sound was coming from while Buff was babbling like Jolly Roger.

Another bloodcurdling scream echoed in the darkness. Nicolas was so frantic to reach Candel that he ran the skiff aground before he realized he was there. The skiff made a grinding "thunk" against the rocks and tree roots, flinging him and Buff forward. Nicolas recovered in a half-second and leaped up as if propelled by a spring, leaving Buff to inform the rest of the rescue brigade.

His jaw set in a grim line, Nicolas forged his way through the brush, tripping over limbs and roots that blocked his path. He felt like a mud-bound wagon spinning its wheels. In the scant moonlight that filtered through the canopy of trees, he could barely make out two shapes thrashing about in the weeds. Fury exploded inside him with killing force as he charged forward like a warrior plunging into battle. A mutinous roar burst from his curled lips when he spied the gleaming barrel of a pistol reflecting the moonlight. Without breaking stride, Nicolas swooped down to retrieve a fallen branch that lay in his path. Hurriedly, he sent the makeshift missile soaring through the air. It slammed into the side of Evan's head, causing him to turn his full attention to the towering giant who sped toward him like an avenging monster from the swamp.

Evan bolted to his feet to turn the flintlock he'd intended to use on Candel toward the dark silhouette that raced toward him. The instant Candel heard the click of the trigger she rolled to her knees to take a swing at Evan.

The blow served to jar his arm and misdirected the bullet which embedded itself in the tree.

A horrified howl escaped Evan's lips when Nicolas made a spectacular leap through the air, knocking both of them to the ground. Nicolas came up fighting. One beefy fist made mincemeat of Evan before the other fist pounded him into putty. Evan knew he was staring death in the face and he swung wildly in answer to the punishing blows. His hands clawed at the pistol on Nicolas's belt, attempting to fire it into his competitor without taking time to extract it from its resting place.

Nicolas clamped his left hand over his weapon just as Evan clawed at the trigger. In the nick of time, Nicolas tilted the barrel of the pistol. Although powder burns stung Nicolas's thigh when the weapon discharged, the bullet missed him by scant inches.

Gasping for breath, Candel grabbed her muddy skirt and floundered to her feet. When she heard the stampede and saw the torches blaze their way through the darkness, she sagged in relief.

"Tiger?" Jean roared as he zigzagged between the torches to reach his friend.

Nicolas delivered one last punch to Evan's puffy face before he pushed himself off the ground. Half-turning, he met the grim expression on Jean's face. In one fluid motion, Jean glided his flintlock from his belt, flipped it over in his hand and tossed it to Nicolas.

Glowing silver-blue eyes fastened on Evan's horrified face. "I warned you that I'd kill you if you ever laid a hand on Candel again," Nicolas growled through clenched teeth. "You know the code in Barataria. The wicked aren't allowed a second chance . . ."

"You bloody bastard," Evan sneered as he rolled to his knees like a wild creature preparing to pounce.

But Evan Rollings never gained his feet. The well-aimed shot took him back to the ground. "Bastard . . ." Evan breathed with his dying breath.

Candel swallowed back a wave of nausea and wheeled away from the gruesome sight. The terrifying ordeal had taken her to the point of collapse. Despite the untold horrors Evan had intended for her, she had the sickening feeling that she was responsible. She hadn't discouraged the lusty sailor while they were sailing on board the *Sea Devil*. She had accepted his attention in an effort to make Nicolas jealous. What foolish ignorance, Candel mused sadly as she slumped against a nearby tree. It was she who had brought Evan to this horrible end. She had invited this mauling and ignited his fiery need for revenge . . .

When Nicolas's fingers curled beneath her chin to lift her face, a mist of tears clouded her eyes. "I'm sorry . . ." she murmured brokenly. "I asked for this, didn't I?"

"Nay," Nicolas assured her tenderly. "Evan Rollings has tested my patience time and again. He disobeyed my orders and he paid for it. The fault lies with him."

When Nicolas wrapped a comforting arm around Candel to lead her to his skiff, the crowd dispersed. Jean Lafitte waited until Nicolas returned his pistol and then stared thoughtfully at him.

"If you deal with all this lovely lass's overzealous suitors in such a drastic fashion, I doubt you will have to fret about other men stealing her away from you again, Tiger," Jean declared with the faintest hint of a grin.

"You included, *mon ami*?" Nicolas inquired after he assisted Candel into the boat.

Jean surveyed the beguiling beauty whose damp clothes clung to her like a second skin. A smile twitched his lips. "*Oui*, but I back away most reluctantly, Tiger. Candel burns with a most hypnotic flame . . ."

When Jean ambled off to his own skiff, Nicolas stared pensively after him. It was going to be hard to let go of Candel, that was certain. But now, more than ever, the obstacles between them seemed insurmountable. War was imminent and preparations had to be made. Candel would be much safer at her family plantation north of New Orleans. After this unsettling encounter with Evan in Barataria, Nicolas didn't dare leave her here. Come dawn, he had to get Candel out of Barataria and send her home where she belonged.

By the time the fleet had returned to Chênière Caminada, Candel had regained control of her emotions. She knew this would be the last night she spent with Nicolas. With the threat of war hanging over them so heavily, Nicolas would have many tasks, none of which included her. She was about to enter yet another phase of her life—one that didn't include this man whom she'd come to love with all her heart. But Candel promised herself one thing: this night, despite her near brush with death, was going to be a night she could cherish in her dreams. Nicolas Tiger was going to remember her, just as she would remember him in the years to come.

Candel was startled when she reached Jean's head-quarters to find Pierre Lafitte looming over her. She had been told that the fair-haired Frenchman's looks had changed drastically after his stroke four years earlier. But the sight of this stout, five-foot-ten-inch privateer who blocked the doorway still knocked her sideways. Although Pierre was reported to be a jolly, affable man, his appearance contradicted what Candel had heard. Pierre looked haggard after his long stint in jail. Besides his tattered clothes, the expression on his bristled face would be frightening to anyone. The stroke had left his eyes crossed and put a strange, fierce twist on his lips.

"So this is the young lass who caused so much commotion," Pierre said, with a chuckle as he stepped aside to allow Candel to enter the cabin.

"My older brother, Pierre," Jean announced as he swaggered into the foyer. "It seems Pierre has had time to rest after his extended stay at the Cabildo." His dark eyes twinkled at his brother. "Pierre, this is Candeliera Junfroi Caron—the Marchioness de Caron, to be specific."

When Pierre's brow shot up, Jean grinned. "Not to worry, *mon frère*. She is nothing like her cousin, thank God. I think we will have one loyal supporter in the Caron household."

Despite his fierce look, Pierre graced Candel with a smile and doubled over at the waist to press a kiss to her muddy wrist. " 'Tis a pleasure, mademoiselle. I am relieved to see that you have been returned unharmed." His gaze darted to Nicolas, who towered over the bedraggled beauty like a guard dragon. "And my thanks to you, Tiger. I had enjoyed the dungeon of Cabildo about as long as I could."

"My pleasure, Pierre," Nicolas replied before he steered Candel toward the bedroom. "Now if you will excuse us, I think the lady would like to bathe and change after her midnight swim."

When the servants had been sent to fetch the tub and clothing for Candel, Nicolas joined Buff, Jean, and Pierre in the parlor to share a bottle of Madeira wine.

"I haven't had the opportunity to thank you properly, Tiger," Jean said between sips. "Our lawyers, Grymes

250

and Livingston, have been trying to effect Pierre's release for months. You found a solution in one night. How the devil did you manage it?''

Nicolas grinned wryly at Buff and Pierre, who smiled back at him. ''Buff and I just happened to be in the right place at the right time, 'tis all. Our document provided plenty of distraction. I only wish we could have freed the other privateers who had been marched off to jail after the American invasion of Barataria.''

Before Jean could press him for details, Nicolas cut to the heart of the matter that concerned him. ''Claiborne was visibly distressed when he read the document. Although he gave me no specific answer, he assured me that he would confer with General Jackson at his earliest convenience. Jackson is recuperating after his grueling battles near Mobile and the long overland journey.''

Jean slumped in his chair and muttered under his breath. ''I have no intention of waiting much longer. If we are to assist the Americans we have arrangements to make for supplies and weapons.'' His ebony eyes focused on Nicolas. ''I have another favor to ask, Tiger. I would like you to deliver a letter to Jackson himself. Take the document along with you. The general may decide that the aid of the Baratarians would not be so distasteful when he is informed of the number of British soldiers who will be crowding the harbor.''

He studied Tiger's handsome face and impressive physique. ''*Oui*, I think your very appearance will change Jackson's opinion of us *pirates*, as he chooses to call us. Claiborne has undoubtedly influenced Jackson and he has the wrong impression, sight unseen. He probably envisions us as a mob of scraggly heathens with eye patches, hooks for hands, spikes for teeth, and blood-stained swords dangling on our hips. You will be good

251

for our image and I will see to it that you are dressed in all the fancy trappings of a proper gentleman when you meet him. Let Jackson turn down such a fine figure of a man!''

"And, of course, you will flaunt all the elegant manners Jean has taught you," Pierre snickered. "Make certain you put on enough aristocratic airs to leave Old Hickory thinking *he* is fortunate to be in *your* company."

"Nicolas ought to take Candel with him," Buff suggested. "One look at her should soften Jackson up."

"A splendid idea," Jean confirmed, smiling.

"An even better idea if she were Tiger's wife," Buff added with a pointed glance at Nicolas.

Jean and Pierre riveted their gazes on Nicolas, who squirmed uncomfortably in his chair. "Marriage, Tiger?" they questioned in unison.

"Curse it, Buff," Nicolas muttered sourly. " 'Tis not the time for another of your lectures . . .''

His voice trailed off when the bedroom door creaked open and Candel emerged in the stunning royal blue gown Jean had generously provided, along with a necklace of priceless emeralds fit for a queen.

"Did I not tell you, *mon frère*, that you had only seen a hint of her extraordinary beauty?" Jean murmured as he rose to his feet to escort Candel to the table.

"I am bewitched," Pierre declared with a dreamy smile. "Truly, mademoiselle, Barataria has never been blessed with such a vision."

Candel wasn't accustomed to such profuse flattery. It made her self-conscious. Unlike most female aristocrats, who soaked up compliments like sponges, Candel merely accepted her looks as nature's gift and went about her business. Nicolas had warned her that life in the states would be different from the island. She had never expected to have men put so much stock in her appearance, wondering if civilized men had so little regard for the intelligence of females that they used compliments for lack of anything else to say. After all, a woman's body and the pleasures she could offer seemed to be all that concerned men.

"Come sit with us, *ma chérie*," Jean urged. "I have a favor to ask of you."

Candel eyed him warily as she sank into the chair across from Nicolas. "I'm afraid to ask what is expected in exchange for all this glowing praise and these generous gifts."

"*Non, chérie*, you misunderstand," Pierre chuckled lightheartedly. "You deserve the praise without payment of any kind. We ask a favor to aid our cause. Nicolas has agreed to take our letter and the document to General Jackson in hopes of granting us the privilege of defending New Orleans. We only request that you accompany him. For Tiger to be seen in such fine company—a bona fide marchioness, no less—will assure Jackson that we are not the wicked, heartless rapscallions Claiborne has made us out to be."

It was such a simple request that Candel nodded without hesitation.

"Nay," Nicolas grumbled. "If the story reaches her cousin's ears, it might not bode well for her. I'd prefer that André never know Candel and I are acquainted."

"And what do I care about my cousin's opinion?" Candel sniffed.

She was annoyed that Nicolas was trying to make her decisions for her when she was perfectly willing and capable of making up her own mind. She loved him, but that didn't give him the right to speak in her behalf without consulting her first.

253

"I had no use for André when I was nine years old. Even as a child I knew he was offensive."

"I say nay!" Nicolas declared in a tone that brooked no further argument.

"Fine, Tiger," Candel replied. "If you don't wish to accompany me then I will take the letter to this Andrew Jackson fellow myself."

"Now there's an even better idea," Jean exclaimed. " 'Tis perfect, in fact. No one will suspect this lovely maid and Tiger won't have to worry about Claiborne's patrols."

"Then it's settled," Candel said with a nod. "I'll see to the errand tomorrow morning." Rising gracefully from her chair, she pivoted toward her room.

"I said . . . you aren't getting involved," Nicolas countered as he bolted to his feet.

Candel half-turned to meet his obstinate glare. "I've made my decision, Tiger."

"We'll discuss the matter in private," he muttered as he latched onto her arm and whisked her away.

When the door slammed shut behind them, Buff chortled in amusement. "Care to place bets on whether the lady goes or not?"

Jean and Pierre stared pensively at the closed door, contemplating the determined expression they had seen on Candel's face.

"My money's on the lady," Jean announced with firm conviction.

"*Oui*. Mine, too," Pierre chimed in.

Buff tucked the coins back in his pocket and sighed. "Aye, so is mine. You're no fun at all. And fool that Tiger is, he still hasn't figured out that she's got him wrapped around her dainty little finger. He's fighting it, but he won't win this power struggle. When it comes to

Candel Caron he can't say nay, not even when it comes to—"

Buff slammed his mouth shut before he blurted out confidential information that the Lafittes didn't need to hear. As far as Buff was concerned, Tiger was an even bigger fool if he didn't marry Candel before some stuffy aristocrat snatched her up.

"You might as well go ahead and write your letter. I'll make the arrangements to take Candel to New Orleans," Buff offered. "If I know that little lady as well as I think I do, she'll be going, even against Tiger's wishes."

Chapter 17

The instant Nicolas kicked the door shut with his boot heel, Candel wheeled to face him. Instead of launching into a fiery argument, as Nicolas anticipated, she pulled the pins from her hair, letting the silky cloud tumble around her. Without bothering with the stays she had fastened herself into, she tugged the off-the-shoulder gown to her waist, revealing the sheer chemise that did more to emphasize than conceal the fullness of her breasts.

Nicolas stood there, caught completely off guard. Rather than argue with her, he simply gaped while she peeled off her clothes. He couldn't even remember what he had intended to say!

"We have only one night left to enjoy each other," Candel reminded him as she tossed the elegant gown over the trunk at the foot of the bed. "We have made no commitments, no promises to each other, but I'm asking for a promise now, Tiger. Make this a night I'll remember always and forever . . ."

She stood before him wearing nothing but the tantalizing chemise that extended just past her hips, looking like every man's erotic fantasy. A fan of thick curly lashes surrounded her glittering amethyst eyes. Nicolas was all too aware of the fact that this was the last night they had. He knew he might never see her again. Although he propelled her into the room to tell her how things were going to *be*, he was struck by the realization of how things really *were*. He had to let Candel go because it was the right thing to do. But it didn't stop him from wishing he were more than just a bastard son who had taken privileges with this titled lady . . .

"Well?" One delicately carved brow arched to regard him curiously. "Shall I summon Jean to take your place? He has generously offered to attend me in any capacity I should choose."

Nicolas tugged off his shirt and tossed it toward a chair, not caring that he missed his target by a mile. "Nay, Jean isn't going to appease your appetite, little witch," he assured her huskily. "He thinks I'll shoot him if he comes near you."

The rakish smile on his lips told Candel that Nicolas wasn't going to be stubborn about accepting her affection, only about accepting her decision to take the letter to Jackson. Perhaps the civilized gentry would gasp if they knew her liberal views about bedding a man with Tiger's reputation, especially without demanding a proposal of marriage. But where Candel had come from, wedlock wasn't an issue or custom. Besides, she loved this blue eyed rogue—heart, body, and soul. That was all that mattered. A legal document wouldn't make her love him more. In times of war, one never knew if there would even be a tomorrow. There was only tonight and Candel wasn't ashamed to admit she wanted to love Tiger just one more time.

When Nicolas scooped her up in his arms to carry her to bed, his gaze fastened on her face, "Candel, I—"

She pressed her index finger to his lips. "Speak to me without words . . ."

His knees very nearly buckled when her eyes focused on him. They were brimming with sweet, erotic promises. He knew he'd never forget the way she looked at him. Nicolas had never known a woman like this. Although she had once teased him about being a pirate and a renegade, she made no judgments about him. And she made no demands he couldn't meet, the way other women tended to do.

Candel didn't give herself to a man, expecting favors or compromises. She was generous and pure of heart, utterly unpretentious and demonstrative of her emotions and affections. Ah, if only they had met at another time and place, if only she wasn't who she was and he wasn't what he was . . .

His rambling thoughts trailed off when Candel stretched out beside him to tantalize him with feather-like kisses. It still amazed him that she could arouse him so easily, making him forget everything that had any semblance to reality. When this sweet nymph was with him it was as if they were marooned on an island in the middle of oblivion. The world shrank, leaving them alone in a universe that fairly crackled with sensual anticipation.

Candel was determined to leave a lasting impression on this renegade who had stolen her heart. Tiger had taught her things she hadn't known about, the most wondrous secrets of life. Now she longed to teach him things he didn't know—things that were the very essence of existence.

Her lips whispered over his cheeks and eyelids while

her practiced hands glided once again over his lips and throat, sensitizing each place she touched, committing every inch of him to memory. Her fingertips speared through the thick hair covering his chest, as she wished she could touch the carefully-guarded heart beneath it.

As courageous and strong as this dark-haired rogue had proved to be, he was a coward when it came to admitting his feelings. His mother's selfish betrayal had hurt him more than he would admit, and Nicolas refused to let anyone close enough to hurt him again. He was afraid of commitment because he believed it wouldn't last. He had constantly insisted that Candel had a lot to learn about the world, but there was much Tiger needed to learn, too. Candel promised herself that she would be the one to teach him.

Nicolas couldn't remember another time when he'd allowed a woman to have her way with him, when he'd permitted a female to take full initiative in lovemaking. But Candel proved to be a most imaginative lover and he let her break every rule he'd established with the fairer sex. He supposed that most men were too conventional to cope with a woman like Candel, who had always played by her own rules. Yet, Nicolas delighted in her role as seductress. He could hardly begrudge the fact that the first intimate moves were hers, not when her tender touch ignited those familiar fires deep inside him.

Candel had never been one to merely accept his passion; she returned it. He liked knowing that he aroused her and she didn't mind showing it with steamy kisses and adventurous caresses. When she loved him, she wasn't afraid to let him know. And Nicolas was certain enough of his masculinity to allow Candel's uninhibited nature to thrive, even in lovemaking . . .

A tormented groan escaped his lips when her roaming

hands swirled around his nipples and then skimmed over the muscles of his belly, headed for more intimate places. His brain ceased to function when her fingertips trailed over his thighs and his body tingled as her warm, moist kisses investigated and aroused him in the most delicious ways.

His heart slammed against his ribs when her petal-soft lips followed the path of her seeking hands, sending flames spiralling through his bloodstream. He would have promised her anything if she would only end this wild, aching torture that instilled such throbbing cravings inside him.

When her hands and lips devoured his body again and again, Nicolas resigned himself to death by exquisite torment. Her hands teased and excited him until he bit his lip to prevent groaning out loud. And when she straddled his hips and leaned down to offer him a kiss that stole what little breath he had left, Nicolas was sure he'd die before she got around to appeasing the monstrous ache that pulsated through the core of his being. He could feel the rosy tips of her breasts caressing his chest, feel her hips moving provocatively above his. The sheer impact of her satiny body upon his drove him wild with wanting. She was so close and yet so intolerably far away that he had to battle the impulsive urge to clutch her to him and devour her.

Candel gave her love so freely, so generously that it devastated Nicolas. When she loved him, she held nothing in reserve. She satisfied him so completely there were no words required. Her luscious body and her honeyed lips conveyed her feelings in a wondrous language that needed no translation.

His hands glided over her hips, moving her exactly where he wanted her. He could feel her absorbing his strength, compelling him closer and closer until his heartbeat was her own, until she comprised the other half of his very soul!

"Candel, I need you . . ." Nicolas rasped raggedly.

Ah, if only he meant he needed her forever, she mused as he became the velvet flame inside her. She longed for more than stolen moments of ecstasy. She adored being with him, observing his various moods. She loved the way he made her feel. Ah, how empty and unrewarding her life was going to become in the weeks and months ahead!

Her tormented thoughts scattered like leaves in a windstorm when Nicolas shifted to draw her beneath him. His lithe body covered hers as he drove into her with mindless urgency, setting the breathless cadence of unrestrained passion. Candel let go with her heart, body, and soul as they set sail across the star-studded universe, soaring on wings of rapture. Indescribable pleasure shook the very foundations of her soul, triggering sensations that left her gasping from sheer splendor. She could feel white hot sparks leap from her quaking body to his and back again, hear the deafening crescendo that built until it burst inside her. Frantically, Candel held on for dear life when she felt herself tumbling through a dizzying whirl of incomparable pleasure. Spasms of ecstasy seized her body as Nicolas shuddered helplessly above her.

If dreams could come true, Candel would have wished to spend the rest of her life suspended in this euphoric world of intangible sensations and hazy contentment. When she was spiralling like an eagle, gliding in motionless flight, nothing could harm her or frighten her. Even Evan Rollings and his cruel treatment seemed no more than a fleeting nightmare. Oh, how she wished these wondrous moments could be part of tomorrow!

"I love you, Tiger . . . I will always love you, no matter how far you wander, no matter how long you're gone. Know that because 'tis true. No one will ever love you the way I do . . ."

Nicolas dropped a whispering kiss to her lips before he eased down to cradle her in his arms. Her words touched him and yet tormented him. He wanted to believe her, but he couldn't see life through her trusting, innocent eyes. "Nothing is forever," he whispered as his lips brushed over her heavily-lashed eyelids. "Never offer promises you can't keep, not to anyone."

"My love is forever," she assured him with great conviction. "You'll see, Tiger. You'll see . . ."

The exhausting ordeal in the swamps, compounded by Nicolas's masterful lovemaking, worked like a sedative. Candel could feel herself drifting in a sea of slumber, bobbing with the waves that carried her far from reality's shore. She had longed to make wild, sweet love to him over and over, but darkness closed in and she found erotic dreams taking up where sweet ecstasy left off . . .

A faint smile pursed Nicolas's lips when Candel's lashes fluttered against her cheeks and she slowly leaned against him in sleep. He studied her exquisite face in the moonlight, marveling at her remarkable beauty, wondering at the lingering sensations that trickled through him. He had to restrain the desire to wake her and love her again. After the harrowing experience she had endured in the swamp, she definitely needed time to renew her strength.

It seemed odd to him that he was always more aware of this woman's needs than his own. He knew he really should have put his foot down and demanded that she refuse to take the letter to Jackson. But she would have defied him again, of course. She always defied him because she was every bit as stubborn and independent as he was. There was no talking Candel Caron out of her decisions once they were made.

Careful not to rouse her, Nicolas inched away to grab his scattered clothes. He really couldn't afford to become so sentimentally attached to this beauty. The minute she returned to her rightful place in society, she would be bombarded with attention and marriage proposals. She would forget him soon enough, he expected. Candel may have convinced herself that she loved him, or perhaps Nicolas himself had planted that seed while trying to draw her out of her shell in Martinique after her unpleasant encounters with Julian and Evan.

A grimace tightened Nicolas's lips as he tiptoed toward the door. He was uncomfortable with the thought of another man sharing the splendor he'd discovered in her arms, but he would get over these possessive feelings when he plunged into the demanding tasks that awaited him. There had been other women who fascinated him for a time. They had all come and gone, just as Candel would do. Truly, she would be better off without him. He would only cause her trouble. He was simply her first experience with passion and she had mistaken her feelings for love. In time she would see their affair for what it was and she would thank him for letting go.

Mulling over that sensible thought, Nicolas eased the door shut behind him and pivoted to see his three friends staring at him in wry amusement. He composed himself and strode at a leisurely pace across the room, only to find himself subjected to more muffled snickers.

"And what, I'd like to know, do you find so damned funny?" Nicolas asked curtly.

Jean poured Nicolas a glass of wine and grinned. "Your shirt, Tiger," he explained. "I really think you should change tailors. Your present one seems to have trouble matching buttons to the correct buttonholes. Why, from the look of things, one might wonder if you didn't hastily wriggle in and out of the garment. Of course, we realize that couldn't possibly have happened since you entered the room to debate with the lady in private.'' With a wink and a knowing smile, he turned to Tiger, who was bright red from embarrassment. ''By the way, Tiger, who won the debate?''

Nicolas snatched the drink from Jean's hand and downed it in one swallow. ''I've decided to let her take the letter to Jackson,'' he muttered to save face.

That wasn't exactly true, but Nicolas wasn't about to admit it to these three snickering clowns!

''I rather thought you would,'' Pierre commented as he sipped his wine. ''But then a man who has put no formal claim on a woman really has no right to make decisions for her, now does he?''

''Nay, he doesn't,'' Nicolas grumbled as he refilled his glass and guzzled it.

''In this particular lady's case, I doubt it would have mattered whether you gave an order or made a request. Candel Caron seems very much a free spirit. She has developed a mind of her own and she uses it,'' Jean remarked.

''Nay, it wouldn't matter,'' Buff affirmed. ''But there are still those among us who think Tiger ought to stake his claim, even if he would always have difficulty maintaining control.''

Nicolas wisely chose to glance the other way before his self-appointed conscience started needling him again. ''I think I'll go to bed and leave you masterminds to your cunning.''

When he ambled off to the room adjacent to Candel's,

Jean chuckled in amusement. "I think Tiger has been to bed already. And André Caron would be none too happy if he knew about his lovely cousin's relationship with a notorious privateer."

"I'm none too happy about it and I'm not even Candel's cousin," Buff huffed. "It isn't right. Tiger should have married her."

Jean swirled the amber liquid in his glass and stared at it thoughtfully. "Do you truly think so, Buff, considering Tiger's ongoing feud with André? No matter what Tiger feels for Candel, he could bring her trouble with her kin. André is a powerful man."

"You're no help," Buff retorted. "You think too much like Tiger does."

"Tiger knows what he is, just as I know what I am. The world is not so forgiving, *mon ami*. Look at Claiborne and Jackson. They have labeled us as criminals. They see only what they want to see and believe what they want to believe. It seems to me that Tiger is being noble to let the marchioness go back where she belongs. Sometimes it has to be enough, just knowing your woman is there, even if she is out of your reach."

"There are things Tiger doesn't even know about himself," Buff said cryptically. "Things that shouldn't even matter, at least not to my way of thinking. But it seems to matter to him. Sometimes a man needs to think with his heart instead of his head. And you mark my words, Jean. Tiger will be damned sorry if he lets Candel go. She's a prize worth keeping." With that, Buff eased up from his chair and headed toward bed.

Jean still wasn't sure he agreed with Buff, not when he knew how difficult life had become since the governor had denounced the Baratarians and refused to allow them to walk the streets of New Orleans without risking capture. Claiborne was hell-bent on making Jean's life miserable. Tiger would face the same difficulties if he were recognized on the streets, especially after he'd plotted Pierre's escape right out from under the governor's nose.

At the moment, the privateers needed loyal friends in the right places. Candel's return to the Caron plantation could prove beneficial if it wasn't known that she had consorted with the Baratarians. Buff was wrong. Tiger had made the correct decision for all concerned. But Buff was a tender-hearted softy who had obviously become so fond of Candel that emotions were clouding his logic. Buff was the one thinking with his heart, and this definitely wasn't the time for that.

Trouble was brewing in New Orleans—the kind that could change history and the lives of Americans forever. Claiborne and Jackson could stand on their stubborn pride if they wished, but they would come to regret it. One day they could very well be begging the Baratarians to defend them. This was no time for arrogant pride, snobbish airs, and personal feuds. This was the eve of a crucial war!

Chapter 18

Candel fastened herself into the exquisite gold gown Jean had provided, along with a gold necklace studded with chips of diamonds. Since the previous night when she had awakened to find Nicolas gone, Candel had resigned herself to the fact that she was about to enter another phase of her life. Although she was reluctant to return to the Caron plantation, she was anxious to lend her assistance to the American cause of freedom. If Nicolas was no longer part of her life, she needed a purpose to ward off depression and provide distraction. In the past weeks Nicolas had come to mean everything to her. Now she had to find something else to fill the void.

The creak of the door brought Candel's head around. An instant smile curved the corners of her mouth when she saw Nicolas's muscular frame filling the doorway. He looked completely different from the image she would forever carry in her heart, but to Candel he was still the handsomest man she had ever seen.

Nicolas felt a jolt all the way to his toes when his gaze roamed over Candel's curvaceous figure and stunning attire. Because of Jean's generosity, she was dressed as elegantly as a queen attending court. All she lacked was a bejeweled crown to complete the picture.

Nicolas knew he was going to miss having this gorgeous woman in his life. But he had to let her go, he had to break all ties. If he didn't, it would only cause both of them trouble. How many more times, he wondered, was he going to have to tell himself that before he convinced his foolish heart?

"I missed you last night," Candel murmured as she moved gracefully toward him. Reaching up on tiptoe, she pressed a kiss to his lips. "I'll miss you forever, Tiger."

Damn it, he thought, why does she have to say things like that at a time like this? It brought out the sentimental tenderness he'd been battling half the night and most of the morning!

"I'll miss you too, imp," Nicolas admitted. Curse it, he'd said so many good-byes in his life. Why was this one so hard? "I sent Otis to fetch your belongings from the *Sea Devil*." Nicolas lifted the two satchels he held by his sides. "Jean gave you another gown . . . or three . . . to tide you over until you get . . . home."

"Jean has been too generous already," Candel insisted.

" 'Tis the way he is, even if Claiborne and Jackson have him pegged as a wicked cutthroat," Nicolas assured her. "In fact, last year Jean rescued an American by the name of Martin when his small sloop was caught in a storm in the Gulf. Some of his men were swept overboard and the boat was already half sunk when Jean reached it. Martin was brought to Jean's home to be fed and clothed. Jean even placed one of his own schooners at Martin's disposal for his trip upriver and stocked it with provisions, including a keg of wine and pineapple cheese as a gift for Martin's wife. 'Tis Jean's kindness and generosity which have won him friends all over New Orleans. He is greatly admired.''

Candel felt the same way about the supposedly notorious Lafitte brothers. And in return for their friendship she intended to convince General Andrew Jackson that they were patriots, not pirates.

"I'm taking you to Jackson's hotel," Nicolas said.

"I suspected as much." Candel smiled impishly as she tugged at the stage mustache and beard disguising Nicolas's dashing features. In place of the tight-fitting linen shirt and snug black breeches that accentuated the muscles of his thighs, Nicolas had donned a homespun vest, blousy shirt, baggy trousers, and a brown cap. Although he was pretending to be a servant, Candel knew perfectly well what kind of man was hidden under his modest attire—more man than she'd ever meet again.

"Candel, I want you to know that—"

Her forefinger grazed his lips as she shook her head, battling a mist of tears. "I love you, Tiger. No more need be said. I only hope you'll remember me now and again in the years to come because I'll go on loving you forever."

Before Nicolas could open his mouth, Candel breezed out the door. Confound that woman! She hadn't given him the chance to say anything. Curse it, did she always have to have the last word?

"Candel!" Nicolas called after her, having not the slightest idea why he felt so frustrated.

She pivoted and her thick-lashed eyes rose to assess his scowl that was partially concealed by his beard and mustache. "Aye, Captain Tiger?"

There was a saucy smile on her lips, despite the mist in her eyes. The sight of Candel standing there like a golden flame, surrounded by dancing sunbeams, hit Nicolas like a physical blow that nearly knocked him to his knees. Before he could formulate a single thought, Jean and Pierre ambled into the room.

"Ah, *ma petite*," Jean said with an appreciative sigh. "As always, you are breathtaking. Jackson himself will have a difficult time denying you anything."

"Let's hope so," Candel replied as she demonstrated her seductive stroll to amuse the Lafittes. "All for the cause, of course."

Jean shook his head in disbelief. Never had he met such a delightfully entertaining woman. She never took him or his flattery seriously, unlike most females who practically begged for compliments. Candel Caron was very sure of herself and in no need of constant praise.

"Mon Dieu!" Jean croaked when he spied Nicolas looming in the bedroom doorway. "What is this? Beauty's beast?"

Pierre burst into laughter when Nicolas strode across the parlor, laden with luggage, looking like a peasant. "You won't have to fret about being recognized in that outfit," he said with another chuckle.

"It appears you've decided to take Buff's place and navigate through the swamps to escort Candel to Jackson's headquarters," Jean remarked.

"I only intend to see that she arrives safely," Nicolas insisted. "I left her in your care last night and we know what happened." He cast Jean the evil eye. "I don't trust Buff, either."

"I was completely distracted by Pierre's unexpected return," Jean said in defense of himself. "You should have told me of your scheme, Tiger."

"I didn't want to disappoint you in case the plan went awry," Nicolas explained as he shifted the luggage to one arm and wrapped Candel protectively in the other.

"I won't forget the favor," Jean assured him. He

270

reached into his vest to extract the letter to be delivered to Jackson. "Nor will I forget that I owe this lovely angel many favors for her assistance *and* for my lack of attention last night."

"You've been more than generous," Candel declared before she tucked the letter into her purse. "And if you require my assistance again, you know where you can find me."

Jean's dark eyes twinkled as he dropped into a courtly bow. "Mademoiselle, 'tis I who anxiously await to assist *you* in any way."

Nicolas rolled his eyes at Jean's gallantry. "Can we get on with this, Casanova?"

"A mite testy this morning, aren't we, Tiger?" Pierre teased.

"You perhaps," Nicolas replied tartly. "I'm in my usual good humor."

On the wings of that exchange he whisked Candel out the door and down the steps. She wasn't allowed to say a word while Nicolas deposited her in the skiff and navigated through the sun-dappled swamps. He was spouting instructions nonstop. Even after he rented a carriage at the docks of New Orleans to drive her to Jackson's head-quarters at the hotel on Rue Royale, Nicolas was still issuing warnings about the dangers of mentioning her relationship with him to Jackson or to her cousin.

"Oh, Nicolas," Candel said impatiently when he finally paused for breath. "I'm a grown woman—"

"Who has a habit of speaking her mind without considering the consequences," Nicolas replied as they passed the Cabildo and veered toward the hotel. "In these times, one must guard one's tongue. I won't be around to rescue you so don't fall into harm's way. And for God's sake, watch your step with the stampede of men

271

who will swarm around you, eager to lay claim to your family's wealth. There are silver-tongued fortune hunters galore in New Orleans who have experience aplenty in wooing women into bed and—''

''You speak from experience, I suppose,'' she taunted.

Nicolas reined the steeds to a halt and twisted on the driver's seat of the landau to glare down into her laughing eyes. ''Aye, I do,'' he admitted frankly. ''There was a time not so long ago when I took women for granted and used them for my own selfish purposes. I know perfectly well how rogues think and behave. It was an amusing pastime until I met a firebrand who changed my ideas about sex.''

''I thought we weren't using that word these days,'' Candel said smugly. ''Or is it only ladies of quality who are not permitted to speak of such things?''

Grumbling at his inability to handle this sassy chit, Nicolas jumped from his perch to assist Candel from the carriage. ''Just don't forget who you are, marchioness. And remember, you still have much to learn about life among the gentry. I won't be around to teach you all the things you'll need to know.''

Candel relished every second of physical contact with Nicolas as he lifted her from the coach and set her on the boardwalk. Her gaze locked with his. She felt her heart lurch in her chest as warm tingles flooded through every fiber of her being. She had tried to make light of every conversation since she had awakened that morning, but she was only playing a charade for Nicolas's benefit. Knowing their moments together were numbered made her soul bleed. He was warning her against the flirtatious attentions of other men, as if she would be susceptible. He still doubted the strength of her love for him. Why couldn't he understand that no other man was ever going to take his place, even if he said good-bye forever?

Nicolas stepped away to keep from giving in to the overwhelming urge to take her in his arms and kiss the breath out of her right there on the Rue Royale. "Deliver Jean's message to Jackson," he ordered brusquely. "I'll be waiting outside for you like a good servant."

Candel picked up the front of her gown as Nicolas had taught her to do so she wouldn't trip on the hem. Tilting her chin upward, she breezed into the lobby. After inquiring as to Jackson's whereabouts, Candel climbed the steps and rapped on the door. She was startled by the tall, gaunt man who appeared before her. Jackson was well over six feet—almost as tall as Tiger, in fact. He wasn't the young, virile general Candel expected to meet, but rather a weary forty-seven-year-old man. He reminded her of a battle-hardened soldier, not a pompous commander who carefully avoided combat and sat upon his steed wearing a plumed hat and carrying a glittering sword. The sun-bronzed lines of Jackson's face testified to his hard life. His reddish brown hair showed signs of turning prematurely white and his shaggy mane was in need of clipping. His tattered uniform was in need of repair and although his blue eyes were bright and alert, the set of his jaw was grim. Exhaustion seemed to hover over him like a heavy cloak.

Composing herself, Candel swept into the room and drew herself to her full stature. "General Jackson, I would like a word with you."

Jackson's brows elevated as he surveyed the dazzling beauty in gold satin. He, like most men of the time, was not accustomed to dealing with such a direct, self-asserting young woman. The shapely blonde intrigued him with her vivacious spirit and stunning good looks.

273

"And if I should refuse you, my lady?" he asked with a wry smile.

Candel replied with a wide smile that made her amethyst eyes sparkle like polished jewels. "Well then, General, I shall just have to badger you until I wear you down. I am not leaving here until I've said my piece and that is that."

Jackson closed the door and gestured to her to take a seat, but Candel motioned for *him* to sit down since he looked as if he could use the rest. Her observation was on the mark. Jackson was deeply tired. He sank down in his chair and sighed wearily. His long bout with malaria fever, the exhausting battle against the British at Pensacola, and the fight with the Indians at Mobile had taken their toll on his health and endurance. He was also suffering from the pain of a shattered shoulder and chest wound that he had suffered during a duel in Nashville.

"What can I do for you, Miss—?" He waited for her to enlighten him, which she did without hesitation.

"Miss Candeliera Caron, Marchioness de Caron," she replied. "And 'tis not what you can do for me, monsieur. 'Tis what I can do for you."

She drew the letter and document from her purse and waved them under his nose. "We are on the verge of war against most difficult odds. According to the latest reports, seasoned British soldiers, who have already defeated Napoleon in Europe and burned the Capitol in Washington, are sailing toward the Gulf to seize this city. There are those in the area who have offered their assistance, but you and the governor have rejected them. It has been said that the Lafitte brothers and the privateers of Barataria are pirates and scoundrels unfit to defend these shores. But I assure you, sir, nothing could be further from the truth! I have spent the past two days

274

in Barataria and I have been treated with nothing but generosity, kindness, and consideration—traits admired in gentlemen all around the world, as I am told.''

Candel took full advantage of Jackson's stunned silence and pushed on. "I am a living instance of the privateers' courtesy and kindness. I was rescued at sea by a privateer captain who safely delivered me to Jean Lafitte's headquarters after it had been smashed to bits by American troops sent by the governor—a man who seems more interested in a petty feud than the defense of New Orleans.''

Amazed that this dynamic female was disarmingly direct and dared to speak her mind, Jackson slumped back in his chair and listened attentively.

"I was fed, clothed, and treated with respect during my voyage and my visit to Barataria.'' Candel purposely omitted the incident with Evan Bollings since a personal vendetta had instigated the encounter. "At first I was prone to refer to these men as pirates, but I have seen the error of my ways and I have also seen them in action. In fact, I was on board the schooner which captured one of the British frigates and confiscated weapons and ammunition for the American cause. Not one British sailor was murdered or even injured in the siege. The sailors were set ashore in the Indies and the much-needed information about the British plans was brought directly to Claiborne. The British have even tried to bribe the Baratarians into fighting with them but Jean Lafitte is an American patriot, despite the vicious lies. Lafitte's request to fight has been denied.

"I am going to be frank with you, General. It seems to me that 'tis pure folly and foolishness to reject the offer of support from Barataria. One should never look a gift horse in the face—''

"In the *mouth*," Jackson corrected with an amused chuckle. "Do go on, Marchioness de Caron. You have my attention."

"I volunteered to bring Jean Lafitte's request to you because I consider it a critical mistake to refuse assistance when the British are gathering forces in the harbor. Lafitte can provide you with able-bodied men and ammunition. It will require a unified effort to rout the British. As I see it, you cannot afford to be choosy or be influenced by personal feelings at such a crucial time."

Jackson assessed the feisty female with narrowed eyes. It was glaringly apparent that Miss Caron possessed determination and nerve. "And you think I'm being stubborn and foolish by refusing these pirates?"

"*Privateers*," she emphasized. "And aye, sir, I'm sorry to say that I do."

She thrust the letter at him. "From the gift horse, General. He can arm your soldiers to the teeth and provide the skilled reinforcements you so desperately need."

This was one very unusual young woman, Jackson decided as he unfolded the letter and read the message. That done, he studied the document which had been confiscated from the *H.M.S. Gallant*. At irregular intervals he glanced up at the lovely woman who stood poised and confident before him. Finally, he nodded his shaggy gray head.

"Very well then, mademoiselle, I will cease being so stubborn about these pir—." He flashed an accommodating smile. "These *privateers* and set my personal opinions aside. Tell Jean Lafitte that I've changed my mind. Although I am obligated to attend the parade and reception tonight, I will confer with Lafitte after my formal duties have been performed. And since I have agreed to your suggestion, I have a counter request."

Candel beamed in satisfaction. "Thank you for being open-minded, General. And in return, I will do all I can to see to your request."

Jackson rose to his feet. "I would like you to be my guest at the reception and dinner. I find it refreshing to be in the company of someone who refuses to say what she thinks I want to hear rather than what she truly feels." He playfully flicked the tip of her nose. "But I hope you will refrain from accusing me of being stubborn and bull-headed in public, Candeliera. It wouldn't be good for my image before battle."

"Candel," she asserted. "My friends call me Candel."

"As well they should." He chuckled in amusement. "You are indeed a fiery flame, my dear lady."

"Thank you . . . I think." She peered up at him through a fringe of curly lashes. "I've been told I'm a mite too plainspoken for a woman. I'm sorry if I've offended you, General—"

"My friends call me Andrew. And nay, my dear, you haven't offended me. You've merely pointed out the error of *my* ways. I shall try to overcome it."

Candel breezed toward the door.

"I'll pick you up at your home this evening at six," Jackson called after her.

"I'll be ready," she assured him before she sailed down the hall to inform Nicolas of the general's decision and the upcoming conference.

"Just like that?" Nicolas blinked, bewildered, when Candel reported on her meeting. "He didn't even want time to consider his decision?"

"I was insistent," Candel replied as she clambered into the landau.

Nicolas groaned as he pulled onto his perch. "Dear God, woman, I hope you didn't lecture the general."

Candel settled her silk skirt around her and adjusted the plumed bonnet Jean had given her. "I merely told him what I thought and suggested that he consider the consequences of allowing his personal opinion to cloud his judgment. I also informed him that I wouldn't leave except by an act of God—or words to that effect."

"How diplomatic," he said with a smirk, even though he was inwardly delighted by Candel's audacity and spunk. Jean was right. Sending this brainy, blond-haired beauty to confer with Jackson had been an excellent idea. She had succeeded where a man might have failed.

"I just didn't see the purpose of talking circles around what needed to be said," Candel replied as she surveyed the city she'd left eleven years earlier. "When I called him obstinate, his very nature opposed the idea. In order to refute my remark he had to become agreeable. 'Twas you who taught me to play to my advantage by preying on a weakness."

Nicolas wasn't sure if he was taking the blame or the credit, but he wasn't about to argue with Candel's surprising and immediate success. Jean had spent weeks trying to arrange a meeting with Claiborne to offer services to the Americans. Candel had taken the request to the very top and changed Jackson's attitude in the span of a half-hour . . .

His thoughts trailed off when he spied the spacious Caron plantation house in the distance. The sight also had a profound effect on Candel. She became pensive while she surveyed her childhood home, lost to memories she had tucked in the far corners of her mind. But the thought that forced its way to the forefront was that this was the last time she would see her handsome companion masquerading as her groom.

When the carriage rolled to a halt, Candel accepted Nicolas's hand and stepped down to survey the immaculate mansion at close range. The plantation was as she remembered it, with the exception of the new east wing with its own private stairway to the outside. Below the grand home was the summer cottage that had once provided distinguished guests with privacy.

While Candel was swamped by memories of her childhood, Nicolas reminded himself that the time had come to break all ties, to burn all bridges.

"It's over," he declared with abrupt finality, unable to force himself to meet Candel's shocked gaze. "This is where we say good-bye, once and for all."

His cold, clipped words hit Candel like a doubled fist in the midsection, stealing the breath from her lungs. She stared up at him, her heart in her eyes. Nicolas suddenly seemed so far removed from warmth and compassion that she wondered if he had only pretended to possess those qualitites when the mood suited him. The chiseled lines of his face looked as if they had been carved from stone and his blue eyes reminded her of chips of ice.

"But Tiger, I love you." Her lips quivered and her mouth suddenly felt as if it were as dry as cotton. "I'll always love you . . ."

A scowl darkened his features as frustrated emotion met noble purpose. Her words were like velvet chains that she hoped would one day bring him back to her. Nicolas knew he couldn't leave her with any hope for the future—any association with him could cost Candel her respectability.

"If you believed in love, then you believed only in

illusion, Candel. As for myself, I try to face reality. I don't want always and forever with any woman, not when the world is teeming with willing females.''

Nicolas forced himself to meet her misty gaze. His hard expression gave none of his emotions away, but he felt empty and dead inside. Saying such brutal words to Candel was killing him. Yet he had to do what needed to be done, for both their sakes.

"If you have your heart set on falling in love, then find some foolish dreamer in New Orleans to accommodate you. I'll never sacrifice my freedom for any woman.''

Nicolas knew damned good and well that there were times when a man had to be harsh in order to be realistic. He couldn't permit Candel to pine away for him when there would be dozens of aristocrats eager to take his place. This was where the marchioness belonged and the sooner she set aside her dreams, the sooner she would adjust. And so would he. Candel was not a part of his life. They had dared too much and he had come to care more than he should have. The fact remained that the marchioness had her own life to lead—a life that could not and would not ever include him. They had nothing in common except a passion that could blaze like a forest fire.

"Whatever we felt for each other is over. You're going back to your world and I'm remaining in mine. That's the way I want it,'' he assured her brusquely. "You were intriguing—an amusement, a careless distraction.''

With firm resolution, Nicolas turned on his heels to gather Candel's luggage. After he had dropped it beside her, he hopped onto his perch and stared grimly ahead.

Before Candel could lash at him for being so insensitive, a faintly familiar figure scuttled up from the cottage below the hill. She brushed back her tears, trying to put a name to the wrinkled face staring at her curiously.

A fragment of half-forgotten memory leaped up. "Nathaniel?" she whispered shakily.

"Miz Candel?" The old man staggered back, clutching his chest with a gnarled hand. "Lord have mercy. Is that you, chile? Yer granddaddy ain't gonna believe it!"

"He's still alive?" Candel felt a breath of hope filling her bleeding heart. At least there was someone who loved her!

"Well, just barely, I'm sad to say," the elderly black man replied. "His health declined drastically after the disaster at sea. He's given up all hope of seein' his family again. But yer return might be just the miracle he needs to breathe new life back into him. I'll take you to him. Lord! I can barely believe yer back myself, even when I'm seein' you with my own eyes!"

When Nathaniel clasped her hand to lead her away, Candel refused to glance back in Nicolas's direction. He didn't blame her. He had deliberately hurt her—for her own good. But watching her walk down the stone path to the whitewashed cottage nestled in the canopy of towering oaks cut him to the bone. Damn, he hadn't thought letting go was going to hurt quite so much, especially since he'd been preparing himself for this moment for the past two weeks. There was an empty ache in his belly and a hollow cavity where his heart had been!

All the way back to the docks, Nicolas pondered consoling platitudes. He'd done the right thing. Her grandfather was still alive and the old man deserved the chance to be re-united with his granddaughter, especially after the emotional trauma they had both endured.

Candel didn't need him, Nicolas assured himself. She had always been assertive and fiercely independent. She would get over her infatuation and adjust to her new life. Her grandfather would see that she lacked for nothing.

Candel would be fine and Nicolas had an important message to deliver to Jean. She was back in her world and he was stuck in his. As the French would say—*c'est la vie*. That's life. He still had his freedom. A man with his heritage couldn't ask for more, now could he?

With that sensible thought, Nicolas returned the rented landau and jumped into his skiff. He was leaving the marchioness in her ivory tower where she belonged. He had severed all ties between them. That was for the best. He just wondered how many times he was going to have to tell himself that before he was convinced, until he stopped missing her. A couple of weeks should do it, he decided. By that time Candel would be properly courted by her own kind and she would be ruling the roost of the Caron plantation. He would be just one of many phases in her life.

But ah, what a time they'd had transforming that lovely nymph into a regal butterfly. His consolation came in knowing that she had fancied herself in love with him once upon a time. It was a flattering memory he could keep forever. And one day, even Buff would have to admit that Nicolas had made the right decision. Of course, Buff would probably prefer to kill himself rather than confess he had been wrong. But fairy tales didn't always come true, especially on the eve of war. That was why those enchanting fantasies wound up in books of fiction. Life wasn't always so kind. And right now Nicolas Tiger was hurting a lot more than he thought he would be! Damnation, why did doing the right thing have to be so painful?

Chapter 19

Candel's memories of her grandfather shattered into pieces when Nathaniel led her into the sun room on the south side of the cottage. Amid a jungle of flowering plants and vines sat a pale, frail, withered man of seventy. The past eleven years hadn't been kind. Gustave Caron, the one-time entrepreneur who had escaped the Reign of Terror in France to amass a fortune in New Orleans, was only a shadow of his former self. His skin had an odd bluish tinge and his muscles quivered constantly as he sat slumped in his wheelchair.

A pang of sympathy stabbed at Candel while she studied Gustave as he soaked up the warmth of the midafternoon sun. His blond hair had turned to silver and the tormented expression that puckered his wrinkled face tugged at Candel's heartstrings.

"Gus!" Nathaniel's loud voice echoed around the room as he nudged the old man. "He's hard of hearing," the servant confided to Candel. "Gus, you have a visitor. Look here! It's your granddaughter Candel, returned from the sea. She's come back to you and she's all growed up. Fine and pretty, just as you knew she'd be."

His lashes fluttered up and bloodshot eyes peered at Candel, making her heart twist in her chest. *"Grand-père,"* she murmured as she dropped to her knees in front of him.

For a half-second the old man rallied and Candel was sure she saw a faint sparkle in his dull blue eyes. But something seemed to sap his energy before he could muster it. Gustave sagged back to breathe a ragged gasp.

"Candel . . ." His crab-like hand folded around hers, giving it a faint squeeze.

A sense of irritation gripped Candel as she stared at her grandfather. His clothes were tattered and worn and they looked as if they were at least a decade old. His thin gray hair was in need of clipping, as was his scraggly beard. It seemed that her cousins—who had been no more than poor, envious relations when she was a child—had neglected the marquis in his declining years. It was Gustave Caron who had generously offered André and Yvonne his wealth when he lost his immediate family. Now Gustave sat like an outcast in the simple cottage while André and Yvonne took up residence in the grand mansion on the hill. This was how they showed their appreciation to the marquis? Candel seethed silently. Now that she had returned things were going to be different.

"Nathaniel, fetch me some scissors," she demanded. "I'll not have my grandfather looking so neglected. And send one of the other servants into town to purchase some new clothes."

A wide grin spread across Nathaniel's face, displaying his buck teeth. "Aye, Miz Candel. It looks as if things are gonna change 'round here. And 'bout time, too. You do remind me of yer granddaddy in his better days. He could walk in and take over and get things done when nobody else could. I'm sure glad ya inherited that fine trait. Yer just what he needs.''

The tap at the door brought Nathaniel's head around. "That'll be the cook with Gustave's supper. I'll have Geraldine fetch a plate for ya.''

Candel flung up her hand to forestall him. "Don't say anything about my arrival to the cook. I don't want my dear cousins to know I'm here just yet. I plan to be well-armed when I do battle with them.''

"Gonna lower the boom and take those two uppity muckamucks by surprise, are ya?'' Nathaniel chuckled delightedly at the thought.

"Indeed I am,'' Candel promised, still fuming over her grandfather's accommodations and unkempt appearance. "If André and Yvonne wish to remain at the plantation, they can take up residence in this cottage. No one is going to shove the Marquis de Caron aside! He built this estate into what it is!''

In response to her fierce declaration, Candel was rewarded with a squeeze of Gustave's hand. She glanced down to see the half-smile on his pallid lips. "And you're going to become your old self again, *Grandpère*. I'll not have you moping about when there's a plantation to run. I'll need your guidance if I'm to assume my rightful place here. You and I are going to take charge,'' she told him loud and clear. "Those cousins of mine have enjoyed the luxury of their positions for the very last time.''

When Nathaniel returned with the dinner tray, Candel scooped up the buttered potatoes to feed her grandfather. Gustave wrinkled his nose distastefully and turned away.

"You have to build your strength,'' Candel insisted.

"Not hungry,'' Gustave rasped.

"His stomach pains him considerably," Nathaniel said. "When he eats he claims he feels worse. He says the food don't taste good."

"Poppycock!" Candel scoffed, drawing the old man's gaze.

The expression had once been a favorite of Gustave's. He actually managed a full smile when Candel spouted *poppycock* at him.

"There is nothing wrong with this food," Candel said with absolute certainty. "It's been carefully prepared. Here, you see, I'll show you how delicious it is."

Candel popped a chunk of potato in her mouth and then frowned at the strange undertaste. The morsel hit her empty stomach like a rock. Before she had chewed and swallowed another chunk a feeling of nausea overcame her. Warily, she scraped the fork over the brownish sprinkles of herbs that she had assumed to be seasoning. She lifted another forkful to sniff the food.

Outrage boiled up inside her when she remembered where she had smelled that strange scent before. The natives of Lost Island had mixed a concoction into which they dipped the points of their spears. In large doses, the potion caused convulsions and paralysis. Unless she missed her guess, and she seriously doubted she had, someone had garnished Gustave's food with the ground powders of poison mushrooms. The *stickhorn*, or *fetid wood witch*, as the natives called it, wasn't as lethal as the *death cup* but it was definitely poisonous. It's stout smell gave it away. The plant grew in abundance in moist climates and was easily obtained in Louisiana as well as the tropical islands.

Candel had seen similar symptoms before in the native children who unknowingly bit into the poison mushrooms. The danger signs were all there—bluish-tinged

286

skin, muscle tremors, and nausea. Candel didn't have to be a genius to guess who would profit from Gustave's ailing condition. Damn that André! He would pay dearly for this!

"Nathaniel, I have another errand for you. I need some herbs and roots that grow wild in the area so I can mix a brew to remedy Gustave's condition. Fetch me some puff balls from oak trees, Dogwood tree bark and blackberry roots . . . and quickly! Gustave has deliberately been poisoned!"

Nathaniel gasped in disbelief as he swiveled his head toward the house on the hill. "They'll pay for that," he muttered angrily. "I swear they will."

Candel shared the same smoldering fury that sizzled through the devoted old servant.

When Nathaniel scurried off to find the items she requested, Candel scooped up the contaminated food and tossed it out the window, silver tray and all!

"I've been wanting to do that for years," Gustave said hoarsely. "But I never could find the strength."

"Well, you'll find the strength when I return with another tray of food. And this time there will be no sour underbite. I promise you that, *Grandpère*."

When Candel wheeled away, Gustave's feeble voice halted her in her tracks. "I'm glad you're back, child," he murmured. "And when I'm feeling better, I want to know where you've been so long. I searched for you constantly before I became too ill to keep the vigil at the harbor."

Candel pivoted to kneel in front of the old man. "There are many things about the past that I chose to let myself forget, but never did I lose the memories of you. I always adored you, did you know that? You used to pull me onto your lap and tell me wonderful stories about your first years in New Orleans. Now it seems we have both been alone forever. But we'll make up for lost time when you're back on your feet."

On that determined note, Candel bolted up to make a beeline for the grand mansion on the hill. As was her custom, Candel set off to right all wrongs. Her first order of business was to confront the cook who had prepared Gustave's meals. She was still seething when she burst through the back door. The hum of voices died into shocked silence when the servants, who had been in service before the disaster at sea, half-collapsed in disbelief. It was several minutes before Candel could proceed with her mission. Questions were flying like bullets. Candel had to offer a brief account of the incident eleven years earlier that landed her on the obscure island. Only then could she make headway on the matter that concerned her most.

"I need to know who prepared and seasons my grandfather's food," Candel finally had the chance to say.

" 'Tis my duty," Geraldine Simmons piped up. "I try to make your poor grandfather's meals as appetizing as possible, but he doesn't eat enough to keep a bird alive."

"And what is that seasoning you sprinkle on his food?" Candel inquired, knowing full well what it was. To her relief, the older woman whom she remembered from childhood didn't look the least bit defensive or wary.

"That's Gustave's medication," Geraldine said innocently. "Since he refuses to take it separately, 'tis added to his meals."

"Please show me the prescription," Candel requested.

"Lady Yvonne has it," Geraldine replied. "She doesn't trust me to add the right dose so she sprinkles the potion on his food three times a day."

A startled frown began to knit Candel's brow. She had expected it would be André who tampered with Gustave's food. But giving the matter consideration, she wondered if André had dried and ground the poison mushrooms, bottled them, and then delegated the task to his unsuspecting wife. Since Nicolas had unpleasant dealings with André in the past, Candel was convinced that her conniving cousin was responsible for this cruel attempt to gain control of the Caron fortune. Yet, she didn't rule out the possibility that both André and Yvonne had conspired to ruin Gustave's health. Damn them! They had schemed to slowly dispose of Gustave in a manner that would draw little suspicion before they took complete control of the plantation and the merchant shipping business.

"The medication is not medication at all," Candel declared. " 'Tis poison mushrooms."

The group of servants gasped in unison.

"My cousins have incapacitated Gustave for their own greedy purposes. See to it that neither of them ever goes near his food again. Don't serve him anything that's been out of your sight for even a second. Because of their ruthless avarice, an innocent old man has suffered a great deal!"

Candel's sweeping gaze was met by nods of acceptance.

"You don't have to fret, Miz Candel." Geraldine said with perfect assurance. "I'll make certain Gustave is served only the best. When I was young, he took me in when I had no place to go. If I'd known I was being used to poison that grand old man I would never have allowed anyone near his food!"

Assured that she had the allegiance of the household staff, Candel turned toward the door. "Where is André? I have an ax to pick with him."

Geraldine's aging face crinkled in a grin. "I believe you mean you have a *bone to pick* or an *ax to grind.*"

Candel half-turned to smile at her. "Thank you, Geraldine. I never can keep those figures of speech straight."

"You couldn't when you were just a little tyke either, Miz Candel." Her dark eyes misted with sentimental tears. "Thank God you're back to make things right again . . ."

Squaring her shoulders, Candel breezed through the spacious dining hall to locate her treacherous cousin. The butler, after recovering from the shock of thinking he'd confronted a ghost, informed her that André was overseeing the workings of the plantation. When she inquired as to Yvonne's whereabouts, Candel was told that the lady of the house was lounging in her private chambers—the new wing which had been added during Candel's absence. Yvonne was primping and preparing for the evening's festivities in honor of General Jackson's arrival.

Candel found her irritation mounting as she stormed up the steps to find Yvonne. Her recollections of her were of a very lovely but vain, prissy young girl who hadn't the least inclination to give a younger child of nine the time of day. Yvonne had spent most of her time playing up to Gustave and Candel's parents in hopes of being included at their social gatherings so she could meet interesting people.

Out of pure spite, Candel hoped Yvonne would take one look at her long-lost cousin-in-law and faint from shock. It would serve that witch right. Enjoying that wicked thought, Candel burst through the door without invitation to find Yvonne fussing over her coiffure at the hand-carved dressing table. Yvonne was attired in the latest, most expensive fashions that Gustave's money could buy. A heavy coat of rouge covered her cheeks, eyes, and breasts, which were overly exposed by the daring décolleté of her silk gown.

Through the reflection in the mirror, Candel noted the shocked expression that claimed Yvonne's sultry features. Her eyes darted momentarily toward the door that stood open between her sitting room and the adjoining boudoir. After a moment, Yvonne composed herself and twisted in her chair with an indignant frown.

"Who are you and what are you doing in my home?" Yvonne demanded haughtily.

Candel wasn't fooled for a minute. Yvonne knew exactly who she was, as did every servant Candel had encountered along the way. "You know perfectly well who I am, even if I'm not a child anymore, Yvonne. I'm not here to play games," she assured the voluptuous brunette who was ten years her senior. "This is no longer your home. I am the rightful heir and my grandfather and I have decided to take up residence in the mansion. You and André are no longer welcome. In fact, I hope to see the two of you rot in jail for what you've done to Gustave."

Yvonne bounded to her feet, her breasts heaving with every agitated breath. "André and I have done nothing to Gustave except care for him in his declining years."

"Oh, yes—didn't you!" Candel sniffed disdainfully. "I know perfectly well about the ingredients you put in that so-called medication you sprinkle on Gustave's food three times a day."

Yvonne jerked up her head and glowered. Not to be outdone, Candel glared right back.

"You took cruel advantage of a despairing old man who had lost his family to tragedy. In his need for compassion and companionship he took you in. And in return for his generosity, you tampered with his food to disable him so André could have control of the fortune.''

''That's utterly preposterous,'' Yvonne snapped, her dark eyes glittering with fury. ''The medication was prescribed by one of the finest apothecaries in New Orleans. You have concocted these lies, just so you can toss us out and take control of this house!''

Candel hadn't seen Yvonne in eleven years and didn't remember how good the brunette was at lying. But she wasn't giving Yvonne the benefit of the doubt. She was sure Yvonne and André were guilty.

''I'm not the one who has reason to lie,'' Candel shot back at her fuming cousin. ''You have settled into this mansion, building additions for your own convenience, as if the Caron fortune were your own. But you will receive no generosity from me when you leave. Your vicious tactics against Gustave are unforgivable and I will see you punished for it.''

''I had nothing to do with anything,'' Yvonne protested vehemently.

''You are also a liar,'' Candel retaliated, only to hear Yvonne gasp in offended dignity.

Candel stalked over to the bureau, pulled open the drawer, and began rifling through Yvonne's lingerie to locate the so-called medication.

With an outraged squawk, Yvonne lunged at Candel, intent on clawing her eyes out. Candel was in no mood to tolerate her malicious cousin. Employing the techniques she had seen Tiger use, she doubled her fist and crammed it in Yvonne's astonished face.

A horrified screech erupted from Yvonne as she staggered back, covering her injured mouth. But in only an instant, she launched herself forward again. Although she stood a few inches taller than Candel and outweighed her by ten pounds, Yvonne was the recipient of another blow to the cheek. When she stumbled back and fell in an untidy heap on the floor, Candel shook the sting out of her knuckles and inspected the second drawer that was jammed full of jewelry, scarves . . . and a suspicious looking bottle . . .

"Voila," Candel declared as she lifted the container for Yvonne's inspection. Popping the cork, Candel took a whiff. Sure enough, the same unpleasant odor wafted its way toward her nostrils, making her shudder in revulsion.

Yvonne admitted to nothing. She merely picked herself up from the floor and glowered at the heiress who had returned from the dead.

"The *fetid wood witch*," Candel hissed as she brandished the bottle in Yvonne's bruised face. "Or *stickhorn*, as some choose to call it. This variety of poisonous mushrooms can be found almost everywhere, even under open steps like the ones that descend from your private quarters. How very convenient . . ."

"You're mad," Yvonne blustered furiously. "I would never do such a thing. The medication is meant to relieve Gustave's pain, not intensify it."

A ridiculing smile played about Candel's lips as she sauntered to the dressing table to sprinkle the powdery substance in Yvonne's glass of wine. With a smile, Candel challenged her cousin. "Drink it. If you survive, you will have my sincere apology, dear cousin."

Yvonne stared at the glass as if Candel had offered her a glass of venom, which of course she had. "I—"

"What's going on here?" André's booming voice reverberated around the room as he barged in.

André pulled up short when he saw his long-lost cousin thrusting a glass at Yvonne. It was obvious that word of

Candel's return from beyond the grave had spread across the plantation fields like wildfire. André didn't seem all that surprised to see her, only bewildered by what he saw.

"I was just offering my cousin-in-law a drink to toast my return to civilization," Candel said sarcastically.

André hadn't changed all that much from Candel's recollection. He still had the look of a dandy, even though he was better dressed than he used to be—before he came into Gustave's money. André had been a man of meager means until Gustave took him in and generously paid his debts. André had always been one to live beyond his earnings as a manager in Gustave's warehouse on the wharf. He bandied the name of Caron about, making the most of Gustave's reputation. But André and Yvonne had little to call their own until the tragedy at sea had left them the old man's only living relatives. It was apparent to Candel that these despicable cousins had taken every possible opportunity to get their greedy hands on the Caron fortune.

"Would you care to join us in a toast, André?" Candel asked with a devilish smile.

André glanced from the bottle in Candel's hand to the bleak expression on Yvonne's face.

"I think you'd better leave, Candeliera," André said through clenched teeth.

Candel set the poisoned drink aside and turned to confront the lean, blond-haired dandy she had never liked, even as a child. "The only ones leaving Caron plantation are you and Yvonne. You are no longer welcome in my home. I will be filing charges against the two of you at my earliest convenience."

"Charges for what?" André smirked, undaunted.

"Poisoning," Candel replied.

André's blond features registered shock. "What are you suggesting?"

Candel was thoroughly stumped by her cousin's reaction. Either he was ignorant of Yvonne's devious scheme or he possessed an uncanny acting ability.

"I'm sure you're well aware that Yvonne has been sprinkling poison on Gustave's food to incapacitate him," Candel said tightly. "In fact, I—"

"What?" André's blistering glare riveted on his wife. Angrily, he stamped over to snatch the bottle of poison from Candel's hand.

"Why you conniving little—" André's thick chest heaved as he fought for composure and glowered at Yvonne.

"I want both of you out of here by tomorrow morning," Candel cut in. "I'll let the magistrate in New Orleans see to the details of this case. Gather your belongings and remove yourselves from the premises!"

Having given her command, Candel sailed out the door and down the hall, leaving André and Yvonne staring at each other. Candel still wasn't certain if André had known about the poisoning, but as far as she was concerned her cousin was guilty by association. He'd married that prissy witch and he'd gotten exactly what he'd deserved.

Chapter 20

A fleeting shadow caught Candel's attention as she whizzed out the front door of the mansion and rounded the corner on her way to the cottage. Her brows knitted in a curious frown when she glanced up at the steps that descended from Yvonne's private domain on the second floor. She noticed a man dressed in a billowing black cloak just as he disappeared from sight. The echo of footsteps resounded on the flagstone sidewalk that led into the tiered gardens which were thick with azaleas, crape myrtles, and oleanders . . .

Candel frowned again. She knew that oleanders— although lovely while in blossom—contained poisonous substances. It would have been a simple matter to mix several deadly plants to feed the unsuspecting Gustave. Perhaps the bottle she found in Yvonne's room contained more than dried mushrooms and caused various symptoms that would be difficult to pin down if one wasn't familiar with the pungent odor of the *fetid wood witch*.

Pensively, Candel switched direction to follow the path that led into the garden. She remembered seeing Yvonne glance toward the adjoining room during their confrontation. It left Candel to wonder if someone had been eavesdropping on their conversation. Unless Candel missed her guess, that same someone had just made a discreet exit down the outside staircase and into the dense foliage of the garden.

She quickened her step, hoping to catch sight of the elusive silhouette she had glimpsed moments earlier. An eerie sensation slithered down her spine as she veered in and out of the dangling ivy draped over the overhanging limbs like thick curtains. A flash of memory leaped out at her and Candel froze in her tracks. An overwhelming sense of presence that was as palpable as her own heart-beat sent tingles of apprehension dancing through her. She couldn't quite put her finger on the cause—it was as if some strange premonition had overwhelmed her, reminding her of something from her past—something dark and sinister and . . .

Candel lurched around and retraced her steps along the flagstone sidewalk, driven by a fear she didn't understand. It troubled her that her conversation with Yvonne and André might have been overheard by someone she hadn't recognized, yet had known sometime in the distant past . . .

Stop this nonsense, Candel said to herself. There were dozens of things to do before General Jackson arrived to escort her to the city's celebration. Her first concern was preparing the herbal teas that could counteract the danger-ous substances Gustave had ingested.

Candel had gained a great deal of knowledge about natural remedies and potions during her life on Lost Is-land. She had been taught to mix the healing recipes that had been passed down through generations in the Indies. As their priestess, she had been called upon to cure illness and attend the sick, not only with voodoo rituals but also

297

with natural remedies. She was determined to treat her grandfather's ills and revive his health. If her predictions were correct, his condition would improve as soon as he began eating foods that hadn't been doctored with Yvonne's deadly potion.

With this in mind, Candel scurried back to the cottage to brew the herbs and roots Nathaniel had gathered. She planned to move her grandfather back to the mansion as soon as possible. Giving orders with her customary tone of authority, Candel sent Nathaniel to gather Gustave's belongings.

Nicolas . . . Candel's hand stalled as she reached for the kettle to boil her medicinal teas. She wondered if he had breathed a sigh of relief after he had gotten her out from underfoot once and for all.

It was obvious that Tiger had only been amusing himself with her, she mused sadly. She hadn't learned to switch her newfound emotions off and on as easily as he. It hurt to know she had been so trusting, that it was only her body that Tiger desired until he grew tired of her independent ways.

While battling her feelings for this love that had turned sour, Candel was up to her neck in other difficulties. Her grandfather was in poor health and her sneaky cousins had kept him lingering near death while they spent his hard-earned fortune. War was about to break loose in New Orleans and she had lost the only man she had ever loved. What else could possibly go wrong? Candel was almost afraid to ask for fear she would find out. All she knew was that Nicolas hadn't been gone a full day and she missed him terribly. Although she had always objected to his making decisions for her, she would have liked to have him beside her offering moral support while she faced this most recent crisis, even if he didn't care as deeply as . . .

"Miz Candel?" Nathaniel craned his neck around the kitchen door as she stood absently stirring her concoction over the fire. "Master André would like a word with you."

"Tell him I'll see him at *my* convenience," she retorted. "It's not convenient now. My grandfather needs my attention."

With a wry smile Nathaniel executed an about-face and strode off to take the message to André. He wished he had the nerve to say such things to the uppity André Caron who delighted in putting on airs since he'd acquired control of the fortune.

André scowled and muttered at the message. Nathaniel's grin broadened when André lurched around and marched away. It served that highfalutin dandy right, he thought. Candel wasn't letting André and his prissy wife off easy. Good for her. Things were changing by the minute at Caron plantation . . . for the better . . . at long last!

"Hello, Candel."

Nicolas halted in his tracks and stared incredulously at the colorful parrot that had been transported from the *Sea Devil* to Jean Lafitte's temporary headquarters on Chênière Caminada.

"Hello, Candel."

"I heard you the first time," Nicolas muttered as he sent the bird a glare that branded him a traitor.

"Need a drink," Roger chattered as he balanced himself first on one spindly leg, then the other.

"That makes two of us."

Making himself at home, Nicolas headed for the liquor cabinet to pour a glass of imported wine. Tugging off his mustache and beard, he swallowed his wine in one gulp and poured another. He felt as if someone had ripped off one of his legs. He hadn't thought that leaving Candel at her former doorstep could cause such feelings of emptiness. He felt just as he had years ago when his mother had dragged him to the docks after the death of his beloved grandmother, who had been the only person in the world who cared. He felt bruised and tormented all over again. He had arrogantly misjudged the hold that blond-haired beauty had on him. Forcing her out of his life so abruptly hurt like hell!

"Hello, Candel," Roger chirped when the door creaked open to reveal Buff.

Buff glanced curiously at the chattering parrot before observing the desolate expression on Tiger's rugged features. Candel's tireless efforts to teach Jolly Roger to say something besides *Tiger* had finally paid off, he thought wistfully. Even the parrot had joined Buff in attempting to make Nicolas realize he needed Candel in his life.

"You should have married her," Buff said softly.

"You're as monotonous as that stupid parrot," Nicolas muttered crabbily.

"He's a smart bird." Buff tossed Nicolas a crooked grin and poured himself a drink. "Roger learned a new word. Too bad you can't."

"Hello, Candel," the bird offered again as the door whined open. "For God's sake," Nicolas complained, "that ball of feathers could get a job as a door bell. He spouts off every time the hinges creak!"

Jean and Pierre snickered in amusement as Nicolas

thrashed around the parlor like lightning looking for a place to strike.

"Where's the rotgut?" Roger chirped as he stretched his wings and preened his feathers.

Nicolas poured a dribble of liquor into a cup, hoping to quiet the babbling parrot. He needed no reminders of the bright, beautiful young woman who had returned to Caron plantation to be reunited with her grandfather.

"Well?" Jean questioned impatiently. "How did Candel's meeting with Old Hickory go?"

Nicolas set the brandy in Roger's cage and gulped down his third drink. "Do you mean before or after she called him a stubborn old fool?"

Jean's dark eyes widened in astonishment, then he chuckled in amusement. "I've wanted to tell Claiborne and Jackson the same thing myself."

He glanced expectantly at Nicolas who was reaching for the whiskey bottle. Although he wasn't known to get drunk often, he was certainly doing a good job of it at the moment. Jean had a pretty good idea why.

"I suppose Jackson rejected my offer again," Jean speculated, tossing his musings aside.

"Nay, he didn't," Nicolas replied between gulps. "He didn't even put Candel off by asking for time to think it over. Jackson agreed to meet with you after the evening's festivities. Apparently Candel sang your praises and accused him of allowing personal differences to influence his objectivity. She told him it was just plain foolhardy to reject your generous offer when faced with such overwhelming odds from the British."

Pierre broke into a snicker. "Ah, that lovely lady does have a mind of her own and she minces no words. I wish I could have been there to see the shocked look on Jackson's face."

301

All this talk of that sassy sprite wasn't doing Nicolas's foul disposition one bit of good. Candel filled his every thought and colored all conversation. There was no putting her out of his mind when her name was on everyone's tongue—even that damned bird's!

"Where am I to meet the general?" Jean asked.

Nicolas shrugged a broad shoulder and took a sip of brandy. "I presume Jackson is waiting for you to make contact and name the place."

"My, my, Candel must have made quite an impression if he became so agreeable so quickly," Buff sniggered, watching Nicolas wear a path across the braided rug. "But that hardly comes as a surprise. She has the same effect on every man she meets. Jackson probably didn't give instructions about a meeting place just so he would have the chance to see Candel again."

"Hello, Candel."

"Shut up, you stupid bird!" Nicolas cried.

The door creaked open and one of Jean's servants breezed inside. Eyeing the scowling Tiger apprehensively, the servant scuttled toward the kitchen as fast as his legs could carry him.

"My, aren't we in a sour mood," Jean noted. The observation earned him a furious glare. "If Jackson has changed his mind, I don't think we should give him the slightest chance to reconsider. We'll monitor his activities this evening by bringing Candel to the dinner party that Grymes and Livingston are giving for him."

"I wonder if Jackson has been informed that 'tis our lawyers who are hosting this grand party for him." Pierre smiled at the irony of the thought. "Candel can be our go-between since she has the remarkable ability to crack old Hickory's stubbornness."

"Since she seems willing to help, perhaps she'll consent to allowing us to use her plantation for a meeting place," Jean suggested. "Tiger, can you contact her with our request?"

Nicolas nodded agreeably, appalled at himself for being so eager to see Candel after what he had said to her. Hell, twenty-four hours hadn't even elapsed since he'd laid eyes on her. If Jean and Pierre hadn't given him a good reason to see Candel again so soon, he probably would have dreamed one up. Out of sight and out of mind was one adage that did not apply in this case.

"Caron plantation would be an excellent location," Nicolas said thoughtfully. "It borders the river. In case this turns out to be some kind of trap, we can cross the river and escape into the swamps."

"Perfect," Pierre declared. "I, for one, have no wish to see the inside of the cells of the Cabildo again so soon." His distorted features puckered in a grimace. "I prefer that Dominique You, Beluche, and the other privateers captured during the American invasion are out of there long before I'm stuffed back in that rat hole again!"

"Caron plantation it is," Jean said with a nod. "We'll wear disguises and take Candel with us to the festivities in New Orleans. She can make the arrangements at the dinner."

While the men went their separate ways to prepare for the festivities, Nicolas leaned negligently against the wall and sipped the remainder of his drink. Candel was probably lounging in the lap of luxury, he mused, reminiscing with her grandfather and surrounded by dutiful servants seeing to her every whim. He imagined the only one who would be chagrined by her return was André. Nicolas hoped that cocky dandy was squirming in his fancy breeches, wondering if he was going to have to step out of the limelight now that the rightful heiress had returned

303

André was about to take a long-deserved step down, Nicolas thought, smiling in wicked glee.

While Nicolas was wishing misfortune on André, Candel was sitting in the spacious parlor which had been redecorated to suit Yvonne's eccentric tastes, listening to André attempt to sweet-talk her into a compromise. Little did André know that Candel didn't compromise once she had made a decision. There was nothing he could say to arouse her sympathy once she had seen her grandfather's pitiful condition.

"After you left the house—" André was saying while Candel half-listened, "I confronted my wife with your accusations. I knew nothing of her devious scheme to incapacitate that dear old man."

Candel arched a dubious brow and regarded her immaculately dressed cousin, wondering how he was going to look in rags. Just fine, she decided.

"Had I known of Yvonne's sinister ploy I would have put a stop to it immediately," André continued with absolute assurance.

"I don't believe you," Candel told him point-blank.

"Why not?"

"Because you had even more to gain than she did," Candel retorted. "You indulged her because you knew she was making sure that Gustave was in no condition to retake control of the plantation or the business, leaving the fortune in *your* eager hands."

It didn't take André long to realize he was wasting his breath. Candel wasn't budging. He decided to switch tactics.

"Then perhaps, dear cousin, you should consider the consequences of your rash decision." His expression held a hint of menace. "You could be jeopardizing your life by threatening to cast us out."

Candel wasn't easily intimidated. "I fail to see how you and Yvonne can be a threat to me while you're mildewing in jail."

André's fingers curled, wishing he could reach for Candel's swanlike throat. The defiance in her eyes practically dared him to try it.

"Damn it, woman, I assumed control of this plantation in your absence," André roared. "The very least you could do is offer compensation for the years I've spent seeing to these matters—"

"If you hadn't poisoned Gustave, *he* would have been in command," Candel shot back as she bolted up to stand toe-to-toe with her cousin. "Consider yourself fortunate that I'm allowing you to keep your personal belongings. And if I had had my way, I'd have forced that poison wine down your scheming wife's throat. She deserves a taste of her own medicine after what she did to Gustave . . . and under *your* orders, no doubt!"

Her arm shot toward the door. "You're wasting precious time. What you cannot carry off before tomorrow morning remains here. If I were you, I'd be searching for residence in another city because I intend to file charges against you this very evening. Your only chance is to escape before the magistrate's men march you away in irons!"

"I had no part in this," André insisted through clenched teeth. " 'Twas all Yvonne's doing!"

" 'Tis a pity you didn't pay closer attention to your wife's activities," Candel countered, eyes flashing.

The remark prompted André to curse under his breath. "Aye, perhaps I should have," he muttered before he wheeled around and stalked off.

Inhaling deeply, Candel counted to ten to gain control of her fiery temper. Lord, what a day, but she was going to get through it somehow. Clutching the hem of her skirt, she strode into the foyer and dashed up the steps to the room her parents had shared long years ago. She surveyed the drawing room adjoining the boudoir. Although Yvonne had redecorated the chambers in bright orchid, Candel couldn't bring herself to take up residence in the rooms that held so many memories. She would use her old room, she decided.

As she walked down the hall, she heard André's booming voice mingling with Yvonne's whine. They were arguing, and before Candel could tiptoe over to eavesdrop, Yvonne burst out of the room.

Candel froze when she confronted the outraged brunette.

"You think you've seen the last of me, do you?" she blared at Candel as if she were deaf. "Well, I advise you to think again, little bitch. And if you—"

"Yvonne!" André appeared in the doorway, glowering at his furious wife. "Mind your tongue."

Yvonne lurched around to return his glare—dagger for dagger. "You'll not use that tone with me, dear husband." She made the endearment sound like a curse. "Perhaps I should tell Candeliera what—"

"I said . . . that's enough!" André bellowed as he stormed forward to clutch Yvonne's arm.

Before Yvonne could blurt out whatever she intended to say in her burst of temper, André whisked her back into her chambers and slammed the door behind him.

Candel couldn't muster an ounce of sympathy for either of them. Each time she thought of the productive years Gustave had been deprived of because of those two schemers, she was more determined to show those two vermin no mercy. They deserved to be hunted down and imprisoned for their viciousness.

Candel returned to her former room, disgusted with the changes Yvonne had made. The woman had no taste whatsoever. Candel called to the upstairs maid to ask the others to help her rearrange the furniture and locate another bedspread.

In the distance Candel could still hear Yvonne and André screaming at each other. They thought she was being too harsh, did they? She hadn't been harsh enough! She should have summoned the magistrate and had them dragged off in chains without warning. But being fair-minded, she had given them a sporting chance, which was a lot more than they deserved after what they had done.

Candel left the servants to prepare her boudoir while she went to check on her grandfather's progress. She had hoped her medicinal teas had improved his condition already. She wanted Gustave to have his former downstairs bedroom as soon as the chamber was ready. With the help of the grooms from the stables, they could move Gustave to the mansion where he belonged. The Marquis de Caron would soon be back in residence and the unwanted clutter—André and Yvonne—would be cleared away.

Chapter 21

After overseeing Gustave's return to the mansion, and assured that her medicinal brew had begun to work its healing powers, Candel scampered upstairs. Hurriedly, she dressed in one of the exquisite gowns Nicolas had purchased in Martinique. Although she still felt restricted by the fashionable garments she was expected to wear in civilized society, she didn't mind fastening herself into this particular dress because it had been a gift from Nicolas. It was all she had left to remind her of him, besides the bittersweet memories. There was something missing in her life and she knew exactly *who* it was, even if that *who* no longer wanted her.

"Ah, Tiger," Candel whispered to the image in her mind. "Why couldn't you have loved me, too?"

She tried to assure herself that her raven-haired lover did care for her in his own way. But he had fought it, tooth and tongue.

Tooth and tongue? Candel frowned, wondering if she had slaughtered that figure of speech, too. For some reason it didn't sound quite right. But what difference did it make? Tiger was no longer around to correct her. He was gone for good.

Tiger was too set in his ways, too entrenched in his cynical theories because of his troubled past. Nothing seemed to soften his hard-boiled heart and he had no intention of changing. Candel certainly hadn't counted on falling in love, but she had adjusted to it. Now she had to nurse her broken heart, and get used to being uprooted from her second life on the island, and replanted in Louisiana soil.

Perhaps she did belong here, especially when her ailing grandfather needed her so desperately. But she missed Nicolas so. She would even have been willing to settle for whatever affection he could offer, just to be near him. She had bent her pride *that* far and still it hadn't been enough! She knew she shouldn't even be giving that rascal a thought after the way he had treated her. "It's over," he'd said with brutal finality. Why couldn't she make her heart believe it . . . ?

The rap at the door jolted Candel from her troubled thoughts. With one last glance at her reflection in the mirror, Candel opened the portal to find the butler.

"The general is here," Potter said. He looked at her in respectful admiration. "Miz Candel, you look lovely. You're the image of your mother . . ." His voice trailed off as he shifted awkwardly from one foot to the other. "Forgive me, my lady. I didn't mean to open old wounds."

" 'Tis all right, Potter. I always thought she was the prettiest woman I had ever seen. I shall take the comment as a welcome compliment."

"As it was meant," he assured her. "She was nothing like Lady Yvonne who was always complaining about the servants. Your mother was loved by one and all. And your father, God rest his soul, was deeply devoted to her . . . and to you.''

Candel felt a pang in her chest as her eyes filled with tears.

Potter gave her hand a compassionate squeeze. ''I'm sorry. Your return has made me a mite too nostalgic. The other servants and I remained here these last ten years for Gustave's sake, even when conditions deteriorated. Like your grandfather, we kept hoping for a miracle . . .'' His golden-brown eyes clouded as he smiled down at her. ''You've made life good again . . .''

Candel reached up to kiss the old butler's cheek before she hurried off to meet the general. Warm yet tormenting memories kept swarming around her, and she was afraid they would depress her. She was in desperate need of distraction to prevent her spirits from nose-diving. Oh, how she longed for Nicolas's protective arms, his masterful touch.

It was odd, Candel mused on her way down the steps. For so long she had prided herself in being strong, independent, and decisive. A great deal of responsibility had been heaped on her in the course of one day. Ordinarily, she would have delighted in the challenge. Now she longed for Nicolas to share it with her. He'd probably laugh if she admitted any such thing to him. He had always complained that she was too self-assertive, too independent and straightforward for a woman. Although Candel had never been one to settle for compromises, she would have accepted one now if she could recapture the happiness she had discovered with Nicolas. She wished she had never discovered how it felt to want and need a man so much.

When Candel floated down the spiral staircase like a

vision from a fairy tale, Jackson sighed in awe. "My dear Candel. You take my breath away."

"Not entirely, it seems, Andrew," she teased, flashing an impudent grin. "I'm sure you say the same thing to all your female escorts."

Although Andrew Jackson, like Jean Lafitte, was known for his sobriety, there were a few individuals who could turn his somber countenance into a smile. Candel Caron was one of those unique people who could put a grin on a man's face and keep it there. Her saucy rejoinders and bright spirit were like an exhilarating dose of summer sunshine.

"Aye, I suppose 'tis impossible to steal my breath completely since I've developed the reputation of being long-winded," he replied as he extended his hand to assist her down the last few steps. "But truly, Candel, you are ravishing."

Candel returned the compliment as he escorted her out the door. "I'm equally impressed by the change in your appearance. You do clean up nicely, General," she added with a saucy wink.

Gone were the mud-caked boots, the faded uniform and tattered cloak. The general had donned a new uniform and appeared to be an entirely different man now that he'd had the opportunity to bathe, shave, and clip his hair. The rough Indian fighter became the dignified army officer Candel had expected to see at their first meeting.

"But to tell the truth—" Candel began, only to be interrupted by Jackson's burst of laughter.

"My dear Candel, when don't you tell the truth?" he teased playfully.

"Rarely," she admitted with a breezy smile. "And being perfectly honest, I never have put much stock in the clothes on a man's back." Where Candel had grown up, clothes were hardly important since every native wore nothing but a loincloth. " 'Tis the man himself who matters most, not his fancy garments. If we all ran around naked, only our character and personality would distinguish us from one another."

Jackson broke into laughter again, which drew an astonished glance from the army private who was acting as his groom for the evening. The general noted his startled stare as he assisted Candel into the landau.

"She's quite an amusing lady," he offered, feeling obliged to explain.

"And extraordinarily lovely," the groom replied.

"Aye. That, too," Jackson agreed as he sank down beside Candel and leaned over to whisper in her ear. "But if it's all the same to you, my dear, I prefer to attend the festivities in full military dress. I think I would cause too much disturbance if I bared all—up to and including my soul."

Candel folded her hands in her lap and smiled sheepishly. Nicolas had warned her to guard her runaway tongue now that she was back in society. The influence of living with the natives for more than a decade was difficult to overcome. Each time she opened her mouth, she spoke as freely as she always had.

"My apologies, Andrew. I've been told more than once that I'm too uninhibited in speech and in spirit. In fact, according to one of my closest acquaintances, the civilized world isn't quite ready for the likes of me."

Jackson took her hand and brought it to his lips. "I find your irrepressible spirit and directness quite refreshing. You're one of a kind, Candel."

"I'm sure that comes as a great relief to most men," Candel replied. "Some of them believe a woman is not to speak unless spoken to, and shouldn't ever debate an issue. I'll probably be considered a misfit."

"To some, perhaps," Jackson remarked before brushing his lips over her wrist. "But to tell the truth, I'm not all that civilized myself."

"Then we shall get along just fine, I expect," Candel said with a nod.

"Aye, I expect we will, too," Jackson concurred with another grin that came so easily to him while he was in Candel's company.

What an exhilarating companion this young lady was, he thought. She was destined to break dozens of hearts and lead some fortunate man on a merry chase if and when she decided to take a husband.

When Jackson noticed Candel staring ponderously at the second-story window of the plantation home, he frowned. He watched her peer up at the silhouette of the female framed by the window. Behind her was the dark image of a man.

"Is something troubling you, my dear?" Jackson questioned, noting the irritation in her eyes.

"Aye," she admitted, tormented by the sight of the dark figure hovering behind Yvonne.

There was something unsettling about that shadow, something Candel couldn't quite understand. She was reasonably certain it wasn't André. The unnerving sight reminded Candel of the stranger she had seen scurrying down the steps and into the garden earlier in the day . . .

"May I be of some assistance?" Jackson prodded when she continued to stare at the woman in the window.

Candel shook herself out of her contemplation. "You have enough on your mind without fretting over me," she replied. "I can solve my own problems."

Jackson didn't doubt that for a moment. Although he hadn't known Candel Caron very long, he knew how decisive and determined she was. "I'm sure you can," he said gently, settling himself more comfortably on the seat. "I wonder if I shouldn't enlist your talent to help me solve *my* problems," he added as the carriage sped down the avenue.

Yvonne watched in fury as Candel disappeared into the darkness. "Something is going to have to be done about that bitch . . . and quickly," she hissed before wheeling to face her darkly-clad companion. "Since I can't convince that spineless husband of mine to dispose of her, the task will fall to you."

Her companion wandered over to pour himself a drink. "The young lass seems to be blessed with as many lives as a cat. It might prove difficult to dispose of her."

"I should think you would be as anxious to be rid of her as I am," Yvonne muttered irritably. "After all, if she ever got a good look at you, she might remember—"

Derrick jerked up his head and glared. "It was a long time ago," he cut in. "She was no more than a child and she probably chooses to forget, just as I do."

"Our future depends on Candeliera disappearing as quickly as she arrived," Yvonne reminded him tartly. "It would be a simple matter for you to dispose of Gustave in his weakened condition. And although that fire-breathing witch might make it difficult, the deed must be done."

Dark, glittering eyes bored into Yvonne's distorted features. "Sometimes I wonder why I've let you keep me at your beck and call all these years. So many promises made and broken," he said with a disgusted sigh. "I've had enough of this lurking about in the shadows while you and your foppish husband enjoy all the luxuries you can't seem to live without.''

Yvonne sashayed over to loop her arms around Derrick's sturdy neck. "I have his name but you have always had my heart," she assured him as her body moved provocatively against his. "You have enjoyed your share of the Caron wealth. I hardly think you and I have struck such a bad bargain."

Derrick set her away from him, none too gently. The sight of Candel Caron had tormented him with memories he had no wish to relive. "I've had my fill of your cunning games, Yvonne," he muttered. "If this love you say you feel for me is so strong and enduring, come away with me and forget about the long-lost heiress and her grandfather."

Yvonne's outraged sneer did her striking features no favor. "I'm asking you to do this for *us*!"

"For *you*," he corrected snidely. "Always for you, Yvonne, never for *us*. You decided to marry André because he was kin to the mighty marquis. I have only been your lover because your husband wasn't man enough to satisfy you. I was young and foolish and in love, willing to do anything to please you, just to keep you with me. But I'm the one who has to slink hither and yon while you flaunt the marquis' wealth and live like a queen in the castle."

With a mocking smile, he continued. "André refused to lift a hand to harm his cousin. Now you want me to see to the dastardly task—once again. Very well, if you want me to make sure the lovely little blonde never comes back here again, you must commit yourself to our affair. After all, it has endured longer than your marriage!"

"Don't be absurd," Yvonne snapped.

She was incensed that Derrick had become as difficult

to manipulate as André, who had hurled threats at her earlier in the afternoon when she made demands. Panic was setting in after all the chaotic events of the day.

"If I lose my allowance you and I will have nothing. We must act quickly to remove Candeliera from our lives forever. She has threatened to have me arrested!"

Derrick remained unmoved by her plea. "If you loved me, you would walk away without looking back, Yvonne. I'm beginning to realize that you've used me just as you used André. You know where you can find me. But this time *you* can come to *me* when you've made your choice." With a hasty glance, he headed toward the steps that led into the shadows of the garden.

"Derrick, damn you, come back here!" Yvonne spluttered as she dashed after him. "If you abandon me in my hour of greatest need, I swear I'll tell Candeliera that you're the man who—"

Derrick wheeled around and glowered murderously at Yvonne. "If you dare, I promise that when I'm through with you there'll be no need for all the luxuries you crave. And I *am* through with you!"

"Are you truly?" Yvonne replied with a ridiculing smirk. "We shall see how long you last. 'Tis I who have kept you in the manner to which you have grown accustomed. If I'm going down like a ship, then rest assured I'll find a way to take you with me!"

Derrick's fingers curled, itching to strangle the life out of her. When Yvonne had finally shown her true colors, the sight of her sickened and repulsed him. What a fool he had been to be blinded by her beauty and corrupted by such evil! "Ah, you're so like the poison you've been feeding Gustave all these years. You destroy everything you touch. But I know enough about you to have you

316

stashed in a cell for the rest of your life. Take that into consideration before you threaten me again.''

"You'll regret this, Derrick,'' Yvonne vowed icily.

"All I regret is that I didn't walk away from you the first time I saw you a dozen years ago. And if you're not careful, Yvonne, you'll regret your vicious threats,'' Derrick hissed.

Damn him! And damn André, too! They had both turned against her. She would make sure they both paid. And curse that Candeliera! Things had been going splendidly until she returned from the dead. Yvonne promised herself to take care of them—one and all. She was not giving up the grand home and luxurious life style without a fight.

Chapter 22

Constantly on the lookout for Claiborne's patrols, Nicolas stood beside Jean Lafitte who was also disguised in homespun attire and a stage mustache. Nicolas was still annoyed that he had been unable to locate Candel at the palatial mansion where he had left her that morning. He had, however, managed to speak with Nathaniel, who informed him that the marchioness was attending the grand celebration. Silently, Nicolas watched the procession, led by Andrew Jackson's carriage and his army from Tennessee and Mississippi. It irritated the hell out of him that Candel was by Jackson's side, right in the thick of things.

His gaze zeroed in on the shapely blonde dressed in the elegant gown he had bought her. She was sitting shoulder to shoulder with the general. Judging by the way Jackson kept smiling at Candel, the man had little thought of anything other than entertaining his escort. Obviously the rumors that Jackson was always serious-minded weren't necessarily true. He appeared to be thoroughly enjoying himself. That rogue, and at his age!

Nicolas felt jealousy nipping at him as the entourage

rolled past the street corner where he stood, inconspicuously surrounded by a crowd of cheering spectators. All of New Orleans was on hand to welcome the general—their hero who had come to repel the British troops.

Candel was also in the limelight. She belonged there. But Nicolas was clinging to the shadows like the other commoners in the streets. It stung his pride that he was considered a criminal, an outsider, while Candel paraded like a fairy princess at the general's side. But what irritated him beyond words was that she hadn't even bothered to tell him about the general's invitation. And why should she, he asked himself crossly. Candel was no longer his concern. He had broken all ties. Seeing her beside Jackson should have driven home the point that Nicolas and Candel were now worlds apart.

"Why so glum, *mon ami*?" Jean inquired as he nudged his brooding friend. "Feeling a mite left out?" He nodded in understanding. "I know the feeling all too well myself. Before Claiborne branded me a pirate and outlaw, I could walk these very streets and rub shoulders with the aristocrats. Now I'm forced to hide behind a mop of whiskers for fear of being apprehended. But for you, it must be even worse since your lady is being escorted around the city by it's newest hero."

"She's not my lady," Nicolas grumbled, even as his eyes followed Candel around the corner into another cheering crowd.

"Nay?" Jean arched a taunting brow. "Buff certainly seems to think the two of you are—"

"Buff isn't a realist. I am," Nicolas cut in sourly. "A bastard son doesn't court a marchioness. Not openly or in privacy."

Jean ambled back to his waiting steed. "Play the martyr if it pleases you, Tiger, but make contact with the marchioness when she arrives at the dinner party. We must make our arrangements with Jackson. All this pomp and pageantry may be good for morale in New Orleans, but the general needs our assistance if he has any chance of defeating the British. The sooner we form a working alliance the better off we'll all be.''

Although Nicolas chastised himself for being aggravated with Candel for parading all over town at Jackson's side, the sight hounded him all the way to Livingston's palatial home. Nicolas's only amusement came in knowing that Jackson was being wined and dined by John Grymes and Edward Livingston, who were Jean and Pierre's lawyers. The money for the ball had been donated by Jean. He wondered if Jackson had any idea or if he was too mesmerized by Candel to care.

If Jackson was so taken with Candel, there was no telling how many dandies would be tripping all over themselves in hopes of gaining her attention. No doubt, she had already realized that the love she *thought* she felt for Nicolas was no more than a passing fancy. She was probably relishing all the attention and no longer needed him. The thought turned Nicolas's mood pitch-black. Even while he assured himself she was where she deserved to be, it still annoyed him that she was enjoying herself while he was miserable. Curse it, she didn't have to adjust to his absence *that* quickly! What incredible resilience she had. Damn her.

Candel found herself enjoying the parade and dinner party even more than she had expected. Her emotions had been on a carousel the whole day. Leaving Nicolas had been difficult and painful. Seeing what her cousins

320

had done to Gustave had infuriated her. Sparring with André and Yvonne had been a thorn in her side. Not only did the social event preoccupy her, but she found it amusing to watch the interaction between men and women in civilization. She was fascinated by society's coquettish customs. It seemed that one was to be polite, even if it meant blandishing compliments and flattery that were unearned and undeserved. From the look of things, it was socially acceptable to say what others wanted to hear, even if it was a distortion of the truth.

Each time the general introduced her to his associates, Candel was quizzed about her recent return to civilization. She found herself surrounded by a dozen young men who looked and listened; actually, they did more looking than listening. Candel felt like a well-dressed doll on display—a newly discovered female to be wooed and won.

For two hours she had been showered with compliments about her lovely head of hair, the intriguing color of her eyes, her flawless complexion, and her siren-like voice. She had been invited out for an evening of wining, dining, and theater, and had an offer to take a stroll through the park—to name only two of the more respectable propositions. It seemed to Candel that aristocratic dandies preferred to avoid reality and ignore war.

Ah, how she missed the days she'd spent with that dashing privateer who challenged her intellect and stirred her emotions without playing all these frivolous games of pursuit and conquest . . .

"Marchioness?" Edward Livingston shouldered his way through the circle of male admirers crowding around Candel. "There's someone who would like a private word with you."

Excusing herself, Candel followed Edward, who threaded his way through the spacious ballroom toward the terrace doors. A curious frown knitted her brow when Edward smiled, winked, and gestured toward the shadowed terrace. Without a word of explanation, he pivoted on his heels and returned to his role of the gracious host.

Candel stepped onto the terrace to search the darkness. There was no evidence of someone awaiting her arrival. For a moment, she stood there in the glow of lamps that blazed through the door of the ballroom, wondering who had summoned her and for what mysterious purpose.

Nicolas lingered in the concealing shadows, watching her in her form-fitting gown—a gown that he had purchased for her. A wave of irritation coursed through him as he studied Candel's voluptuous figure and her glorious cloud of hair. For the past half hour he had been peeking in one window and then another, watching her hold court in the ballroom while her foppish admirers drooled all over her. Available bachelors and married men alike had been sniffing at her heels each time she sashayed near them. And worse, each time one of her ogling admirers held her in his arms to dance, there was almost no space between them.

Although Nicolas had reminded himself that he had no right to be envious and possessive, he was. True or not, Candel had said she loved him. And if she really did—which he doubted—it seemed to him that she had certainly recovered from her infatuation quickly enough.

"It seems the New Orleans gentry has eagerly accepted you," Nicolas muttered sourly. "And you have quickly learned your new way of life."

Candel flinched at the unexpected sound that rumbled from the shadows. Her eyes searched the darkness to locate the growling Tiger. When she spied the moonlight reflecting in his blue eyes she impulsively rushed forward, only to have him agilely side-step her embrace.

"Don't play games with me, Candel," he grumbled. "You needn't gush at me, either. I'm not your most recent conquest."

Candel was confused by Nicolas's harsh tone. She was the one who should have been snide and sarcastic after he'd jilted her. She had tried not to hold a grudge, but Tiger was doing a splendid job of it. How ridiculous!

"If anyone deserves to be bitter it should be me, not you," she insisted. "What's wrong with you, Tiger?"

Nicolas had grown so irritable that the slightest provocation or inconvenience annoyed him. It seemed the harsh words he hurled at Candel were actually directed at himself. He was suffering from an unaccountable case of resentment, anger, and frustration. But it was all *her* fault, Nicolas thought crankily. He wouldn't have been in such a foul mood if she hadn't looked as if she were having such a grand time without him.

"I've missed you, Tiger," Candel openly admitted as she reached up to limn the shadowed features of his face. It was all too easy to remember the heated closeness of their bodies in more intimate moments and she longed to recapture the wondrous pleasure.

Again, he eluded her touch as if the thought of physical contact repulsed him. Candel cursed herself for confessing feelings Tiger had no wish to hear. How many more ways did he have to tell her that he wanted nothing to do with her before it finally soaked her thick skull.

"Of course you missed me," he snorted sardonically. "That's why you're having a marvelous time without me tonight. In fact, you didn't even bother to tell me that you would be the general's companion during the festivities. It certainly didn't take you long to adapt to the life of the rich and famous, did it? You seem to be determined to become as much of a rake as I am. And from all indication, you're succeeding admirably!''

Was that jealousy she heard in his voice? Candel smiled in satisfaction. Nicolas may never come to love her the way she loved him, but he cared enough to be annoyed.

'' 'Tis only that I find the social edicts in civilization fascinating,'' she explained with a lackadaisical shrug. She was going to be nonchalant and see how that worked.

Candel ambled along the railing to stare into the night, making no more attempts to touch him. Jean Lafitte had told her that romantic courtship was played like a battle—advance, retreat, pursuit, and capture. For too long she had been doing the chasing. She had been open, honest, and demonstrative about her affection and her needs. Although Nicolas scoffed at the games people played she wondered if he participated. Perhaps she had been too easy a conquest for a man who thrived on challenge. Maybe he would be interested if she became more elusive and less obvious. No man loved a challenge more than Tiger. He lived for danger, intrigue, and excitement. Maybe she could once again pique his interest if she played hard to get. After all, wasn't it part of human nature to want what one thought one couldn't have? Wasn't she living proof of that herself?

Nicolas's narrowed gaze followed her as she glided across the terrace. He was growing madder by the minute and he wasn't even sure why! What the hell was wrong with him? He was acting like a jealous lover. *He* was the one who had set Candel free, so why should he be irritated because every gentleman in Livingston's mansion had been devouring Candel as if they were rats and she was the cheese?

"I'm not sure I'll ever fit in here again, but I'm trying to adjust because I have no other choice," Candel went on to say. "The good citizens of New Orleans have been reasonably tolerant thus far. Even when I commit a *faux pas* or a breech of aristocratic etiquette, I'm forgiven with a reassuring smile."

"By the *men*," Nicolas specified. "And only because they have no wish to dash their hopes of getting you into their beds."

Candel responded with a reckless shrug. "If I become lonely, perhaps I'll let them think they have won their games of conquest. After all, sex is sex, no matter who delivers it—"

Nicolas was upon her like a starved dog on a bone. He spun her around to face his menacing snarl. "You are *not* going to become any man's whore."

She stared him squarely in the eye, even though the ominous look on his face would have tongue-tied the average female. "I was *your* whore for a time, Tiger. You have had other women. What's good for the duck is fine for the goose."

"What's good for the *goose* is good for the *gander*," he corrected with a gritty growl.

"I'm glad you agree," she replied as she wiggled her arm from his vise-like grasp.

"I wasn't agreeing. I was correcting your idiotic idioms and maddening metaphors!" he shouted irritably.

"Did you come here to criticize my clichés or did you want something important?" Candel questioned, highly amused by the black scowl consuming his handsome face.

Nicolas was so agitated that he couldn't stand still. Seeing Candel enjoying the limelight while he slinked around in shadow was infuriating. And hearing her theories on casual sex rankled him every time. For a woman who once claimed to love him she was taking rejection too damned well!

"You said you loved me," he blurted out, and then cursed his runaway tongue.

"Is that what you came to remind me of?" She flashed him a mischievous grin. "I do love you, Tiger. I always will. But that doesn't necessarily have anything to do with simple sex, now does it?" she queried. "You didn't love any of the women you had sex with, did you?"

Nicolas couldn't listen to another word. "Curse it, Candel. You just don't get it, do you?"

"Will it make you feel better to know that I'll probably see your face when I close my eyes and surrender to the man I take as my lover? I'll love you, even if you aren't the man providing the physical pleasures of passion. Now are you satisfied, Tiger?"

With tremendous effort, Nicolas suppressed the overwhelming urge to curl his fingers around her throat for those infuriating remarks. "Jean sent me here to arrange a meeting between him and Jackson at your plantation tonight," Nicolas said through clenched teeth. "We've sighted more frigates in the Gulf. Time is of the essence."

Candel cast all teasing aside and nodded agreeably. "I'll relay the message to Andrew."

"*Andrew?*" One thick brow arched. "Now it's Andrew, is it? I hope you can remember the general is married, even if his wife remained behind in Nashville. And let's not forget the ugly rumor that Andrew wed Rachel while she was still married to her first husband. It does leave a man to wonder if any female is safe in the general's company."

Candel rolled her eyes at Tiger's snide remark. "I'm perfectly aware of Andrew's marital status. And he's

326

devoted to Rachel, even if *devotion* is something you know nothing about. And if I want to have sex, there is an abundance of eligible young bachelors other than Andrew who—''

''Stop bandying that word about!'' Nicolas snapped.

''You're the one who brought it up, not once but twice,'' Candel pointed out, delighting in his reaction.

She had pledged her loyalty and love to him but he cherished his freedom more. She had every right to torment him, she decided. He was definitely tormenting her! Nicolas cared only enough to be jealous and possessive, as if she were a prize he had acquired. He didn't want her forever but he wanted no other man to have her, either. What a preposterous attitude, thought Candel.

This conversation was getting Nicolas nowhere. Gnashing his teeth, he turned and strode across the terrace to leap over the railing.

''We'll be waiting at the cottage at midnight,'' came the clipped voice from the shrubs. ''While you're organizing all your intimate tête-a-têtes with your long line of suitors, don't forget to deliver the message to dear Andrew. Governor Claiborne is also invited to attend, that is if he can forget his private feud with Jean long enough to listen to logic.''

Candel heard nothing more than the quiet rustling of limbs and leaves as Nicolas made his retreat. It could have been the wind—she wouldn't have known the difference.

A spiteful smile pursed her lips as she headed toward the ballroom. She hoped she was the cause of the irritation in Nicolas's voice. It was only fair that he was annoyed since she was hurting so on the inside. All she had really wanted was to dash into his arms. But Nicolas hadn't allowed her near him. He seemed determined to remain just out of her reach—and out of her life.

After her dealings with her cousins and the shock of learning what they had done to Gustave, Candel could have used a little comfort and compassion from Tiger. But he offered nothing but torment.

Damn him, she thought. She really should accept the invitations she'd received this evening. It would serve Tiger right! Too bad the thought of suffering another man's kiss was so distasteful. If Nicolas was such an imbecile that he didn't realize she couldn't surrender her body to someone else when she was totally and completely in love with him, then Nicolas knew nothing whatsoever about this thing called love. And if he didn't understand the meaning of love it was because he hadn't come to love her at all while they were together.

"You're the imbecile," Candel muttered to herself as she breezed into the ballroom.

Nicolas stamped back to the spot where Jean Lafitte waited in the tangle of trees and vines. Jean looked worried when he saw the moonlight splattered across Nicolas's scowling face.

"More problems?" Jean questioned anxiously.

"Nay, everything is fine," Nicolas snapped, his tone belying his words. "Candel will see to the arrangements and make sure Claiborne has been invited to attend the conference at the plantation."

"If everything is fine, why do you look as if you've bitten into something sour?" Jean quizzed in bemusement.

"This is my natural expression," Nicolas muttered as

he swung onto his steed. "I always look this way. You just never bothered to notice."

When Nicolas wheeled his horse around to zigzag through the bushes, Jean studied his friend's rigid back. "Does this have something to do with your ladylove?"

"She is *not* my ladylove," Nicolas protested more harshly than he intended. "She's not my anything and I would appreciate it if you never mentioned her name again!"

"Does that mean there is an open season on shapely blondes? If there is, then I should like to go a-hunting," he teased.

"You lay one hand on Candel and you'll wind up just like Evan Rollings," Nicolas snarled.

"I see," Jean murmured.

Nicolas swiveled in the saddle to glare at Jean. "Just what is it that you see?"

"I see a man who's too stubborn to admit he's in love," Jean replied perceptively. "Obviously you don't really want to be in love and you're terribly uncomfortable with the feelings. To borrow from Shakespeare— even if the poor chap was a bloody Englishman—methinks you protest too much, Tiger."

"Me thinks you talk too much, Lafitte," he hurled back.

"Not when I'm with a lovely, desirable woman, I don't," Jean needled his scowling friend. "If you don't want her, then let her go—completely. You're wearing yourself out trying not to think about her. In times like these, 'tis best for a man to make peace with himself before battle. Unsettled emotions affect a man's logic and that can get him killed. Make your peace, Tiger, one way or the other."

Irritated though Nicolas was, he did take time to consider Jean's advice. No other woman had been able to stir emotions deep inside Nicolas. But when battle broke out in the Gulf, he needed a clear head. It was time he analyzed the turmoil and put his life back into perspective.

Candel Caron was a survivor, just as he was. She was also extremely intelligent and independent. In the weeks that followed they would each settle into their separate niches where they belonged. Nicolas was going to let Candel go—finally, completely, and without regret.

Even if Jackson and Claiborne did agree to join forces with the Baratarians, Nicolas and Jean were still fugitives from justice. Candel was still, and would forever be, a marchioness. Nothing would change, Nicolas reminded himself realistically.

Let Candel take men to her bed to appease her physical needs. What did he care? As she so bluntly reminded him, he'd had other lovers. So why couldn't she? He was going to get over that sassy blonde, just as he'd gotten over his mother's betrayal and her lack of affection. If Candel wanted to become mistress to half the male population of New Orleans, then let her!

In fact, he would probably be better off if he stuffed that feisty female into the same category with his mother so he could hate both of them good and proper! He could then look upon Candel as he had all women—necessary evils. All she was to him was one of the many females who had flitted in and out of his life. She could bewitch and bedazzle every man in the city, General Jackson included. He wasn't going to waste any more emotion on that frustrating female. Indeed, he should take the passion Candel could offer for his own selfish pleasure and then walk away from her for the very last time tonight.

330

After all, nothing could ever come of this emotional torment. And furthermore, he had a war to fight and he needed to channel his thoughts and energy into seeing that the Americans kept New Orleans from British rule! Now there was a noble cause and a challenge to take his mind off that violet-eyed imp!

Chapter 23

The clatter of footsteps on the flagstone path heralded Candel's and Andrew Jackson's arrival at the cottage. A single lantern blazed in the parlor of the quaint home. Drawing himself up to full stature, Jackson opened the door to see Jean and Nicolas sitting in the shadows. Before Candel could make the introductions, more footsteps clicked along the stone path. She glanced over her shoulder to see Governor Claiborne, whom she'd met earlier in the evening, striding purposefully forward.

Taking command of the field, Candel swept into the house. "Governor Claiborne, General Jackson, I would like you to meet Jean Lafitte and Nicolas Tiger."

The four men sized each other up and nodded politely.

So far so good, thought Candel. Nicolas and Jean had changed into formal clothes in hopes of making a good impression. Thus far, all four men were trying to be reasonably courteous and cordial.

"Since you have so much to discuss on such important issues, I will leave you to the serious matter of the city's defense." Candel stared meaningfully at each one of them, just as she had done when settling squabbles among hostile natives. "It seems to me that petty personal conflicts have no place in this room. Now is the time to bind yourselves to a common cause. What you decide here tonight must be for the good of this struggling country, not your personal pride. After all, there won't be much dignity in America if this country falls subject to British rule."

With that thought, Candel turned around and walked out. To her surprise, Nicolas followed her outside.

"You aren't staying?" she asked.

"Jean can handle Jackson and Claiborne well enough, I should think," Nicolas declared as he accompanied Candel to the mansion. "I prefer to celebrate this history-making conference in other ways."

Candel stopped short and peered up into Tiger's shadowed face, baffled by the comment. His lean fingers traced the sultry curve of her lips, the delicate line of her cheek and jaw. Nicolas had changed moods since she had seen him a few hours earlier. What a confusing man he had become of late!

"I want you," he said simply and directly. "Or have you already enlisted a new acquaintance to pleasure you this evening, marchioness?"

Candel decided then and there that her attempt to win Nicolas's attention by telling him about other men had worked to her disadvantage. Somehow she had become no more than the place Tiger went for physical satisfaction. It hurt to realize she'd made such a foolish blunder. She had put herself on the same level as all the other women he'd known.

Since she had already made such a stupid mistake, she decided to keep silent for once in her life, difficult though it was. Whatever she said to Nicolas was always wrong. Hadn't it always been? He had certainly been right about her, from the very beginning. She had been away from civilization so long that she was socially retarded. She didn't function well in society and she obviously didn't know how to win a man's love. Capturing this blue-eyed Tiger was a lost cause and she was a hopeless misfit!

Lifting the hem of her skirts, Candel headed toward the house on the hill. Before she could take her third step, Nicolas grabbed her arm and swung her around.

"I asked you a question. Answer it," he demanded gruffly. "Am I first in line tonight or last?"

"Let me go!" she muttered, refusing to dignify the question with an answer.

"That's what I've been trying to do—in my own way," Nicolas retorted.

Candel stared into his stony features, wondering if perhaps she should revert back to her old theories. Maybe if she tried to respond to his passions the way the natives did, she could get over this hopeless attraction. She would treat him the same way he treated her—like a plaything to be used and discarded when passion ebbed. For once, it would be only physical desire that overcame her. She would look upon him just as he looked upon her—as a temporary amusement. Tonight she was going to get him out of her system, once and for all. She would become just like him and perhaps at long last she could truly understand him.

"Very well," Candel agreed in a tone that conveyed all the indifference she could muster. "If you're having an attack of lust, then I shall appease it as any courtesan would do. But you'll have to curb your desires until after I visit my grandfather." While Nicolas muttered at her annoying remark, she led the way to the mansion. "My cousins have been sprinkling poison in his food for the

334

past few years so he couldn't take full control of the plantation.''

Nicolas gasped in disbelief as Candel hurriedly continued. ''I have prepared several potions to counteract the poisons, but it will take time for Gustave to recover. I ordered André and Yvonne out of the house with the promise that I would file charges against them this evening . . . which I did. I have found myself with a plantation to run while Gustave recovers . . . *if* he recovers from such cruel treachery.'' She tossed Tiger a quick glance as they climbed the steps. ''I hope you'll forgive me if I seem distracted during our tête-a-tête. I have a great deal on my mind.''

Did she sound distant and aloof enough? She hoped so. After being burned once, Candel had decided she would never leave herself open to heartache again. She would try Tiger's tactic of loving only with her body, but never again with her heart.

Nicolas's composure cracked upon hearing what had happened to Candel. His attempt to bring all his emotions for her under control failed when he stared down at the old man who lay asleep in his bed. He felt a fierce tug on his heartstrings.

''Any change?'' Candel asked Nathaniel.

The old servant nodded and smiled. ''The marquis ate every bite of the supper Geraldine prepared.'' He gestured toward the medicinal tea on the nightstand. ''He even asked for another dose of the potion ya brewed for him. Yer return has given him the will to fight again, Miz Candel.''

Candel smiled at the servant before directing his attention to the handsome man standing behind her. ''Nathaniel, this is Nicolas Tiger. He's the sea captain who brought me back from the island.''

335

Nathaniel bowed respectfully before Nicolas. "I can't begin to thank ya enough, Cap'n Tiger. Returnin' Miz Candel gave the old marquis hope. The faithful servants who've tolerated André and Yvonne have seen their prayers answered at long last. You'll always be welcome here because ya brought Miz Candel back to us."

Nathaniel gave Candel a gentle nudge toward the door. "You've had a long day, missy. Now don't ya worry none 'bout yer grandpa. I'll be right here by his side. Just get some rest and don't fret 'bout nothin'."

Just as Candel and Nicolas turned to leave, they heard a sharp gasp from Gustave. He had momentarily opened his eyes and his stunned gaze was riveted on Nicolas, as if he'd seen a ghost.

Nicolas couldn't imagine why the old man had reacted in such a peculiar fashion. The ailing marquis uttered inarticulately and lifted his hand toward Nicolas. His failing strength seemed inadequate to express the emotion that had leaped into his eyes.

Just as quickly as he had roused, Gustave slumped into a deep sleep that prompted everyone in the room to make sure he was still breathing. Whatever Gustave had tried to say was lost for the moment.

Candel gave Nicolas a strange look after she noticed Gustave's alarm. She was pensive as she moved into the foyer. Gustave's odd behavior made no sense whatsoever.

The strange encounter troubled Nicolas, too. All the way up the spiral staircase, he cursed himself for leaving Candel at her doorstep that morning. The least he could have done was take stock of the situation she was walking into. Things had been worse for her than he'd ever imagined!

"I'm sorry," Nicolas murmured inadequately as he followed Candel into her boudoir. "I didn't know—"

"You have no need to apologize," Candel interrupted as she pulled the pins from her hair and shook the golden strands loose. "As you said, this is my world and I have to deal with its problems. You have enough difficulties in your world." She cast him a fleeting glance and smiled callously, leaving Nicolas to wonder if she were a mirror reflecting his own image. "If you wish our relationship to be purely physical, then it shall be. As on Lost Island, and in your domain on the high seas, there are no lasting commitments. You're here only to help me forget my troubles and I'm here only to satisfy your desire. 'Tis nothing personal, only sexual . . ."

The last word tumbled off her lips in a rush when Nicolas yanked her against him, her hips in intimate contact with his. "Stop it, Candel," he pleaded. "Don't shut me out. You did that after Julian St. Croix and Evan Rollings attacked you at Martinique. I hated watching you retreat into yourself."

"But isn't that all you really want?" she questioned, trying to ignore the familiar sensations that the touch of his muscular body triggered. "You have no other use for me other than to appease your physical needs. I asked for more and you couldn't give it. I loved you and you couldn't accept it. Now I'm going to give you exactly what you've always wanted—"

His mouth came down hard on hers—twisting, devouring, stealing her breath away. She didn't retreat, nor did she surrender. She was determined to share no more than desire, to hold her heart and soul out of his reach. This was all Nicolas had ever really wanted and tonight that was all he would receive. She would close her eyes and pretend he was any of the other men who had attempted to seduce her. This romantic interlude wouldn't mean a thing—only the joining of bodies to satisfy mutual needs.

When Nicolas received no response, he raised his head and stared into her impassive features. Damn this unpredictable, totally impossible woman! She was tearing his heart out by the taproot! She had needed his support during the day and he hadn't been there. He had thrown her to the wolves—her cousins, that is. And then he had left her to the score of eager men at the ball who were entertaining lusty fantasies of getting her into their beds. Now she was building a wall around herself again, just as she had in Martinique.

Nicolas was exasperated—he wanted to take her to bed as if she were one of the many somebody elses in his past. And yet, he wanted to draw out the open, honest, and very demonstrative woman he had first met. Candel was changing, evolving right before his very eyes! But she could never be like the other women. She operated on theories based on her life with a primitive culture. Its basic structure was in direct contrast to the world she was in now. As always, Candel thought she had to shoulder all the burdens in life because she was a woman. Yet, in civilization that was supposed to be a man's job—at least that was what Nicolas had been taught to believe.

Coping with her constantly turned him inside out! Hell, he didn't know what he wanted or expected any more. All he knew was that nothing seemed right unless he was with Candel. He always felt an exasperating loss when she withdrew and refused to respond to her honest, giving nature. Candel made him contradict himself time after time. No wonder she didn't know how to act with him—he didn't know what he expected himself! Since both of them acted rather than reacted, they always wound up butting heads. They were too equally matched. That had always been the problem. She was too much woman and he'd always hated that.

With a frustrated sigh, Nicolas moved away from her. "I think I'd better leave."

"Aye, perhaps you should," Candel agreed. She turned away before the mist in her eyes betrayed her. "I think maybe you were right, Tiger. Good-bye is best. I have responsibilities here and you have so many duties awaiting you."

Even as she spoke the words it was impossible to convince her aching heart. She was trying to be strong and sensible, just as she had always disciplined herself to be. But deep down inside, she wanted someone to lean on, to depend on, if only for this one night.

Candel clung to her crumbling composure as she listened to his quiet footsteps retreating. When the door eased shut behind Nicolas, a sob wracked her body. Muffling her tears, she paced the floorboards, determined to regain control of her chaotic emotions. Tiger wanted to get out of her life and nothing she could do would bring him back and make him love her. It was high time she faced that and let go of her dreams. It was officially over, Candel told herself fiercely. She wasn't going to forget that again, even if she went mad listening to the tormenting echo in her heart.

Candel tugged off her gown and let it fall where it would. After fluffing her pillow a half-dozen times she sought a comfortable position in which to sleep. Finally, she gave up the idea entirely. Tossing her legs over the edge of the bed, she donned the velvet robe Jean had given her. Although Nathaniel had insisted he would remain with Gustave, Candel decided to check on her grandfather. When she stepped into the hall, she noticed the lantern light glowing around the edges of the door to Yvonne's private chambers.

Candel was both irritated and puzzled. She had hoped her cousins had gathered their personal belongings and were prepared to leave at break of day. If the rooms still looked as they had early in the afternoon, she would know her cousins hadn't taken her threat seriously. Squaring her shoulders, she padded barefoot down the hall to inspect the private chambers. Without announcing herself, Candel barged into the room to find Yvonne wobbling dazedly, leaning against the wall for support. There was a blank look in her eyes and a bluish tinge on her lips. Her whitened features turned a lighter shade of pale as she half-collapsed into a nearby chair. When her arms dropped loosely by her sides, Candel rushed forward.

"What happened?" Candel asked, giving her cousin a firm shake.

Yvonne's head rolled limply against her shoulder. With great effort, she raised her arm and gestured in the direction of the ornately carved cabinet that stood in the far corner. "The drink . . ." she breathed weakly.

Assuming that Yvonne was asking Candel to fetch the half-empty glass of brandy on the cabinet, Candel retrieved it. She had only taken three steps toward Yvonne when a ghastly expression fell over Yvonne's features. Her body flinched once and then twice before she slumped in her chair.

"Yvonne?" Candel's befuddled gaze settled on her cousin's pallid skin and the glassy stare in her eyes. Hurriedly, Candel brought the glass to Yvonne's lips, urging her to take a sip.

Candel jerked up her head when she heard footsteps

in the hall. The creak of the door heralded André's arrival. With a bewildered expression he glanced from Candel—who hovered over his collapsed wife—to the glass of brandy in her hand.

"What did you do to her?" he queried sharply. "Were you repaying her for tampering with Gustave's food?"

"Don't be ridiculous," Candel snapped as she set the glass aside to check Yvonne's pulse.

Shock registered on Candel's face when she was unable to detect a heartbeat.

"Get away from her," André growled as he stormed over to shove Candel aside. He placed his palm on Yvonne's neck to monitor her pulse but he came to the same grim conclusion Candel had. "She's dead! You've killed my wife!"

"I did no such thing," Candel insisted. "I came to see if you had gathered your belongings for tomorrow morning's departure."

"And since Yvonne has refused to leave the premises as you demanded, you decided to give her a taste of her own medicine, just as you threatened to do this morning," André snarled.

"Get out of here!" Candel fumed at her raging cousin.

"Does the command imply that I'll also be poisoned if I refuse?" André sneered. "You vicious bitch, I was outraged to learn that my wife had been sprinkling poison on Gustave's food, but I never thought you would go to such drastic measures to make sure we were gone from the plantation!" His wild-eyed gaze flew to his wife before he stamped toward the door. "Don't think for one minute that your title and position will save you from this crime, cousin."

Muttering like a madman, André suddenly reversed

direction. He dashed over to retrieve the glass of brandy from the end table and took a sniff, his glittering gaze riveted on Candel. "Evidence, dear cousin," he spat.

With that, André stalked out of the room, rousing the servants to attend his departed wife. "You'll pay for this, Candeliera!" His thundering voice boomed from the hall into the room where Candel stood staring bewilderedly at Yvonne's lifeless body.

In the adjacent room, Candel heard the quiet click of the door to the outside staircase. The vision of the darkly-clad figure spiriting away from the mansion earlier in the day popped into her mind. Someone had obviously been in the next room, waiting for Yvonne. Or perhaps someone had been waiting for her to collapse after she had sipped the poison-laced drink.

Frantic to apprehend the mysterious stranger, Candel stumbled over the furniture that seemed to leap out of the bedroom to trip her up. When she stepped onto the balcony, she spied the fleeing man at the bottom of the stairs. Barefooted, she raced down the steps two at a time. When the intruder darted into the garden, Candel dashed off in hasty pursuit. She could hear his footsteps pounding on the flagstone path.

Again, as before, Candel felt an eerie premonition. There was something about the unidentified stranger that struck a chord . . .

A sharp gasp filled Candel's throat when a hand shot out of the thick bushes lining the path. Her terrified gaze locked with the dark, angular features beneath the shadowed brim of a hat. Another stab of memory sizzled through her like a lightning bolt. Suddenly she was transported back in time to that stormy night at sea. Through the eyes of a panic-stricken child of nine, she stared up at the looming figure swathed in a flowing black cloak.

Then, as now, Candel felt a shudder ripple all the way to the bottom of her soul. The hair on the back of her neck stood on end and her heart seemed to stop.

In the scant moonlight that filtered through the canopy of trees, Candel stared at the featureless face in fanatical fascination. She was a child again, petrified with fear. She was hounded by the instinctive need to run from the danger but her body was frozen. The same shadowed face loomed above her, now as then.

Candel screamed at the same instant that she found the will to fling herself out of the man's grasp. Her head slammed against a low-hanging limb of the tree behind her, causing her skull to explode in blinding pain. The world and the terrifying memories from childhood faded into oblivion. She wilted at the mysterious stranger's feet, a victim of her own terrified reaction to his reappearance.

Derrick glanced in every direction at once. For a half-second, he towered over the crumpled young woman. When he heard thrashing in the bushes on the far side of the garden, Derrick wheeled around to disappear into the darkness like a disembodied spirit.

Chapter 24

Icy dread slithered down Nicolas's spine when he heard the bloodcurdling scream in the distance. In less than a heartbeat he had switched direction. All thoughts of attending the meeting with Lafitte, Claiborne, and Jackson faded. The only sound to filter into his brain was the echo of terror in Candel's voice.

Helplessness sliced through him like a double-edged sword as he fought through the tangled vines. In the distance he could hear the thunder of hooves. His heart stalled in his chest when he spied Candel's motionless form lying on the earth. Nicolas's murderous gaze swung to the rider who blazed across the meadow like a demon bounding back to hell. Still panting, Nicolas squatted to run his hand over the back of her head. Sure enough, there was the beginning of a magnificent goose egg.

Carefully, he rolled her onto her back to check for wounds and, thankfully, he found none. Breathing a sigh of relief that Candel hadn't been stabbed, Nicolas scooped her limp body into his arms and headed toward the house.

"Curse it, Candel, for such an intelligent woman,

you certainly don't have the sense to stay out of trouble,'' Nicolas mumbled, knowing she didn't hear a word.

Moonlight sparkled in the gray hair of the stoop-shouldered servant who had scuttled outside at the sound of the high-pitched scream. Nathaniel gasped in dismay when he spied Nicolas striding grimly toward him, holding Candel protectively against him. Her blond hair glowed in the faint light as it cascaded over Nicolas's arm. Nathaniel's legs nearly gave way beneath him at the sight.

"Is Miz Candel still alive? God have mercy! First Miz Yvonne and now—"

"Yvonne?" Nicolas frowned as he glanced at Nathaniel, who had fallen into step beside him.

"Aye, Cap'n Tiger,'' Nathaniel affirmed as he scurried around to open the door. "Somebody poisoned Yvonne. André has been stormin' 'round the house, makin' all sorts of accusations.'' He gulped apprehensively. "André says he saw Miz Candel bendin' over his dead wife with a poison-laced drink in her hand.''

"What?'' Nicolas cried in astonishment.

Nathaniel nodded gloomily. "Aye, sir. The man was beside hisself with grief, rantin' and ravin' that Miz Candel was tryin' to get even with Yvonne for destroyin' Gustave's health so she could live in the mansion and prance 'round like a queen.''

Hurriedly, Nicolas mounted the steps to Candel's room. When he had settled her on her bed, he sent Nathaniel to fetch smelling salts. The mansion was in a state of chaos. Servants were dashing hither and yon to tend Yvonne as André had instructed and to check on Candel, whom they were sure was either dead or dying. While the servants who had rushed to the bedroom to check on

345

Candel babbled nonstop, Nicolas drew the lantern close to examine her injury.

"Here ya go, Cap'n Tiger." Nathaniel thrust the salts at Nicolas and waited anxiously beside the bed.

"Don't tell Gustave anything that happened tonight," Nicolas murmured as he waved the smelling salts beneath Candel's nose.

"Nay, sir. I wouldn't do that to the old marquis. The shock would surely kill him."

When Candel stirred slightly in response to the strong potion, Nicolas cast the worried servants a reassuring smile and shooed them toward the door. "She'll be all right. She's hardheaded. It would take more than one blow to crack that skull."

"Aye, Cap'n Tiger," Nathaniel affirmed with a faint smile. "She always was a mite headstrong, even when she was a child. She was the apple of her papa's and her grandpa's eyes, to be sure. But there was no doubt at the tender age of nine that she had a mind of her own. Smart as a whip she was, too." His gaze lingered fondly. "That's why her folks kept totin' her off to Europe for schoolin'. I always wondered if she hadn't learnt more than she could ever hope to understand for one so young."

Nathaniel's hand brushed over the tangled mane of golden hair that spilled over the pillow. "The Lord works in mysterious ways, don't he, Cap'n? He made sure Miz Candel learnt all she could before she was washed onto that remote island. Then He gave old Gustave enough will to keep holdin' on, to keep prayin' for a miracle, even when that ruthless female tried to dispose of him little by little so it would look natural-like."

After a long moment, Nathaniel stepped away from the bed. "I better check on the marquis. I hope all the commotion didn't rouse him, 'cause he'd be likely to ask questions I'd rather not answer.''

When Nathaniel and the last of the servants had taken their leave, Nicolas stared down at Candel, reflecting on what the old servant had said. He sat there a long time, lost to his memories, wondering why this feisty lady seemed to be blessed with the devil's luck when the only luck he had known was the kind he made for himself. She had as many lives as a cat, that was for sure. By all rights she shouldn't have survived all her brushes with catastrophe the past eleven years. But Nicolas was certainly glad she had. After coming to know her so well the past month, he couldn't even begin to image what life would be like without her.

Candel hovered between dreams and reality after Nicolas had aroused her further with the smelling salts. Her head throbbed fiercely, and fragments of half-remembered horrors leaped out at her. Her ears rang with the roar of the windblown surf and the rumble of thunder. She could feel herself being dragged up the companionway to the steps of the waterlogged schooner. Stark fear seized her when hands like bands of steel encircled her, forcing her over the rail of the ship into the engulfing waves of the sea. Above her was that shadowed face that was to become her last memory of the life she had once known.

Candel sobbed as she felt herself falling into infinity. Wildly, she thrashed to anchor herself to the railing before the sea swallowed her alive. She could see her parents tumbling toward her the instant before she plunged into the dark abyss . . .

"Candel!" Nicolas howled when her arms fastened around his throat, very nearly strangling him.

347

Another terrifying face loomed over her, frozen in a vicious snarl. Candel could feel Evan Rollings' harsh breath as he clawed at her, intent on tearing her garments to shreds, determined to abuse her and dispose of her. Frantically, she shoved him away, struggling to disentangle herself from his firm grasp.

"Candel! Oooff!" Nicolas exclaimed when her elbow plowed into his midsection.

Lord amighty! Nicolas shuddered to think how many nightmares had converged on Candel from all corners of her fuzzy mind. One moment she was clinging to him like a drowning cat, the next she was fighting for freedom. And before Nicolas could recover from Candel's well-aimed blow, her wild eyes flew open and she flung up her arms as if to protect herself from an oncoming attack.

When the cobwebs cleared from her mind, Candel peered up into the still-blurry face that hovered over her. Impulsively, she shrank away before she was struck on the cheek, but when her senses cleared, she recognized Nicolas's handsome features. Instinctively, she surged off her pillow to hug him.

Deep laughter rumbled in his chest as he nuzzled the top of Candel's head. "I hope this means you're coherent enough to recognize me. You aren't planning to hit me again, are you?"

She couldn't swallow the lump in her throat in time to respond. Nicolas was trying to tease her into good humor. But after the torment she'd been through the past hour, nothing could improve her mood except the feel of Nicolas's protective embrace. She'd gone from hell to heaven, she mused shakily. Since her return to so-called civilization, her emotions had been stretched to the breaking point, leaving her feeling out of control. Just when she thought she had her feet on the ground, another catastrophe knocked her to her knees.

Like metal to a magnet, Nicolas was helplessly drawn to the wild-eyed beauty who trembled convulsively in his arms. He knew it would have been wiser to leave her with her devoted servants and be on his way. But there were so many questions. And yet, finding answers didn't seem half as important as holding Candel close, reassuring himself that she had survived another calamity.

The feel of strong arms enfolding her shattered what was left of Candel's self-control. Oh, what a hypocrite she had turned out to be! Earlier in the evening she had been intent on sending Nicolas on his way and now she was clinging to him as if she could never let him go.

And this time, when Nicolas's dark head moved steadily toward her lips, Candel made no attempt to restrain the emotion bottled up inside her. His kiss was hot and hard and forceful—she couldn't remain indifferent. He mattered too much. Despite what she had said to irritate him, no other man could stir her the way he did. She had compared her male admirers at the party to Nicolas and they had all fallen short. What she wanted was Tiger's love and she was settling for sharing his passion, if that was all he could give.

The instant Candel's sensuous lips melted into his, Nicolas knew he was lost. His mind was sinking into a cloud of pleasure and he could think of nothing except quenching the maddening thirst that had hounded him throughout the long day. His hands roved over her body, remembering each time he'd made wild, sweet love to her. Almost immediately, his body was quivering with barely restrained desire.

It had always been like this with Candel, he realized as he sank down beside her. She always left him teetering

349

on the edge of total abandon. She was the flame that sparked the fires within him. One touch and he was burning alive. One kiss and his desires fed upon one another—there was no rhyme or reason for these sizzling sensations riddling his body. They were simply there—like the moon in the star-spangled sky. It was as if this need had existed for a hundred thousand years, waiting to burst into life and consume him.

The events of the day made Nicolas impatient. He still didn't know what had happened in the garden to cause the swelling on Candel's head. But at the moment, his curiosity wasn't half as demanding as his desire. Gnawing hunger made him desperate to peel away the garments that separated them. Nicolas couldn't wait to rediscover every inch of her, to bring her passions to the same urgent pitch that hummed through his body. His lips skimmed the rose-tipped crests of her breasts before he drew a bud into his mouth to savor the soft, sweet taste. His hands roamed everywhere at once, teaching her far more intimate things than he'd ever dared before. He wanted to do more than taste and touch. He longed to brand her with his kisses and caresses until she was aware of nothing but him and the pleasures he could offer.

Never before had Nicolas cared whether he made a difference to a woman. Despite what he had said, he did need Candel's love, even if it couldn't be a part of his future. He needed to know she cared. When he prepared himself to defend the country against British invasion, he needed these wild, sweet memories as inspiration . . .

The thought swirled away like a gust of wind as Candel returned each kiss and caress as only she could. His body welcomed her imaginative touch. He lived for the feel of her velvety lips spreading butterfly kisses over his skin, crippling his mind and body with heart-stopping sensation. She seemed intent on discovering all the ultrasensitive places he liked to be touched. Her hands coasted over the rugged terrain of his body, bringing every inch of him to life. Ah, how quickly he had become a prisoner of these pulsating needs that riveted him like rapid-fire bullets. Ah, how he reveled in the feel of her satiny skin only a hairbreadth from his. Nicolas couldn't contain his moan of maddening torment when she stroked and teased him with her body, lips, and tongue. The knot of longing uncoiled inside him, leaving him to shudder in deep spasm of helpless response.

The instant before Nicolas lost his last shred of self-control he hooked his arm around her trim waist and rolled to his knees to draw her supple body beneath his. When she lifted her arms to welcome him, just as she had on the terrace at the party, Nicolas responded eagerly. Earlier he had been tortured by wounded pride and jealousy, but nothing could have kept him from her now. He needed this violet-eyed angel as he had needed nothing else in this world. She gave him life and breath.

"Candel, I—"

His words trailed off into a ragged sigh when her pliant body arched toward his and she guided him to her. But the thought of what he had almost said exploded in his mind. With a moan of frustrated torment, Nicolas drove urgently into her. She answered each hard, demanding thrust as she buried her head against the pounding beat of his heart. Never had Nicolas known a woman who responded with such wild abandon. Never had another woman been able to draw so much emotion from deep inside him, leaving him completely vulnerable. He could feel himself reaching up toward an elusive sensation that hovered just beyond his understanding and his grasp.

351

The tempestuous winds of passion seemed to blow the stars around, leaving Nicolas hopelessly disoriented. Again, he felt himself reaching for that unexplainable sensation that transcended all physical boundaries, and to his stunned amazement he found it within his grasp! This fiery female with hair like sunbeams and moonlight had taken him higher than he'd ever been before, showing him new dimensions of existence. Ah, the natives of Lost Island were right about Candel. She did possess a mystical quality, a supernatural gift that touched others' lives . . .

Nicolas felt the surge of hot, wild desperation engulf him as they moved in perfect rhythm. A gasp of utter disbelief tumbled from his lips as he clutched Candel so tightly to him that neither of them could breathe.

Candel's responsive body matched each spasmodic shudder that seized him as they leaped over rainbows and tumbled into clouds. It was much later when Nicolas found the strength—or the will—to move. He could have lingered on the shores of oblivion for an eternity with Candel in his arms, reliving each rapturous sensation.

Absently, her tapered fingers glided over the sleek muscles of his back and hips before retracing their leisurely path. This magnificent specimen did indeed remind her of a sleek tiger. Oh, he'd never admit that he needed to be stroked and petted and loved, despite his invincible strength and determination. Beneath that mass of explosive energy beat the heart of a man who considered it a weakness to surrender his heart.

The cruelties and disappointments of life had hardened Tiger to the point that he never allowed himself to trust or depend on anyone but himself. And no matter what he was feeling for her in the aftermath, Candel knew he'd talk himself out of it later. He always did. Nicolas Tiger

as infuriatingly stubborn about trusting in love. He re-
used to believe that he and Candel could make each other
happy, that they could fill the empty corners of each
others' hearts. Damnation, she thought bitterly, why
couldn't he try to create a life for them? Why must he
deny these silken chains that bound them together—body
to body and soul to soul?

It was obvious now that Candel could never truly talk
herself out of loving this man. The feelings were soul-
deep. It seemed this blue-eyed Tiger was destined to be
her first and last love, but she knew she couldn't hold
him forever. Loving a man like Tiger was like clutching
at moonbeams.

When Nicolas finally rolled away to gather his clothes,
she felt cold and alone. Each time they made love he
lingered a little longer than the time before, but never
quite long enough to satisfy her. She yearned to call him
back, to beg him to stay the night. But she knew he
had other obligations. The conference in the cottage was
critical to the future of New Orleans and Barataria. She
was being selfish to want Nicolas to remain with her when
he was needed elsewhere.

After he dressed, Nicolas ambled back to brace his
arms on either side of Candel's bare shoulders. He was
afraid to speak for fear of what he might say. Instead, he
blessed her with a whispering kiss before he withdrew.
For a long moment, he stared at her, forcing himself to
concentrate on the incident that had brought them together
rather than the feelings that threatened to melt the ice
around his heart.

"Do you feel up to talking about what happened tonight?" Nicolas questioned, his voice raspy with emotion. "Nathaniel said some very disturbing things to
me."

353

"I can take care of it," she assured him determinedl "Jean is probably wondering where you are."

Nicolas sank down on the edge of the bed and frowne "I distinctly remember asking you not to shut me o again. What the hell happened, Candel?"

Although she resented his tone, Candel explaine "After you left, I saw a light burning in Yvonne's chan bers and went to see if she was packing." Absentl she massaged her throbbing temples and attempted organize her thoughts. "I found her stumbling around h room, then she collapsed. I think she was trying to te me that someone had poisoned her drink before the dead potion took full effect. But I had assumed she had bee drinking heavily and that she only wanted me to fetch h glass so she could finish drinking herself into a coma. was poised over her with the glass in hand when Andr barged in and leaped to the wrong conclusion. He bega ranting and raving that I had murdered Yvonne for tryir to poison Gustave. I tried to explain but he was too frant to listen. After André stormed out, I heard the door sh in the adjoining room. I saw a man—"

Candel stopped short, wondering if she should divulg her suspicions about the mysterious stranger to Nicola Nay, she decided. He had too many things on his min And besides, she couldn't even describe the man wh reminded her so much of a nightmare from her pas He was no more than a feeling of deja-vu which wa impossible to explain to anyone who hadn't experience it. She much preferred to keep Nicolas in the dark whe it came to the feelings and premonitions she had exper enced while she was chasing after that mysteriou stranger. But unless Candel missed her guess, he ha slipped the poison into Yvonne's drink before disap pearing into the night . . .

"And?" Nicolas prompted impatiently. "Have you een this man before?"

"Aye, this morning," she hedged. "He was sneaking om Yvonne's private chambers. Or rather I thought I aw the shadow of a man." Candel sighed deeply and nspected the knot on the back of her head. "I don't feel p to this, Tiger."

Gently, he brushed his hand over her brows. "You eed to rest. I'll come back tomorrow to—"

"I can handle André," she insisted.

Nicolas rose to his full stature and stared at Candel for moment. "If you need me, send for me."

She needed him but not in the way he meant. And vhen he finally realized he needed her for all the right easons, *he* could come for *her*.

"Promise me," Nicolas said authoritatively.

"You told me not to make promises I can't keep, 'iger," she mumbled, wishing her headache would go way.

"Cast-iron daisy." He chuckled softly as he traced er lips with his forefinger. "Always prepared to fill a nan's shoes in this world, aren't you? Don't let that ndependent streak get you into trouble . . . Sleep well, Candel."

"*Good-bye*, Tiger."

He glanced at her sharply. Her voice carried a note of inality that cut to the quick. She was showing him the loor again, assuring him that she didn't need him to be er white knight. That's what he wanted, wasn't it?

When Nicolas left, Candel moaned in exhaustion. Her houghts kept leaping back and forth between Tiger and he cloaked stranger in the garden. She had definite suspi- :ions about who had disposed of Yvonne . . .

Candel huddled beneath the quilts and stared at the

shadows on the wall. Confound this nagging headach
she thought. She couldn't think straight. Tomorrow sl
would have to fit all the pieces of this puzzle togethe
but not now. The memory of Tiger's lovemaking wa
fresh and lulled her into dreams . . . With that tantalizii
thought, Candel gave way to exhaustion . . .

Nicolas didn't have long to wait at the cottage befo:
the conference adjourned. When the three men amble
out the door, talking amiably to each other, Nicolas kne
the outcome. Claiborne and Jackson had agreed to enli
the aid of the Baratarians to defend the threatened city

"I would like your men to block all the bayous b
tween New Orleans and the Gulf," Jackson requested
Jean and Nicolas. "I'll see to the training of the loc
army of regulars with my militia."

"According to the reports from our scouts, the Briti
are already approaching Chandeleur Island," Nicol:
said grimly. "We haven't much time to prepare for
full-scale battle. General Pakenham has twelve thousar
seasoned British soldiers under his command—more tha
we first believed to be approaching."

"Our most serious need is for weapons and ammun
tion." Jackson sighed as he stared out into the nigh
"We have no flints for our rifles. Somehow, I don't thin
we'll be able to send thousands of British into retreat
we have to beat them back with clubs and sticks."

Jean smiled as he peered at the disgruntled genera
"If flints are what you need, then you shall have then
There are still a good many guns and muskets hidden i
the swamps. I'll put Tiger in charge of gathering the flin
and delivering them to you posthaste."

"The Baratarians not only have a stockpile of weapor

ut they are expert at maneuvering the swamps and marshes with the stealth of Indians,'' Nicolas added. ''Our spies will keep us posted on the movements of the British fleet while you train your militia. Thus far, the English have found the bayous difficult to cross. The Legion will continue to hamper their progress, buying us precious time.''

''There is also one other matter I would like you and Claiborne to consider,'' Jean said firmly. ''After the American attack on Barataria a few weeks ago, eighty of my men were locked in the Cabildo. They are seasoned fighters who could be of great assistance if you see fit to let them go. If they are released, there will be more than a thousand fighting men from Barataria who will be eager to join this alliance.''

Jackson glanced at Claiborne, who had been responsible for the invasion and capture of Lafitte's privateers. After a moment, Claiborne nodded. ''The doors of the Cabildo will be opened wide in the morning. Your men will be free . . . provided . . .'' The faintest hint of a smile hovered about the governor's lips. ''Provided you rescind the fifteen hundred dollar reward on my head.''

''Done,'' Jean confirmed. ''and what of *my* head, Governor?''

''Considering your generous offer to provide supplies, I'll allow you to keep your head,'' Claiborne declared.

Although the situation in New Orleans was far from settled, Nicolas was greatly relieved that the Baratarians had been allowed to come out of hiding to help defend the city. While he and Jean made their way through the swamps to relay the information to the other privateers, Nicolas wondered how Candel would fare when battle broke out. He hoped she had the good sense to remain out of the crossfire!

357

The trouble at Caron plantation should keep her occupied, he assured himself. Candel was concerned about her grandfather's health. Yet, Nicolas had the inescapable feeling that she hadn't told him everything. She probably had a pretty good idea who had disposed of Yvonne, but Candel was keeping her own counsel. Surely she wouldn't try to take matters into her own hands. Of course she wouldn't, Nicolas reassured himself. Even Candel wasn't *that* foolish and he wouldn't be around to rescue her. She knew that as well as he did.

"Has the marchioness settled into her life without difficulty?" Jean questioned as they negotiated the vine-choked swamps. "I'll be forever indebted to her for changing Jackson's mind. Perhaps I'll send her a gift of appreciation."

"Candel has taken the mansion by storm," Nicolas assured Jean. "I'm sure she'll manage the threat of impending war, just as she manages all else."

He wasn't sure if he was trying to convince Jean or himself. But when he remembered that determined glint in Candel's eyes before he left her in her room, he knew she would meet any crisis that came her way with her customary courage and spirit. Candel would be just fine. She was a survivor, after all. Look at what she'd already endured. Aye, Candel could take care of herself, Nicolas thought confidently. And she was going to have to.

Chapter 25

Although Nicolas awakened the following morning assuring himself that Candel was safe and sound at Caron Plantation, she was not. While Nicolas scurried around to collect the flints Jackson needed, Candel was confronted by the constable and his armed guards who had come to arrest her for Yvonne's murder.

Behind the grim-faced law officers stood her cousin André, glaring at her in condemnation. It was apparent that André had been so distraught over the death of his wife that he hadn't been thinking clearly. He already held a grudge against Candel for evicting him from his home of eleven years. That, compounded with his anguish over Yvonne's death, had obviously sent André over the edge. He had stormed to the Cabildo, carrying the glass of poisoned brandy, demanding Candel's immediate arrest.

"You're making a mistake," Candel protested.

"That's what they all say," the constable countered before he clamped the manacles around her wrist.

"My cousin doesn't have his story straight," she insisted. "I tried to chase down a mysterious intruder who slipped out the private exit while André was stomping

around like a crazed maniac. He was too busy accusi
me of a crime which I didn't commit to notice the mar
presence or his hasty retreat.''

When the constable wavered indecisively, And
snorted. ''That's ridiculous. I caught you red-hande
Candeliera, and now you're grasping at excuses to sa
yourself. I should have expected as much from you.'

Nathaniel's widened eyes focused on Candel as
constable's men led her away like a common crimin
When she noticed the haunted look on the old servan
face, she stopped.

''Don't tell Gustave about this,'' she ordered Natha
iel. ''It will only upset him and impede his recover
Keep giving him the potions I prepared. I'll be back soo
You can count on that, Nathaniel.''

Nodding bleakly, Nathaniel watched the officers le
her away while André marched along behind the proce
sion. Nathaniel didn't know what kind of tale he w
going to invent to explain her absence. The old marqu
seemed to have come to life earlier that morning wh
Candel was sitting with him, briefing him on the ever
that had taken place during the last decade.

Heaving a troubled sigh, Nathaniel ambled down t
hall to Gustave's room, trying to project a cheerfulne
he didn't feel. He prayed Candel would return hor
quickly, for her sake as well as Gustave's. With Cand
gone, the responsibility of the plantation would again f:
the André. Ah, if only someone else could corrobora
her story and save her from this humiliating degradatio
It was outrageous to even think Candeliera Junfroi Car
would commit such a crime! Nathaniel would never ha
thought she would be held responsible for Yvonne
death. He knew she was innocent. What fools those la
officials were!

True to his word, Claiborne ordered the release of the eighty Baratarians who had remained behind bars since the American invasion of Lafitte's headquarters. Although the privateers filed out while Candel was being locked away to await trial, they were completely unaware of her relationship with Tiger and Lafitte. Indeed, they were too busy celebrating their own good fortune to consider the lovely young woman who was taking their place in the musty prison.

For three days following the alliance formed by Jackson, Claiborne, and Lafitte, a steady stream of Baratarians poured into the city to join the American forces. Even the French and Spanish Creoles, who had never truly considered themselves Americans, responded to the threat of British domination. Every able-bodied man armed himself to the teeth. Many of the Baratarians were put on guard in the swamps to repel the British forces while other privateers were placed at the head of Jackson's artillery division.

Nicolas had begun making lists of all the tasks required of him. He and Jean had spent a great deal of time at Jackson's headquarters on Rue Royale, organizing their defenses while Pierre took command of the forces in the bayous.

Despite all the defensive barriers set up on Last Island, Grande Terre, Grand Isle, and The Temple, the British still thrashed their way through the marshes, moving steadily toward New Orleans. With so many waterways and routes into the city, the Americans couldn't block them all and dispatchers were constantly being sent out to gather information.

Nicolas was disappointed to learn that the five American gunboats which had attacked the British frigate off Chandeleur Island had been defeated. More depressing news arrived at Jackson's headquarters within the next few days: the British had surged onto the mainland and had camped seven thousand soldiers at Villere Plantation, which lay only nine miles from the heart of the city. Nicolas knew the British were moving closer but he was shocked to learn they were *that* close!

When Jackson decided to attack the British at Villere plantation, Nicolas was put in charge of the division that was to circle through the swamp to form the flank. Even Governor Claiborne had been assigned the corps of soldiers who guarded Gentilly Road, which led into the city. Jean was requested to return to the forces at The Temple and prepare his men for battle.

News of the British advances prompted scores of citizens to take arms. The streets of New Orleans were packed with men and boys from sixteen to sixty, all of whom were determined to defend their homes.

Candel heard the cheers and cries to arms from the window of her cell. But after more than a week of solitary confinement, she began to wonder if she would still be locked away long after the battle ended. She had sent letters to John Grymes and Edward Livingston, who served as Jean and Pierre's lawyers, but she had received no response to her requests for counsel. She supposed the threat of war had prevented them from answering her messages. The hours of uninterrupted monotony were intolerable. Candel had been so active all her life that confinement weighed heavily upon her. If she were forced to withstand too many more days of this, she was sure she would die of sheer boredom.

In those moments when frustration and depression nearly swallowed her alive, Candel felt abandoned and alone, just as she had after the tragedy at sea. Each time those tortuous thoughts assaulted her, the dark face of the man she had confronted in the garden sprang to mind and she froze in fear.

The more she thought of it, the more she speculated on the relationship between Yvonne and the unidentified stranger who seemed to be a specter from her past. Intuition told her he was the one who had heaved her overboard during the storm eleven years earlier. The fact that the stranger had access to Yvonne's private chambers caused suspicion to cloud Candel's mind.

If she were speculating, she would bet that Yvonne had something to do with the catastrophe at sea. It made sense that Yvonne and the unidentified stranger were somehow involved. Perhaps Yvonne, who had tried to poison Gustave, had also plotted to dispose of the Carons while they were at sea. Perhaps Yvonne was even the one who had sent the black-clad stranger and his accomplice to do her dirty work for her!

Knowing how shrewd and greedy Yvonne could be when money and position were involved, Candel couldn't help but wonder if that vicious witch had intended to lay the blame on her henchman when Candel miraculously returned from the dead. Maybe Yvonne had lost her life after she had threatened to expose the mysterious stranger in order to save her own neck.

There were so many questions. But now, as luck would have it, she was locked in a dingy cell and Yvonne's murderer was free. Candel might not live long enough to uncover the truth. And if André had his way, she would spend the rest of her life in this musty cubicle. André was overwrought with grief and he was so bitter about Candel's order to oust him that he refused to listen to reason. She was doomed. From a remote island to

363

solitary confinement, Candel thought dispiritedly. What had she done to deserve so much torment? It would have done wonders for her if she could have Tiger's love. But she didn't have that, either. Indeed, for a woman who was heir to a fortune, she couldn't buy a friend or her freedom!

While Candel was conjuring up and discarding a dozen theories to explain Yvonne's death, Nicolas and Buff led their army brigade through the swamps and crawled through the underbrush to provide reinforcements for Jackson.

In the cover of darkness, they took their position on the perimeters of Villere Plantation. A disguised American frigate under Captain Henley's command had sailed innocently into the harbor to dock nearby. The British soldiers mistook the ship for an ordinary merchant vessel, but to their surprise, heavy cannonfire exploded in the darkness. The British scurried into position to return the volley while Nicolas and the other American troops crept closer to the distracted enemy who erroneously presumed their only threat came from the sea.

The well-precisioned attack came from all directions at once, sending the British into a furor. After an hour and a half of intense battle, the British retreated to their headquarters at the plantation home.

Nicolas cursed the dense fog that had rolled in from the sea. The last half hour of battle had been damned near impossible because it had become difficult to tell friend from foe. Since the British outnumbered the Americans, it would prove disastrous if he and his men attacked each other by mistake!

Weary though Nicolas was, he left Buff in command

of the ranks while he rode off to Rodriguez Canal to confer with Jackson. Jean arrived a few minutes later to report that the Baratarians had driven the British to the edge of the swamps. When the night-long meeting ended, Nicolas returned to his command. For two days he found himself involved in hit-and-miss skirmishes while the main corps of British erected a stronghold along the river.

Jackson had given Nicolas and several other officers free rein to employ guerilla warfare to pester the British. The American army slithered through the marshes like vipers to pick off British sentries and small bands of unsuspecting soldiers.

"It amazes me that the British insist on using their European style of fighting," Nicolas commented as he accepted the cup of coffee Buff offered. "They march in formation, pounding their drums and making themselves easy targets. They are either incredibly foolish or remarkably brave."

" 'Tis fine by me if they want to reveal their location and tromp shoulder to shoulder in their fancy red coats while we crouch in the brambles and pick them off like ducks," Buff snorted.

"One of the prisoners complained to me that we Americans are too sneaky and uncivilized to fight a war with Her Majesty's Royal Army," Nicolas smirked. "According to the British we aren't playing by the rules."

"Aye, maybe they're right," Buff murmured as he cast Nicolas a pointed glance. "Maybe we aren't as civilized as you keep telling Candel we are. There aren't as many differences between any of us Americans these days—you and Candel in particular."

Funny, wasn't it, how Buff could take an unrelated

topic and manage to work Candel's name into the conversation. He had a one-track mind, Nicolas thought in disgust.

"How is Candel, by the way?"

Nicolas rolled his eyes heavenward and heaved a tired sigh. Despite the intermittent skirmishes and excessive duties, Buff constantly needled him about Candel. The man had developed the infuriating knack of harping on Nicolas's responsibilities every five minutes.

"In case you're too shellshocked to notice, there's still a war going on here," Nicolas grumbled as he stared at the contents of his coffee cup. "Now's not the time to badger me about my love life. Candel's alive and well and living in the lap of luxury with her grandfather, surrounded by a host of faithful servants who treat her exactly like the natives on Lost Island."

If Nicolas had known Candel was in the dungeon of the Cabildo, growing weak from the dismal meals and lack of activity, he would have been outraged. He was laboring under a false sense of security where she was concerned.

"Well, don't think that just because there's a battle going on I'm going to let you forget your obligations," Buff declared with another meaningful glance. "And if you don't do right by Candel, I've half a mind to march myself up to the marquis and tell him just how friendly the two of you became on board the schooner. We'll just see how long the marquis allows you to shirk your responsibility when the smoke clears around New Orleans!"

"Enough!" Nicolas exploded, drawing the curious stares of the soldiers under his command. "I've got far too much on my mind to put up with your constant harassment. Candel is exactly where she needs to be."

"Where she needs to be is confined to the institution of marriage to you, if you ask me," Buff retorted.

"You weren't asked."

"I'm still entitled to my opinion. There isn't a law against it, so far as I know," Buff retaliated belligerently. "I'm not making a threat, Tiger, I'm making a promise. When this is all over, I'm going straight to the marquis!"

Flinging Buff an irritated glance, Nicolas rolled to his feet to mingle with the troops. He didn't need Buff bandying Candel's name about. She was on his mind more often than naught as it was. In fact, the intensity of the skirmishes was all that preoccupied him and gave him some relief. Aye, he missed not having that rambunctious woman underfoot. But curse it, their ill-fated affair was over and done. He had seen that look of determination in her eyes the last night they had been together. Candel had discarded any romantic fantasies she might have had. Now she knew her place and she had come to realize that he was cut from a different scrap of wood. He would never belong in her world.

She was a blueblood and he was a mongrel who didn't have the slightest idea who his father was. He wouldn't shame her more than he already had. She deserved better . . .

"You're every bit as good as the marchioness, but you won't let yourself believe it," Buff muttered as he ambled past Nicolas. "You're a fool, Tiger."

"Thank you for the insult," Nicolas snarled at Buff's departing back.

"You're welcome," Buff yelled over his shoulder as he headed to the serving line for supper.

"Stubborn old goat," Nicolas muttered sourly.

"I heard that." Buff wheeled around to flash him a condescending glare. "Someday, you're going to rile me

367

enough to tell you what I promised not to tell. And then maybe—''

Buff snapped his jaw shut so fast he very nearly bit off his tongue. Cursing under his breath, he stomped off to eat his meal, leaving Nicolas to stare bemusedly after him.

If not for the arrival of a messenger with news and orders from Jackson, Nicolas might have drilled Buff full of questions after that cryptic remark. But the British were gearing up for a strong offensive and Nicolas was forced to gather his men and scramble to the projected battle site.

The British had erected a barricade along a ditch at Chalmette Plantation, not far from Jackson's main division. According to the alarming report, the British battery was only six hundred yards away from the infantry of Baratarians and Tennessee militia. Because of the dense fog that had settled in the lowlands, the British and Americans couldn't see far enough in front of themselves to open fire. The fog gave Nicolas and the other division the chance to pull up stakes and circle to rejoin Jackson and Lafitte.

This new development should take Buff's mind off his annoying lectures, Nicolas thought as he navigated through the swamps. And if Buff didn't stop his harping pretty damned quick, Nicolas was seriously considering giving that old buzzard to the British. Maybe they could do something with him. Nicolas certainly didn't seem to be able to!

By the time Nicolas and his men forged their way through the fog the British had opened a heavy cannonade. Nicolas was concerned by the fusillade of gunfire that was dangerously close to the American lines. Despite the fact that he was only a recently commissioned officer on Jackson's staff, he went straight to the general to express his concern about potential American losses. Jean and Pierre Lafitte and Dominique You were already in conference at headquarters. Without preamble, Nicolas marched inside and cut straight to the heart of the matter—a tactic he'd picked up from Candel and had begun to use extensively without realizing it.

"General, 'tis my opinion that our main force should retreat to another location," Nicolas declared. "The enemy fire is so intense that we risk losing too many men. Considering the odds against us, we can't afford a single soldier."

Jackson, who had eaten only four tablespoons of rice to relieve his nausea, lifted his head from where he lay sprawled on the sofa. This was no time to be suffering another attack of chronic malarial fever and he found little relief. With an anguished sigh, Jackson nodded his gray head.

"Aye, Tiger. I know we're in a dangerous position," Jackson concurred in a feeble voice.

"To complicate matters, we came upon a division of infantry that was on its way to Piernos Canal," Nicolas went on to say. "If we're not careful, they'll have us surrounded."

"My scouts have also returned with the message that the British are in the process of digging out Canal Villere," Pierre Lafitte added bleakly. "It looks as though the British plan to use the canal for passage from their headquarters."

"We need to keep our guerilla fighters near enemy

lines to hamper their progress," Jean told the ailing general. "It looks as if the English are preparing for a major offensive from all directions at once."

Jackson pondered what he'd been told for a long moment. With extreme effort he heaved himself into an upright position. The endless days he had endured in the rain and fog were taking their toll on his strength and his health. He and his men had been sleeping in the mud like creatures of the swamps, surviving on rations of rice and stale bread. What little in the way of supplies they had received had come from the women of the city who sent blankets, extra shirts, and cloaks—anything that could be found to clothe the tattered army.

"All your suggestions are well-founded," Jackson murmured as he staggered to his feet. "I see no other recourse but to retreat a few miles and prepare for the inevitable confrontation. The Baratarians and Tennesseans can handle the guerilla fighting while we set up headquarters and build barricades." He stared at each somber face. "Inform our men that we will relocate to a more advantageous position. I'm told there is more than a million dollars worth of cotton, ten thousand hogshead of sugar, and other valuable goods stored in the city. The British aren't going to get their hands on it and turn a profit on this war. And you can tell our men that the only way our enemies are going to get into New Orleans is over my dead body! I may retreat to regroup but I will *not* admit defeat to those bloody British!"

The outburst forced Jackson to wilt back to the sofa to muster his strength. While he rested, the officers trooped outside into the fog to pass the orders. Dominique You clutched Nicolas's arm to detain him and then chuckled when he wound up with a hand full of mud. "Conditions in the swamps appear worse than in this slime brought on by the rain,'' Dominique said as he wiped his fingers on his soiled breeches and sighed at his inability to find one clean spot.

"Aye, I've been slogging around in the muck so long I expect to grow fins,'' Nicolas admitted as he wiped the smudges off his face with his shirt sleeve. "But then, our enemy has already accused us of fighting dirty. And so it seems we are.''

"I would still rather be up to my knees in mud and fighting British redcoats than sitting out this battle in the Cabildo,'' Dominique assured him. "I imagine that feisty young chit whom the guards marched into prison while we were tromping out would prefer the uncertainty of battle to the monotony of jail, too. She was throwing such a fit about being locked up for a crime she loudly announced she hadn't committed that the guards put her in chains. Poor lass,'' he added with a compassionate sigh. "I know exactly how she feels. When one is accustomed to freedom those barred doors and windows can drive a body to the brink of madness.''

"I wouldn't waste much sympathy on the wench, Dominique,'' Nicolas advised. "The male of the species would probably be better off if all the females on the planet were behind bars.''

Dominique chortled as he and Nicolas slopped through the mud to reach their divisions. "Aye, perhaps. But all of us would probably beat down the prison doors to get to them. If I wasn't a happily married man I'd be eager enough to do time with that gorgeous blonde in the Cabildo.''

Nicolas's footsteps stalled in the slime for a half-second before he lengthened his stride to walk abreast of his long-time friend. A sickening feeling settled in the pit of Nicolas's belly. He kept reassuring himself that there were dozens of attractive blondes in New Orleans besides Candel Caron, but knowing what he did about the incident at the plantation two weeks earlier caused uneasiness to engulf him.

"What did this wench do to land in jail?" Nicolas queried urgently.

Dominique arched a thick brow and grinned wryly. "Do you plan to pay her bail after the battle is over, Tiger? I admit the spirited lass is just your style but she could be fatal if the accusations were true. They say she poisoned—"

"What?" In shocked dismay, Nicolas stared down at his short, stout friend. His worst nightmare materialized in his mind's eye. "Poisoned?" His voice wobbled with astonishment. For one wild moment Nicolas stood there, up to his ankles in mud, glancing in every direction at once. "It can't be!"

Nicolas had obligations aplenty but impulse bade him to thunder into New Orleans to determine whether or not it was Candel who was rotting away in prison.

A muddled frown settled into Dominique's rugged features. "Tiger, are you all right? I hope you aren't coming down with the same affliction that hampers General Jackson!"

Nicolas had no time to comment. The British artillery struck up with a booming tirade and a solid sheet of flame roared against the gray fog. Men scattered everywhere, gathering their gear to retreat to higher, safer ground. The house Jackson used as his headquarters suffered a direct hit from an exploding cannonball. Debris rocketed into the fog and the house burst into instant flame. Luckily, Jackson had marshalled the energy to leave before disaster struck.

Firing orders like bullets, Nicolas raced toward his

men who were scrambling for cover. "Buff!" Nicolas shouted over the crack of rifles and the whine of cannonballs. "Follow Dominique's men to our new location!"

Buff watched Nicolas race over to clutch the reins of the nearest horse. "Where are you going?" he questioned as Nicolas leaped into the saddle.

Nicolas offered no explanation, but raced down Gentilly Road. The thought of Candel rattling around in that stinking jail where Dominique, Pierre, and the other privateers had been penned up like animals outraged him beyond words. It was obvious that André Caron had been so bitter and vengeful after his wife's death that he had leaped to ill-founded conclusions about Candel's involvement. She had become the scapegoat. It was just like André to place the blame on everyone but himself. That fool—surely he didn't believe Candel was capable of murder!

Nicolas sorely wished he hadn't been content to simply loosen a few of André's teeth during their encounter the previous year. He should have knocked some sense into that prancing dandy. Candel was no more a murderess than Nicolas was a titled lord. When he got his hands on that dolt he was going to choke the life out of him for sending Candel off to jail.

With fanatical haste, Nicolas cut through the fog to the deserted streets of New Orleans. He was armed to the teeth and prepared to battle his way through the halls of the Cabildo if he had to. But he was going to free Candel if it was the last thing he ever did.

Chapter 26

Candel shivered beneath the grimy animal skin quilt while she sat huddled on her cot. Absently, she stared at the ceiling where a spider was meticulously spinning its web. Her eyes darted to the snake that slithered up from the cracks between the rough planked floor to stick its forked tongue out at her. The spider and snake were the only companions Candel had to break the drudgery of despair. Little by little, though Candel had valiantly fought to keep her spirits up, she could feel herself withering away, just as her grandfather must have when grief, depression, and Yvonne's poisoned meals ate away at him. There was nothing to break the monotony except the arrival of her food which consisted of stale bread and rancid bacon floating in its own grease.

The sound of distant cannons rumbled, momentarily drawing Candel from her reverie. Listlessly, she rose from her cot to peer out into the soupy fog that still blanketed the city. She longed to know how Gustave was faring and what excuse Nathaniel had dreamed up to explain her extended absence. She wondered where Nicolas was, if he was still alive—

Candel stifled that unthinkable speculation before it took root like so many of her other dispiriting thoughts. Nicolas Tiger, though too daring for his own good at times, was a survivor, too. He would weather the storm as he had endured everything else. He had an incredible inner driving force that defied even death . . .

The sound of footsteps on the cobblestone street outside her dungeon window jostled her from her musings. All Candel could see was mud-caked boots and the hem of a damp black cloak. To her disbelief, a gloved hand appeared between the bars. A ring of keys clanked to the floor in front of her, followed by a small pistol. And then without a word of explanation or identification, her mysterious visitor's footsteps retreated into silence.

Candel didn't have the faintest idea how or even why she had been granted the opportunity of escape, but she wasn't about to question her good fortune. With renewed spirit, she glanced over her shoulder to make sure none of the guards who paced past her cell every half-hour had heard the clank of the falling keys. Hurriedly, she stabbed the keys into the lock until she found the one which unshackled her manacles.

A band of raw flesh surrounded her wrists to remind her of her captivity. She massaged her chafed skin as she inched toward the door to check for passing sentinels. Stretching up on tiptoe, she wormed her arm through the window of the door to reach the outside padlock. She had to contort her body to wrestle the keys into the lock until she located the right one. After a few minutes the door gave way, whining as it swung open to the corridor that fronted the long row of cells.

After scooping up the pistol—a weapon she'd never used in all her twenty years, Candel inched down the hall. In the distance she could hear the murmur of voices

and the scuffling of feet. The guards were oblivious t
her presence as she edged toward the steps that led t
freedom.

Candel hardly dared to breathe for fear the soun
would give her away as she cautiously navigated th
stone steps. Stealing glances over her shoulder at irregula
intervals, she ascended the stairs and squinted to adjus
her eyes to the pale light after two weeks of gloom
darkness.

Her pulse pounded uncontrollably when she spied th
door that led to freedom. When she heard the sound o
footsteps, she shrank back into the shadows of the stair
case, waiting until danger passed. As soon as the coas
was clear, Candel focused on the door that opened ont
the street. She took off at a rapid pace, intent on burstin
through the portal and making good her escape before th
roving guards and officials realized she was gone.

To her dismay, the door lurched open, seemingly o
its own accord. Candel barreled into the hard, unyieldin
body that was barging in while she was plunging out
She collided with solid flesh, but in a flash, Candel recov
ered to spin away and dash off. When a steely han
clamped over her forearm and spun her around, sh
pushed her tangled hair from her face and clutched at th
pistol she had stashed in the bodice of her battered gown

Stunned, Candel peered incredulously into Tiger'
smudged features and then let her gaze wander over hi
mud-stained body. Nicolas only spared her a quick pe
rusal before he latched onto her arm and practicall
dragged her toward his horse.

Candel's first thought was that Nicolas was the on
who'd somehow managed to swipe the keys and dro
them into her cell. But in an instant she realized tha
Nicolas wasn't wearing a black cloak, or leather gloves

True, his breeches were smeared with slime all the way to his thighs and grime clung to his soiled shirt like a second skin, but he definitely wasn't the one.

When Nicolas hurriedly scooped her up into the saddle, Candel caught a brief glimpse of the shadowed silhouette that hovered at the corner of the Cabildo. Again that strange feeling of intuitive terror trickled down her spine. A hidden face loomed beneath the brim of a hat and unseen eyes stared at her through the fog. The shapeless black cloak and mud-caked boots assured Candel that this was the man responsible for her release. But why?

Before Nicolas had time to settle himself behind her in the saddle, Candel gouged the steed in the flanks to race toward the mysterious stranger who had been tormenting her thoughts for weeks.

"Argh!" Nicolas yelped as he clawed at the horse in an attempt to balance himself before he tumbled onto the street. "Curse it, Candel, I came to rescue you. The least you could do is have the courtesy to wait until I mount!"

Candel had no time for explanations. She was intent on discovering the identity of the man who haunted her past as well as her present. When the cloaked stranger saw her thundering toward him, he wheeled around to dash off, his cloak swirling around him. His footsteps died beneath the clatter of hooves. Before Candel could run the man down, Nicolas snaked out an arm to jerk the reins from her grasp.

"Hell and damnation," he breathed down her neck. "What do you think you're doing?"

"Chasing him!" Her arm shot out to indicate the spot where he had evaporated into the fog.

"*Him?* Who?"

Nicolas peered at her skeptically. He was honestly beginning to wonder if her brain had been affected during her sojourn in jail. Nicolas's probing gaze surveyed the fog-filled alleyway and he cocked his head to listen for a sound. Either the roar of cannons had deafened him or Candel was hearing things. He rather suspected the latter to be the case.

"It was the man who released me from jail," Candel muttered as she fought for the reins, but to no avail. Nicolas refused to give them back. "That's the same man who murdered Yvonne and let me take the blame for it!"

With a curse Nicolas listened to the shouts and howls of the guards who had just discovered their prisoner had escaped. He took absolute control of the reins to wheel the steed in the opposite direction. "We don't have time to chase shadows," he said as he forced the horse into its swiftest gait.

A congregation of outraged guards trampled over each other in their haste to reach the street. Bullets spit into the fog as Nicolas pushed Candel against the saddle to protect her. He swerved around the corner to Rue St. Louis and clattered down the street as if the hounds of hell were nipping at his heels.

Candel yelped as the motion of the horse jammed her from one direction and Nicolas slammed against her from the other. After several agonizing minutes, he straightened and pulled Candel back against him.

"How the devil did you manage to escape?" he wanted to know as soon as they were safe. "From the report I received, you were in chains and locked away."

"I already told you the man in the black cloak helped me," she replied. "He dropped the keys through the cell window. He's the one you wouldn't let me chase."

"You little fool," Nicolas snapped at the back of her matted blond head. "Did you stop to think this mysterious man whom you believe to be responsible for Yvonne's death might have set you up for the kill? Maybe he wanted you to escape so that either he or those guards could shoot you down. You seem to be the only one who's seen him, the only one who claims he killed Yvonne. Curse it, Candel! When you saw him you should have run *away* from danger, not *toward* it!''

''Why? You never do—''

The last word was ripped from her lips when Nicolas cut a short corner to thunder down Rue de Chartres. Unprepared for the hairpin turn, Candel came dangerously close to being catapulted from the horse, which was traveling at breakneck speed. If not for the sinewy arm that was clamped around her waist, Candel was certain she would have been skidding across the cobblestones.

When they reached the outskirts of town, Nicolas slowed his wild pace. Impulsively, he twisted Candel around until she was half-reclined across his lap. His mouth came down on hers in a searing kiss. He felt like a starved, desperate man devouring a long-awaited treat. He'd ridden hell-for-leather to reach the Cabildo to rescue Candel. He'd dodged flying bullets to make his escape. And now his reward was the taste of honeyed kisses that he'd longed for since he last saw her.

''Mmm . . . I needed that,'' Nicolas murmured when he finally came up for air. ''It's been a long two weeks.''

It annoyed Candel that Nicolas had declared their affair to be over when he had dropped her on her former doorstep. And yet, he kept coming back, wanting the pleasures of a woman's body—any woman's body. Candel had plenty of time in prison to mull over the one-sided love she felt for this blue-eyed Tiger. She had assured herself that she was only in for more heartache if she kept carrying a torch for this fascinating man. Although her traitorous body still craved his masterful kisses and caresses, Candel refused to express her love ever again.

"I want to go home," she said with her customary air of authority.

"Why?"

He was annoyed that she had retreated inside her shell again, shutting him out. He hated it when she did that, when she took away the love she had once freely offered him. He felt like a lost sheep.

"If I take you home, André will only get the constable to lock you up again and attempted escape will be added to your crimes." He stared into her defiant features. "Nay, Candel. You're coming with me and that's the beginning and end of it. At least I'll know you're safe."

Candel stared at him as if he were insane. "Safe on a battlefield? Really, Tiger, you've been in the swamps too long. And anyway, I'm no longer your concern. No matter what happens to me, it's no sweat off your forehead."

"No sweat off my *brow*," he replied in correction. "If you can't keep those damned cliches straight don't use them. And you're still coming with me, like it or not."

"Which I don't," she fumed.

Nicolas tightened his grip when Candel tried to leap off the plodding steed. "Damn it, hold still. While the other women of New Orleans are praying for their men and sending supplies, you're doing your damnedest to destroy the morale of one soldier in particular—yours truly."

Candel ceased her struggle. It was a waste of energy. "You certainly don't need moral support from me. You need nothing and no one. My grandfather wants and needs me and that's where I prefer to be."

"Candel?"

"What?" she asked testily.

Nicolas tipped her grimy chin to his smudged smile. "If you'll try to be agreeable for the next few crucial hours, I'll take you home and make sure that demented cousin of yours listens to reason."

"I don't need your assistance."

She swatted his hand away as if it were a mosquito, refusing to succumb to his tender touch and devastating smile. Never again would she be a fool for love. Tiger had taught her valuable lessons, and she vowed never to forget them. He alone had the power to hurt her and he was not going to do it again! She had made herself that promise in prison. He had said it was over and she had finally begun to believe it.

Nicolas dropped the subject. He would make sure that Candel stayed where he put her because he had the physical strength to see that she did. She might not like it—which she obviously didn't—but he would have to force her for her own good.

Candel swallowed all further argument when they reached the farm house that had become Jackson's new headquarters. What she saw disturbed her to such extent that she set her personal conflict with Tiger aside. The sight of tattered soldiers slogging through the mud in barely enough clothes to keep them warm stirred patriotic feelings inside her. She had sulked around her prison cell, wallowing in self-pity and frustration. And here were these brave men, risking their lives to rout the redcoats.

The instant Candel spied Jackson among his weary troops, she cursed herself for refusing to accompany Nicolas to the front lines. The ailing general looked exhausted. His poor health was evident in the strained lines that bracketed his eyes and mouth. It was as if he and his officers were carrying the weight of the world on their shoulders. Lord, what impossible odds these Americans faced!

Despite her own weariness and concern for her grand-father, Candel hopped to the ground and marched off to set a dozen pots of coffee brewing over the campfires that dotted the soggy meadow. She offered an encouraging smile to each and every battle-worn soldier, along with a cup of steaming liquid. When she handed a cup to Jackson, he smiled fondly at her.

"A lovely rose among the thorns," he said softly. " 'Tis just what we all needed." When he sipped his coffee, he glanced over at Dominique You, who had given Candel his own private coffee supply. " 'Tis better than we usually get. You didn't by chance smuggle it, did you, Dominique?"

The stocky privateer grinned wryly before he winked at Nicolas, who was sprawled beside the campfire. "That may be, General," he replied. "Indeed, you could well be sipping brew that was meant for the British. One never knows."

Candel glanced around her, surveying the men who crouched beside the fires to absorb the warmth. "I'm glad you brought me here, Tiger," she said.

Nicolas's thick lashes swept up to meet her peace-treaty smile. "I thought you would be. We're all glad you're here. You remind us of what we're fighting for— the homes and the loved ones who remained behind."

Candel was touched by his simple yet eloquent remark, but she didn't have long to ponder it. Buff slopped through the mud to request a refill and tossed out the loaded question like a grenade.

"Did you take time to marry Candel before you dragged her out here?"

Candel's head snapped up to see Buff glaring at Nicolas and when her gaze swung back to Buff there was a glitter of mischief in her lavender eyes.

"I have no more wish to wed Tiger than he does to wed me. He's married to his freedom and as far as I'm concerned he's welcome to it," she insisted in a loud voice.

True, she would undoubtedly love this big, blue-eyed renegade forever. And true, she did delight in lambasting Tiger, just to rile him. It was one thing for her to criticize Tiger, but she found herself amazingly defensive when someone else tried to do it. Candel wasn't about to have Tiger browbeaten into matrimony by his well-meaning friend. She never did take to having anyone make decisions for her. And besides, Nicolas Tiger wouldn't know love if he met it head-on, which he already had.

"Now wait just a damned minute," Nicolas said as he rolled to his feet, balancing his coffee cup in one hand. "I don't need any woman speaking for me. I'll decide if and when I wish to marry."

The nerve of this woman! She didn't have to broadcast that announcement to the whole damned army!

"Then by all means speak for yourself," Candel remarked sarcastically before glancing at the soldiers who were all ears and smiles. "And while you're at it, tell Buff he doesn't need to protect me. I can take care of myself without some man trying to tell me where to go, what to do, and when to do it."

Dominique You burst out laughing at Candel's spirit. With an expansive gesture, he toasted her feisty temperament. "Any woman who can talk to Tiger like that and get away with it has my respect. Give him hell, lass."

Nicolas hadn't realized their verbal swordplay could do so much for the morale of the men—they were all chuckling in amusement. And Candel, quick-witted as she was, seemed to have sensed that long before he did. Indeed, he began to think that part of her reason for tossing around those sassy rejoinders was to distract the soldiers from the miserable conditions and impending doom.

"Thank you, sir. I do believe I shall let him have it with both muskets," she commented to Dominique.

"With both *barrels*," Buff corrected.

"Aye, that too," she allowed with a lift of her belligerent chin. "I don't know that I would follow Tiger through the jungles of battle, either. He'd likely lead me in circles. I pity these men."

"Aye, Tiger did lead us on a merry chase just last night," one of the men under Nicolas's command piped up. "But we happened onto a legion of redcoats and we had ourselves a dandy time sending them slogging off through the swamps in retreat."

"Because of *your* and the *other soldiers'* bravery and valor, I'm sure," Candel said sweetly. "Why, the lot of you are undoubtedly responsible for giving Tiger credibility that he doesn't deserve as a military strategist."

"To be sure!" another soldier teased playfully. "And never mind that he felled the two redcoats who tried to run me through with a bayonet—"

"Or the dragoons who tried to separate me from my scalp," someone else chimed in.

"Fine, gentlemen," Candel concluded as she looked Tiger up and down. "Then you can keep this muddy marine of yours since you seem to think he's worth his salt on the battlefield. But I wouldn't advise you to marry him. From the sound of things, Tiger makes a better commander and soldier than he would a husband. I expect there are those among you who would be better at both."

When she sauntered off to refill another dozen cups and fraternize with the troops, Nicolas watched the hypnotic way she walked. He definitely wasn't alone. Every male head moved in synchronized rhythm as Candel sashayed by, casting out smiles like welcome sunbeams in the fog.

"Buff is right," Dominique remarked as his gaze lingered on Candel's shapely derriere. "You ought to marry her. Not only can she brew a good cup of coffee, but she would also quench a few other thirsts."

Just as Dominique brought his cup to his lips, Nicolas smiled devilishly. "Beware that you don't drink too deeply, my friend," he advised. "Or have you so quickly forgotten where you first met this woman? She's the one who was dragged to jail for poisoning some poor departed soul's glass of brandy."

Dominique choked on his coffee and spit out a showering spray that stained his rain-dampened cloak.

"Is she guilty or innocent? What do you think, Dominique?" Nicolas snickered as his friend wiped his chin with his sleeve.

Leaving the good-natured Dominique chuckling at being taken in by the joke, Nicolas wandered off to keep an eye on Candel. When she breezed past him with another steaming pot of coffee, he tugged at her ragged sleeve.

"You're just what they needed, marchioness," he murmured quietly. "But I think you knew that before you staged that scene, didn't you?"

Candel peeked up at him from beneath long curly lashes. "And you didn't mind that I made *you* the brunt of *my* jokes?"

Nicolas gave his dark head a shake. "Nay. You gave the soldiers food for thought in the process. You reminded them that they were there for me and that I was there for them. They all needed inspiration, knowing what tomorrow will bring.''

He stared across the distance that separated the Americans from the British lines. The fog had lifted just enough to reveal the army of redcoats drilling for the inevitable battle. The sound of hammers being used to erect scaling ladders echoed in the twilight.

"It looks to be a brutal battle," Candel mused as she stared at the Americans' fortifications, which had been constructed of boards and cotton bales. "Despite what I've said in hopes of distracting, amusing, and entertaining the men, I'll be praying for you."

With that Candel ambled off, leaving Nicolas to stare pensively after her. She knew that her parting remark was just the inspiration *he* needed on the eve of battle. He chuckled softly and asked himself just how the hell he was going to get along without her for the rest of his life.

The more he thought about it, the more he wondered if it could be done . . .

Chapter 27

Thanks to General Jackson's generosity, Candel had bedded down in the farm house which had become the American's headquarters. Sometime during the night Nicolas had sneaked in through the window to join her. They had shared no more than the warmth and security of each other's arms. His simple gesture of cuddling her protectively against him had touched her heart in ways she hadn't expected. Whether that billy goat of a man realized it or not, he had expressed special affection by not taking her body.

Candel shrugged out of her thoughts and slipped into the gown she had washed before retiring for the night. This was not the time to muddle through thoughts about Nicolas. She needed to provide encouragement and enthusiasm among the ranks before another battle broke out. Although she didn't look her best when she walked outside to serve food and drink to the soldiers, she did look a damned sight better than she had when Tiger retrieved her from the gloomy dungeon of the Cabildo.

Sporting a cheerful smile, Candel breezed out the door. Her beauty and her vivacious spirit brought all activity to a standstill. After watching her for a long moment, the men waved, blessed her with smiles, and tossed a few lighthearted comments at her, which she returned in double measure. Candel's presence, Nicolas observed while he stacked more cotton bales and planks on the embankment, made these crucial hours tolerable.

Nicolas turned his attention back to the makeshift wall that had been erected to hold off the British. Although the fortification was twenty feet thick, it was twenty feet tall in some places and only eight feet tall in others. Nicolas wasn't certain that a wall of cotton would discourage the British. But it was a damned sight better than nothing, he decided as he heaved another bale onto the barricade.

When he turned around he found Candel waiting with a plate of food, a cup of coffee, and an endearing smile that smoothed his troubled soul. "You've become an angel of mercy," he said softly as he began to munch on his meal.

"You must have an unusual idea of angels," Candel replied airily. "I thought I'd been a wee bit impudent in my comments to the other soldiers."

"You've teased them into distraction without overmothering them," he commented between bites. "It seems angels work in mysterious ways, but you're an angel all the same."

When he saw Candel thoughtfully studying the wall of cotton bales, he smiled wryly. "David took on Goliath with only a slingshot. The Americans plan to battle the British with cotton. 'Tis a rather unsettling thought, I'll admit, but you'll be safely tucked in the cellar just in case this wall doesn't hold."

"I've spent two weeks in a dungeon already. I'll not be stuffed underground again," she told him in no uncertain terms. "Perhaps I don't have the skills to fire muskets or cannons, but you can teach me to load rifles for the men."

Nicolas frowned. "Now, Candel . . ."

"Now, Tiger . . ." She used the same intimidating tone and tactic. "I am neither a soldier under your command nor your obedient wife. And even if I were one or the other, I would not allow you to dictate to me. You brought me here and I have chosen to stay. But I refuse to hide like a gunshy rabbit. Where I come from, women stand beside men in battle, even though females are the dominant, more intelligent gender."

"Look around you," Nicolas demanded with an expansive wave of his arm. "Does this look like the place you came from? The natives of Lost Island have been isolated for decades. They haven't had to do battle since the days they fled the butchering of the Spanish in the Indies. You aren't prepared for what's about to happen, I assure you. There's nothing worse than unnecessary heroics. Battle is brutal and bloody—and I don't want you hurt!"

"And I don't want to see you or any other soldier wounded, either," she blared as if he were deaf. "None of you are planning to hide in the cellar and neither shall I!"

Jackson overheard the heated exchange, along with every soldier who was within earshot. In precise strides, he approached the twosome.

"My dear lady," Jackson said in a tone that was a bit too patronizing to suit Candel. "We appreciate your willingness to stand beside us through thick and thick—"

Before he could say *but*, Candel flashed him a sweet smile and cut him off. "Thank you, General. I intend to do just that." Wheeling about, she walked toward Dominique You. "Dominique, you're the artillery and ammunition expert around here. I should like you to teach me to powder the muskets.''

Dominique glanced over Candel's blond head to meet Nicolas's glittering glare and the decisive shake of his head. Candel snapped her fingers in front of Dominique's nose, demanding his absolute attention.

"You do not need permission from Tiger, nor do I. Will you teach me or must I search elsewhere for an instructor?''

Jackson and Tiger stared at Candel's rigid back. That particular part of her anatomy always indicated when she refused to bend or compromise . . . which, Jackson duly noted, did not happen very often.

"Our only other option is binding and gagging her, then dragging her to the cellar,'' Jackson murmured to Nicolas.

"I'll get a rope,'' Nicolas replied.

"Will all of you deprive me of my need to do my part in defending our homes and families?'' She put the question to the army at large. "I would not reject *your* right to fight for *your* freedom.''

Dominique shot another quick glance over Candel's head to Nicolas. His bronzed features were now creased in a pensive frown. The faintest hint of a smile tugged at one corner of his mouth before he inclined his head discreetly.

"As you wish, my lady,'' Dominique replied a moment later. He clutched Candel's arm to lead her toward the stockpile of ammunition and spare rifles. "It isn't wise for me to deny you for fear you might lace my drink with poison.''

"I hardly ever poison drinks before going into battle,'' Candel insisted with a mischievous grin.

"I didn't think you did,'' he assured her with a wink.

390

"And had I known who you were when I saw you at the Cabildo, I would have seen to it that you never set foot in that intolerable rat hole."

"Snake hole, actually," Candel added.

Dominique's thick brows arched in question as he escorted her toward the arsenal. "A long, skinny, black snake?"

"Aye." Candel chortled as she matched the stout privateer step for step. "I saw him swallow two mice during my captivity. He's the only creature there who didn't go hungry."

Dominique peered at the pert beauty teeming with irrepressible spirit. "I like the way you laugh at what you can't change and live with all the rest," Dominique murmured. His smile evaporated as he placed a musket in her waiting hands. "I only hope you can live with what you're destined to see here today. Prepare yourself, Candel. It won't be a sight that's easily forgotten."

Candel tilted her chin to stare him squarely in the eye. "I'll manage, Dominique. I'll manage . . ."

The privateer surveyed her for a long moment before nodding his head. "Aye, I do believe you will." He clutched a sack of gun powder and set to work teaching Candel to load the muskets quickly and efficiently.

"I hope she knows what she's doing," Jackson murmured half-aloud while he watched Candel follow Dominique's instructions.

"Never fear," Nicolas assured the general. "Candel Caron knew exactly what she was doing when she debated with me and then made sure her comments were heard by every man within shouting distance. She was assuring one and all that she had the utmost confidence in their ability to repel attack. She was also providing them with the extra incentive to protect her as well as themselves,

391

and those loved ones who remain in the city." Nicolas never took his eyes off the shapely blonde who was listening intently to Dominique's every word. "That woman's intelligence and insight astound me."

Jackson pondered Tiger's assessment of Candel's actions and then grinned. "I do believe your first mate is right. You really should marry that woman. I know from firsthand experience that a wife's unwavering devotion and support are rare blessings." He half-turned to survey his army of "dirty shirts," as the British mockingly referred to them. "I intend to see that my wife still has a husband when this battle is over. She will also have a country that stands for freedom." His gaze drifted into the distance and his thoughts focused on the battle ahead. "Prepare your men, Tiger. The British are coming . . ."

At six o'clock, just as dawn paled the sky, a British rocket soared across the space that separated the enemy troops. A human wall of red-coated soldiers moved across the frost-white field of sugar cane stubble. From the cypress swamp that bordered one edge of the flat plain to the levee on the river which formed the other boundary, seasoned British regulars marched sixty men abreast in closed ranks, keeping precise rhythm with the pounding of their drums.

Candel fumbled her attempt to pour gunpowder into the barrel of the musket which she was in the process of loading when the American cannons exploded like thunder, ripping openings in the red columns of soldiers who marched toward them. Despite the British belief that European fighting customs could win battles anywhere, Candel scorned the tactics as a preposterous waste of human life.

She swallowed back the feeling of nausea that rose in her throat when bodies fell beneath the cannonade. In spite of the fallen soldiers, the British were relentless with their pomp and pageantry. Staring certain death in the face, they continued to advance and closed in around the fallen ranks. Candel felt a shudder of dread slither through her when the well-precisioned army marched within two hundred yards of the line of waiting American rifles. Jackson had ordered the core of his infantry to hold their fire until the British became easy targets. Only five small batteries of men, commanded by Dominique You and Nicolas Tiger and three other officers, blasted away at the enemy from their crude barricades.

A sense of panic overwhelmed Candel when British gunfire set the cotton bales ablaze. She held her breath and prayed nonstop while Tiger and his men scrambled from their protected positions to drag the burning bales away before the entire fortification exploded in flames.

Again the cannons roared and rifles cracked in the cold December air. The British refused to abandon the battle plans until the devastating number of fatalities broke their spirit. When the redcoats were at close range, Jackson gave the order for his front line to take aim at the V of the British cross-belts.

When Jackson shouted "Fire!" at the top of his lungs, it looked to Candel as if the entire embankment had burst into flame. The deafening explosion sounded like the rifle cracks of a gigantic firing squad. The end result was just as deadly. Behind the first lines, a second battalion fired in relays, giving the stunned British soldiers the impression the Americans were equipped with some strange kind of reloading rifles. Little did the British know that Candel was blistering her fingers on hot muskets, frantically loading the weapons and sending them down the line.

The sickening sight of so many fallen redcoats caused

Candel to grimace as she glanced up from her task to monitor the battle. Some of the redcoats had broken from their ranks to flee, even while the officers on horseback drove the men with a vengeance, slapping the reluctant ones with the flat side of their swords.

Candel cringed again when the league of Scottish Highlanders, bagpipes wailing and plaid kilts flopping, marched across the meadow of death in drilled military precision. Under Jackson's order, the American lines fired again, as if one man, one weapon had been triggered by a single impulse. A sickening groan tumbled from Candel's lips when the mournful sound of bagpipes died into deathly silence and men pitched forward on the ground to build a human bridge over which the trailing infantry walked.

If Candel had been in command of the enemy troops, she would have raised a white flag and waved it in defeat. The British death toll had climbed into the hundreds. Instead of acknowledging a battle lost, the British General Pakenham sent a company of West Indian Negroes forward with their scaling ladders. The solid sheet of flame that rolled from the muzzles of American rifles like a holocaust spelled impending doom.

Candel turned away from the firing lines when the enemy was cut down, as if a gigantic fire-breathing dragon had unleashed its fury on them. The soldiers who survived were devastated by the gruesome sight. They scattered in frantic confusion, despite the bellows of officers who tried to order them back into formation. Only when General Sir Edward Pakenham himself fell mortally wounded in an attempt to rally his scattering forces did the survivors retreat.

When the smoke lifted from the breezeless battlefield two hours later, Candel was appalled by the magnitude of victory and the devastation of life. Hundreds of wounded redcoats stumbled forward to give themselves up. Candel once again became an angel of mercy, just as Nicolas had claimed she was. Compassion put wings on her feet as she dashed onto the battlefield, determined to do what she could for the wounded. The stench of death filled her nostrils and put tears in her eyes, but she was driven to comfort those who suffered in ways she knew she would never fully comprehend.

Frantically, she ripped pieces from her petticoats and gown to stop profuse bleeding. Wiping tears from her eyes, Candel found Nicolas beside her. His face was smeared with splatters of mud and soot from exploding rifles. His expression was grim and yet filled with concern for her and the prisoners who begged for relief from their pain.

Nicolas battled back the tangled emotions that swirled inside him while he watched Candel administer first aid to the wounded and dying. Although her hands and lips trembled, she greeted each tortured face with a reassuring smile and a soothing voice. He was certain that those who survived, and maybe even those who didn't, would long remember this golden-haired angel of mercy who did everything within her power to ease the enemy's plight.

While Candel and Nicolas were concentrating on their ministrations, Jackson sat upon his steed, watching the British retreat. With a tired sigh, he turned back to congratulate his men. Although impossibly outnumbered, the Americans had engaged in the kind of strategic battle for which the orderly ranks of British had no defense. Jackson had lost only thirteen men while the English casualties numbered twenty-six hundred.

Candel found it difficult to calculate the amount of

time she spent tending the seriously wounded who didn't have the strength to retreat to their ships. She worked feverishly until she collapsed in exhaustion. Two weeks of indigestible meals and confinement in a dreary dungeon had finally caught up with her, not to mention the grim sight of the dead and wounded on the battlefield. Candel suddenly wilted in a faint before she even had time to realize the world had turned as black as pitch.

"Good God," Nicolas muttered as he stared down at the disheveled woman collapsed at his feet. "You never did know when to quit, did you?"

The wounded British soldier whom she had been tending glanced up at Nicolas with a pained grimace. "What's this angel's name?" he rasped.

Nicolas kneeled to finish fastening the bandage around the man's leg. "Candel," he murmured. "I do believe she's been burning from both ends for so long that her flame went out." He patted the soldier's shoulder and offered him an encouraging smile, just as Candel would have if she hadn't keeled over in exhaustion. "But don't fret. She'll be up and around again in no time, just as you will be, too."

After scooping her up in his arms, Nicolas strode toward the farm house to put Candel to bed. With a fond smile he peered down at her face, which was covered with mud. It could have done with a good scrubbing, but Nicolas wasn't about to rouse Candel when she was in dire need of rest. Now that other citizens from New Orleans had come to offer aid to the fallen British, Candel could be spared, even if she didn't think she could.

Nicolas hadn't been able to bear a grudge against the British, and neither had Candel nor the American soldiers. It seemed as if they had been fighting a group force, not the individuals themselves. In past battles where hatred and cruelty drove him and his men at their enemy with a fiendish vengeance, Nicolas had been forced to kill or be killed with murderous intensity. But the Battle of New Orleans was like nothing he'd ever experienced. With perfect military precision the British had bravely walked into a bloodbath. He pitied those poor souls who were too proud and stubborn to change their ways . . .

Nicolas missed a step as he plodded across the porch, very nearly hurling himself and his unconscious cargo across the wooden planks. The British soldiers had been so set in their ways after their European wars against Napoleon that they had refused to switch tactics to counter the Americans' strategy. And he, fool that he was, had been too stubborn and set in his ways to change tactics when dealing with an unconventional female who roared into his life like a flaming cannonball, blasting holes in his defense. He, like the British, had been subjected to absolute defeat. Nicolas knew it for certain when he stared down into that bewitching face that appeared so often in his dreams, even when he valiantly denied his tender feelings to the bitter end.

Aye, he certainly hadn't planned it. He had marched confidently forward, just as the British had. He'd been so sure he wouldn't fall victim to Cupid's arrow. But Cupid had struck with the same devastating force as the American firing line. Candel had hit him right between the eyes and squarely through the heart. Of course, he'd been too blind to see what was happening to him until it was long past too late. He had been so busy denying his emotions that love had sneaked up on him from all directions at once!

Of course, nothing had changed, Nicolas reminded himself. He still wasn't an appropriate match for a titled heiress because of his background. But logic hadn't kept his carefully guarded heart from attacking his wary cynicism from within. And sure enough, he'd wound up falling for this rambunctious misfit with the saucy smiles and sharp tongue. She had touched that one vulnerable corner of his heart and crumbled the foundations of his soul. Tenderness had taken root in him until his need, desire, and affection for her coursed through every fiber of his being.

"Is Candel all right?" Buff queried when Nicolas shouldered his way through the front door. His scrutinizing gaze rose from Candel's waxen features to Tiger's stunned expression. "Hell, forget this little firecracker. I know she'll survive, just as she always does. Are *you* all right, Tiger? You don't look well at all."

The remark drew stares from the congregation of men gathered in the parlor. Jean and Pierre Lafitte were there, along with Dominique You, Claiborne, and General Jackson. They all paused with drinks in hand to survey the cryptic expression on Tiger's rugged face.

"Nay, I'm not all right," Nicolas confessed as he carried Candel toward the bedroom where she had spent the previous night. "I just engaged in another battle and I'm sorry to report I wasn't on the winning side."

When he disappeared into the back room, Buff turned to stare bemusedly at the other men. "What the devil do you suppose that meant?" he asked.

"You ought to know, Buff," Jean replied with a sly grin. "After all, you're the one who's been telling Tiger he's been fighting a lost cause with the marchioness."

"Indeed," Dominique snickered, his dark eyes twinkling with mischief. "I would say Tiger's been burning on a bright flame and it has just dawned on him that he's never going to be able to put this particular fire out." He lifted his glass to toast the occupants of the back room. "To Tiger and the fire Candel set within him."

"Well, I'll be damned . . ." Buff croaked. "Do you really think—?"

"Aye," Jackson confirmed. "Cupid's flaming arrow struck me on a flatboat bound for Natchez. I went along to protect Rachel from the maniac she had first married." He sank down in his chair and glanced back through the window of time to the incident that had brought him and Rachel together. "Lewis Robards had ordered Rachel out of their house in one of his many fits of jealous rage. She returned to her mother's boarding house where I was staying in Nashville. When Lewis came to beg forgiveness in one of his saner moments, his suspicious eye and unfounded accusations fell on me. He and I came dangerously close to a duel. When he vowed to carry Rachel off by force and punish her for indiscretions she hadn't committed, she feared for her life and decided to flee to Natchez. And that's where my noble intentions ran amuck and Cupid struck."

Jackson calmly sipped his brandy before continuing the tale that had sent rumors flying about his so-called sordid affair with Rachel Robards. "During the long journey, that which Lewis Robards had imagined and what I suppose I had refused to admit to myself all along, came true. I fell hopelessly in love with Rachel, despite the obstacles between us. After we reached Natchez, we received the news that Lewis had divorced Rachel. I asked for her hand in marriage, only to discover later that lunatic Lewis had merely voiced the announcement in one of his wild rages and he hadn't followed through with the divorce proceedings."

"And what did you do when you discovered you were

wed to a married woman?'' Nicolas asked as he pushed away from the doorjamb where he had been listening.

"I did the only thing a man could do when he's in love,'' Jackson replied without batting an eyelash. "I married Rachel a second time, after that imbecile Robards finally did as he claimed he had done two years earlier.''

"And the moral of that story—'' Buff declared, focusing intently on Tiger, "—is that you should marry the marchioness before some other eager knave weds her first and complicates matters.''

"Wise advice,'' Jackson agreed. "I told myself I was only doing the noble thing by defending and protecting Rachel from that madman she had consented to marry without really knowing him at all. And I assured myself that I only accompanied her to Natchez to ensure her safety from river pir—'' He glanced at Jean Lafitte, remembering that Candel had insisted that the word *pirate* be stricken from his vocabulary while in a privateer's presence. "Protect her from river robbers,'' he amended with a sly smile. "I was too stubborn to face the real reason I had accompanied her.''

Jackson focused his intense gaze on Tiger. "Sometimes, my friend, a good soldier has to know when to accept defeat,'' he said philosophically.

"Well, it will probably kill me to admit it to her,'' Nicolas muttered as his gaze strayed toward the bedroom. "I've never said any such thing to a female in all my life. 'Tis difficult enough just to discuss my feelings with the lot of you!''

That was an understatement if ever there was one. Nicolas felt horribly awkward standing there revealing his innermost emotions to this group of men. He had never found himself involved in such a personal conversation. He had always kept his private feelings to himself.

"Perhaps you should practice on her while she's asleep," Pierre suggested with a snicker.

"I'd let you practice on me," Dominique teased, "but imagine how my wife would react if she got wind of it."

Nicolas was not amused by the playful taunts directed toward him. "A marchioness and a bastard's son with a price on his head?" he questioned with a distasteful snort. " 'Tis not exactly what one could call a match made in heaven."

"And what about a match between a bigamist of a wife and a rakehell who supposedly defied the lawful bounds of matrimony to seduce a wedded woman?" Jackson queried scornfully. "I've lived with those nasty rumors wherever I go. But I can tolerate them so long as I have Rachel's love and devotion. And you can rest assured that before long you and the Lafittes will not be considered criminals in any state of this nation. You will never be labeled as outlaws again, but rather courageous heroes. I'll see to that, Tiger."

"And you can also rest assured that you and the Lafittes will be requested to attend the Victory Ball in New Orleans," Governor Claiborne piped up. "You'll be honored guests. It seems to me, Tiger, that you have no excuses left. In fact, I might just put a reward on your head if you *don't* marry that remarkable young lady."

"Claiborne is just the man who can do it, too," Jean razzed his one-time enemy.

"Knowing this wily rascal, Jean will probably increase the price, just for the sport of it," Claiborne retorted.

While the officers filed out to oversee the gloomy tasks that followed battle, Nicolas helped himself to a drink . . . or three. Despite Jackson's moral support—and it sounded as if the general had endured plenty of difficulty

401

in his romantic affairs—Nicolas still had serious reservations. What if Candel had gotten over her fascination for him? What if her grandfather became outraged at the thought of a commoner marrying his only true heir? What if she were subjected to the same painful ridicule Rachel had suffered because of vicious gossip? What if . . . ?

Nicolas threw down another drink. Curse it, he'd never been so unsure of himself in all his born days. The thought of admitting he loved Candel like hell on fire was as unsettling as the prospect of stripping naked and tramping down the streets of New Orleans! He had never said those three words—ever!

What did he have to offer Candel now? The raid on Barataria had destroyed his home and possessions—just as it had demolished the Lafittes' belongings, which had been confiscated by American authorities. Chances of recovering the property and valuables were slim. No doubt Nicolas would be ridiculed as a fortune hunter if he asked for Candel's hand when he had nothing left but a schooner and a babbling parrot that chirped "Hello, Candel" every other minute! There was nothing about him that Candel could be proud of—not his background, not his breeding, not his previous occupation as a privateer.

"Well, damn," Nicolas muttered, tossing another drink down his gullet. All he had to offer the Marchioness de Caron was his love. His pride and dignity kept insisting that love wasn't enough.

Nicolas had always considered charity something worthy and honorable . . . until he found himself on the receiving end. Accept money from a wealthy heiress? The very thought of living off Candel's fortune sent a shudder through him. By God, he couldn't do it! Jackson was obviously a better sport than Nicolas was. He wasn't sure he could endure the ridicule and snide innuendo from the upper crust, whom he had always loathed. He would be itching to challenge every smart-mouthed aristocrat to a duel.

If he had any sense at all, he would pack up and leave before Candel awoke. Nicolas swallowed down another gulp of brandy and tried to convince himself that he still had some common sense left . . .

Chapter 28

After what seemed like a decade-long nap, Candel pried her eyes open to find herself staring at the ceiling of the bedroom in Jackson's field headquarters. She felt years older after witnessing the historic battle that sent the British limping back to their frigates in the Gulf. Forcing herself to sit upright, she rolled off the bed and strolled into the parlor to find the house abandoned. When she stepped outside, a saddled mount awaited her. Instinctively, her gaze swept the meadow in hopes of seeing Nicolas among the soldiers who had remained behind to tend the casualties.

It looked as if Tiger had performed his vanishing act without bothering to say good-bye before he walked out of her life—again. She was learning to expect that from him. Resolutely, Candel hoisted herself into the saddle and guided the steed toward Caron Plantation. Along the way she encountered many soldiers returning from the field. But still no Tiger. Wherever he was, he obviously had no intention of seeing her.

The reception Candel received at the plantation did much to lift her sagging spirits. Gustave looked like a new man—at least more like the one she remembered from childhood. Although he was still too weak to walk around the house under his own power, there was heightened color in his cheeks, a lively sparkle in his eyes, and a smile on his lips.

After Candel gave her grandfather an affectionate hug, Gustave's smile disappeared. "And just where have you been so long, young lady?" he asked in that authoritative tone she recalled from days gone by.

Candel glanced quickly at Nathaniel, who stood behind the wheelchair, silently prompting her. "There's been a war going on," she reminded Gustave in a loud voice as her gaze settled on Nathaniel, who was pantomiming the act of wrapping bandages around imaginary wounds on his arms. "I've been tending the wounded."

Little did the old servant know it was no lie.

"On the battlefield?" Gustave queried anxiously.

"Aye," Candel assured him with a grin. "That's usually where wounds are sustained."

"Nathaniel told me that's where you'd gone, but I refused to believe him," Gustave grumbled. " 'Tis no place for a woman."

"A woman's place is wherever she decides it is."

Gustave peered into the lovely face he had long believed to be lost to him forever. "Aye, my little Candel," he said, his voice wobbling with sentimentality. "I suppose it is. After what you've been through this last decade, it seems you have more than earned the right to name your place. 'Tis only that, having lost you once, I cannot bear the thought of losing you again. You're all I have left."

Candel felt a mist of tender emotion cloud her eyes as she stared at her grandfather's wrinkled features. How she wished Tiger felt such fondness for her. She had

Gustave's unconditional love but she would never earn that from Tiger. She *had* to let him go. Her life was here with Gustave and she had to learn to be satisfied with it.

When Candel excused herself to bathe and change, Gustave reached out a gnarled hand to detain her. "Do you have the faintest idea what's been going on with André these days?" He glanced at Nathaniel and frowned. "I've just recently been informed of Yvonne's death. I realize André is beside himself, but he's been storming in and out like a madman. What's the matter with him?"

Well, at least André had been considerate enough not to tell Gustave he had sent her to prison, Candel thought. Of course, André would probably hit the ceiling when he realized she had escaped . . . or perhaps that knowledge was what had made him so angry . . .

André hit the ceiling much sooner than Candel had anticipated. When she turned around she heard his furious growl echoing in the foyer. It seemed her cousin was determined to make a scene, even at Gustave's expense. Curse the man!

"You!" André raged as he stalked into the parlor. "I've turned this town upside down trying to find you. But don't think I won't have you arrested again, murderess!"

"Murderess?" The color drained from Gustave's cheeks. He had no trouble hearing André's words, since the man had all but shouted them. "André, curb your tongue," the marquis snapped. " 'Tis a preposterous accusation. And what is this business about Candel being arrested?"

His probing gaze riveted on Candel. It was no use— she was forced to confess the truth. And if the explanation caused a setback in Gustave's condition, she would poison André's drink, and with plenty of malice and forethought! She had definitely spoken too soon and had given André far more credit than he deserved. Obviously, the only reason he hadn't approached Gustave before now was that he'd been too busy trying to find her. He didn't have the decency to speak to her in private, away from Gustave, who had just set foot on the road to recovery.

"In André's extreme duress, he leaped to the erroneous conclusion that I was responsible for Yvonne's death," Candel explained without taking her eyes off her fuming cousin. "She died from an overdose of the same poison she'd been sprinkling on your food."

Gustave gasped in disbelief and his wide eyes swung to André.

"I had no knowledge of Yvonne's treachery," André insisted. "And although I was infuriated by Yvonne's subterfuge, Candel spitefully repaid my foolish wife by lacing her drink with poison."

"I did no such thing!" Candel loudly protested and then counted to ten in hopes of controlling her flaming temper. "I think the dark-cloaked man I saw sneaking from Yvonne's chambers was responsible for her demise."

"Ah, of course," André smirked, refusing to accept her explanation. "A dark phantom? What a flimsy excuse, Candeliera. How is it that no one else can corroborate your preposterous story?"

"There's one person who can," Candel shot back, thoroughly disgusted with her cousin for putting Gustave through this emotional ordeal.

André eyed her coldly. "And who might that be, my dear cousin?"

The fact that Tiger hadn't actually seen the dark-cloaked stranger at the mansion or the Cabildo was unbeknownst to André, and she preferred to keep it that way. Candel hoped the announcement would shut him up nonetheless. "Nicolas Tiger."

"Tiger!" André exclaimed. "The infamous pirate who robs unsuspecting vessels and then sells the booty at outrageous prices in the swamps? With his lack of credibility, you'd be laughed out of court if you called him as a witness."

The shock of hearing of the events surrounding Yvonne's death and the possibility of an embarrassing court battle caused all color to ebb from Gustave's features.

Cursing under her breath, Candel waved André away. "I ordered you out of this house for conspiring with Yvonne. Now get out, André. Even if I'm marched off to prison again for a crime I most certainly didn't commit, you'll never get your hands on the Caron fortune. I'd sooner give it away!"

"And I'd sooner let her." Gustave leaned forward in his wheelchair, even though his face had turned white and his body trembled from overexertion. "You have already enjoyed eleven years at my expense. It seems to me you're all too eager to accuse Candel of the crime so you'll be in charge of my investments."

"I'm eager to see justice served because Candeliera is guilty!" André thundered, his face purple with rage. "She killed my wife! Do you think I'll forgive her for that? That would be an insult to Yvonne's memory. I will not and cannot let Candeliera go scot-free. She must be punished!"

"Get out," Candel hissed when Gustave half-collapsed, struggling to catch his breath.

André stared at the old man for a long moment, then

glared at Candel. Their eyes locked like clenched fists. His chest still heaving with indignation, André turned a stiff about-face and stormed out.

"I'll take care of the marquis," Nathaniel volunteered. "Go on upstairs and rest, Miz Candel. After all you've been through you deserve a decent night's sleep. I'll have Geraldine send up yer supper tray and prepare yer bath."

Nodding appreciatively, Candel ascended the steps. Ah, how simple life had been on the island where disputes were relatively easy to solve and bloody battles no longer existed. Since Nicolas had whisked her from Lost Island, she had dealt with dozens of unfamiliar incidents and emotions. But she had to admit she loved being in the thick of things. But she couldn't seem to come to terms with the unrequited love she felt for Tiger. The man had taken up permanent residence in her heart. She was never going to fall in love again, Candel promised herself. Once was enough—and she was never putting herself through it again!

"Hello, Candel."

"Shut up, featherhead," Nicolas growled as he flung Jolly Roger a glare. The very last thing he needed at the moment was to hear Candel's name echoing around the room.

"Where's the rotgut?" Roger's question was accompanied by a fluff of feathers and several piercing wolf whistles.

Mechanically, Nicolas ambled over to the liquor cabinet in the cottage at Chênière Caminada. Tormented by his thoughts, Nicolas poured himself and Roger a drink.

The creak of the cabinet door caused the parrot to emit one more *Hello, Candel*, followed by Nicolas's muttered curses.

It was a conspiracy, Nicolas decided. Not only were his friends and acquaintances heckling him about that violet-eyed beauty, but so was the damned parrot. Everywhere Nicolas went there were constant reminders. She had even intruded on the battlefield because he had constantly been aware of her presence, and was determined to protect her in case disaster struck. Watching her stride across the field to offer compassion to the wounded enemy had touched him in ways he hadn't expected. Her very presence had provided moral support and inspiration to the American forces before, during, and after the battle.

Despite her feisty temperament, Candel was a caring, demonstrative, totally unpretentious individual who could accept responsibility and make quick, intelligent decisions. In Nicolas's opinion, there wasn't another woman in the world who could compare to her. She had amazing resilience and a fierce, independent nature—to name only two of her lovable characteristics.

Nicolas nursed his drink while Roger chattered and sipped his grog. Hours ago, Nicolas had left Candel to manage on her own. He had stifled the urge to ride off to New Orleans and pound some sense into André for even thinking Candel had been responsible for his wife's death. For all André knew, it might have been an accidental poisoning that wasn't meant for Yvonne. But Nicolas knew full well that Candel preferred to take care of herself without his interference. Any further involvement in her life would make it even more difficult for Nicolas to back away. She was and always would be better off without him . . .

"Hello, Candel."

Jolly Roger announced Buff's arrival. A look of disappointment crossed Buff's face when he spied Nicolas sitting alone in the cottage. Citizens of Barataria and New Orleans were celebrating what had become known as an Old Hickory Victory. War heroes had turned out in the streets in droves, and Buff had hoped Tiger had been celebrating the victory by admitting his affection for Candel. So much for Buff's hopes.

"So here sits the coward," Buff said as he ambled over to pour himself a brandy. "You didn't tell her you loved her, did you? I wondered if you had the courage to face Candel with your true feelings. Obviously you didn't."

Nicolas flashed his long-time friend an aggravated glance. "I have nothing to offer the marchioness," he reminded Buff. "Perhaps she's been away from society for a decade, but she would be quick to understand how it felt to be snubbed if she wound up with a husband or suitor like me. I'd ruin her chances for respectability."

Buff was quiet for a long moment. Only the sound of Jolly Roger's occasional chirp and squawk broke the silence. Buff had sworn never to repeat the story he had seen unfold almost thirty years earlier, because it would only have caused hard feelings. Nicolas would have tortured himself for no good reason that Buff could see. But these feelings of inferiority which Nicolas harbored were unfounded and they had to stop! Tiger was a far better man than he gave himself credit for. Those to whom Buff had promised silence and discretion were gone and he alone was the keeper of certain secrets. Perhaps the time had come for Tiger to hear the tale—it might make a difference in his life if Tiger's heart was in the right place. Buff was determined to know if it was.

"Do you love her, Tiger?"

Nicolas spoke not one word. He merely stared at the contents of his glass.

"I asked you if you love her," Buff persisted. "Answer me."

Nicolas sighed deeply. "Aye," he admitted, though most reluctantly.

"Then say it," Buff insisted. "Say the words. I want to hear them loud and clear. I want to hear you say you love her, despite all obstacles, despite everything you believe and feel!"

"What sort of torture is this?" Nicolas muttered sourly.

"Just say it, you stubborn fool. I need to know if you truly mean it."

Nicolas glanced at Buff who had leaned forward on the edge of his seat, anxiously waiting for a forthright answer. For some unexplainable reason, Buff seemed determined to hear words of love from Tiger's lips. As if that would change anything, thought Nicolas. Well, hell, if it meant so much to the old coot, Nicolas would say the words. He didn't give a damn about anything anymore.

"Aye, I love Candel." The word felt strange on his tongue and even stranger to his ears. *Love* had been the only four-letter word that *didn't* pass Tiger's lips on occasion. "I love her enough not to tell her. I love her enough not to give her hope for something that cannot be. I love her enough to let her go, Buff. But if you start badgering me again, I swear I'll—"

Buff threw up his hand to deter Nicolas. "Sit back in your chair, Tiger. I have a story to tell you."

"I'm not in the mood for one of your homespun yarns, Buff," Nicolas groused. "I said what you wanted to hear, though why it was so imperative that you know how I feel about Candel I'll never know." With an enormous sigh he gulped down his drink. "Just leave me be."

Buff had no intention of leaving Tiger be. Now that he was sure of Tiger's deep feelings for Candel, he could tell his story. Tiger's admission guaranteed that this emotions were based purely on the whispers of his heart and the longings in his soul. Tiger had come to understand the meaning of love. Now he could know the truth that had been kept from him all his life.

"I'm sure you don't recall much about the first years of your life," Buff began, causing Nicolas to stare at him in bewilderment. "You weren't American-born as you'd been told. The first four years of your life were spent with your parents, enjoying all the luxuries of the nobility in France."

That certainly got Nicolas's attention. He slumped back in his chair as if he'd received a devastating blow. His mouth opened but he said nothing. It was true that he had no recollections of his early childhood. He had been told that he had been born in the poor sector of New Orleans and he had also known what his mother had done to earn a meager living for him and his grandmother. What Buff was saying was in direct contrast to all Nicolas had believed. The comments had caught him completely off guard and commanded his undivided attention, just as Buff hoped they would.

"It was the time of the French revolt," Buff continued after he lubricated his vocal cords with a sip of brandy. "The expenses France had incurred to help fight the American Revolution used up all the funds in the King's treasury, which had been on the verge of bankruptcy before the war. When the peasants rebelled against Louis

413

XVI's devastating tax policies and his effort to squelch their bid for freedom, disaster struck the feudal lords and nobility. Although your father had the foresight to know his life and that of his family was in grave danger, he tried to create a working compromise between the King and the commoners. He had already witnessed the execution of many of the noblemen who had also served as the King's ministers. Rumors were even spreading that King Louis XVI and Queen Marie Antoinette would be beheaded for betraying the country. Conditions began to crumble very rapidly in France.''

Buff took another sip of brandy and watched Nicolas sink a little deeper into his chair. Even Jolly Roger had ceased his babbling and remained calm on his perch. ''The King tried to escape with his family but he was recognized at Varennes and dragged back to Paris. The radical leaders of the revolution used the King's thwarted escape attempt to arouse the suspicion and anger of the commoners. Stories spread that Louis was plotting against France with his ministers, many of whom had already fled to other countries. The revolutionists sent out spies to ensure those who had left the country before they could be executed would not plot to destroy the new regime.''

Nicolas leaned out to grab the nearby bottle and poured himself another drink. He wasn't sure he should believe what Buff was telling him, considering the old buzzard could spin a wild yarn better than anybody he knew. And yet . . .

''Your father made arrangements to escape, as did the other noblemen who had been threatened,'' Buff went on to say, drawing Nicolas from his pensive musings. ''Stéphane Rouchaud made plans for his wife Colette, his young son, and himself to sail to New France or the merchantman which was under my command. But disaster struck on the eve of their planned departure. Peasants stormed the manor and there was no time to gather supplies or belongings and flee. Like so many other noblemen of the Reign of Terror, Stéphane was executed without mercy. But his last deed exemplified his courage. He provided a very important distraction while he battled the score of peasants, buying precious time for those he loved to make their escape.''

Nicolas swallowed his brandy and gulped hard. Buff was painting a ghastly picture. The fact that Nicolas had just taken part in a bloody battle made it far too easy to imagine the scene Buff described.

"You and your mother owed your life to Stéphane and to the devoted maid who gathered peasants' garb and concealed your identity before she whisked you through the angry mob. The terrorists stole everything of worth while they searched the chambers for you and Colette. They confiscated food, furniture, jewels, and wine before they set a torch to the manor and burned it to the ground. The fact that Marquise Colette had escaped with her young son outraged Maurice Sartre, who led the mob to the manor. According to what I had been told, Maurice had been dismissed from Stéphane's services and severely punished because he had forced his attentions on your mother. Maurice wanted more than a rebellion—he wanted personal revenge. When he failed to locate your mother, he was furious. He had fully intended to make Marquise Colette his mistress and behead her son.''

Buff peered somberly at Nicolas. "When I saw your mother come aboard that night with her maid, she was hysterical and overwrought with such anguish and grief that I wasn't sure she would survive the long journey at sea. She was a beautiful but very delicate woman. The

415

unspeakable horrors she had witnessed broke her spirit and totally devastated her.''

Nicolas's blue eyes bore into Buff's weather-beaten face. ''She didn't survive, did she, Buff?''

Buff sighed deeply, as if he had just dropped a heavy burden that had weighed him down for years. ''Nay, Tiger, she didn't. She had already endured the death of one of her brothers and a sister who had been carted off to the guillotine. Watching her husband being beaten and mutilated by a mob sent her over the edge. It was the maid, Hélène, whom you were led to believe was your grandmother, who brought you to New Orleans. The fortune and the property which was to be yours were gone and so was your family. Hélène was afraid for her own life as well as yours. She had been branded a traitor to the cause when she aided in the escape.''

''My God . . .'' was all Nicolas could think to say. He was thunderstruck by the gruesome tale.

''Hélène was desperate to save you and herself from the spies who had been sent out to find you. Colette had told Hélène that they were to make contact with one of the noblemen who had fled France before the crux of the blood bath began, but she was never given the name of the family who offered assistance.'' Buff gazed at Nicolas, imagining how very different his life would have been if Hélène had been able to make contact with the family who had offered assistance to the Rouchauds. ''Hélène was most hesitant to ask questions in New Orleans for fear word would reach Maurice Sartre in France. Since she was unable to make contact she sought work to support the both of you. All she could find was the job of a maid in a lowly bordello.''

Nicolas frowned. ''But who was the woman whom

416

believed to be my mother, the one who gave me her name? Or was it just an alias that Hélène dreamed up?"

"The woman who became your mother was no more than a young French girl whom Hélène had taken pity on during a serious crisis in her own life. Cecile agreed to the ruse to return the favor to your so-called grandmother, though Cecile was never told the reason for the mysterious request. When Hélène became gravely ill, she sent a message to me in hopes that I would honor her plea to take you in and raise you. I alone knew the secret she had refused to share with anyone in New Orleans.

"It was no accident that Cecile was ordered to bring you to me. I did what I could to make a man of you. I taught you all I could about the sea so you could have a life of your own. And when you had learned your lessons well and had received the best education I could provide, I stepped down to let you take control of the ship. You became the son I never had, Tiger," Buff said with a sentimental smile. "I don't know what happened to Cecile Tiger after she brought you to me. But if you resented her lack of emotion toward you, it was because she was only fulfilling an obligation to a kind-hearted old woman. You are not a bastard's son, but rather the son of a titled lord who met his death during the cruel Reign of Terror."

"Why didn't you tell me this years ago?"

Buff stared him squarely in the eye. "So you could grow up bitter about the violent tragedy that befell your family and stripped you of your title and wealth? Why, Tiger? So you could stomp through life with a chip on your shoulder, thinking the world owed you a big favor instead of pulling yourself up by your boot straps and making your own way by your strong will, talents, and strength of character?"

417

Buff gave his wiry red head a somber shake. "Nay, Tiger. I couldn't do that to you. There are far too many men like André Caron who slide by on a name and never develop the initiative to make something of themselves. André is a leech. He survives only because of the strength of a well-known name. Had I told you the truth, you would have spent your youth wishing for something that was lost and gone forever instead of taking control of your life and your destiny. Now I can tell you the truth of your heritage because Maurice Sartre is dead and most folks prefer to forget those years of stark terror. You are already a man of character and you have earned respect from others because of what you are, not what you might have been if your family had survived."

After a long moment of silence, Buff peered solemnly at Nicolas. "Now history has repeated itself. All your worldly possessions were destroyed by the invasion of Barataria." Buff leaned forward, demanding Nicolas's absolute attention. "Tell me this, Tiger. Are your worldly possessions, and your lost title and fortune you have just discovered you once had, more important than what you feel for Candel Caron? Do you love her less because her family fled France before it was too late? Do you resent what she's got that you haven't?"

"Of course not," Nicolas answered. "What I feel for her has nothing to do with fortunes gained or lost."

That was exactly what Buff hoped he would say. Tiger cared for all the right reasons. Now all Buff had to do was clear away the last of Tiger's excuses and make him realize that his affection for Candel was all that truly mattered.

"The fact is that the only real difference between you and Candel is that her grandfather pulled up stakes and left France to begin life in New Orleans before he lost his possessions—and his life. Do you begrudge his foresight since your father remained in France to the bitter end, hoping to save his native country from revolution?''

"Nay," Nicolas answered. "One man was wise and conscientious and the other bold and courageous. Gustave Caron suffered in his own way, especially if his family's death at sea was related to the French Revolution, as some have speculated.''

"Aye, Gustave has lived through his own hell on earth, even if he managed to hold onto his fortune and put down roots in New France," Buff agreed. "And, no doubt, Gustave would have gladly given away all he had if he could have had his family back. His love for them was all that really mattered.''

"What is your point, Buff?"

"The point is money means nothing without loved ones to share it," Buff declared with perfect assurance. "Now take a good long look at Candel, who spent her life on an island with primitives. She had no concern for her lost title and fortune. She learned to live with money and without it in two drastically different cultures. Because of her contrasting experiences, she can function quite satisfactorily in most any situation. She came to feel something for you, despite your notorious profession as a privateer. 'Tis the man you are that made you something special to her. Even your bitterness toward all females, because of what you were led to believe, didn't affect her feelings for you. Indeed, Tiger, you're lucky to be alive at all and most fortunate that such a remarkable woman cares so much for you that she was willing to let you go because she thought that was what *you* wanted most.''

"But even if I came from prime stock, I have nothing to give a marchioness,'' Nicolas insisted.

Buff had talked until he was blue in the face, un-earthing ghosts from the past in order to make Tiger see the light. But that muleheaded moron still couldn't let go of his damnable pride! "Damn it, Tiger, you can give Candel the only thing she really wants—your love! And even if you're too foolish to set your pride aside and follow your heart, don't you think Candel at least de-serves to know that you truly care for her? She had the courage to love you, even when you built walls between you! Where's *your* courage, Tiger? Buried under a moun-tain of pride?"

Scowling, Buff slammed his empty glass down on the end table and bolted to his feet. Tiger's monumental stubbornness had worn him down. "Maybe you don't deserve Candel," he blustered irritably. "You're more concerned about your colossal pride than your feelings for her and her love for you! Well, fine, Tiger, just sit here on your solitary throne. I'm going back to New Orleans to celebrate our victory. I hope you and your pride enjoy yourselves. Good night!"

Having delivered his parting shots, Buff stamped out and slammed the door behind him.

"Hello, Candel," Roger chirped.

Nicolas sat there for a long time, staring straight ahead, seeing nothing but the images of violet eyes, a halo of silver-gold hair, and a smile that burned as brightly as the tropical sun.

"Well, hell," he muttered a good while later.

Buff was right. Foolish pride could make a man miser-able and deprive him of happiness. It was time he fol-lowed his heart.

"Need a cracker," Roger babbled as he performed one of his famous acrobatic maneuvers on his perch.

Nicolas gave Roger what he wanted before he marched out into the darkness. He hoped it wasn't too late for him to find the only woman who could make his dreams come true. All Roger needed was a cracker, but as for Tiger, he needed Candel to put the light back in his life . . .

Chapter 29

The sounds of a creaking door and muffled footsteps brought Candel up from the depths of slumber. Her breath froze in her throat when her lashes fluttered up to see a darkly-cloaked figure looming over her. Before Candel could voice the scream in her throat, a gloved hand clamped over the lower portion of her face. She winced at the feel of the cold steel blade that pricked her throat. Roughly, the intruder dragged her from bed and propelled her across the room.

Even with the moonlight that filtered through the sheer curtains, Candel couldn't make out the man's features beneath the wide-brimmed hat. He was as much a mystery to her as he had been a decade earlier, and as he had been since she saw him lurking around the plantation. And yet, there was something different about this stranger that Candel couldn't comprehend—something only pure instinct detected, despite the seeming similarities.

Whoever this man was, Candel knew she was being marched to her death, and only God and this elusive intruder knew the reason why.

Despite the fact that Candel tried to make it as difficult

as possible for her abductor to steer her through Yvonne's private chambers, she was herded along at a rapid pace. But to her bewilderment, the mysterious stranger paused long enough to slash the canvas portrait of Yvonne which hung over the mantle. The portrait crashed to the floor. It seemed a peculiar act for a man who had been acting in silence and who had refused to allow Candel to make a sound since he had first approached her.

The instant the black-cloaked stranger reached around her with one arm to open the door, Candel raised her hand to shove the blade away from her throat. But before she could push herself away, his hand grasped her hair, giving it a painful jerk and twisting her neck to an unnatural angle to meet his waiting dagger. To her dismay, she found herself shepherded onto the balcony.

Why her abductor tarried unnecessarily long on the gallery Candel couldn't imagine, either. It seemed the man actually wanted to be seen and heard before he committed murder. If she had been the one determined to commit the dastardly crime and escape punishment, she certainly wouldn't have waited around for an audience. It became alarmingly apparent that she was dealing with a madman whose actions were impossible to predict!

Before Candel could come to terms with that terrifying thought, she was shoved across the balcony and forcefully dragged down the steps. And yet, the stranger still appeared in no particular hurry to vanish into the night. It seemed he was still waiting for someone to spot him, or even to pursue him. What kind of trap was he setting? And for whom? Was she to be the bait or the victim?

Boldly, Candel glanced over her shoulder, hoping to make out the shadowed features of a face that had eluded her for over a decade. But as fate would have it, she couldn't discover the stranger's identity. His face was covered by a black mask. Life, it seemed to Candel, was full of mysteries. She would probably go to her grave never knowing who had killed her or why.

A muffled shriek escaped her lips when her captor gave her hair another painful pull. At the risk of having it pulled out by the roots, Candel gouged her abductor in the midsection, provoking a startled grunt. With a vicious snarl, he whipped Candel around to level a blow to her cheek. Her head snapped backward and her senses reeled as she stumbled to clutch at the balustrade. Tripping on the hem of her nightgown, she tumbled down the remainder of the steps. That was the last thing she remembered before the night turned a darker shade of black and piercing pain exploded in her skull . . .

While Candel was falling into oblivion, Nicolas was up a tree. It had been his intention to sneak into Candel's second-story boudoir for an unexpected midnight visit via the giant oak that loomed beside the north corner of the mansion. By the time he spied the two silhouettes on the gallery at the opposite end of the house he was out on a limb.

The sight of the dark-cloaked man clutching Candel in his arms sent icicles of dread shooting through Nicolas. It only took an instant for him to remember Candel's references to the mysterious man in black. Terrified, Nicolas clawed his way down the tree trunk with more speed than caution. Twice he very nearly toppled from the towering branches.

Darting regular glances in the direction of the outside stairway, Nicolas hopped down from the crotch of the tree and bounded off in pursuit. By the time he reached the steps, the man in black had slung Candel's unconscious body over his shoulder and disappeared. From the balcony overhead, shouts of alarm blared in the night. Nicolas recognized Nathaniel at the head of the steps, holding a lantern to search the swaying shadows.

Hurried footsteps pelted the flagstone sidewalk, attracting Nicolas's attention. He took off like a shot, frantically racing after the blur of black that mingled with the shadows of the night. In the distance he heard the nickering of a waiting steed and he burst into his swiftest pace before the fiend managed to escape with Candel.

Stark, blood-pumping fear pulsated through Nicolas's veins when a female shriek filled the cool night air. He was sure his heart was about to pound his ribs to splinters as he raced through the tangled vines and shrubs that seemed to leap out to block his path. Nicolas suffered the torments of the damned as he forged through the thicket toward the terrifying sound.

In that moment of terror, Nicolas knew beyond all doubt that it no longer mattered who he was or what he had to offer Candel. All that truly counted were these intense feelings of love and concern that churned inside him. He loved her as he'd loved nothing in all his life. She could have been a royal princess, an island priestess, or a common peasant and he wouldn't have given a damn. Nor did he care that he had been denied his rightful inheritance. All he wanted was that lovely woman back in his arms—safe and sound. But what scared the living daylights out of him was that he might never be able to save his heart's desire.

From the unnerving sound of things, Candel had roused before her intended murderer sent her to her grave. Nicolas was terrified that he might not be allowed the chance to save her and she would never know that he loved her more than life itself. He had been captivated

425

from the first moment he had seen her standing among the natives on Lost Island, looking like something from a fairy tale. He had fought all these tender emotions from the beginning and now it was too late . . .

Another bloodcurdling scream shattered the night and Nicolas felt the sound vibrate through every nerve and muscle in his body. It was as if he were moving in slow motion, willing wings to sprout on his feet, and finding none.

"Candel!" His tormented voice boomed like the cannons on the battlefield as he plunged through the jungle of vines to reach the frightened sound of her voice . . .

Candel had roused just as her abductor tossed her over the saddle and bolted up behind her to hold her in place. Frantically she had struggled to hurl herself to the ground and dart to safety, but her captor held her fast. She was aware of the thrashing in the underbrush which seemed to come from all directions, but she didn't have time to wait for possible rescue. Her wild eyes were riveted on the dagger gleaming in the moonlight. She twisted atop the steed and flung up her arm to deflect its downward thrust as it swished toward her. Her agonized scream was gone before she could bite it back. Pain seared her forearm and blood soaked the sleeve of her nightgown. She instinctively recoiled and then willed her injured arm to rise again before the deadly blade buried itself in her chest.

Before the dagger swooped down a second time, a gloved hand clutched at her abductor's arm. Through pain-glazed eyes, Candel glanced over to see yet another darkly-clad stranger struggling with the man on horseback. There were two of them—just as there had been two of them that night on the schooner!

The frightened horse swerved, stamped, and snorted at the struggle taking place on his back. Furious snarls and grunts mingled with the steed's protests. Candel felt herself being shoved sideways to such an extent that she rolled over the horse's neck and collapsed. Pushing her tangled mane from her eyes, she watched two identically dressed men battle for control of the knife. The man on foot lunged at his opponent with such unexpected ferocity that he caught his challenger off guard. The blade swerved toward the horseman's chest and a gurgle of terror froze in his throat.

The steed reared up, thrashing the air as his rider collapsed upon him. Candel saw the hooves coming at her but a daze of pain and confusion prevented her from reacting quickly enough to avoid being trampled. In the nick of time, a gloved hand gripped her arm and dragged her from beneath the frightened steed.

Muffled hoofbeats pounded the soft ground as the horse circled, its wounded rider clutching wildly at the reins. Candel could see the panic in the horse's luminous eyes as it shifted, bolted, then finally lunged away, uncertain of its rider's commands.

The sound of rustling bushes to the north caused Candel's most recent captor to scoop her up and shove her into the thicket. She didn't see Nicolas burst through the vines that marked the boundary of the garden.

In the moonlight, Nicolas spied the steed cantering ahead of him. The steed broke stride, danced sideways, and then shot off, only to skid to a halt before prancing a tight circle. Nicolas assumed Candel was draped over the saddle, but it was impossible to tell for certain as the rider's cloak was billowing in the wind and he was hunched over the skittish steed.

Howling every curse word in his vocabulary, Nicolas charged after the horse and rider, unaware that Candel was being carted off in the opposite direction.

Gasping for breath, the man in black skidded to a halt and set Candel on her feet. When he shoved her to the ground and glanced around to determine if he was being followed, Candel tensed. She knew for certain that *this* man in black was the mysterious stranger from her past, not the one who had abducted her from her bedroom. She was totally confused by the fact that he had saved her from the other stranger. Before she could puzzle out what was happening, her captor sank down atop her to pin her to the ground.

" 'Twas André who murdered Yvonne because of me," he rasped raggedly. "He wanted you to take the blame for his wife's death so he could control the Caro fortune."

. Candel couldn't stop shaking or staring at the shadowed features of the man who hovered over her. Her paralyzed brain refused to send orders to the rest of her body, demanding that she bolt and run before disaster struck again. She simply lay there, peering up at him uncomprehendingly.

"Aye, you have every right to despise me, Candeliera," he assured her as he reached out to brush his hand across the welt on her cheek. "I do not dare ask forgiveness for the torment I put you through those long years ago. I have lived with a torment all my own because of what I did, or rather what I was supposed to do to that terrified little girl of nine." Bitter laughter filled the night air. " 'Twas all in the name of blind devotion to a woman who knew all too well how to manipulate me to see her evil will done.''

Candel felt the tenseness ebb from her body as she listened to the tortured voice that whispered in the night.

" 'Twas Yvonne who sent me and my brother Evan to dispose of you and your parents, and to make it look like a disaster at sea,'' he confessed, watching her eyes grow round with astonishment.

"Aye, Evan recognized you and sent word to me from Martinique that you had survived. He had intended to bring you back to collect the reward before he disposed of you as I was supposed to have done that night on the schooner.''

"She planned it all? Just to acquire my family's fortune?''

"Aye, it was only when you returned that I learned of her scheme to poison the marquis. All these years she stayed with André while she vowed her love to me. She even demanded to have the new addition built onto the mansion so I could come to her private rooms without being noticed. And I stayed with her these long years, bound by my tormented conscience, telling myself I deserved no better after what I'd done.''

"It was Evan who killed my parents?'' Candel choked out as the haunting memory exploded in her mind. "And you shoved me into the sea?''

Derrick nodded grimly. "I was ordered to kill you, but when I looked down into the frightened face of that lovely little girl, I couldn't do as Evan had done. I gave you a fighting chance by tossing the wooden keg into the sea after you. If I hadn't pushed you over the railing, Evan would have turned his knife on you as well because I had hesitated too long and he cursed my sense of de-

cency. But I couldn't take your life. I couldn't . . .''
His voice broke from the anguish of years of pent-up
emotions.

Candel's eyes were swimming with tears as she stared
into the dark features of the man from her nightmares.
''It was you who released me from jail, wasn't it? Why?''
she asked in a wobbly voice.

''Because André had bribed the guards to starve you
half to death and he had confiscated the letters you had
written to the lawyers. He meant to see you tried and
convicted so he could regain control of the plantation.
With you out of the way, Gustave would have been forced
to leave his fortune to André.''

Assured that he had Candel's undivided attention, Derrick eased down beside her, but he refused to turn his
face toward the moonlight so she could see his features.
''When you returned, Yvonne demanded that I dispose
of you, just as I was to do in the beginning. I refused,
despite her threats. Knowing you were still alive was like
a key that unlocked me from my torment. I had made too
many sacrifices for Yvonne and I vowed to make no
more. She flew into a rage and assured me she had only
kept me around to do her bidding and to provide the
passion she couldn't enjoy with André. She had only
married him for his name, hoping he would one day
receive part of the Caron fortune. But she grew impatient
as a poor relation and set out to change her fate by disposing of your family.''

Candel squeezed her eyes shut against the flood of
tears. Her parents had died violent deaths because of
Yvonne's obsession for wealth. Candel couldn't understand why prestige would be so important to Yvonne that
she would take innocent lives to acquire it. The woman
was obviously so vain and greedy that she didn't care

430

who she hurt or what she had to do to get what she wanted. For all of Yvonne's sultry beauty and pretended charm she was a wicked witch who cast evil spells on the men who dared to love her.

Derrick brushed away her tears with his gloved hand and sighed heavily. "Yvonne also demanded that André dispose of you to save them from humiliation. I heard them arguing while I hid in the adjoining room. She meant to place the blame on André, too. He became desperate to silence her because he was also involved in the scheme to poison Gustave. No doubt, André also saw his chance to repay Yvonne for her infidelity as well. He knew about my affair with Yvonne, but he could no more let go of her than I could. She bewitched the both of us. As evil as she could be, there was something utterly intriguing about her that drew a man against his will. It was like chasing some deliciously wicked . . ."

The words trailed off and he shrugged, as if uncertain how to describe the mystical hold Yvonne had on him as a man.

"I tried to spare your life when you were a child. It was my hope that you would somehow survive. You will never know how long and hard I prayed you would."

His voice wavered with a torment Candel wasn't sure she even understood. But something about this mysterious man still haunted her, just as the memory of what he had done and why continued to torment him.

"I have spared your life a second time, Candeliera, because you have been the innocent victim of vicious games of power and ill-fated love. The spell Yvonne cast over me, and even over André, has ended. It was he who abducted you from your room tonight, intent on killing you and placing the blame on the mysterious stranger you had claimed to see. And although you will never be able

431

to forgive me, I hope you can forget what I cannot. I will take my sins with me to my grave. Until then, I will continue living my hell on earth . . ."

"Candel!" Nicolas's voice shattered the darkness.

Like a phantom drifting off into the night, the mysterious stranger who had saved Candel from certain death became one of the swaying shadows. She blinked back the tears and struggled to her feet, only to find herself swept into Nicolas's arms.

"Dear God!" Nicolas croaked, completely out of breath. "I thought I'd never find you."

After he'd whirled her around in his arms until she was dizzy, he set her on her feet and planted a swift kiss on her lips. "Are you all right?"

Candel blinked to clear away the stars circling around her head. "I'm fine," she managed to say, even while Nicolas pressed her face into his shoulder to give her another energetic hug. For weeks now, he had done his damnedest to keep a safe distance between them for fear his lust would overcome him. What was the matter with Tiger? He was behaving rather strangely, she thought.

"I found your mysterious man in black," he murmured as he held her to him, as if to reassure himself again that she was safe. "It was André."

Nicolas had raced across the meadow on foot, refusing to give up. It was only when the cloaked rider toppled off his steed that Nicolas realized Candel wasn't with him. Nicolas had been startled to find André's blanched face beneath the mask. He had also been terrified to think Candel had stumbled off into the garden, a victim of a stab wound slowly draining the life out of her. He had presumed she had managed to sink the dagger into André's flesh before she limped away. There was no other explanation.

432

Only Candel knew the truth about the harrowing incident, but she couldn't bring herself to explain the complicated details just yet. She realized now that André had purposely lingered on the balcony and steps, intending the servants to see him—or at least see the mysterious man in black to whom she had referred on occasion. André had every intention of disposing of her for the fortune and allowing Derrick Rollings to shoulder the blame for both Yvonne's and Candel's deaths. Now his reasons no longer mattered. The threat to her and to her grandfather had died with André . . .

When Nicolas's hands gently touched her wounded arm, she instinctively pushed him away. In the darkness, he studied her, wondering at her odd detachment and her refusal to let him touch her. He mistook her reaction for rejection. With a deep sigh he peered down at her in the darkness.

"Have I spoiled every chance of going back to the way we were, Candel?" he murmured softly.

She cocked her head to assess his strange expression. "I didn't think you cared about the way it was when I loved you, Tiger. If you only came back to make sure I resolved my conflict with my cousin, there's no need to stay. André will cause me no more trouble and you're free."

He watched her like a hawk, baffled by her behavior and the fact that she kept casting distracted glances at the swaying shadows. "Is something else wrong?"

Candel pushed forward, brushing his shoulder as she headed toward the mansion. It was only as she passed through the spray of moonlight that he noticed blood stains on the sleeve of her gown.

"You're hurt!" he gasped.

"Brilliant observation, Tiger," Candel muttered as

she breezed past him. "Before I bleed to death, I think I'll tend my wound."

Her wound wasn't all that serious, but it was an excuse to leave before she humiliated herself with Tiger as she had done so many times before. It was over and she was going to let it stay that way, no matter how it hurt to lose the only man she'd ever love.

"Thank you for coming around, Tiger. But as you can see, I have everything under control."

Under control? Nicolas gaped at her in disbelief. She had very nearly gotten herself killed and she thought she had her life under control?

"You can move on without fretting over me," Candel assured him before she wheeled around and marched away.

Nicolas stood like a marble statue, totally baffled by Candel's strange preoccupation with the shadows and her lofty tone of voice. He seemed to be a million miles away from her thoughts and that cut him to the bone.

Bowing his head, Nicolas marched after her. He wasn't about to give up on this blond-haired firebrand, not after all the mental struggles he'd gone through to face the truth of his feelings. As Buff had said, this woman deserved to know how he felt. He may have spoiled all his chances of going back to the way it was when she loved him, but he would find a way to tell her how he felt, even if he fumbled miserably. He had come this far and he wasn't turning back now! There was too much at stake—his one and only chance of happiness!

Chapter 30

Before Candel reached the flagstone path, Nicolas grasped her good arm and swung her around. "I have something to say and you're going to listen," he said tersely.

"Then kindly do it before I bleed to death."

Damn the man! Why wouldn't he simply go away and let her forget him as she had been trying to do? Did he enjoy torturing her, knowing how she felt about him? He had told her it was over but he wouldn't let it be over! Tiger was impossible!

Nicolas ripped the hem off his shirt to provide a makeshift bandage for her injured arm and carefully secured it in place while he formulated his thoughts. "Candel, I—" He struggled with the word that clung to the tip of his tongue. He knew now that he should have rehearsed for this moment, just as Dominique and Pierre had suggested.

"You what, Tiger?" Candel prompted impatiently.

"Must you make this more difficult than it already is?"

He was annoyed with her for badgering him and at

himself for fumbling like a tongue-tied idiot. It would have helped if Candel had cut him a little slack. But then, when had she ever?

She gazed up into his moonlit features, hurting in ways that had nothing to do with the throbbing pain in her arm. "I'll make it easy on you, Tiger," she said, struggling to keep her voice from cracking with emotion. "You can leave here with a free conscience and peace of mind. You delivered me to my grandfather, just as you vowed to do. I'll see to it that you're given the reward Gustave promised. You're released from all responsibilities . . . *all* of them."

There. She had given him his precious freedom. She hoped he was happy, even if she was miserable.

"Curse it, Candel, I don't want the reward," Nicolas snapped in frustration. "All I want is you!"

Her chin jutted out and her violet eyes flashed. There had been a time when she had assured herself that she would settle for whatever scraps of affection this rugged renegade could offer. But it was no longer enough. Candel couldn't cling to her liberal theories about sex. She had changed drastically the past two months. It seemed she wanted all or nothing where Tiger was concerned and she refused to settle for anything in between.

"Well, you'll no longer have me at your beck and call," Candel said firmly. "You can find all you'll ever need with dozens of somebody elses. I fought tooth and gum to convince you of my love for you and you constantly threw it back in my face. You've wanted it to be over and now 'tis over!"

"Tooth and *nail*," he automatically corrected her. His massive chest swelled with so much exasperation that he very nearly popped the buttons off his shirt. "Candel, I love you! I can't even remember when I didn't love you,

436

though I was afraid to let it show for fear of getting in way over my head . . . which I did anyway. All I want is for you to love me back, even if I don't deserve you," he all but yelled at her.

Candel blinked in amazement. Had he actually said what she thought he'd said? Had her ears deceived her? She had waited so long to hear him admit he cared that she was afraid she had only imagined it.

His hands framed her face and he gazed deeply into her astonished eyes. "I love you," he whispered softly, sincerely. "I truly love you, Candel. You've become a constant flame that burns inside me. I've tried letting go because I thought it was best when I had nothing to offer you. But like a moth, I keep fluttering back. I want you any way I can get you." He stared at her for a long, anxious moment. "Have I waited too long to speak what has been in my soul? Have I hurt you so many times that I've destroyed what you once felt for me?"

Despite her wound, Candel flung her arms around his neck and reached up on tiptoe to give him a sizzling kiss. She feared her heart would burst with joy. Ah, how long she had waited to know Tiger returned her love!

The answers to Nicolas's questions were in the sparkle in her eyes and in the eager response of her kiss. With a moan of relief, he clutched her to him, feeling her luscious body melt familiarly into his. Determined to express all the love and desire he had bottled up inside him, Nicolas scooped her up in his arms to find a secluded place to . . .

The patter of footsteps on the flagstone path halted Nicolas in his tracks. He pivoted, still clinging possessively to Candel. A raised lantern illuminated the rescue brigade of servants commandeered by Gustave, who was being propelled along at dangerous speeds in his wheelchair. How the old man had rallied in his weakened condition was a mystery to Nicolas. But the marquis was there, determined to save the granddaughter who kept mysteriously disappearing from his life.

Damn, thought Nicolas. He was never going to get Candel alone to express all this pent-up emotion that boiled inside him. Ah, what he wouldn't give to be marooned on a tropical island right about now!

"And just who the hell are you and what do you think you're doing with my granddaughter?" Gustave demanded as he rolled toward Nicolas, who looked like a huge oak tree from where the marquis sat.

"I, sir, am the man who loves your granddaughter," Nicolas admitted to Gustave and the congregation of startled servants.

It was getting easier to say the words each time, and Nicolas wanted the whole world to know he was in love for the very first and only time in his life, despite the fact that he had nothing to offer Candel. But that didn't matter, he reminded himself. He would find some means of support without living off Candel's fortune.

"Say what?" Gustave cupped his hand around his ear, demanding that Nicolas repeat himself.

"He's hard of hearing," Candel prompted.

"I said . . . I love Candel with all my heart," Nicolas practically shouted at the marquis.

Nathaniel leaned down to inform the marquis that Nicolas was the ship captain who had found Candel on the island and who had dashed off earlier to save her from the mysterious man in black.

"Candel?" Gustave peered at his granddaughter who was still being carried in Nicolas's arms. He squinted into the shadows, trying to get a closer look at Nicolas. "And just how do *you* feel about this man?"

Candel's gaze never wavered from Nicolas's. "I love him, too," she loudly declared with genuine emotion.

With a flick of his wrist, Gustave dismissed the servants clustered around him. "Put my granddaughter down and come out into the light so I can see you, young man," the marquis demanded with his customary tone of authority.

Nicolas obeyed, knowing full well where Candel had inherited that authoritative voice of hers.

When Nicolas ambled out of the shadows to confront Gustave, the marquis gasped for breath and clutched at his chest. A fragment of memory leaped out at him, momentarily rendering him speechless.

"Stéphane . . . ?" Gustave chirped after his vocal apparatus began to function. "Stéphane Rouchaud?"

Nicolas had secretly wondered if Buff had invented that tale about his family, just to reassure and encourage him. But judging from the way Gustave gaped at him—as if he were staring through a door through time and space—Nicolas had the inescapable feeling that *this* was the patriarch who was to have been Rouchaud's American connection. That would certainly explain why Gustave had reacted to Nicolas as he had a few weeks earlier. The incident in the marquis' bedroom had befuddled Nicolas. Now it all made sense.

"Nay, that can't be right," Gustave babbled as he wracked his memory. "But you look amazingly like your father. 'Tis Nicolas, isn't it? Nicolas Rouchaud. My God, I can scarcely believe it! I was told that you and your family . . ."

Gustave's eyes misted over as he glanced from the handsome suitor to his lovely granddaughter, who was frowning in total confusion. "Two miracles in one lifetime," he murmured as his shaking hand fumbled for his handkerchief to wipe his eyes. "Somehow it seems as if all my suffering has been doubly rewarded . . ."

Although Gustave was showing signs of fatigue, he rolled his wheelchair toward the mansion and gestured for Nicolas to push him forward. "Nicolas, I have something for you that I have kept for your family for twenty-five years."

Totally bewildered, Candel followed her grandfather into the house. To her further astonishment, Gustave opened his safe and presented Nicolas with the deed to the land that Stéphane Rouchaud had instructed Gustave to purchase along with the jewels and coins that had accompanied the letter. Gustave explained that the property had been farmed as part of the Caron plantation, even though he had never put the unclaimed Rouchaud land in his own name.

"Your father made contact with me a week before he was to leave the country," Gustave explained. "When I received no more correspondence from him, I feared . . ." He smiled sympathetically. "I'm so sorry, Nicolas. Your father was a fine man. He and my son had been close friends before I pulled up stakes and came to New France. I deeply regret what happened, but you will have part of your lost inheritance back, as well as my blessing in marriage. It will be a fine match—one that must surely have been arranged by the departed angels who have been watching over both of you."

Gustave requested that Nicolas push the wheelchair back to the bedroom. The marquis bid his future grandson good night and crawled into bed, thoroughly exhausted but completely at peace. After years of heartache and suffering, Gustave fell asleep, content with the world at long last.

Nicolas lingered in the foyer, wanting very much to

accompany Candel to her room, and yet hesitant to over-step the bounds of propriety, especially after all the kindness Gustave had bestowed on him. With a wry smile Candel watched Nicolas glance from Gustave's bedroom to the spiral staircase and then to the front door.

"There's another set of steps . . . in case you've forgotten," she quietly reminded him before she turned toward the stairs.

"Will you be waiting, marchioness?" he asked as he leaned against the balustrade with a roguish smile.

Candel turned on the landing to return his provocative grin. "Haven't I always been waiting for you, Tiger? Why would tonight be any different?"

Nicolas's appreciative gaze slid over the gossamer gown that did more to tantalize than conceal. "I love you . . ." he murmured softly, sincerely.

"Truly?" With an impish smile she turned toward her room. "Prove it, Tiger . . ."

Nicolas forced himself not to race out the front door. But the instant he reached the porch, he dashed around the side of the house.

The moment Nicolas eased the door open, his knees very nearly buckled. The quilts had been drawn back invitingly and Candel lay abed, covered with a silk sheet and wearing only a welcoming smile.

"It took you long enough, Tiger," she purred as she stretched seductively.

Her quiet comment carried a double meaning and Nicolas was quick to note the mischievous twinkle in her amethyst eyes. "Aye, it did," he admitted, undressing on his way to bed.

It had taken him almost three months to realize that

this lovely siren was his destiny and he wasn't wasting another moment.

The bed creaked as Nicolas stretched out beside Candel to devour her luscious curves with his eyes, hands, and lips. He longed to reacquaint himself with every inch of her exquisite body, to love her for all the times he'd wanted her in the past and had denied himself. *I love you* was communicated in each adoring kiss and caress, spelling out the words he had too long contained, printing the phrase on her silky flesh until he had given a delicious new meaning to *love letters*. For the first time in their stormy affair, there was no hint of reluctance or regret. Nicolas let go with his mind, body, and heart to express his innermost feelings for this violet-eyed beauty. He compensated for all the times he'd cursed this strong-willed woman who had the courage to love him in ways he still wasn't sure he deserved.

Candel thought she'd scaled passion's highest peaks each time she was in Tiger's arms, but nothing compared to what she was feeling at this wondrous moment! Her body was ablaze with fiery sensations, glowing with the rapture of his loving touch. When his powerful body settled over hers, she felt as if the dark world had opened to swallow her up, submerging her in a whirlpool of ineffable sensation. When the hot, sweet ache of desire consumed her, she clutched at Nicolas as if he were the only stable force in a universe of heart-stopping tremors and wild, mindless urgency. And in that frantic moment, a warm flood of contentment bathed her quaking flesh. The unconditional love Tiger offered was like a comforting balm that soothed every burning ache.

As the tide of passion ebbed, Candel sighed deeply, marveling at the kaleidoscope of feeling that had ribboned through her before she found the quintessence of sweet release. It was a long, breathless moment before the splendorous whirlwind cleared and she could formulate thought. Numbing pleasure still lingered like a mystical spell that refused to be broken.

"I want you with me now and forever, Candel," Nicolas whispered in a voice that quivered with the aftereffects of sublime fulfillment. "Before you came along I needed nothing. Now I need nothing but you. These feelings for you run soul-deep." The tenderest of kisses emphasized his words. "I want to start all over again with you, Candel. And this time, I don't intend to hold anything back. I want you to be the sun when I wake and the moon when I drift off to sleep. I want to love you with every beat of my heart for all the days of my life. If there is such a thing as forever, I want to spend it with you."

Candel was touched by his words. It was still difficult for her to believe this proud, stubborn man had finally bowed to the power of love. Ah, it seemed as though she had waited an eternity for him to offer his heart as freely as she had given hers to him.

"Love me, for now and always," Nicolas murmured as his hands and lips drifted over her body once again to convey the maelstrom of emotions she had aroused in him.

"I do love you, Tiger," she assured him, her voice thick with pleasure. "I always have and I always will. You'll never have cause to doubt it . . ." With a smile of pure satisfaction he drew Candel's curvaceous body beneath his to teach her a few more techniques in the art of lovemaking. When he was in the magical circle of her arms the flame burned higher and higher, casting shadows on the world around him, sending him soaring into infinity.

It no longer mattered that Nicolas had lost his title and

443

all his worldly possessions, or that Gustave had restored part of his inheritance. This bewitching woman was more precious than a royal pedigree or buried treasure. Candel had become his living flame of love that burned bright against the night, lighting his way to eternity. She could make a man a king. She could crown him with riches more priceless than diamonds or gold. She had become his very reason for existence!

As for Candel, she had learned early in life to survive on the barest of necessities. She could live with or without riches. The only gift Candel wanted and needed to make her life complete was Tiger's tender touch. He was the only man who could keep her own flame of love burning . . . Always and Forever. . .

A Note to my Readers

I hope you enjoyed this fast-paced adventure with Candel and Nicolas. I took advantage of the unanswered questions in history in the telling of this tale. No one seems to know for certain how Pierre Lafitte escaped from jail. Nor do historians know exactly where General Jackson and Jean Lafitte met to form the alliance, or why Jackson suddenly changed his mind about accepting the aid of the Baratarians. But who knows? Perhaps it was the Nicolas Tigers and Candel Carons of the world who played their part in these history-making events. In any event, I hope this story brought you a few hours of reading pleasure and an occasional smile.

Happy reading,
Gina Robins

PINNACLE BOOKS HAS
SOMETHING FOR EVERYONE—

MAGICIANS, EXPLORERS, WITCHES AND CATS

THE HANDYMAN   (377-3, $3.95/$4.95)
He is a magician who likes hands. He likes their comfortable
shape and weight and size. He likes the portability of the hands
once they are severed from the rest of the ponderous body. Detective Lanark must discover who The Handyman is before more
handless bodies appear.

PASSAGE TO EDEN   (538-5, $4.95/$5.95)
Set in a world of prehistoric beauty, here is the epic story of a
courageous seafarer whose wanderings lead him to the ends of
the old world—and to the discovery of a new world in the rugged,
untamed wilderness of northwestern America.

BLACK BODY   (505-9, $5.95/$6.95)
An extraordinary chronicle, this is the diary of a witch, a journal
of the secrets of her race kept in return for not being burned for
her "sin." It is the story of Alba, that rarest of creatures, a white
witch: beautiful and able to walk in the human world undetected.

THE WHITE PUMA   (532-6, $4.95/NCR)
The white puma has recognized the men who deprived him of his
family. Now, like other predators before him, he has become a
man-hater. This story is a fitting tribute to this magnificent animal that stands for all living creatures that have become, through
man's carelessness, close to disappearing forever from the face of
the earth.

*Available wherever paperbacks are sold, or order direct from the
Publisher. Send cover price plus 50¢ per copy for mailing and
handling to Pinnacle Books, Dept. 647, 475 Park Avenue South,
New York, N.Y. 10016. Residents of New York and Tennessee
must include sales tax. DO NOT SEND CASH. For a free Zebra/
Pinnacle catalog please write to the above address.*

FEEL THE FIRE IN CAROL FINCH'S ROMANCES!

BELOVED BETRAYAL (2346, $3.95)

Sabrina Spencer donned a gray wig and veiled hat before blackmailing rugged Ridge Tanner into guiding her to Fort Canby. But the costume soon became her prison—the beauty had fallen head over heels in love!

LOVE'S HIDDEN TREASURE (2980, $4.50)

Shandra d'Evereux felt her heart throb beneath the stolen map she'd hidden in her bodice when Nolan Elliot swept her out onto the veranda. It was hard to concentrate on her mission with that wily rogue around!

MONTANA MOONFIRE (3263, $4.95)

Just as debutante Victoria Flemming-Cassidy was about to marry an oh-so-suitable mate, the towering preacher, Dru Sullivan flung her over his shoulder and headed West! Suddenly, Tori realized she had been given the best present for a bride: a night of passion with a real man!

THUNDER'S TENDER TOUCH (2809, $4.50)

Refined Piper Malone needed bounty-hunter, Vince Logan to recover her swindled inheritance. She thought she could coolly dismiss him after he did the job, but she never counted on the hot flood of desire she felt whenever he was near!

Available wherever paperbacks are sold, or order direct from the Publisher. Send cover price plus 50¢ per copy for mailing and handling to Zebra Books, Dept. 647, 475 Park Avenue South, New York, N.Y. 10016. Residents of New York and Tennessee must include sales tax. DO NOT SEND CASH. For a free Zebra/Pinnacle catalog please write to the above address.

DISCOVER DEANA JAMES!

CAPTIVE ANGEL (2524, $4.50/$5.50)
Abandoned, penniless, and suddenly responsible for the biggest tobacco plantation in Colleton County, distraught Caroline Gillard had no time to dissolve into tears. By day the willowy redhead labored to exhaustion beside her slaves . . . but each night left her restless with longing for her wayward husband. She'd make the sea captain regret his betrayal until he begged her to take him back!

MASQUE OF SAPPHIRE (2885, $4.50/$5.50)
Judith Talbot-Harrow left England with a heavy heart. She was going to America to join a father she despised and a sister she distrusted. She was certainly in no mood to put up with the insulting actions of the arrogant Yankee privateer who boarded her ship, ransacked her things, then "apologized" with an indecent, brazen kiss! She vowed that someday he'd pay dearly for the liberties he had taken and the desires he had awakened.

SPEAK ONLY LOVE (3439, $4.95/$5.95)
Long ago, the shock of her mother's death had robbed Vivian Marleigh of the power of speech. Now she was being forced to marry a bitter man with brandy on his breath. But she could not say what was in her heart. It was up to the viscount to spark the fires that would melt her icy reserve.

WILD TEXAS HEART (3205, $4.95/$5.95)
Fan Breckenridge was terrified when the stranger found her near-naked and shivering beneath the Texas stars. Unable to remember who she was or what had happened, all she had in the world was the deed to a patch of land that might yield oil . . . and the fierce loving of this wildcatter who called himself Irons.

Available wherever paperbacks are sold, or order direct from the Publisher. Send cover price plus 50¢ per copy for mailing and handling to Zebra Books, Dept. 647, 475 Park Avenue South, New York, N.Y. 10016. Residents of New York and Tennessee must include sales tax. DO NOT SEND CASH. For a free Zebra/Pinnacle catalog please write to the above address.